The Collected Shorter Supernatural & Weird Fiction of Algernon Blackwood Volume 8

Algernon Blackwood

The Collected Shorter Supernatural & Weird Fiction of Algernon Blackwood Volume 8

Seven Short Stories, and Three Novelettes of the Strange and Unusual Including 'The Man Who Lived Backwards', 'S.O.S.', 'The Lane that Ran East and West,' and 'Elsewhere and Otherwise'

Algernon Blackwood

LEONAUR

The Collected Shorter Supernatural & Weird Fiction of
Algernon Blackwood
Volume 8
Seven Short Stories, and Three Novelettes of the Strange and Unusual Including 'The
Man Who Lived Backwards', 'S.O.S.', 'The Lane that Ran East and West,' and
'Elsewhere and Otherwise'
by Algernon Blackwood

Leonaur is an imprint of Oakpast Ltd

Copyright in this form © 2024 Oakpast Ltd

ISBN: 978-1-916535-74-9 (hardcover)
ISBN: 978-1-916535-75-6 (softcover)

http://www.leonaur.com

Publisher's Notes

Contents

Alexander Alexander

His Christian name and surname were the same, and the fact that he insisted upon their proper use, respectively, made things of ten most unpleasant. His sombre dignity forbade familiarity. If, greatly daring, I said "Hullo, Alexander!" using his Christian name, he would assume a stern and frightening air:

"*Alexander!* If you please," he would say icily. "Use my right name."

Herein lay, perhaps, the heart of that dark secret which deceived mean for so my years, as also the essence of that horror his double masquerade concealed: Whereas, between Alexander and *Alexander* none knew which was which, he—alone of all the world—*he* knew!

To me, as a little girl, there was something portentous about him always. More than a common man, he was a Personage, a Figure. With the passage of the years my conception of him grew, for his bulk and stature grew at the same time, until, more than man, or personage, or figure, he became almost that emanation of legendary life—a Being. Although the original sharp outline remained, he spread himself out somehow over an immense, dim background, against which that first outline yet held itself fixed in vivid silhouette. I conceive him as both remote and very close, as shadow and substance, an unreality yet dreadfully composed of solid flesh and blood.

This confusion in my own mind added enormously to the mystery of his strange existence; but it was the mistake in the use of his name that remained chiefly serious, a crime of untold import, since it was I myself who first—christened him. To call him by a wrong name, therefore, was an insult to his actuality, a careless and unpardonable sacrilege that trifled with the essential nature of his personality.

I lived with an uncle, who was also my guardian, and this mystifying double role contributed, no doubt, an element to the birth of Alexander *Alexander*. Some childhood's divination dramatized itself perhaps. If so, this earliest creative drama had a prophetic, even a clairvoyant, quality that enabled him to endure until he had fully justified his dark existence. Both Alexander and Alexander persisted through my girlhood. Only at the threshold of womanhood, when I came of age at twenty-one, did the dreadful pair pass hand in hand to their final distressing dissolution.

He—*Alexander*—often came to see my uncle, who, I divined, was a good deal afraid of him—a fact that impressed me painfully. He was tall, dark, angular, and so thin that he always looked cold, even in the sunshine; as though, having left off his flesh, as others leave off their thick underwear, he was for ever shivering in his bones. Of those mummied Pharaohs he reminded me. He had the great square jaw, deep eyes, heavy cheek-bones, and copious hair those gloomy figures of prodigious personality bear tirelessly with them down the ages. He walked on his toes a little, adding thus to the appearance of his height. He took, too, an immense and swinging stride, with an easy gliding motion that seemed to flow. His extraordinary swiftness of movement made me think of running water.

Oh, Alexander—or do I mean *Alexander?*—how you impressed me when I was about six years old! Which "Alexander"? I don't quite know, to tell the truth. Years passed before I got even an inkling.

The names still flow, like parallel rivers, down and through my consciousness, to lose themselves in the depths of some mysterious dream-ocean where, at length and at last, they become merged, I believe, in one. There were certainly two of them—once. There was Alexander, and there was Alexander. I can swear to it.

It was his—*Alexander's* copious hair that impressed me vividly at the age of six. It was smoothed down with shiny grease whose faint, but not unpleasant, aroma came into a room before its wearer, and hung about in the air long after he had left. Hair, perfume, grease, all fascinated me.

"That's *pomade*," explained my nurse, answering a question and using a strange new word. Then, fearful of some wrong use I might make of the information, she added: "and no business of yours, remember, either." The queer word seized me; it remained hanging about my mind . . . pomade, pomade. How vividly, with what lasting depth and sharpness these early impressions score the mind of a child, so tenderly receptive. No wonder the psychologists dive after them to explain the irregularities of nerve and memory that emerge in later life. The name Alexander, to begin with, carried me away. It bore me along with it. There was movement in it. Jones, Green, Brown, one syllable names, are stationary and fixed; but "Alexander" had a glide. It was a watery movement; I always connected it with water. It flowed round and through and under me.

It bore me easily away with it. I saw a rapid stream, whose undulating surface had no actual waves, owing to its speed, but swept along in rhythmic rise and fall, like a brimmed rivulet across a sloping meadow. My feet gave under me, and I was off. "Alexander, *Alexander*, oh, why cannot you meander?" I used to murmur to myself, using another strange new word I had discovered, a suitable word since it was the name of a river that also flowed. I saw copious hair, pomade, a lean, dark, careering figure on its toes, swinging rapidly down my mind with a pulse of hurrying water.

He was a solicitor, I imagined, and the name only half understood, somehow to me suggested prison; and my uncle, who was also my legal guardian, I fancied had done something wrong. It was rather confusing having an uncle who was guardian too. It puzzled me. My uncle was reserved, secretive—that is, as "guardian," he was reserved, secretive; for as "uncle" he was affectionate, playful, kind, and very dear to me. I had this mingled fear and love.

The name had a strange power. I was, perhaps, nine years old when the goose frightened me in the yard behind the stables, and some undigested fairytale made me think its clacking beak was going to bite me into pieces. Pulling down my little skirts frantically to protect my bare legs, I found the bad rhyme instantly, though I may have shaped it actually a little later:

Alexander, Alexander,
Oh, come down into the yard!
For I'm frightened at the gander—
Oh, come quick with your pomade!

And he came. That was what lived with me for years, increasing enormously his influence. He came at once. The glass door of the conservatory opened, and out he poured with amazing swiftness, on his toes, turning his thin, dark face and head towards me. His great stride brought him up to me in a moment. He was, I believe, really looking for my uncle, who was in the stables just then, examining the horses. But it was in answer to my cry that he was beside me in a second. I caught the whiff of the pomade.

"Oh, Alexander—!" I cried, relieved, but also alarmed.

"*Alexander,*" he corrected me sternly, his deep eyes staring, while the gander retreated and left me safe at once. Yet, when I turned round again from watching the retreating bird, he—Alexander—had disappeared, and my uncle—or was it my guardian?—was coming towards me from the stables with a smile. The incident, at any rate, left a deep impression on me. The use—the correct use—of the great name evidently carried away with its own movement. I saw him only occasionally as I grew older; during holidays, when home from school, and later, from a year in Paris to improve my French and acquire manners and deportment. He was aged in the eyes, and skin, and gait.

The stream of his name no longer brimmed its banks as formerly. But the spell remained. And the pomaded hair kept young as ever. My uncle, I now realised somehow, welcomed his visits, yet while dreading them. I thought of the two at the time, I remember, as driver and driven in some mysterious enterprise of financial kind. They were. But Alexander was the driven, and *Alexander* held the whip. And once, lying half asleep in bed, a horrible suspicion came to me that my uncle—or was it my guardian?—knew. Knew what? Why "horrible?" I could not say, I felt it, that's all.

A week after my return from Paris—I was to be of age next day—I was standing in the passage when he called. Thomas was leading the way. It was just outside the study door.

"Mr. Alexander to see you, sir," I heard him announced.

The visitor glowered with vexation. "Mr. *Alexander*," he rebuked the servant in a low tone, as he swung through the door on his toes into the study, where my uncle, or my guardian evidently awaited him. And as I heard the name, in the way *he* uttered it, a sudden wave of cold anxiety, more of acute distress, broke over me. As that lean, dark, pomaded head flowed round the open door with its extraordinary swiftness, and vanished, I felt afraid. The footman went past me with an expressionless face, but it seemed to me that his face was ghastly white.

He disappeared in the empty hall beyond; I heard the green baize door into the nether regions swing to behind him with its customary gulp. But the draught of its closing came to me across all that distance; so that I felt it on my cheeks. And its touch was icy. I stood there shivering, unable at first to move or think. A vague dread and wonder held me. What were Alexander and *Alexander* saying to my uncle and my guardian?

What steps to take I knew not. For I was aware that I ought to take steps at once. My hesitation was caused by an inexplicable fear. It was the fear of my guardian, but *for* my uncle. Is that clear? While dreading my guardian, I felt, I knew, that I must help my uncle. Two courses seemed open to me: to enter the room, or to follow the footman and ask him an awful question.

I chose the latter. In a moment I was through the green baize door that led into the servants' quarters; but, as I ran, a new suspicion fastened on me. It fastened on my spine where the shivering was. I was amazed and horror-stricken. For the suspicion was so complete that it must actually have lain in me a long, long time already.

"Thomas," I said, breathlessly; "the gentleman you showed in just now—who was it?"

"I beg pardon, Miss," he said, staring blankly. I asked the question a second time. "Showed in, Miss," he repeated stupidly.

"The tall, dark gentleman," I insisted, in a failing voice, "you just showed in to——" (I could not, for the life of me, say "my uncle's")— "into Mr. Burton's study—Mr.—Mr.—?" I stammered and stuck fast.

The man paused a moment, with a puzzled air. He stared at me. "I showed no gentleman in, Miss," he said, a trifle offended, his voice firm and decided. "Mr. Burton rang for——" (it was his turn to hesitate)—"for something to drink, Miss. And I just took it in to him."

I knew then. I knew it all at once, complete. I tore back. But my thought raced faster than my legs. An elaborate fabric built most carefully, and standing firm for years, collapsed into ghastly ruins. The footman's face, I remembered, was always white. My nurse, now dead, had always fallen in with my fancies. My uncle was tall and thin and dark, and had always worn pomaded hair. But it was only when I reached the study door that the final film cleared off, letting in the appalling light. For I suddenly remembered another thing as well; he acknowledged to a buried name. Hidden away among several others, he owned a name he never used. His full name, of course, was Frank Henry *Alexander* Burton.

I stood transfixed outside the door.

But precious minutes were passing. "Oh, Alexander, *Alexander*," rushed down my mind. The childhood's rhyme was about to follow, yard, gander, pomade and all, when a sound inside the room sent the ice again down my spine. It made my will tighten at the same time. I might be too late even now. Without knocking, I rushed into the room. The desk was strewn with documents and papers. A decanter of spirits stood beside them, with a half-emptied glass. The French windows were open on the lawn. The summer air came in. There was a faint aroma of pomade. But I was too late. The room was empty. "Oh, Alexander!" I gasped, petrified by the emptiness, and was about to add *"Alexander"* when a horrid weakness came over me and a blackness rose before my face. My legs collapsed. I fell into a dead faint on the floor. . . .

It was "by water" of course, and the verdict was death by drowning while of unsound mind. I saw the body next day. It was my uncle's, not my guardian's body. The hair, for the first time, I saw tangled.

Oh, *Alexander*, Alexander! Merged at last in one! You, Alexander, left me a pauper. But for you, Alexander, I have still kind memories of a weak, affectionate, and sorely tempted uncle. . . .

Adventures of Miss De Fontenoy

As an occasional reader for a friendly publisher, I have come across strange stories sometimes that made me wonder about the writers and whence their material had been drawn. And by "strange" I mean uncommon, odd, unusual, entirely out of the ordinary. Had the stories been lived, or merely invented?

First novels, I knew, were by a large majority autobiographical: the writers had thrown their own experiences into the third person, often brilliantly. But such novels would be rarely followed by a second, for the personal experiences had been used up, and the creative faculty that imagines new ones was not present. A good story, however, even when the treatment fails, is there, though for lack of creative imagination it may remain raw.

It was some "raw material" by a writer called Janet de Fontenoy that caught my attention one day by this quality of strangeness, making me wonder about the writer, and whence she drew the experiences she described. Badly written, poorly presented, they somehow bore the stamp of having actually happened, for signs of imaginative faculty there were none, and they were assuredly not invented. Were they autobiographical, I asked myself? How did she compose such strange adventures? They were so utterly incredible.

My curiosity was stirred. There was an atmosphere about the tales that testified to something lived. Had there been evidence of craft, I might have doubted; it was the conviction that I was reading first-hand experiences that woke my interest to know more about their author. I could not recommend the stuff for publication, but I could write a word of tentative encouragement and suggest an interview. And this I did. Miss de Fontenoy accepted my invitation to talk about her "raw material" with a reader who had been unable to "recommend its acceptance for publication," and came to tea one afternoon in my flat.

I felt a trifle guilty, to tell the truth. Her literary talent being nonexistent, I could not honestly encourage her to continue writing and the motive behind my invitation was solely curiosity. I wanted to see what she was like, to ask about the experiences I had read, to ascertain wherein exactly lay the oddness of her mind, to judge for myself, in a word, what manner of character and personality it was that could claim to have known such things direct and at first hand. Though she had adopted the device of making the adventures happen to a man, the feminine touch seemed clear. I was too experienced, I flattered myself, to be deceived by that.

That she was not one of those glib women who create a fantasy world to compensate for a life that has disappointed them, I felt equally positive. The mental and emotional fantasia many disappointed women so easily create is unmistakable, for the ego struts and preens itself always as the central figure; but of such tiresome fantasia I could detect no sign. I was, thus, inclined to accept that Miss Janet de Fontenoy had known experiences of rarest kind, had moved, indeed, in a world not realised by the majority. These, for some reason, she had set down baldly on paper. My own training and interest in experimental psychology sufficiently explains the curiosity I felt.

I think I expected the door to admit a small, elderly woman, with glasses, a grave face rather, a pointed chin possibly, and dressed in unfashionable attire, so that when I saw a tall, broad-shouldered young man, hefty, with clear blue eyes, stride in, I confess that it rather took my breath away. After the first surprise, however, my instinctive reaction was one of relief. I was actually relieved to find that Janet de Fontenoy was a healthy looking, upstanding young male. Was there disappointment too? I think so, though it had nothing to do with the sex of my visitor, but rather with his appearance.

Fancy had played, no doubt, with a picture of someone who would suggest the mysterious, even the uncanny: there would be a hint of a queer mind, an interestingly unbalanced personality, behind dreamy eyes that saw beyond the common things of life, an atmosphere of the ghostly, even the other-worldly. Whereas this fellow was an athlete surely, a football forward, a diamond sculler, or on his way to the centre court at Wimbledon. There was nothing mysterious in the figure towering above the armchair with cushions I had placed for an elderly lady.

His mind seemed as straightforward as his physical appearance.

"I must apologise for pretending to be a woman," he began at once in a good deep voice. "I ought to have told you, I'm afraid. But"—he hesitated a fraction of a second, smiling like a shy boy rather—"I

14

knew you'd not be so interested to see a man. And I wanted to come. I hope you will forgive me."

A shade disturbed by his penetration, I smiled inwardly over my faulty judgment, and assured him there was nothing to forgive and made him sit down.

"I'm not literary either," he went on, "as you already know. I've got the mathematical mind, I believe. At least, figures are my best point. My father's an actuary, and I'm in his office."

He was direct as a poker. The little armchair, intended for a frail lady, creaked ominously as he sat down. I poured out the tea, feeling a tankard of ale or a whisky-and-soda might have been more suitable.

"Your—your work interested me," I told him, choosing the noun wrongly, for while it was not literary, it equally was not work. The writing was done surely of necessity, I knew, functional as eating, and eating is not work. "I rather wondered, you see," I stammered, "what made you try to write these experiences."

I met his directness, that is, with similar directness.

He laughed. "Try is the right word," he replied. "But I'll tell you why. I wanted to get it out of my mind on to paper. I'd have preferred to build a model, but that was impossible of course. So, I chose words—as plain and true as I could make them."

"You found expression of some kind a relief——" I suggested.

"I suppose so, yes," he said slowly. He reflected a moment. "The fact is," he went on, "I think I wanted to find a formula—an hypothesis that would cover my experiences. Writing it all out in words and sentences, setting it down in another medium, I thought, might clear my mind a bit. Besides, I wanted—I——"

I encouraged him with a nod and an understanding smile, and waited. To my amazement, a slight flush came to his brown cheeks.

"You see, I knew you would read the stuff and ask me to come," he finished, face, voice and eyes as honest as those of a schoolboy.

"Ah! You knew that," I repeated. "Knew it in advance, you mean?"

He looked straight at me, nodding his head in turn.

"I knew you'd believe them, too," he added.

"Believe the experiences—believe they really happened?"

"That's it, yes."

"You deliberately picked *me* out, then?" I asked, showing no hint of scepticism, because I felt none. "You knew my mind, my attitude?"

"Yes—up to a point, that is. I knew your mind was open, without preconceptions. You had no prejudices, I mean, against such things

15

happening." He took his second piece of cake, having scorned mere bread and butter and the hot trifles I had expected to see a spectacled lady nibble daintily.

I watched him with increasing interest, not sorry to find the direction of the talk could be left to him, and I was aware already that my mind had decided of its own accord neither to argue or deny. I found myself accepting at face value, so to speak, whatever he might tell me. The Adventures I had read in MS. rose before me vividly, forming a background to his straightforward, almost boyish personality, producing perhaps a sense of incongruity somewhere, yet nowhere of doubt. It was not easy, I mean, to reconcile "other-worldly" experiences with this stalwart, hefty fellow eating his cake with zest and with an appetite as honest as his eyes and manner.

Nothing dreamy or uncertain emanated from this very fit young man—twenty-eight to thirty years I gave him at most—whose fitness reminded me of newspaper advertisements of Grecian youths who wear "health-giving" underwear, or eat some divine patent food. Nothing fanciful lay in him, no hint of the charlatan, no touch of mystery. Desire for notoriety, as the hero of unusual adventures——a common motive of inferiority-complexes that can achieve peculiarity in no other way—was certainly absent. If this fellow claimed that he had lived unordinary things, he had lived them.

Thus, when he asserted quietly that he knew my mind in advance of meeting me, I found myself disposed to take it as true. The word "incredible"? did not again offer itself. What did offer itself, oddly enough, was the idea that his appearance and his adventures were not so entirely irreconcilable after all. This idea rose in me suddenly: that his appearance and personality, so obviously genuine, were an epitome of what he claimed, a simile rather. Behind this "obvious reality" I gazed at, a deeper reality lay concealed. Life, nature, the universe, are but a fractional, imperfect representation of an actual reality behind we never know. Their "obvious reality" is false. Similarly, behind this Janet de Fontenoy crouched another, more real being.

I remember this notion shooting across me, as I watched him enjoying his cake. While my mind, untouched by criticism, held his astonishing claim that he had known me in advance of meeting, a judgment formed itself as well. So swift are intuitive processes, that it rose, like Minerva from the head of Jove, complete in a second. Here, I felt, was a nature at one with itself, made of a single piece, homogeneous, uninjured by any grit, mental or emotional, that crept in to disturb rhythm. His machinery ran smoothly as a complete whole, its simplicity unmarred by any extraneous influence that might cause wavering. Such human beings, I knew, were of necessity extremely rare. To have reached his age intact would, indeed, constitute him almost a freak.

The poison of thought alone, of sex, if of no other activity, destroys this unique quality early. His mind, he had mentioned, was mathematical. Was he, then, acquainted with symbols only? My own thought, at any rate, made this sudden jump in speculation. That he had gauged my own, at least, was certainly true. He had deliberately picked me out as a reader of his MS. in advance. He had known that I should invite him to call, that I expected a woman, that I should be interested, and more, that I should believe. And his claim to have foreseen this scrap of the Future I indeed found myself accepting at its face value. No hostile criticism, such as normally must have been the case, stirred in me.

Having finished his cake and set down empty his third cup of tea, he declined a cigarette, asking if he might smoke his pipe.

"You've had no direct experiences of your own," he remarked, as a statement rather than a question. "If you had, you would be more than open-minded only—you'd be convinced. Wouldn't you?"

I raised my eyebrows merely, for this further evidence of penetration, of accurate knowledge rather, was again disturbing. But I made no comment. I wanted him to talk first, my own questions could come later, though I already began to have the feeling that these would be answered before I had even stated them. Did I feel that my thoughts were open to him? Hardly that perhaps. It was rather that his power of anticipation was extraordinary. Such trivial evidence of thought-transference, in any case, I reflected, was common enough between minds in sympathy. "You took that out of my very head, I was just going to say it," is a commonplace, of course.

And the sympathy between us was indeed definitely there, for while the visit, the precedents leading up to it, were of a kind to produce a certain tension, if quite easy tension, this was not present. We might have known one another for years. There was a sincerity and naturalness about him that made me think of trees: I might have been sitting in a calm, deep beech wood, communing with nature on a windless day. This sort of peace and reality he brought with him. No disturbance of any kind broke a certain stillness he produced. The simile of a deep wood on a windless day returned—no single leaf was ruffled. Yet my mind was actually seething with questions I meant to ask—about himself, about the experiences I had read, about

how, why and whence they came to him, how they affected his being, his reactions to such strange occurrences in his ordinary life, and
what, indeed, his "ordinary life" consisted of. My curiosity, my questions, however, somehow did not qualify what I call this stillness. It
remained undisturbed between us.

One must pay attention to his actual words. Each phrase held so
much.

"I've had them, at intervals, since childhood," he remarked. "At
intervals, of course. They are more real than my ordinary life. Though
they come as interruptions in my ordinary life, it's my ordinary life
that seems the interruption. As though daily life was 'being asleep,' and
I wake up suddenly. An Experience is when I'm awake. When it's over,
I fall asleep again—into ordinary life."

I did not wish to check him. I merely slipped in a quick question
by the way about his sense of time. Did time, during an Experience,
seem the same as time in ordinary life? Was the sense of duration similar in both? He smiled with pleasure.

"Of course, you ask that," he said, "because you know already.
Years are very short periods that only seem long. The Experiences last
longer, ever so much longer, but in quite another way." I left it at that,
watching him pressing his pipe down, with an air of having said all
that was necessary.

"Nothing in my parents explains anything," he went on quietly
between puffs. "My mother, a Russian now dead, was emotionally religious; my father lives only for his work and is rich. I get my turn for
figures from him. I could always add several columns at a glance, and
extract cube-roots, like the prodigies, at sight. That's what I meant by
having a mathematical mind—only figures really. The reasoning that
belongs to mathematics I don't possess. I have no reasoning power at
all—none. No sex either. Sex has never developed in me. I see nothing
that even begins to waken it——"

I interrupted, for he was going too fast—in the sense that I should
never remember all the mental notes I was making for questions later;
for, let me repeat—one should pay attention to his actual words.

"An ascetic, are you then? A virgin—still?"

He smiled, his eyes bright with a laughter that was more of surprise
than shyness.

"Continent—oh, yes—always," he answered. He seemed to reflect
a moment, as though perhaps trying to find the exact words he wanted. I, too, reflected—as swiftly and intelligently as his pregnant speech

18

permitted. Sexual energy, the basis of all energy, primarily intended for the occasional procreation of children, had long since deteriorated into a mere physical enjoyment of frequent recurrence. The waste of valuable energy to the individual, to the race, to humanity as a whole, was incalculable.

"The energy goes somewhere else," he went on, as though picking up my own fleeting thought. "Goes in another direction, of course. It all gets used—I know that much. It leaves nothing over for w—— for lovemaking," he quickly changed the word, and though there was no hint of contempt in his voice, there was a rather nameless quality I thought of as—not pity precisely, so much as pitying.

"Could you express that in your formula?"

He shook his head. "I've never got as far as a proper formula," he answered.

I used the laconic shorthand he evidently preferred, though what he had just said provided a text I could have commented upon with deep interest and at great length. Above all, I felt, argument must be avoided. He surely was telling me, rather casually, things he knew, and argument could only bewilder him. It was his simple direct utterance I wanted, the rest must wait. My visitor, of whom I knew little enough indeed, should be accepted on his own terms. My questions, I decided, must be few, but fundamental. I wished, that is, to establish one or two general principles in my own mind before going into detail. The conviction that I had come across something of rarest interest and value meanwhile deepened. I was aware of uncommon thrill.

"Naturally," I commented. "I understand. And wisdom needs no formula."

I gazed into his blue eyes through the tobacco smoke, and he returned my gaze as steadily. It was, I believe, my own eyes that fell first. Not that there was the faintest suggestion of any so-called hypnotic nonsense about his state, but that there was, for all that, some quality I found stimulating to the point of being disconcerting, since I hold "disturbing" to be too strong a word. Yet only remotely so, and perhaps the *mot juste* after all would be *inspiring*. It was as though, deep down in me and far out of sight, an odd quiver tried to rise, an eager quiver of intense excitement.

His eyes, if extremely direct, did not look through me; it was not that; nor did they, so to speak, see something behind me. That they seemed more aware, more conscious, gazed into a more extended, ag a different field, than the one I knew, expresses it best. The phrase "worlds not realised" flashed across my mind as my eyes fell from his, and the thrill I have already mentioned included in that moment a further reaction still, so that I felt spidery legs running up and down my spine, and I acknowledged the shiver we call goose-flesh.

Instantly, again, I had myself in hand, strap-hanging, as it were, to a sensible question:

"Your Experiences cannot be induced, I suspect?" I asked, though my exact meaning, it was clear, escaped him. For he had no reply at first.

"Induced?" he repeated, in his steady voice.

"Can you bring them on at will," I explained, "or when you want them?"

He shook his head decisively. "Oh no," he said, "I can't do that."

"So, you haven't trained yourself in any special way, I take it? Training of attention or will, for instance? Concentration, breathing, breath-control—what the East calls Yoga?"

He stared for a moment, wondering evidently what I was talking about. "I am ignorant, I'm afraid," he replied, "for I don't know what all this is. They come, or they don't come. Out of the blue they come——"

"Without warning?"

That made him laugh again, a jolly laugh it was, too.

"No bell rings exactly," he said, "but I'm given notice, if you like. There are warning signs as you might call it, a sort of warning thrill. Something rushes over me—*all* over, I mean."

"And what starts the thrill?"

"Well—colour or sound usually, I think, music—outline, too, sometimes." He broke off, hesitating a little. "A combination, it seems."

"Beauty?" I ventured.

He nodded at once. "Beauty, yes, that's it. Loveliness. I get a shock, you see, first."

If he talked rather as a schoolboy talks, that was what I preferred and welcomed.

"That, too," I suggested, "refused to come into your formula?"

He chuckled, the shy expression passing across his face again.

"I used the word formula before without knowing exactly what it means," he confessed. "Anyhow, I don't know properly the combination of colour and sound and emotion that bring on an Experience. They are usually the first sign of the change coming—that's all I can say."

20

I gave an understanding nod, as it were, yet not daring to pretend in any slightest degree, for he would see through any camouflage, I felt positive, and I should lose his confidence. Beauty, I mentioned, was well known to heighten and intensify consciousness with sensitive people, producing an exaltation of the faculties. "And this 'combination' you speak of," I asked, "is loveliness of one kind or another that makes you feel deeply first?"

"That's it," he agreed promptly. "The kind that really hurts—you know—gives you a stab, a wound."

"What you called a shock just now, yes; and the shock shifts your whole being, so that your consciousness finds a way open suddenly—well, elsewhere?"

His face lit up with pleasure. "Splendid!" he exclaimed, almost as though he cried "Well hit, sir!" at cricket. "I knew, of course, that you would talk to me just like this. It's what I came for really."

To gain time, perhaps to cover a momentary confusion, I lit a cigarette. My own mind, I felt, had been rushing far ahead of my strange visitor's, while yet the feeling grew upon me that his own was actually in advance. What I had thought out and reasoned, I mean, he seemed to know as naturally as a child plays with a ball. Speculations I had wildly indulged for years seemed to meet corroboration halfway in his Experiences. Dreams and visions my subconscious had beckoned from the stars came almost to earth as I watched and listened. My critical faculties, however, were not dulled entirely, for as I lit my cigarette and saw its blue smoke rise, I found myself questioning that "shock" that beauty gives—to the young, at any rate. Children, I remembered, are not susceptible to loveliness, they are not aware of beauty, they do not perceive it. At what age, I wondered, had his Experiences begun to show themselves?

"I am intensely interested," I said, after this slight pause. "But tell me—if you can remember—were you consciously aware of recognising beauty, loveliness, as a child? Did these shocks come to you as a youngster, for instance?"

For the first time he seemed to stammer.

"I—I——" he began, then stopped. Yet it was not stammering, nor was it, properly speaking, hesitation even. "As a child," he went on, presently, "in early youth—*I*—*I* did, yes, get these shocks," emphasising the pronoun peculiarly, "but—not I," repeating the personal pronoun with no emphasis at all.

His meaning came to me, though not instantly.

21

"Another 'I'—a different 'you,' of course?"

He merely nodded. It was as obvious to him as the sugared cake on the table beneath his nose.

"It's a longish time ago, you see," he observed quietly. "I was little more than a boy when the first thing happened—about seventeen—and I'm over forty-five now."

Why, I caught myself wondering, did this statement, this astonishing statement, hardly even startle me? Why did I not feel bewildered, puzzled? I ought by rights to have known a reaction of amazement, incredulity, laughter, of sceptical disbelief at any rate. Some exclamation of blank surprise, of utter doubt, should have found spontaneous expression: "Over forty-five! What d'you mean? You're not even thirty yet!" Instead of which, his statement, offered so quietly and naturally, dropped into the pool of my mind as a thin stone slips into water with scarcely a ripple. Not a leaf stirred—to use the simile of the wood again. I was the one who acknowledged to over the half-century mark, and I was talking with a youth, a young man, who yet claimed to be nearly my own age as naturally as though he said: "Yes, I'd like a cigarette," or "I feel hungry, too."

It was this absence of the normal reaction in myself that then simultaneously flashed an explanation that was similar, rather, to his stammering choice between "*I*" and "I" a moment ago. It is less easy, perhaps, to set down this hint of explanation, but the essence of it lay in time. His Experiences took place in other, in different, time. In *that* he was indeed "over forty," a hundred, a thousand. His statement was made out of a different time-scale. I now caught myself acknowledging that I had already been aware of age in him, of something old, old, of something ageless rather, even while I sat there chatting with a lad who wore the full bloom of youth.

It had lain unrecognised in me hitherto. I searched his face, his physical appearance, keenly for signs that nearly half a century should have traced; and as I did so there again stole over me that sensation as of little feathers that brushed my skin along the spine, stirred by a breath of cooler air, the touch of the unearthly. . . .

"Yes, of course," I found myself saying quietly after a certain pause, and as much pursuing a thought of my own as addressing him directly, "the careless waste of sexual energy ages us, no doubt, yet it's not the question of storing it up alone, but the way—the direction—in which to use it afterwards that is important."

"Is that it?" he replied. "I had never put it into words."

While he refilled and lit another pipe, and while my own thoughts went diving and soaring a little wildly perhaps, I got the impression that his own mind lay quite inactive, uncharged with thoughts of any kind. It came to me that he really did not think at all. He waited, anyhow, for me to speak. And this time I made a plunge for it:

"And life, as we find it and know it," I asked, following my own line of ideas somewhat at a venture again, "does life interest you—are you thrilled, I mean, or bored with it? Do you enjoy being alive? Does it seem to you worthwhile, for instance, or the reverse?"

It was, of course, a fundamental question. His relations to living involved a keynote theme. I wanted to know his main reaction to finding himself upon the planet, conditioned in time and space with a given order of faculties and senses, as human beings are. Had he an object in being alive? Was he ambitious? Was life of value, of importance, to him? Did it seem to him merely a rather futile dream, or filled with meaning?

The question demanded a reply. He gazed into my eyes. Why did I attach such importance to what he might say? I hardly knew. Had I already persuaded myself that this strange and rather casual visitor experienced—occasionally, at any rate—a different kind of life?

"It's wonderful—isn't it—merely to be alive," I added, helping him to a reply, "even if the meaning is not clear."

His eyes withdrew to the lighting of his pipe, then returned calmly to my face again, and I cannot explain why his quiet, steady gaze increased that faint tickling down my spine.

"Yes," he answered, "I do enjoy it." He hesitated. "Knowing there's a way out makes all the difference, though—doesn't it?"

I had expected his reply to be of this kind; he knew, moreover, that I had expected it. A smile began, then vanished; but behind the great sunburnt bulk of him I saw another thing steal up, something I can only describe as light and fiery, and of amazing swiftness. It was gone even as I stared.

"Your Experiences you mean, point to a way out?"

He nodded.

"A way of escape—from what would otherwise be—intolerable?"

He nodded again, giving the slightest possible shrug of the shoulders.

"From what's almost a mechanical state—a state where we just respond automatically to external *stimuli* of various kinds?" I insisted. "Like machines, rather—automata merely?"

23

A puzzled expression crossed his face. We laughed a little.

"They're real, you see. "I'm awake then. Wide awake," he put in.

"Ordinary life seems something of the dream-order by comparison, you mean? Semi-conscious almost?"

He nodded again, shrugging his big shoulders, and it was as though he said: "I suppose so." Evidently, he had never thought of putting it into words before. He gave a kind of long-drawn sigh. "There's a way out anyhow," he said, "and once we know that, we can manage to stick the rest—to enjoy it even."

He puffed his pipe, at any rate, as though he enjoyed *that*. His manner was as quiet and easy as if we had been discussing cricket averages, or styles at tennis. A pause fell between us, lasting probably longer than I realised, for I was rather intensely occupied with my own thoughts, and these thoughts dived in headlong fashion into somewhat deep recesses of my own field of psychological research. It was after a considerable interval that I heard my own voice again, but as if speaking to myself rather than to him, so that I hardly expected an answer. I was not even certain that I had spoken out loud. His comment startled me, therefore, all the more.

"Shall we ever get any further?" I was thinking. "Will our knowledge ever really advance? Shall we ever know more about essential things. . . ." And, apparently, I spoke aloud.

"Not by any method we're using at present," came the startling comment. "We shall go round and round in the same old circle as for thousands of years. Humanity as a whole, I mean. Not individuals, of course."

Was it telepathy again, or had I uttered actually? In any case, it did not matter; he had taken my own thought whole: that nothing *real* could ever be known by intellect or reason. It was the wrong instrument.

"We possess no faculty, as we are now, for knowing anything real. That's what you mean?"

He nodded, pressing the tobacco down into his pipe with one finger. "It's useless *that* way," he remarked, as though he criticised a man's service at tennis in relation to his improvement. "It's only adding the same kind of knowledge to the same kind of knowledge."

He lit a match and puffed vigorously for a moment. "To know more," he repeated between puffs, "we—we ourselves—must change."

And on this our conversation abruptly came to an end; it stopped, as though a climax had been reached beyond which nothing useful could then be said. Perhaps that was true, I found myself reflecting, as I saw him rise from his chair and knock the ashes from his pipe which had refused to light again properly. He replaced it in his pocket, his clear blue eyes gazing down at me. I sat gazing up at him a moment, after the most astonishing talk of my life. That this well set-up young fellow was nearly as old as myself seemed, of course, was incredible. The conversation just ended was, of course, even more incredible.

Cryptic, almost like some shorthand known only to the two of us, it must have sounded unintelligible to any third party who had heard it. For I had spoken as though communing with myself, uttering the final results of many years' difficult experiment and thought, but omitting all process of argument by which these results had been reached. And yet he had not only completely understood me, but had confirmed, even added to, my deep convictions. He had taught me something too.

Something in me felt breathless. Something had emanated from him all this time that almost literally took my breath away.

"You'll jot down notes about your further adventures," I remarked, walking beside him to the door, "and let me see them? "

"I'll come and tell them to you, please," he answered. "We may hit on the formula together then. You have the time."

So, he knew that too. It was true that I only "read" queer, out of the way, even outlandish MSS. for my friend, the publisher, "reading" them for my own interest without a fee.

I put no unnecessary questions to him, least of all how it was he knew so much about my mind and habits. That my hobby combined research and experiment along psychological and physiological lines was obviously no secret to him. But one question I did ask, as we reached the door into the street.

"Your name—you might as well tell me," I suggested. "Your address, of course, I have."

"Smith-Jones," he replied at once. "John." And I watched him go striding away down the street with the quiet energy and ease that belong to youth alone. He had left his MS. in my room, but purposely of course.

1

The Experiences assuredly, I reflected, were by no means all of them significant, in the sense that they added anything to life either by way of happiness, knowledge, or human faculty. Some, indeed, were little better than ghost tales, if of rather unordinary kind.

There was, thus, the matter of the mackintosh, or properly speaking, of the mackintosh and hat, an experience capable of more than one fairly obvious explanation that will occur to all, while yet, I hold, of not entirely satisfactory kind. The obvious explanations, that is, explain away better than they explain.

The account of what happened is simple enough; in the version John Smith-Jones set down on paper most would call it banal, trivial, dull. Its schoolboy English, however, could not quite conceal another quality that somehow crept past the style, the errors of punctuation, even the faulty grammar. It was this quality that caught my attention, surviving all the weaknesses of composition. Was I right concerning this "quality," I asked myself? Did I not perhaps supply it myself, imagine it?

It only to satisfy myself that it was, or was not, my own contribution, I persuaded him, oh, easily enough, one day to repeat it verbally to me. The written account lay clearly in my memory as I listened. The "quality" not only survived, but became intensified.

It was one of the earlier experiences, John somewhere about eighteen years of age, his nose well on the grindstone of his father's actuarial business, involving office work which began at the comfortable hour of ten every morning. His father, preferring his semi-country little house in Richmond, did not sleep in town, and John had a room in his aunt's apartment near the Marylebone Road in Devonshire Terrace.

Breakfast, dinner and bed he found thus with his father's unmarried sister, whose alert nowhere intrudes into what happened beyond the fact that one late October she went to Paris, taking her maid with her, and providing an opportunity for the cook, an old family servant, to take a holiday at the same time. John, thus, was left alone in the apartment, with room and breakfast attended to by the porter's wife. He rather enjoyed it; to dine in a restaurant for a change appealed to him as well, the sense of privacy, as though he owned the flat, amused him; he was the only person with a latchkey.

It afforded him pleasure, he mentioned, to find the place empty and unoccupied on getting home in the evening, or at night after dining on the way, if work had kept him late. And it was the word "unoccupied" rather than "empty" that he stressed. His account contented itself with this slight emphasis, in passing as it were, but drew no deduction from the little point. On my pressing him for a word of further explanation, he merely shrugged his shoulders. I put my question because here, it struck me, was a specific instance where the "quality" I have already mentioned stole out of the loose end his written version had failed to gather up later. "Oh," he replied, "there was a continual sort of coming and going in the place. No, not of any disturbing kind—I mean, nothing that concerned me personally—merely that I was aware of it"—which was all that I could squeeze out of him, and for the simple reason that it was all that he could tell me. The rooms were, thus, unoccupied, yet, in some sense or other undefined and indefinable, did not seem entirely empty.

Is it a distinction without a difference? I think not. The aunt, only referred to in this single regard, was a kindly ego-centric, whose voluble personality filled every corner and cranny she had left behind her. She was of the type that could talk about herself to a visitor for an hour without stopping, nor talk uninterestingly perhaps, yet add when saying goodbye: "but you've told me nothing about yourself! How are you getting on?" with an interest wholly sincere. In my own mind I ascribed John's "coming and going" to what may be called "atmospherics" left behind her.

To this unoccupied suite, at any rate, he returned one afternoon towards the end of October, made himself a cup of tea with the things left out by the porter's wife, read for an hour, dozed for another hour, and then felt it was time to go out and get his dinner. The weather was raw and squally; he chose a restaurant at hand; he chose also a rather worn grey felt hat and carried a mackintosh over his shoulder, and the mackintosh was both new and of a very light fawn colour, so light, indeed, that he remembered hesitating when he bought it, with the thought that a darker shade would wear better by not betraying the London grime so easily. And now, as he left the restaurant soon afterwards, the rain was coming down with a steadiness that prophesied a stormy autumn night, with gusts of angry wind and a raw touch of cold.

A miserable, gloomy night, it was. He walked the few hundred yards, but was glad to reach the shelter of the building, shaking himself in the vestibule like a wet dog. The porter took him up in the lift and wished him goodnight. He let himself in with his latchkey, flung his wet mackintosh and grey felt hat upon the ottoman in the corridor just outside his door, and made himself comfortable with a book in the deep armchair of his small sitting-room.

It was perhaps about ten o'clock, the gusty rain driving against the windows. But the rain and wind, shouting the end of summer dismally enough, could not trouble him, for his chair was comfortable, his voluble aunt was far away, the next day, being Sunday, allowed of breakfast in bed, and his book, *Arabia Deserta*, enchanted, even indeed, enthralled him.

In this pleasant receptive state, his thoughts a vivid picture of the coloured scenes he was reading about, John paid little attention to autumn's gusty violence, nor noted particularly the passage of time, for the idea of breakfast at any hour he happened to wake next morning rather broke time's usual tyranny. It was thus a sound in the street that first disturbed his easy enjoyment of Arabian deserts—the music of someone playing upon a fiddle that drew his attention, by slow stages, from his vicarious travels to things closer at hand. He had recognised Tchaikovsky's *Andante* even before he named it to himself, but having once named it his thoughts had then been deflected outwards.

Laying the book down upon his knee, he listened, and the exquisite and poignant melody, sighing out its soul upon the dismal street at night, plunged deeply into him. Its gracious melancholy stirred him profoundly. He imagined the homeless player, homeless and hopeless too, for who would be passing ready to give alms at such an hour in the darkness?—he saw the poor instrument, damaged to ruin by the streaming rain, he felt the soaked clothes and soggy boots . . . and opening his window he called out loudly above the wind, while he threw down half-a-crown wrapped up in a sheet of old newspaper.

The wind blew both voice and newspaper at an angle, but he saw a shadow crawl out of other shadows, pick it up, and retreat into the night . . . and when he was back in his chair again, the enchanting book ready to be resumed, he discovered that its haunting power had evaporated, something different having replaced it. There was emotion in him of disturbing kind that denied the desire to read. What were precisely its ingredients? He could not say.

There was pity, an aching pity; there was yearning, a homeless yearning; a bitter sense of desolate frustration, with a desire to escape, though not for himself primarily, from miseries due to some intolerable slavery. A pang of violent, unearthly nostalgia swept over him, that was accompanied by an icy realisation suddenly of the futility of life's brief span and its ludicrous limitations. All of which emotions, powerful and searching, grouped themselves about a vivid picture of that wretched shadow fiddling hopelessly in the cold rain and darkness.

A moment this swept over him, a moment merely, and it was while occupied with it that he caught another, closer sound, not in the street this time, but in the flat, in the corridor indeed just outside his door. He was aware of it, no more than that, for it did not draw his attention particularly, and he merely noticed it with enough vague interest to say to himself "Now, what was that, I wonder?" but caring nothing about the answer. He listened. A mouse, a stray cat dropping from a window ledge, a letter pushed beneath the front door or through the flap. There was, however, no conscious attention in his listening, his mood still under the sway of that haunting music, that aching yearning pity, with the mournful, homeless shadow crawling in the rainy darkness.

He did listen, none the less, with a certain deliberation, and then, the sound not being repeated, he picked up his book again and went on reading. And he was half-way down the page when it came back to him sharply that no mouse or cat had made that sound. It was a footstep. This did not interrupt his reading; it was merely that another part of his mind recognised the fact while he still read—until he reached the end of the page and laid the book down abruptly because the sound had suddenly been repeated.

He listened now with close attention. A footstep had passed along the corridor immediately outside his door, a very quiet, soft, almost a stealthy, footstep. It was not audible now. It had stopped.

That he was alone in the empty flat then came over him, the front door locked, the porter gone, the lift no longer running, for it was after eleven o'clock, and that the only latchkey was in his pocket, and—that there was somebody in the corridor. This slight increase of awareness came over him. "Who can *that* be, I wonder?" ran a second question across his mind, yet again a question he asked himself quite casually. There was no trace of nervousness in him anywhere, as he laid his book down and got out of his armchair to have a look for himself.

"I'll just have a look round," was the way he put it to himself, as he rose in leisurely fashion and crossed the carpet.

Opening his door, he stood staring along the dark passage, turning on the electric switch the same second. There was no one there, the corridor was empty. He strode along it, looking into each room in turn with the light full on—his aunt's bedroom, the drawing-room, both draped in dust sheets, the kitchen, the bathroom too. Under the beds he looked and into the cupboards. He even went out on to the iron landing beyond the scullery where the tradesmen hoisted up the food. There was no one. Nor was there any open window through

29

which a cat might have crept. The entire place was empty, silent, apparently unoccupied, so that he turned out the various lights and went back to his reading, feeling quite sure he was alone in the apartment. And it was then, while reading, that another part of his mind let loose an unexpected whisper:

"There was a change in that corridor, a difference in it, something you noticed, but didn't realise quite."

It was true. He now realised it. There *was* a slight alteration in the corridor, a detail missing, something that had been there when he came home from dinner had disappeared. This detail, whatever it might be, was no longer there. The same moment he was out of his chair and in the corridor again, searching keenly with his eyes and memory, and as he looked at the low divan where he had flung down his mackintosh and old grey felt hat, he instantly detected what the alteration was.

The fawn-coloured mackintosh lay where he had flung it, patched with wet, one sleeve hanging down, the other sprawling over a cushion. It was the grey felt hat he could not see. The hat was gone.

So there had been someone in the flat. His search had not been thorough enough. He must look again. He did so, and ended with the positive certainty that neither man nor mouse, burglar least of all, was in hiding. He closed the door of each room in turn behind him, fastened the chain along its groove in the front door as well. He did this very thoroughly. The hunt for the missing hat was equally conscientious. It had neither slipped behind the divan, nor fallen to the floor, nor become mixed up with the mackintosh. It had been lying, he remembered distinctly, on the top of the wet mackintosh, for he had taken it off last and tossed it there, and, since it was now gone, somebody had taken it.

Somebody, yes, but who? Had, perhaps, the front-door catch failed to work when he came in, so that a hand could slip through quietly? Not only was the distance too great for any hand to reach, but the front-door was securely fastened, and the only available latch-key was in his pocket.

Moreover, he had definitely heard that stealthy footstep.

A moment longer he stood looking down at the mackintosh, which he then folded differently so that another side of it should dry, and then he went back slowly to his sitting-room and calmly resumed the reading of his *Arabia Deserta*.

Calmly, yes. For somehow, the little incident did not disturb him particularly, did not really puzzle him unduly, as it must have disturbed and puzzled, probably alarmed as well, anybody else. Not that he had the faintest idea how that hat had vanished, nor any explanation of the footstep he had indubitably heard, but that strangely—in some strange way—he knew it was explicable. He understood that it was all right, using both words precisely in their true meaning. The notion of a thief or burglar left his mind entirely. The agency by which the hat had been removed was, literally, all right.

That it was being worn now in the gusty rain and wind, as he felt positive it *was* being worn, he knew equally, was all right. His mind and pen used the schoolboy phrase, where a more lettered choice would doubtless have used "natural." For "natural" as against super-natural was assuredly what he meant. The positive assurance of its rightness and naturalness, he mentioned, was "all over him."

The reading of *Arabia Deserta*, therefore, continued easily and de-lightfully, and it must have been fully an hour later when a sound again caught his absorbed attention. It was, again, indubitably a foot-step, again just outside his door, where someone was walking quietly along the corridor. He heard a gentle click. The same moment he laid his book aside and was out of his room in the little hallway. The light, he saw, to his astonishment was turned on.

Perhaps fifteen seconds was the interval between hearing the sounds and standing in the hallway. The corridor was empty, the chain hung securely in its iron groove, no door banged or was stealthily closed, but there was another alteration in the detail of the familiar scene that this time he detected at once. The mackintosh, the fawn-coloured mackintosh, no longer lay on the divan. It had disappeared. Following the old grey hat, it had been taken too.

Someone who had taken the hat had now come back and taken the mackintosh as well. That was as plain as the nose on his face. Both articles had been removed while he sat reading his book, removed by someone who had found an entry into the flat twice in succession, and who, similarly, had left it again twice in succession, each time with extraordinary rapidity. This was clear and positive; but it was equally clear and positive that there was no conceivable way of entry or de-parture, no possible way by which any human being could have got into the flat and out of it again. The same positive certainty applied to the question of hiding. Faced with which definite and perplexing certainties, he yet was fully aware that the whole puzzle was explicable as simply, above all as naturally, as though he had himself opened the

31

front door and given away the missing articles with his own hands.

Standing in the passage, now flooded with light, he found other positive assurances in him too, and these were as definitely certain as the fact that his wrist-watch showed the hour of one o'clock. These positive assurances admitted of no arguing, needed no consideration even; they merely presented themselves to his mind as knowledge. He was convinced of them as he was convinced that his watch face showed one o'clock:

Both hat and mackintosh had been removed by human agency. The taker had not been secreted in the flat beforehand, but had entered and left. This taker, moreover, strangely, was still here, still in the flat, even though he had left. The impossibility of this presented no difficulty somehow. The taker, indeed, stood at this actual moment very close to him, as close as hands or feet. This conviction of intimate proximity did not disturb him.

"It is all right," he heard his mind saying to itself, "is quite all right and natural. . . ."

The taker, he realised further, was not a thief, but someone who needed both hat and mackintosh, someone who could use them, wear them, with a clear conscience, someone who was using and wearing them at this very moment—now.

With such positive and convinced knowledge in him, he did not therefore waste time in making a further useless search, but stood there in the lighted corridor, dealing with these inconsistent and incredible facts. For facts they were, though how precisely he "dealt" with them lay beyond his powers to describe. Not with his mind assuredly, he asserts, nor with any faculties of reasoning or analysis. His medium of expression in words, in literary form, here failed him completely; he used the term "dealt"? and made no more exact attempt at description. The incredible inconsistencies and obvious impossibilities, he says merely, did not exist. Neither fear nor nervousness of any kind came near him. He accepted the blazing absurdities quite calmly, standing motionless for a moment, listening, watching. Then he glanced at his watch. It was 2.30. The "moment," therefore, actually had been an hour and a half.

"It didn't surprise or startle you?"

He shook his head and smiled.

"And that hour and a half you were standing in the passage—you've any recollection of it? Ninety minutes—I mean, or just a moment? Did it seem long or short? Did nothing happen to you in all that time?"

He answered simply, and without hesitation:

"Well—rain and wind were in my face," he told me. "It was cold. My feet were wet, my body ached like hell, I remember sneezing and shivering. Then there came the comfort of warmth, the heat of a warm bar in a dirty pub., and two or three glasses of beer—of bitter, rather. I dislike bitter very much."

"Sleeping"? I asked. "Do you remember sleeping anywhere? Lying down? Going to bed, for instance?"

He laughed a little. "In a dim way, yes," he said. "I changed half-a-crown and the bed was ninepence, but that was somewhere else. And they took a fiddle from me, a fiddle and case, and gave me a ticket. Only, the room was packed with lousy men and stank so that I—sorry—I was sick on the floor———"

"That's a positive memory?"

He nodded with a rueful smile. "I looked at my watch just after it," he said, grinning again. "It was 2.30 and I was standing in the corridor."

Sense of an interval, I gathered next, there was none; yet a sense of duration, apparently, there was.

"You found yourself exactly where you were when you left your book to look for the possible intruder?"

"In the same spot."

"Any thought, any recollection, of the fiddler in the rain still in your mind?" I asked.

"None whatever."

"You had forgotten his existence?" I insisted.

There was a moment's hesitation, as though he wanted to be extremely accurate.

"No thought or picture of the man came to my mind," he said. "He didn't crop up once. I thought of him later, of course—next day, I mean. But in the corridor—nothing."

"And the missing hat and mackintosh—the possible thief or intruder—did that bother you?"

"Oh, I remember that passed through my mind," he admitted, with his frank, delightful smile, "but—I had no feeling of bother———"

"Or question?"

"Or question," he agreed.

"You felt comfortable and happy—normal?"

After an instant's hesitation he accepted that. "I felt a sort of inner relief," he found his words. "Relieved, yes, that's the word. Sort of pleased and comforted, you know." And then he repeated the first adjective: "relieved."

"Any sign of your having left the house and been out of doors?" I fired at him.

He answered instantly. "Soaked to the skin." He laughed outright then. "And a little sick—a touch of nausea perhaps." He grinned like a boy who had eaten sweet things unwisely. "What I did then? What I did next? Oh, I got out of my wet clothes, had a hot bath in auntie's lovely bathroom, and went to bed and slept like a top till nine o'clock next morning."

Such a detail as the notorious licensing hours seemed hardly worth mentioning, I felt, though it was in both our minds, of course. In an experience where Before and After held no meaning, where a single individual, it seemed, could operate in two different places simultaneously, argument about such different time and space struck me as useless. I let it pass. I lit a cigarette and looked hard at him with an examining eye across the smoke. His own expression and manner betrayed no doubt or hesitation of any kind.

He was frank and honest as a child. Nothing veridical anywhere, absolutely nothing, I thought to myself. Aloud I then said: "You see now why a written account of all this could not interest anyone—because of its utter, its hopeless, incredibility. To the ordinary man even normal, linear time is muddling enough sometimes. Most folk are rather disturbed, too, by any too vivid visualisation of the past, but a glimpse of the future means almost consulting a mental specialist. The two together, just baldly written down——"

We laughed together, but while he laughed he began fumbling in his pocket and a moment later produced a scrap of dirty paper and handed it across to me.

"I found this when I woke up," he said. "It was on the floor beside my bed."

It was a doss-house ticket in the name of John Doe, the date stamped on it by a rubber stamp, with the words "One fiddle and case."

"The date is right," he mentioned quietly. "The address—well, you've read my manuscript."

I left this detail too till later, since it was a verifiable one, and in due course *was* verified by myself, for I called at the doss-house, presented the receipt, and now have a fiddle and case in a cupboard of my library.

34

I took up some further questions first. About sleeping, for instance: had he, to his knowledge, ever fallen asleep in an upright position? He had not. Then, were his dreams as a rule actual and vivid? They were not, and for the simple reason that his sleep was always dreamless. He had never once dreamed, he assured me, in his whole life.

"I have never known a dream," he told me, adding that of course that might only mean that he never remembered them. "My eight hours' sleep every night go just like that," and he clicked his fingers in the air. "I shut my eyes, I wake up. It's like a minute. A dream would probably be as strange to me as—as, say, the taste of alcohol. That's probably why the bitter made me sick that time."

The pause between us, though it lasted several minutes, had nothing awkward or embarrassing about it. The prolonged silence was as natural as if I had been sitting in a wood with trees all round me. Oak, beech and pine may overcharge a receptive mind with communications of a rather pregnant silence to which no comment by way of audible response is possible.

I jumped back to something his written account had dismissed with a dozen words:

"The taker, as you call him—were you conscious, when standing in the corridor, of his presence?"

"Of his existence, yes," he answered.

"As another person?"

"Another—no," came the prompt reply.

"One?" I asked.

He nodded emphatically. "Just one," he agreed with decision.

"Very close to you, very near, you felt him?"

"We occupied the same space—as close as that." Then he laughed. "And how can we get that into a formula?" he asked me with a grin.

It was some considerable time later, the voluble aunt back from Paris, when a sort of climax appeared: a "sort" of climax, for in his written version it was evidently intended as such, though its crude, brief manner of presentation made it merely the addition of another wholly incredible episode.

He was strolling along Jermyn Street shortly before one o'clock to a luncheon engagement, and he was dressed accordingly in what he called his "best," tidy at any rate and looking a very presentable, even handsome, figure, and being ahead of time he was idling along rather. He carried only a cane. It was a sunny day, the air soft and warm, with the lovely radiance of an Indian summer snatched from June. The light creamed over almost into blossom, the sweetness was like perfume.

"Your mind occupied?" I enquired, since there was no mention of his mood. "Particularly occupied, I mean?"

He shook his head. "Just hungry," he said, "and looking forward to lunch, while enjoying the day, of course—I mean, you couldn't help *that*. It changed the street and houses so——"

"A change in yourself too of any kind?" I put in quickly.

"A bit, yes. I felt a change coming—something or other in me—trembling a little——"

When his attention was drawn suddenly to a figure across the street and slightly ahead of him, the figure of a tall man looking into a shop-window. But his attention was not merely drawn, apparently, it was definitely arrested, so that he stopped dead on the kerb and stared. For some seconds, half a minute possibly, he stood quite still, watching the figure, staring at it, as it moved to the next shop-window a little further on. The man, in spite of the warm sun, was wearing a light fawn-coloured mackintosh, and on his head was an old grey felt hat. Only the back of the figure was visible, as the man stooped over and peered into the windows, pacing slowly along, and now and again returning a little on his steps.

He watched the figure with the keenest possible intentness for perhaps another minute or so, and then realised that the person was no longer the same. It was not the same figure, something had happened, it was another, a different, person pacing to and fro. He declared that he knew instantly who it was, this changed figure, knew instantly, too, that he must cross the street and join him. He must be very quick, he must go over immediately without a second's delay. It was imperative beyond all doubt or question to act at once, as imperative—he used a striking simile here in his written version—as to seize a flung rope when you were just sinking for the last time.

And he obeyed the impulse, yet even while doing so, while dodging the rather slow traffic, he had time to become aware of another thing as well. His reference to it was brief, a passing mention merely, but its importance to me seemed vital, and I linked it in my mind with his hearing of the Tchaikovsky *Andante* in the wet and windy street earlier in the adventure.

It was music, though music of a kind that would have left the majority unaffected: a group of four men, singing for alms, had turned the corner up from St. James's Square into Jermyn Street, and their voices, if rough, were good. They sang in tune, they sang with feeling, there was pathos, even beauty, in the Irish air that only just overrode the traffic rumble.

He caught it as he crossed, and the change he had already mentioned in himself 'became intensified. This change he had felt coming a moment earlier now abruptly established itself. It was all over him, within him, definitely there.

"You can put a label to it?" I asked. "Describe it?"

He nodded, a smile of peculiar radiance flashed to his face and vanished.

"Loveliness," he whispered softly.

This was the word used in his manuscript, but mentioned without further elaboration, and I wanted to hear if he could add to it. Questions and answers may be summarised, and what he said was good and easily understandable up to a point. For the beauty of the morning, of which he had already been quite aware, fell upon him with a sudden abruptness for some reason that held shock. With a rush it came over him, "like a burning flame of fire," as he put it, and the music of those singing voices seemed a spear-head that pierced him to the core. This intensification was due, apparently, to the combination of the light and colour, and the sound. This "loveliness," which had nothing to do directly with the figure he was watching, burst upon him with its overwhelming, shattering appeal. And he tried to explain, in answer to my questions, that a fellow's normal state held no machinery adequate for dealing—using the verb he favoured so often—with such loveliness, for it strained almost to breaking point every receptive faculty a man possessed.

"So, I went across to him," he continued, "diagonally over the street, dodging the traffic, and came up with the figure very rapidly, and looked over the man's shoulder as he stared into the shop, and saw by the reflection of the face in the window who it was. The two pairs of eyes met fairly and squarely in the glass."

And here, without worrying him with the numerous questions that worried myself, I went straight on to the next point in the Adventure exactly as his manuscript description took it.

"In which instant," I said, "you found yourself—not in Jermyn Street at all?"

Although we both knew the answer, it came naturally and promptly:

"I found myself in one of those little side-streets that run off Baker Street, perhaps a mile and a half away, and it was raining quite heavily, and I was mighty glad that I was wearing my mackintosh and my old grey felt hat, and I had something in my hands, though it was too dark—oh, yes, it was night of course—too dark to see exactly what it was, and a window was flung open suddenly far above me on the opposite side, and someone threw out a coin wrapped in a piece of white paper which the wind blew away sideways, and just as I crept after it and picked it up, I found myself in the lobby of a restaurant in Jermyn Street again, my host a few yards away waiting, while I pocketed a cloak-room ticket from a page-boy, and I had just said to this boy 'Both hats—you took both hats?' and the boy was answering with a grin, 'There was only one, sir—a black felt hat and a cane,' as I stuffed the ticket in my waistcoat pocket entirely satisfied that the boy was right."

<h2 style="text-align:center">2</h2>

It was sufficiently easy, of course, to check a good many of his statements, and I did this thoroughly enough to satisfy at least myself. Beyond this I felt no interest, for in examining cases of such abnormal kind the verdict of the man in the street seemed to me valueless. Judgments of the herd, being expressions of the herd-instinct, are invariably negative, self-preservation making all innovation abhorrent and dangerous. Anything that attacks the established order must be crushed out. Nor had I any desire to justify experiences that would hold in a court of law. What interested me, frankly, was this chance personal justification of ideas and theories my own research and speculation had led me to think might not be wholly impossible.

In the sense that a mad mind is a mind out of relation with its environment, John Smith-Jones was madder than any Carrollian hatter. He was a crazy man, suffering from acute paranoia, a victim of absurd, incurable delusions, while yet a saner man, a mind more perfectly in relation with its environment I swear I have never met. Environment indeed is here the master word, for his environment was unquestionably an extended one. It was an environment otherwise conditioned, familiar with expansion in space and time.

I made few notes of what had so far come my way from his accounts. Strictly speaking, only one or two conclusions seemed definite enough to be worth setting down on paper, and these I arrived at after hearing a number of his Adventures, not merely the one just sketched. And the first is easily stated: he possessed another way of "knowing," a way not open to ordinary folk, though affirmed in the *Yogi* teachings

of the East to be accessible to those who can dare the necessary training. Apparently, to stop thinking is the first essential, in other words
to arrest the ordinary method of knowing and to get behind thought.
Obviously, to cease thinking is a labour of Hercules that, open poten-
tially to all, can be achieved actually by extremely few. John Smith-
Jones managed it easily and naturally.

The second conclusion I arrived at was also clear enough: that an
Adventure only followed when certain antecedent conditions were
precisely right. Unless these exact conditions supervened, his life was
as normal and commonplace as yours or mine, but with their arrival
he slipped into a state of other consciousness as naturally as one slips
from waking into sleeping, or *vice versa*. All moved on oiled ball bear-
ings, there was no jerk, no hitch, no shock or sense of violent transition. And once in the Adventure, once experiencing it, the intense
reality of it was overmastering. It held a shattering intensity of conviction that made it seem his usual state, his daily life in comparison a
dream-like kind of brief semi-consciousness.

These antecedent conditions, moreover, were easily recognisable,
and can be summed up in a single word: beauty. A message of beauty
flamed upon him and he was off! Whether the message came by sound,
form, or colour made no difference. Loveliness was the key, and loveliness, blazing upon him as with the power of some awful lightning,
fused the limitations of normal consciousness and introduced him
into a state of changed consciousness where another way of knowing
operated and where time and space lost their pitiful limitations.

The power of beauty to heighten susceptibility and intensify consciousness is, of course, established; but in his case there was more than
this. Not merely an intensification, but a different type, of consciousness altogether supervened.

The Adventure in Gloucestershire was induced apparently by the
intoxicating loveliness of the May in an ordinary English Spring. What
layer of time and space he tapped here, whether medieval, or perhaps
not even strictly his own, is not for me to say. That I followed it at all
was due to some out of the way reading I had done. To the ages of
superstition, of course, belongs the alchemist's notion that man is a
fourfold combination of the elements, then limited to four instead of
over ninety, and that while his physical body was the vehicle for manifestation on earth, it held also three other vehicles for manifesting,
respectively, in air, water, and fire. Sylphs, undines, salamanders remain
today the nursery myths of what was once, no doubt, believed in all

sincerity and, who shall prove, not based upon authentic experience?

The Adventure, at any rate, sprang from the quite commonplace opportunity of a lift by motor a friend offered him into the wilds of Gloucestershire, and the friend was a brown-eyed woman who meant no more to him, he told me, than the girl in the box-office of some cinema where he might buy a ticket.

"The May's rather poor this year, don't you think..." she remarked.

On the way out of London this seemed true, the hedges thinly covered, or without any blossoms at all, but as the car crossed Buckinghamshire it gave signs of rising to the surface, in Oxfordshire it showed still thicker, and when Gloucestershire was reached the fragrant white blossoms poured in shining creamy cataracts down the sloping meadows. There was this suggestion of careless rioting. In old-world gardens, too, as the car rushed by, the laburnum, with its pools of dripping gold, was lavish, even to wantonness, while such a glory of buttercups, he thought, he had never seen before.

"The A.A. men are such a decent class, I always think. . . ."

If only she would have let him enjoy it in peace and without interruptions. It was kind of her, of course, to give him this lift on her way to Broadway Village, a score of miles beyond where he had to go; she drove well and safely too, so that, much as he disliked motoring, he felt confidence and was free to enjoy the scenery without worrying about corners and traffic. If only she would leave him to his enjoyment. It was her stream of comments, dealing with the obvious top of life, that broke with interrupting jerks into his deep pool of intense delight and ruined its clear surface, making a rejoinder of some sort necessary.

For this Spring loveliness, always a disconcerting experience, brought its customary sweet pain. Today, after months in a London street, the sunshine over this riot of flowers came with a kind of shock. There were foaming torrents of wild hemlock too, the beech leaves at their tenderest, and the grey stone villages rose through a dream, beauty shining everywhere with a poignancy that hurt.

"Wonderfully well marked, the roads, aren't they?" she commented, as they sped through a stretch of loveliness that seemed hardly of this world at all. . . . .

Inside him lay a glass, a mirror, some medium at any rate in which was transmuted all he saw and felt into an ineffable shimmering glory of delight, hinting at transcendental meanings he almost captured, yet never quite.

"Thirty-five's quite fast enough, isn't it? We're ahead of time. . . ."

plopped with a little splash into his silent inner pool just when something of translucent gauze and brilliant wings flew towards him with a sudden revelation.

"Oh, rather—quite—it's just right, I'm sure," he managed to jerk back with the proper polite interest, turning his head awkwardly towards her as he did so, for it had been precisely in just this fraction of a second that he was first aware of the change about him. It came stealing up and over, yet with its customary instantaneous swiftness, for it was already there, increasing, growing possibly in power, yet definitely established in a flash. It rose from some inmost and viewless centre of the day itself, from that deep heart of painful loveliness, that central power of stinging beauty, through which the car sped with its purring sound.

Purring, yes; that was precisely the right word. The voice, too, was purring. . . .

She had just said something, another remark, and he wondered if he had heard it correctly at first: "Here lies our shell of fire, air, water, earth. . . ." Was that what she said? A phrase so meaningless could not have left anyone's throat, hers least of all, at such a time and place. He had misunderstood; the car needed water, with more petrol, Shell of course, opening a window for fresh air—anything but what she had seemed to say and he had seemed to hear.

Then turning to glance at her, this thin, brown-eyed woman, he had sharply realised in the same instant that she was comely. The idea had never entered his head before. He had merely known in a vague kind of way that her voice was pleasant, soothing rather, her smile, if crooked slightly yet not disfiguringly, lit the face oddly, and that the eyes were clear shiny brown. Now, as he stared into them, they held a touch of fiery amber, though that must have been the sun of course.

"Eh?—oh, yes—" he stammered, bewildered by his having possibly mis-caught the words, and then heard his voice adding in quite another tone, a tone that held something whispering about it: "It's fire with me, remember. I move most easily in that———"

"Fire!" she laughed. "As if I didn't know it already! I'm air, of course. We are friendly then. Air and fire work together. . . ."

A grinding noise like the roar of a lion, a sudden jerk that shot him forward against the windscreen, interrupted, so that he caught his breath and shielded his face with outstretched hands. There came no crash, however. The car had stopped.

"Hulloa!" he cried, withdrawing his eyes from hers with a kind of difficulty, and wondering why his voice had turned hoarse and trembling. "Not an accident, is it?" He heard her give a quick choked-off laugh in her throat as she said "Sorry! These four-wheel brakes. I forgot. We're wrong anyhow—our last turn, I think——" She turned her head round. "You might go and ask that old man where this road goes."

Her voice died away, as he got out and made his way, as in a dream, to the figure leaning against a gate, an old fellow in gaiters who eyed his questioner good-humouredly enough. A lurcher at his feet got up and sniffed at his approach. "No," growled the old fellow, showing broken teeth in a grin intended to be friendly, "this road don't go any further'n the farm yonder." He pointed with his stick to a scattered group of grey stone buildings fifty yards ahead. "That's where the man fell over the edge," he added with his growling chuckle.

"Fell over the edge!"

The old fellow repeated the chuckle that was half grunt, half growl. He seemed amused, as though the man who fell over the edge had only got his deserts. "He thought it went on. It don't. The road ends sudden," he explained curtly enough. "But you can get shelter there maybe. They'll take you in."

He turned his attention to his lurcher to signify that was all he wanted to say, and the other gave his thanks and swung back towards the car, noticing as he did so out of the corner of his eye a stretch of bare down above the buildings, where against the skyline a gaunt single tree stood out, a big torn branch hanging down loosely and swaying in the wind. Only the car, as he now turned back to report the old man's words, no longer stood there.

No vehicle at all was there except an open cart of sorts, with a tired horse in the shafts, the reins held by a woman wearing, he saw, some shoddy cheap fur about her neck. The brightness and the gay morning sunshine, too, were gone. That lonely tree, it struck him, stood out now against a sky of leaden clouds. The entire scene was gloomy, and with a rising wind that struck cold against the cheek. The dusk was falling fast.

He approached the cart slowly, the woman's eyes watching him steadily, the only portion of her face visible, as they peered out through a welter of wrapped shawls about her head and shoulders. But the woman, he knew, for all her shoddy clothes, was comely. He was aware of silken hair. At the same time those staring eyes, rather intently fixed, made him think of a feline that looks for prey, an unwelcome notion he could not by any means account for.

"Come on out," he said in a voice of pretended control, for he was frightened, though the slight shiver running over him might well have been due to the bitter wind. The woman, he felt suddenly and sharply, was somewhere too strong for him. She was very sure of herself. "We're lucky. We can get shelter in that farm. The horse is done, anyhow. Get out—will you?"

She unwound her shawls a little as he helped her out, but she missed the yielding iron step and a length of fine leg appeared in a grey worsted stocking that yet could not hide its shapeliness. He made her take his arm, while his other hand led the stumbling, weary nag, and at that moment, as though from under her very skirts, a large tawny cat, that seemed to have sprung from the old cart, ran past and ahead of them with a silent dancing gait. It had, no doubt, emerged from the hedge, he hurriedly told himself. It disappeared in the deepening shadows towards the old grey buildings. A column of pale blue smoke rose from the main chimney, but almost at once turned downwards, sinking rapidly, as in sign of coming bad weather, floating in sullen, heavy coils, then, past the lower mullioned windows.

"I'm air . . . and that means we're friendly . . . for air helps fire . . ." rang on in his ears as he approached the old grey building, knocked, and enquired about shelter.

"I'll put the 'oss away," he muttered, as the old *beldame* opened the door and accepted the benighted couple, nor did it occur to him even that he said "'oss," or that he stepped in hesitatingly. He only noticed, to tell the truth, that his friend, the slim, brown-eyed woman, brushed past him with rather a masterful air as though she had a right to shelter here, perhaps expected it, and that his nostrils caught a whiff of perfume, half artificial, half of sweet warmish animal fur, as she went by him into the lamp-lit room.

It occurred to him suddenly, while these two talked together of the stormy night, and the blind road that ended in a sudden drop where horses, sheep and cattle too easily went lost, that he had left his flint-lock in the cart. And while putting the 'oss to stable he now hid it beneath his heavy coat and brought it back into the house. What made him do so he could not rightly say. There was uneasiness in him, a fear of some sort, a fear of uncommon things, and that was all he knew, a fear that, like the wind, came suddenly and also, like the wind, was rising. . . .

The thick onion soup had a welcome, fragrant smell when he

came back, and he sat down to his bowl without a word or question, and broke his coarse bread into it hungrily. Then, looking up, he noticed how hungrily she, too, gulped her soup, yet daintily, and how delicious her moist red lips were. Even when she blew across her big spoon to cool the steaming mixture, she did it invitingly, her brown eyes gleaming above the succulent mouthful. His strange uneasiness grew as he watched, but something else rose up to meet it. A light shudder ran through him.

"God! Am I so weak and easily taken? . . ." passed through his mind, for he knew that, even if weak and trembling at an offer so perilously easy, this was something he did *not* mean to yield to. As a Disciple of the Order, as a wrestling and struggling Aspirant, this casual loss of valuable energy, above all else, must not dare to tempt him. Oh, he felt sure of himself and his vows, confident enough in all conscience. With some vehemence he gave himself this hurried assurance. When the scene was gaily set, he reminded himself, among lights and music, wine and colour, he had no fear, for danger was too obvious and flaunting.

But it was this chancy, so unlikely setting, in a gloomy farm upon a wayside road, seeking shelter merely for a few hours from an ill-omened night and threatening weather, and with a woman who, for all her soft brown eyes and comeliness, was surely but of passing acquaintance, it was this very casualness, hiding a stiletto beneath the homespun, that made him tremble.

He gave an involuntary start as her voice reached him across the table:

"You brought in the flint-lock," she said suddenly between her draughts of soup. "Is it then a cat you are afraid of?" her soft laugh showing her white even teeth. "A yellow-backed farm cat?" Her eyes held his without wavering.

"A cat?" he asked thickly, taken by surprise. "Did you see a cat?"

"There's always a cat in these old farmhouses," she told him, taking a mouthful of the fried ham and eggs now set before them. "If you don't meet a barking dog, it always means they keep a cat, and they're generally amber-coloured." Her eyes still held him.

"I brought in the gun," he admitted a trifle sullenly, "because—this is the sort of place that favours the highwaymen for a night's lodging. And tomorrow, even sooner, we may be glad of it, for you never know."

"Tomorrow," she repeated, without lowering her steady eyes. "Yes,

44

tomorrow maybe," and she wiped her lips, which gleamed moistly in the lamplight.

The coffee was drinkable, the rum still better, and when he complained of the cold she mixed his second glass, and then his third, having swallowed a sturdy two herself. Her breath, drawing towards him across the narrow table where her elbows rested, her face thrust forward, seemed to mingle with the sweet-flavoured liquor; and it was when the old farmwife, *beldame* as he first thought her, came in to ask if all was to their liking, that he caught the abrupt swift certainty that the two women were not unacquainted, not strangers to one another.

And on the instant, though he gave no outward sign, his whole being rose in sudden, alert challenge. He knew, of a surety, the brown-eyed woman had led him here with purpose. The old tired horse, he remembered now, had made to take another turning as of habitual instinct while she had persuaded it, aye and himself too, otherwise along the rough trail below the down.

'It's an old beast, eh, that tawny cat of yours?" he asked abruptly of the farmwife, aiming to take her by surprise. "A fine creature too," he added admiringly.

"Cat!" she replied. "There's not a cat within a twenty mile of here. I mislike the things and wouldn't have one about me."

"A stray cat, dear," put in the brown-eyed woman quickly, but not so quickly that the quick sharp glance between the pair was lost upon him. He emptied his glass to hide the awkwardness with some natural gesture.

"They do come strayin' over the hill sometimes," the old woman was saying, "but they don't stay long," she added significantly, "for they know I won't abide 'em." And she got up and began to clear away the dishes.

"Yet you have a power of mice," he put in. "They're useful to you—a good sharp cat, I mean."

She never raised her eyes. "Useful to some, maybe," she mumbled, "but they're more'n of this world and best put away, to my way of thinkin'."

He shivered, without knowing exactly why, so that the brown-eyed woman—she was not really thin at all, he noticed again, but most sweetly and comfortably covered—poured him out a glass of yellow rum. "It makes me shiver too, dear," she murmured soothingly, "and this will just make us sleep good and proper. It was a cold job putting the 'oss to stable, I'll be bound."

He swallowed it heartily enough, determined to give no sign if he could help it that he realised something here to do with cats he did not welcome, knew also that he was betrayed, and the amber of her soft brown eyes, he was aware, again slipped stealthily into the gleaming contents of his glass, so that he drank that down too with the rich liquor.

This acceptance and refusal he felt in him, this strength and weakness, lay beyond his entangling; it was as though a portion of his being was growing slowly a little numbed, and he could not be sure whether the rum soothed or stimulated the deep uneasiness that growled out of sight within him. . . .

Their rooms were far apart, at opposite ends of the old building, and as he went to bed, he heard that rising wind pass alternately sighing and roaring over the grey tiles and naked downs beyond, an unholy wind, he was persuaded, renewing the faint shudder in his mind with the vivid thought of that old tired tree against the skyline. He saw again the loose dangling branch swinging creakily.

"Goodnight, dear," he heard her voice at the corner of the landing when they parted, candle in hand, and saw her amber eyes gleaming brightly in the unsteady flame.

It was the increasing tumult of that violent, unholy wind beating against the narrow casements of his room that mingled with her last words as he stood on the boards by the light of a single candle, hesitating whether to undress or not. The rum worked in his blood, but something else worked too, and instinct, since alcohol dulls the reasoning faculties, was expressly alert. This instinct played a game as it were, a game that lacked form, but assuredly did not lack meaning. It played with several counters, and these counters, if a trifle confused, were insistent in the claim they made upon his attention. He could visualise them distinctly, he could name them correctly, all three of them: that large yellow-backed cat, the understanding between the two women, and the flint-lock.

His mind took each in turn and dealt with it after a fashion.

The gun—he had, after all, left it downstairs; the cat—he had not seen it again; the two women—at the remote end of the house, yet, he somehow knew, far from being in bed and asleep. But it was the gun that chiefly held his attention. He wanted it near, he wished he had it ready to his hand in this dim-lit room. It lay in the hall, he remembered, beneath his overcoat on the settle. The next thought was easy: he would go down and get it. Obeying the instinct, he stole across the floor on tiptoe and cautiously opened his door, and then, without knowing why, he hesitated. He stopped dead. He listened intently.

What made him hesitate? What caused the moment's uncertainty? Thought, of course. He had begun to think. It was reason that blocked the flow of automatic guiding instinct. Was he, then, afraid of anything, he asked himself? Of anyone? Of highwaymen, least of all, he told himself. Of a great cat with a yellow back? Assuredly not. Then why did he want the gun? He could not use a gun against a comely woman with amber eyes; nor for that matter, he swore to himself again, did he need any means of defence against such temptation except his own firm confident will.

For a second, as he stood hesitating by the door, such thoughts tumbled about in him, and the next second, dismissing them, he passed through the door and crept softly along the landing, lit by the gleam from the candle left behind him. Silent and dark the landing was, though the wind outside made a mighty howling as its gusts stormed against the walls. These passed, leaving a silence deeper than before. He crept along, knowing that the creaking board, if anyone listened, would be put down to the blustering wind. Stealthily, he moved. Remembering the way, he turned right and left when necessary, following the next dim landing correctly, till he reached the stairs that led down into the black well of the hall.

Peering down into this murky space, no single outline was discernible. Nothing stirred, there seemed no movement. Both women were safe away in their distant beds. He crept forward down the stairs, and was already more than half-way down when he caught a faint glimmer of light below him by the settle where the gun lay underneath his overcoat.

It was so faint, however, that he doubted his eyes, and, there—even while he stared—it was gone again! Reaching the lowest step without seeing it return, he was certain he had been mistaken. He crossed the hall on tiptoe, came to the corner where the gun lay hidden below the overcoat, stretched out his hand to grope for it, and in that instant his fingers touched something warm and soft and furry. He was aware of perfume, a tiny point of light appeared as well, and the flint-lock was placed deliberately into his outstretched hands.

"I was just bringing it up to you," a low pleasant whisper startled him. "For I knew you would like it near you this night." The same moment the point of light grew into a sudden little flare that died out as soon as born, yet not before he had caught the swift picture of a face, two cupped hands shading a match, and the gleam of two amber-coloured eyes that peered into his own.

"You are cold," he faltered, muttering the words in his throat, shivering himself as he spoke, for he realised that the soft warm thing he touched was a strip of shoddy fur about the neck. "Why should *you*——"

"Hush!" she interrupted in a whisper, placing a hand gently on his mouth, covering her figure at the same time with his overcoat from the settle, then drawing him backwards more deeply into the corner and making him crouch low beside her. Her warm body lay close against him, her breath perfumed his cheek, as they sank down and hid against the wall. His arm had fallen naturally about her, as she half knelt, half sat, with her weight upon his side. And then someone, shading a light with a thin bony hand, the lines of the fingers visibly marked, came stepping cautiously down the stairs towards the hall.

So suddenly, so quickly, all this happened that it left him worse than bewildered. He stared. His eyes never left that slowly approaching light. The sweet comfort of the woman's warm body against his own bemused clear vision still further. Yet what chiefly darkened his mind, fluttering thought, emotion, judgment, was the friendly offer of the gun, supporting so unexpectedly his own desire and intention. For how had she thus forestalled his purpose so adroitly, how even become aware of it? Was this a move in her game, a sinister move that mere chance had enabled him to surprise? Was she then with him, after all, rather than against him? Who was the friend and who the enemy?

He was warily on guard and alert, but any clear solution failed to present itself. Could she have divined, this amber-eyed woman, that his own will and strength made him invulnerable, that his vows were not so easily rendered vain? Did she seek, perhaps, merely to place a dart, then twist it later in a burning wound that would find alleviation only upon its withdrawal—by her own fingers?

This flashed across him while he watched the descending light creep farther down the stairs towards the hall. Who bore that light he could not see. The holder moved without a sound, the boards were silent, no single creak was audible. The soft breathing against his ear was all he heard, the beating of another heart against his own.

The light reached the last stair and passed slowly, as with a gliding motion, across the hall towards them, then paused within a dozen feet of where he crouched. But now the vague shape behind it was not so vague that he could not distinguish it, and he recognised the bent, huddled outline of the old farm woman.

It was curious then that, simultaneously with this recognition, another picture leaped with startling significance before his eyes, but before the eyes of memory, and he saw for a vivid second that gaunt sinister tree on the brow of the naked hill, and realised that the torn loose branch dangling in the wind was a body and no branch at all. This mental recognition gave him a startling, uneasy twist of horror, but it vanished swiftly under the strain of yet greater horror that now followed instantly, as he witnessed something he had always known about, but yet had never seen actually with his own eyes.

He saw it happen a dozen feet in front of him, though in light so confused and dim that outlines were blurred and no sharp edges showed. For the *beldame*, as she shaded the faint rushlight, became most singularly transformed. Abruptly her figure shook down, as it were, into another figure, a figure much closer to the ground, an animal figure, a creature on all fours.

The point of light shivered an instant, then became twin lights, a pair of shining eyes that gleamed out of a bluntish muzzle below two sharply pointed ears. They were fixed steadily upon his own staring face, but vanished the same moment as though turned aside, so that their light was lost. A light, quick pattering, as of scuttling paws, came straight in his direction, shooting across the floor to the corner where he lay in darkness. "The cat, the monstrous cat," slashed in letters of fire across his brain.

"To the Sabbath," rose a whisper that yet held the quality of a shriek kept somehow in abeyance, for it was a shriek in exultation. "The wind delights, there are no stars, the brow of the hill is waiting! Bring the sacrifice, dearie, and let the Master see him burn!" From the very floor against his feet the awful voice came rushing.

A terrific gust of wind that shook the building, shook him into a clearer understanding perhaps as well. He felt the warm fragrant body quiver against his own, he felt the weight and pressure become heavier, and was aware in the same instant that the fur he had called shoddy covered not the neck and shoulders only, but spread now over the whole shape completely, covering it indeed from head to tail.

"Two of them—a pair!" his thought gasped frantically, as he gave a violent, spasmodical jerk. He remembered the huge, tawny cat, that yellow beast which sprang so strangely from the cart, if not from his companion's very skirts. He remembered other awful changelings too, the hare, the fox—and a shiver as of death convulsed his body.

49

"Keep still, my pet, keep quiet," came the purring voice against his smothered ear, while the weight upon him increased with sudden, horrifying pressure. "You are safe with me, I hold you fast, and fire and air work friendly."

He could hardly breathe, such was the suffocating smother of warm fur upon his face and lips; it was wellnigh impossible to stir a foot or leg. The weight took the very air from his mouth, and almost the last resistance from his very heart as well. The heat, the stifling heat, overcame him.

"I'll come," he mumbled thickly, fighting for space and air.

"You must," was the answer that he heard, his helplessness knowing it for true, but in the same instant precisely heard also the pair of them whispering and muttering between themselves. No words, much less sentences, not even syllables indeed, reached his mind, but he caught, despite his smothering, the tone of utterance. And an awful realisation crashed in upon his weakening faculties. A forgotten phrase leaped into memory: "the utterance of demons is indistinct, thin and hoarse."

And the horror of the memory, salved from what seemed now distant, almost forgotten teaching, passed like forked lightning into his final store of energies. He made a gigantic effort. The weight was lifted from him by a fraction, shifting itself, at any rate, to another angle — and a hand, as by magic, became partially released. How he contrived it lay utterly beyond him, how his fingers lay suddenly clutched upon the flint-lock, how they contrived the priming, found and pressed the trigger, bringing the flash and explosion in the darkness, timing with the roar of the storm outside—all this he never knew. He only knew that the suffocating weight relaxed, and that a wild, high, dreadful scream, half animal, half human, crashed against his very ears. . . .

"'We must have gone wrong at the last turning," she was saying. "If you'll get in again, I'll back her up. It's only a few hundred yards. The old man is right about: the road ending suddenly. We don't want to go over the edge. . ."

He climbed back into the car, which she then deftly manoeuvred up the little incline till they reached the fork where the mistake had been made. As it swung slowly round, the brow of the bare down filled his open window for a moment, and he saw the gaunt ugly tree where the dead branch had dangled, only now no branch was there, and only the shattered outline of the ancient tree broke against the blue sky of spring.

It caught her eye too, apparently, though her attention was centred

50

on the car.

"That hill and tree," she remarked casually, her gaze fixed chiefly on the ditch and width of road for turning, "there's something about it in the map. They used it for hanging witches once, or burnt them on that hill—I forget exactly what."

As he consulted the route map provided by the A.A. and confirmed the reference, she turned her head, so that he saw the blood on her cheek—a long, thin, reddened line as though a bullet had just grazed it. He made no reference to it, nor was she, apparently, aware of it, but an hour later, when she set him down at his point on the road, he saw her, from a little distance as she drove away, wiping it with a handkerchief which she first moistened on her red lips.

Malahide and Forden

1

Our three-months' tour was drawing to its close—the Company playing in a midland town at the moment and Forden was chatting with me in the wings during the second act, when Malahide's great voice boomed in my ears as he hurried to his entrance. It startled me; the audience must surely hear it too. Forden gave me his quick smile, an understanding wink added to it.

"Hubert, old man!" cried the voice. "There's a place called Barton I want to see—Barton-in-Fabis. Let's go tomorrow. There's a train at 10.15. Forden, you come too!" His eyes blazed at us with an odd glare through the grease-paint, his great shoulders swept round the canvas, and he was gone on to the stage, where at once his voice became audible in the lines that ten-weeks had made rather too familiar.

I experienced a twinge of surprise. Walking was little to Malahide's taste. He usually spent his spare time playing golf, and in the afternoon, he invariably slept for a couple of hours, so as to be rested for the evening performance. That he should propose a whole day's walk, therefore, was unexpected.

My companion and I were left staring at each other.

"Does he mean it—d'you think!" I asked in a low voice. "It sounds such an odd name. You think it's real!" I laughed a little.

"A lovely name, though," came the whispered answer. "It's real enough. Yes—I've heard of it—"

"Oh, you've heard of it?" I interrupted, looking up at him.

He nodded. Always absent-minded rather, he was also always truthful. An expression on his face now puzzled me. He looked perturbed. I repeated my remark, anxious to press him for some reason.

"People make pilgrimages there—sometimes—I believe. There's an old church—" Then his cue sounded, and he moved quickly away, but flinging over his shoulder, again with his quick smile, a final whisper: "Oh, it's real, yes, quite real. We'll go."

So, it was the church and the odd name that had caught Malahide's romantic fancy. Yet such a flat and empty name, I thought, without the adjunct, which alone gave it atmosphere. "In fabis," I gathered from one of the local supers, meant "among the beans," and Barton was a village "with a lot of historic interest," he informed me proudly. The name and the historic interest, evidently, had taken Malahide's vagrant fancy. He was an incalculable fellow; but he was not a man to ply with questions. His temper was insecure as a wayward child's. I, therefore, asked no questions.

Forden, too, was an elusive creature, where questions were concerned. There are people who instinctively detest having to give definite information in reply to definite questions. All the more, then, was I surprised to hear Forden ask one of Malahide—about the expedition. We passed the latter's dressing room as we left the theatre to walk home together, and the door was open.

"Ten-fifteen, remember, Central Station," boomed Malahide, catching sight of us. "Single tickets to Stanton. We walk from Stanton." It again surprised me; he had actually thought out details.

It was then that Forden asked his question:

"I—I suppose," he ventured, faltering a trifle, "there's a train back all right?"

The evening performance of course, involved an early meal, and the question seemed so natural that I thought nothing, but Malahide looked up from pulling on his big boots as though it startled him. He seemed taken by surprise. His eyes held the same blaze, the touch almost of glare, I had noticed before, but the startled air was added.

"We'll work round. What can it matter anyhow— provided we get there?" was all he vouchsafed, and in a tone that did not invite cross-examination.

So, it was to be 10.15, with single tickets to Stanton, a walk thence to Barton among its Beans, with its old church and historic interest, and we were to "work round" to another station, and so home. Malahide had planned it all in advance. He wanted to go. Forden also wanted to go. It all seemed natural enough, ordinary, no exceptional feature anywhere about it beyond the trivial detail that Malahide did not care for walking as a rule.

It is strange, therefore, that somewhere in my being lurked a firm conviction that the whole business *was* exceptional. For one thing, I felt sure that both Malahide and Forden did not really want to go.

That they had to go, and meant to go, was the impression left upon my mind, not that either of them actually "wished" it.

During our supper of cold tongue, salad and beer, for instance, we made no further allusion to the expedition. Rather than actually avoided, it was just tacitly assumed, Forden, I partly gathered, realised that I still did not quite believe in the Barton walk, but was too delicately loyal to discuss our friend's delightful irresponsibilities. In his own mind, too, I fancied, lay the thought that Malahide would not turn up, and that he would lose his morning's sleep for nothing, but that he meant to keep the rendezvous none the less. My fancy may have been quite wrong, yet this, anyhow, was Forden all over. He was of finest material, something transparent and a trifle exquisite in him; and even when poorly cast—as in the present play—this quality shone beautifully through his acting.

We went soon to bed, but Malahide kept late hours, and Forden and myself were asleep long before he turned in. In the morning, however, he was waiting at the station when we got there. He had left the hotel before us. "I've been to look at the churches," was his unexpected explanation. "One of 'em was open, and I went in and sat a bit. A wonderful atmosphere of peace and stillness. By Jove, it makes one think," and he gabbled on about the charm and atmosphere of an empty, ancient church. It was surprising, of course, and it left us without comment. Yet I had known him before in this odd mood—when he was frightened about something, frightened usually, of death.

Malahide, I understood, was frightened now, and his thoughts, for some reason, ran on death. In his eyes, moreover, I noticed, though veiled a little, a trifle deeper down, the same blaze I had seen the night before. And all the way to Stanton he gazed out of the window, humming to himself, the heap of morning papers beside him all untouched. The criticisms of his own performance, as, equally, mention of the Company, though of importance to the week's business, had, for once, no interest for him. His mind lay, evidently, upon other matters.

He looked extraordinarily happy—happier, I thought, than I had ever seen him before; there was a careless indifference, a lightness, something, too, of a new refinement-to use a queer word his vehement personality did not ever suggest—thought were new, yet all this lit, as from below, by the gleam of hidden fear I most certainly detected in him. And it was these contradictions, I think, these incompatibilities almost, that affected me so powerfully. Impressions began to pour and pour upon me. Emotions stirred.

Things going on at a great speed in Malahide were things that I could not fathom.

To me, this short train journey to Stanton, *en route* for Barton among its Beans, already had the spice of something just a little unusual, of something a trifle forced. Unexpected touches played about it, as though a faint unknown light shone from the cloudless sky of that perfect April morning, but from *beyond* it. Forden, behind the transparent mask of his rather beautiful face, betrayed more than his customary absent-mindedness, sometimes to a point I could have thought bewilderment. Each time I spoke to him—to Malahide I did not once address a word—he started a little.

In him there was no attempt at adjustment, no analysis, no effort to explain or query. He asked himself, I am sure, no single question. Whatever life brought him he accepted always. He was receptive merely; a recipient, but an extremely sensitive recipient, leaving all problems, all causes, to his God. Though without a formal creed, Forden was a deeply religious nature. And Forden now seemed to me—let me put it quite plainly as I felt it at the timepreparing, making himself ready, getting himself in hand, to meet something. Yes, to meet something— that is the phrase. And it was the search for this phrase, its discovery rather, that made me aware of an incomprehensible stress of subconscious excitement similarly in myself.

We were a queer enough trio, it may be, even in our normal moments. In myself, at any rate, being of different build to both Malahide and Forden, numerous little wheels were already whirring, gathering speed with every minute. This whirring one usually calls excitement. My own personal reactions to what followed are all, of course, that I can report. Though caught up, more or less, with the other two, I remained always the observer, thus sharing only a small portion probably of what my companions experienced. Another man, of different calibre, placed as I was, might have noticed nothing. I cannot say.

My problem is to report faithfully what I observed; and whether another man would have observed the same thing, or nothing at all, is beside the mark. . . . Already before the train stopped at Stanton I felt— well, as if my feet did not quite touch the ground, and by the ground I mean the ordinary. It may, or may not, be an exaggeration to say that I felt both feet slightly off the earth. That my centre of gravity was shifting is, perhaps, the most truthful expression I can find.

By the time we reached Stanton, at any rate, the whirring wheels had generated considerable heat, and with this heat playing all through my system I had already begun to see and feel in a way that was not quite the ordinary way. I perceived differently: I experienced, as it were, with a heightened consciousness. Perception seemed intensified a trifle; but more than that, and chiefly, it seemed different.

Different is the right adjective, I think. Malahide and Forden were "different" to the Malahide and Forden I knew comfortably from long acquaintance. Very, very slightly different, however, not radically so. I saw them from another angle. There was nothing I could seize or label. The instant my mind fastened on any detail, it was gone. The "difference" escaped me, leaving behind it a wonder of enquiry, a glow of curiosity I could not possibly define.

One sentence, perhaps, can explain my meaning, both in reference to the men and to the inanimate things they moved among: I saw *more* of everything. . . .

The fields, through the carriage windows, were of freshest green, yellow with a million buttercups, sparkling still from a shower that had followed sunrise, and the surface of the earth lay positively radiant in its spring loveliness. It laughed, it danced, it wept, it smiled. Yet it was not with this my mind was occupied during the half-hour's run to Stanton, but rather with the being of my two companions. I made no effort to direct my thoughts. They flowed of their own accord, with poignant, affectionate emotions I could not explain, towards Malahide and Forden. . . .

2

Played about them, over them, these thoughts did, lovingly rather, and directed by a flair, so to say, of understanding that was new in me.

Neither would ever see forty again, yet to me they seemed young, their careers still in front of them; and each, though without much energy, groping a way honestly toward some ultimate meaning in life that neither, I fancied, was ever likely to discover. If not dilettanti, both shrank from the big sacrifices. They were married, and each, in this fundamental relationship, unsatisfied, though each, outwardly at least, had mastered that dissatisfaction. Accepting, that is a responsibility undertaken, they played the game. There was fine stuff in them.

And both sought elsewhere, though without much energy as I have said, an outlet marriage had accordingly failed to provide. Not immorality, of course; but a mental, maybe a spiritual, outlet. They sought it, I now abruptly judged, without success. Their stream of yearning, whatever its power, went lost among the stars and unremunerative dreams. The point, however, remains: this yearning did exist in each. Its power, I conceive, was cumulative.

Similarly, in their daily work as actors, and uncommonly good actors, one with a streak of fine inspiration, the other, Malahide, with a touch of fiery genius, both accepted an art that both held, mournfully, and secretly rather, was not creative. They were merely interpreters of other men's creations. And, here again, lay deep dissatisfaction. Here, indeed, lay the root and essence of a searching pain both shared—since, God knows, they were gifted, honest beings—that a creative outlet, namely, was denied to creative powers.

This fundamental problem—the second one—lay unsolved in both; hence both were open to attack and ready for adventure. But the lesser adventures, refuge of commonplace fellows, they resolutely declined. Were they, perhaps, worthy then of the greater adventure that circumstances, at length, with inexplicable suddenness, and out of the least likely material, offered to them . . .?

Somewhat thus, at any rate, I saw my companions, as the train jolted us that sparkling April morning, many years ago, towards Stanton, Malahide humming his mood idly through the open window, Forden lying at full length, reading the papers with listless eye. But I saw another thing as well, saw it with a limpid clearness my description may not hold: something ahead—an event—lay in waiting for them, something they knew about, both not desiring, yet desiring it, something inevitable as sunrise.

We move towards and past events successively, calling this motion time. But the event itself does not move at all. It is always there. We three, now sitting in the jolting carriage, were approaching an event about which they knew, but about which I did not know. I received, that is, an imperfect impression of something they saw perfectly. And in some way the accumulated power of their combined yearnings, wasted as I had thought, made what happened possible.

It was an extraordinary idea to come to me with such conviction, and with this atmosphere of prophecy. I glanced at the two men, each like myself the victim, I remembered, of a strange, unhappy weakness. These weaknesses, too, I realised, contributed as well: un-balance, instability, were evidently necessary to the event. To steady, heroic types it never could have happened.

The train was stopping, and Malahide already had the door half-open. Forden, in his turn, sprang up.

"Stanton!" cried the former, as though he spoke a line of tense drama on the stage. "Here we are. Come on, you fellows!" And he was on the platform before the train drew to a standstill. His vehemence was absurd. He used it, I knew, to help him make the start, the fear I have mentioned prompting it.

And Forden, like a flash, was on his heels. I followed, pausing a moment to collect the papers in case Malahide should ask for them, and then, thank heaven, as we stood on that ugly platform and asked the porter the way to Barton, my own strange feelings, heightened perception with them, dropped back with a jerk into the normal again. The uncomfortable insight was suddenly withdrawn. It had seemed an intrusion into their privacies; I was relieved to see them again as two friends merely, two actors, out for a country walk with me to a village called Barton-inFabis on a brilliant April morning.

One last flash only there was, as I followed them out, one final hint of what I have called "seeing more" of everything, seeing "differently," rather. The three of us left the carriage as described, in sequence; yet to me it flashed with definite though illogical assurance that only one got out. Not that one was gone and two were left, but that the three of us got out as one, simultaneously. One being left that carriage. The fingers of a hand, thus, may move and point in several directions at once, while the hand, of which they form parts, moves forward in one direction only, as a whole. The simile occurred to me I perceived it, moreover, through what I can only call a veil of smoke.

3

"Oh, about three to four mile, maybe," the porter was telling Malahide, "an' you can pick up the Midland at Attenborough to get back Yes, it's a nice day for a walk, I dessay."

The name made us laugh, but the instructions as to paths, stiles, signposts, turnings, I, personally, did not listen to. I assumed, as most do, an air of intelligent comprehension. Forden, I saw, wore a similar expression, from which I knew that he, too, was not listening properly, but was leaving it to Malahide, wondering, like myself, how the latter could carry in his great slumbering mind so many intricate details whereas, actually, he was doing nothing of the sort. Malahide was merely acting, intent upon some other matter that was certainly not here and now.

We started off, therefore, with but a few details of our journey secure:—"a mile and a half down the road, and bearin' to the right, you'll see a signpost to Barton across the fields, and if you foller that a little way, bearin' to the left a bit now, you'll see a gate on the right just past some trees, but you don't go through *that* gate, you go straight on, bearin' to the right always, till you come to a farm, and then, through another gate . . ."

There was a definite relation between the length of description and a tip in the porter's mind, upon which Forden commented wittily, as we swung down the road, each relying upon the other two, and then exclaiming confidently, but with blurred minds, as we reached a signpost: "Ah! Here we are!" while we scrambled over a stile into enticing fields of gold.

We spoke little at first. "We must bear to the left, remember," mentioned Malahide once, to which Forden and I nodded agreement, adding however: "till we reach the gate," with Malahide's firm reminder: "which we do *not* go through," followed by my own contribution: "past some trees, yes, to another gate,"—and then Malahide's conclusive summing up: "always bearing to the right, of course . . ."

We jogged on happily, while the larks sang overhead, the cuckoos called and the brilliant sunshine flooded a countryside growing more and more remote from signs of men and houses. Not even a thatched cottage or a farm-house broke the loneliness from human kind. . . .

We spoke little, I have said; but my companions, presently, fell into a desultory conversation about their own profession, about present and future conditions on the stage, individual talent, rents of theatres, and so forth, to all of which, being an interloper merely, I listened with slight interest. It was the odd smell of burning, I think, that held my curious attention during this preliminary period, for I saw no cause for it, no smoke of rubbish being consumed, no heath-fire certainly. Malahide, I remember, coughed a little once or twice, and Forden sniffed like an animal that scents an untoward element in the atmosphere, though very faintly.

They made no comment, I offered none. It was, obviously, of no importance. The beauty of the day in its fresh spring brilliance absorbed me wholly, so that my thoughts ran on of their own accord, floating on a stream of happy emotion, careless as the pleasant wind. The sentences I caught from time to time did little more than punctuate, as it were, this stream of loveliness that poured through me from the April morning. Yet at intervals I caught their words, a phrase or a sentence would arrest me for a second; and each time this happened, I noticed what I can only call a certain curious change, a change—in distance. Their talk, I mean, passed gradually beyond me.

There was incoherence, due partly, of course, to the gaps I missed; and once or twice, it seemed to me, they were talking at cross-purposes, although tone and demeanour betrayed nothing of the sort. I remember that this puzzled me, that I registered the fact vaguely, at any rate; also, that an occasional comment of my own won no rejoinder from either Malahide or Forden—almost as though, momentarily, they had forgotten my existence and seemed unaware that I was with them.

Deeper and deeper into my own sensuous enjoyment of the day I sank accordingly, glad that I might take the beauty in my own little way. One thing only pierced my personal mood from time to time: the picture of Malahide's great head thrust forward a little when I glanced at him, the eyes turned upwards, carrying in them still that odd soft blaze, the glare, as I called it, now wholly gone; and that upon Forden's delicate face was a gentle expression, curiously rapt, yet with a faint brush as of bewilderment somewhere among the peering features. This impression, however, came back to me later, rather than held my attention much at the actual moment. We moved on deeper and deeper into the lonely countryside. With the exception of a man some fields ahead of us, I saw no living soul.

4

Our path, meanwhile, crossed a lane, and a little later a road, though not a high-road since no telegraph poles marred it, and then Malahide remarked casually: "But, I say! It's about time, isn't it?" He stood still abruptly, staring round him. "It's about time—eh?"

"For what?" enquired Forden gently, not looking at him, a touch of resignation in his voice.

"That signpost, I mean. We should have come to it by now."

"Oh, that signpost," echoed the other, without interest.

Neither of them included me in this exchange, which had broken in upon a longish conversation, and I found myself resenting it. They had not so much as glanced in my direction.

"Signpost!" I exclaimed bluntly, looking straight at Malahide. "Why, we passed it long ago." And as I said it, my eye again took in the figure of the man three fields away, the only living being yet seen. Out of the corner of my eye I saw him merely, and a breath of sharper air, or something like it, passed quickly over my skin. "It said 'To Barton,'" I added, a flavour of challenge in my tone. I purposely kept my gaze hard on Malahide.

61

He turned slowly, with a look as though, casually, he picked me up again; our eyes met; that sharper air seemed in my mind now.

"We passed *a* signpost," he corrected me; "but it merely said 'Footpath.' And it pointed over there— behind us. The way we've come."

Forden, to my amazement, nodded in consent. "Over there, yes," he agreed, and pointed with his stick, but at right angles to the direction Malahide had meant. "And it said: '*From* Barton.'"

This confusion, produced purposely and in a spirit of play though of course it was, annoyed me. I disliked it, as though somewhere it reached a sad, uneasy region in my mind.

It was Malahide's turn to nod in consent. "Then we're all right," he affirmed with unnecessary vehemence in his deep voice. And that vehemence, again, I did not like. "Besides," he added sharply, pointing ahead, "there he is!"

A wave of vague emotion troubled me; for an instant I felt again that sharper air-and this time in the heart.

"Who?" I asked quickly.

He replied carelessly: "The man." "*What* man?"

Malahide turned his eyes full upon my own, so that their soft blaze came over me like sunshine, almost with a sense of warmth in them. On his great face lay a singular expression. I heard Forden, who stood just behind me, laughing gently. There seemed a drift of smoke about them both. I knew a touch of goose-flesh.

"What man do you mean?" I asked with louder emphasis, and this time, I admit, with a note of exasperation that would not be denied, for the nonsense, I thought, had gone far enough, and there was a flavour in it that set my nerves on edge.

Malahide's reply came easily and naturally: "The man who plants them," he said without a smile. "He sticks them into the ground, that fellow. He's going about with an assortment of signposts 'To and From Barton,' and every now and again he plants one for us."

"We're standing under one now," Forden breathed behind me in his purring way, and looking up I saw that this was true. I read in black lettering upon a white background: "To Barton." It indicated the direction we were taking.

It occurred to me suddenly now that we had already walked at least four miles, yet had seen no farm, no trees, no garden. I had been sunk too deep in my own mood to notice things perhaps. This signpost I certainly had not noticed until Forden drew my attention to it. Malahide was tapping the wooden arm with the point of his stick, reading the lettering aloud as he did so:"'Footpath *From* Barton,'" I heard him boom. And instantly my eyes fixed tightly on it with all the concentration that was in me. Yes, Malahide had read correctly. Only, the arm now swung the other way. It pointed behind us! And I burst out laughing. Sight and memory had, indeed, fumbled badly. I felt myself for a moment "all turned round," as the saying is. Malahide laughed too; we all laughed together. It was boisterous, not quite spontaneous laughter, but at any rate it relieved a sense of intolerable tension that in myself had reached a climax. This fooling had been overdone, I felt.

"So, you see, we *are* all right," Malahide exclaimed, and swung forward over the meadow, already plunged again in the conversation with Forden which he himself had interrupted. They had enjoyed their little game about the signposts, Malahide, in particular, his touch of fancy about "the man who planted them." It all belonged to the careless, happy mood of a holiday expedition, as it were—the nonsense of high spirits. This, at least, was the ready explanation my mind produced so glibly, knowing full well it would not pass the censor of another kind of understanding, a deeper kind, that sought hurriedly, even passionately, for the true explanation. It was *not* nonsense; nor was it acceptable. It alarmed me.

I repeat: this confusion about directions, the two men agreeing that opposite directions were one and the same, was not the nonsense that it sounds; and I affirm this in view of that heightened perception, already first experienced in the train, which now came back upon me in a sudden flood. It brought with it an atmosphere of prophecy, almost of prevision, and certainly of premonition, an atmosphere that accompanied me, more or less, with haunting persistence to the end.

And its first effect was singular: all that a man says, I now became aware, has three meanings, and not merely one. The revelation arrived as clearly as though it were whispered to me through the shining air. There is the literal meaning of the actual words; there is the meaning of the sentence itself; and there is the meaning, above and beyond both these, in which the whole of the utterer is concerned, a meaning, that is, which the unconscious secret part in him—the greater part—tries and hopes to say.

This last, the most significant of all three, since it includes cause as well as result, makes of every common sentence a legend and a parable. Gesture, tone of voice betray its trend; what is omitted, or between the lines, betrays still more. Its full meaning, being in relation to unknown categories, is usually hidden both from utterer and hearers. It deals simultaneously with the past, the present and—the future. I now became aware of this Third Meaning in the most commonplace remarks of my companions.

It was an astounding order of perception to occur to me, and the difficulty of reporting it must be obvious from this confused description. Yet it seemed to me at the time so simple, so convincing, that I did not even question its accuracy and truth. Malahide and Forden, fooling together about the contradictory signposts, had betrayed this third meaning in all they said and did. Indeed, that it appeared impossible, absurd, was a proof, perhaps the only possible proof, of its reality. Momentarily, as it were, they had become free of unknown categories.

5

My own attitude contained at first both criticism and resistance; it was only gradually that I found myself caught in the full tide that, apparently, swept my companions along so easily. A first eddy of it had touched me in the train, when my feet felt a little "off the earth"; now I was already in the bigger current; before long I had become entirely submerged with them . . . . Fields and lanes, meanwhile, slipped rapidly behind us, but no farm, no trees, no gate, as the porter described, had been seen. We were lost, it seemed, in the heart of the sparkling April day; dew, light and gentle airs our only guides. The day contained us.

I made efforts to disentangle myself.

"Barton's not getting any nearer," I expostulated once.

"Barton-in-Fabis," mentioned Malahide with complete assurance, that no longer held a trace of vehemence, "is there—where it always is," while Forden's breath of delicate laughter followed the flat statement, as though the larks overhead had sung close beside my ear.

"D'you think we're going right?" I ventured another time. "Our direction, I mean?"

Again, with that ghostly laughter, Forden met me: "It's the way we have to go," he replied half under his breath. "It's always a mistake to trouble *too much* about direction—actual direction, that is." And Malahide was singing to himself as though nothing mattered in the world, details as to direction least of all.

It was just after this, I remember, as our lane came to a stile and we leaned over it comfortably, all three, that the odour of burning touched my mind again, only with it, at the same time, a sight so moving, that I paused in thought, catching my breath a little. For the field before us sloped down into the distance, ancient furrows showing just beneath the surface like the flowing folds of a shaken carpet. They ran, it seemed, like streams. Their curve downhill lent this impression of movement. They were of gold. Every inch of the surface was smothered with the shimmering cream of a million yellow buttercups.

"Rivers of Gold!" I exclaimed involuntarily, and at the same moment Forden was over the stile in a single leap and running across the brilliant grass.

"Look out!" he cried, a bewitched expression on his face, "it's fire!"—and he was gone.

It was as though he swam to the neck in gleaming gold. He peered back at me a second through the shining flood—and it was in this instant, just as I caught his turning face, that Malahide was after him. He passed me like a wave, still singing; there was a rush of power in his speed. I followed at once, unable to resist. The three of us ran like one man over and through that flood of golden buttercups, passing, as we did so, every sign the railway porter had told us to look out for: the farm, the trees, the gate, the second gate—everything. Only, we passed them more than once. It was as though we swung in a rapid circle round and round the promised signs, always passing them, always coming up to them, always leaving them behind, then always seeing them in front of us again, yet the entire sequence right, natural and—possible.

Now, I noticed this. I was aware of this. Yet it caused me no surprise. That it should be so seemed quite ordinary—at the time. . . .

We brought up presently, not even breathless, some half-way down that golden field.

"Nothing to what I expected," exclaimed Malahide, interrupting his singing for the first time.

"There was no pain," mentioned Forden, his voice soft and comforting, as though he spoke to a little child.

There was an instant of most poignant emotion in me as they said it; a certainty flashed through me that I could not seize; a sudden wave, as it were, of tears, of joy, of sorrow, of despair, swept past me and was gone again before I had the faintest chance to snatch at any explanation. Like the memory of some tremendous, rather awful dream, it vanished, and Malahide's quick remark, the next second, capped its complete oblivion:

"And there *he* goes again!" I heard. "He's stuck another one in!"

He was pointing to a hedge at the bottom of the field where,

65

behind the veil of its creamy hawthorn, I just made out the figure of a man ambling slowly along, till the hedge, growing thicker, finally concealed him. But the signpost, when we reached it a few minutes later, showed an arm rotten with age, and only the faded legend on it, hardly legible: "Footpath." It pointed downwards—into the ground.

6

We swung forward again, without a moment's delay, it seemed, my companions talking busily together as before, their meaning, also as before, far, far beyond me. They were talking, too, on several subjects at once. The odd language they had just used, the way we swung forward instantly, without comment or explanation, touched no sense of queerness in me—then. No comment or explanation were necessary; it was natural we should go straight on.

Their talking on "several subjects simultaneously," however, did occur to me—yes, as marvellous.

Foolish, even impossible, as it must sound, it yet did happen; they talked on more than one subject at the same time. They carried on at least a couple of conversations at once without the slightest difficulty, without the smallest effort or confusion. My own admission into the secret was partial, I think; hence my trouble and perplexity. To them it was easy and natural. With me, even the strain of listening made the head swim. The effort to follow them was certainly a physical one, for I was aware of a definite physical reaction more than once, almost indeed of a kind of dizziness akin to nausea.

To report it is beyond my power. For one thing, I cannot remember, for another, the concentration necessary left me a little stupefied. I can give an instance only, and that a poor one. They used "third meanings," too.

Malahide, thus, while voluble enough in his normal state, was at the same time usually inarticulate. His verbosity, that is, conveyed little. The tiny vital meaning in him fumbled and stammered through countless wrappings, as it were. These wrappings smothered it. Now, on the contrary, he talked fluently and clearly. It was I who was puzzled—at first— to find the subject he discussed so glibly. And Forden, usually timid and hesitating in his speech, though never inarticulate, now also used a flow of fearless words in answer. Yet not precisely "in answer," for both men talked at once. They uttered simultaneously—on two subjects, if not on three:

"We all deserve, maybe," Malahide's deep voice thundered, "a divine attention few of us receive— God's pity. We are not, alas, whole-hearted. Few of us, similarly, deserve another compliment. Due to splendour—the Devil's admiration."

His voice, for once, was entirely natural, unselfconscious. There was the stress of real feeling and belief in what he said.

"I for one," he went on, "I take my hat off to the whole-hearted, whether in so-called good or evil. For of such stuff are eventual angels wrought . . ."

Angels! The word caught me on the raw. Its "third meaning" caught me on the raw, that is, and with a sense of power and beauty so startling that I missed the rest. The word poured through me like a flame. Of what he spoke, to what context the strange statement was related, I had no inkling; yet, while he actually spoke the words, I heard Forden speaking to Malahide, who heard and understood and answered—but speaking, and simultaneously, on another matter altogether. And this other matter, it so chanced, I grasped. Remote enough from what Malahide was saying, and trivial by comparison, it referred to an Alpine sojourn with his wife a couple of summers before. Malahide, too, had been with them:

"Often, after the hotel dinner," Forden said contemptuously, "I heard them mouthing all sorts of lovely poetic phrases; yet not one of them would make the slight sacrifice of personal comfort necessary to experience that loveliness, that poetry, in themselves . . ."

To which Malahide, though still developing "God's pity" and the "Devil's admiration" in phrases packed with real feeling, contrived somehow to answer, but always simultaneously, his friend's remark:

"They bring their own lower world," he boomed, "even into the beauty of the mountains, then wonder that the beauty of the mountains tells them nothing. They would find Balham on great Betelgeuse"—a tremendous laugh rang out—"and Clapham Junction on fiery Vega!"

"*Her* pity," came Forden's words, talking of another matter alto-gether, yet uttered simultaneously with his friend's laughing rhetoric, "is self-pity merely. She does these out-of-the-way things, you see, without sufficient apparent reason. It is not a desire for notoriety—that would shock her—but it *is* a desire to be conspicuous. Life, which means people, did not make a fuss about her in her youth. But the law of compensation works inevitably. Late in life, you see, she means to have that fuss."

It is the phraseology, perhaps, that enables me to remember this sin-gular exchange. My head, of course, was spinning. For Malahide made a reply to this, while still discussing the poseurs in the Alpine hotel. And while they talked thus on two subjects simultaneously, Forden managed to chat easily too *with me*—upon a third.....It was as though a second dimension in time had opened for them. Between myself and Forden, again, there was plainly some kind of telepathic communication. He had my thought, at any rate, before I uttered it aloud.

Of this I can give two instances, both trivial, yet showing that simultaneously with his Malahide-conversations he was paying attention to my own remarks, and—simultaneously again—was answering them. It was absolutely staggering.

Here are the instances memory retained:

Some scraps of white paper, remnants of an untidy picnic party, lay fluttering in the thick grass some distance in front of us, and at the first glance I thought they were not paper, but—chickens. Only on coming nearer was the mistake clear. Whether I meant to comment aloud on the little deception, or not, I cannot remember; but in any case, before I actually did so, Forden, glancing down at me with his gentle smile, observed: "I, too, thought at first they were chickens." He hit them idly with his stick as we passed.

The second instance, equally trivial, equally striking at the same time, was the gamekeeper's cottage on the fringe of a wood. It suggested to my mind, for some reason, a charcoal-burner's hut in a book of German fairy-tales, and I said so. This time I spoke my thought. "But, you know, I've just said that," came Forden's comment, his eyes twinkling brightly as before. And it was true; he had said it a fraction of a second before I did. During this brief exchange between us, moreover, he was still talking fluently with Malahide—on at least two subjects—and simultaneously.

Now, from the fact that I noticed this, that my mind made a note of it, that is, I draw the conclusion that my attention was definitely arrested, surprise accompanying it. The extraordinariness of the matter struck me, whereas to my companions it was ordinary and natural. I was, therefore, not wholly included in their marvellous experience. I was still the observer merely. . . .

Immediately following the telepathic instances with Forden, then, came a flash of sudden understanding, as though I were abruptly carried a stage deeper into their own condition:

I discerned one of the subjects they discussed so earnestly together.

This came hard upon a momentary doubt-the doubt that they were playing, half-fooling me, as it were. Then came the swift flash that negatived the doubt. I can only compare it to the amazing review of a man's whole life that is said to flash out in a moment of extreme danger. This quality, as of juggling with Time, belonged to it.

Malahide and Forden, then, I realised, were talking together of Woman, of women, rather, but of individual women. Ah! The flash grew brighter: of their own wives. Yet that Malahide spoke of Forden's wife and that: Forden discussed Mrs. Malahide. Each had the free *entrée* into the other's mind, and what each was too loyal to say about his own wife, the other easily said for him. This swiftest telepathic communication, as with myself and Forden, they enjoyed between themselves. With supreme ease it was accomplished.

It was an astounding performance. This discussion of their wives was actually, of course, a discussion of—well, not of Mary Forden and Jane Malahide individually, but, through them, of the deep unsolved problem of mate and sex which each man had faced in his own life—unsuccessfully. The fragments I caught seemed meaningless, because the full context was lacking for me. I got a glimmer of their Third Meanings, however, and realised one thing, at any rate, clearly: they were giving one another help. Forden's honeymoon, I remembered, had been spent in the Alps, whereas Malahide's wife had the lack of proportion which made her conspicuous by a pose of startling originality.

This gave me a clue. Time, however, as a sequence of minutes, days and years, did not trouble either speaker. The *entire* matter, regardless of past and present, seemed spread out like a contour-map beneath the eyes of their inner understanding. There was no picking out one characteristic, dealing with it, then passing on to consider another. To *me* it came, seriatim, in that fashion, but *they* saw the matter whole and all at once; so rapidly, so comprehensively, too, that the sentences flew upon each other's heels as though uttered simultaneously by each speaker.

They were it seemed, poised above the landscape of their daily lives, and in such a way that they were able to realise present, past and future simultaneously. It was no longer exactly "today," it was no longer necessarily "today." Temporarily they had escaped from the iron tyranny of being fastened to a particular hour on a particular day. They—and partially myself with them—were no longer chained by the cramping discipline of a precise moment in time, any more than a prisoner, his chains filed off, is fixed to a precise spot in his dungeon. *Where* we were in time, God knows.

It might have been yesterday, it might have been tomorrow—any yesterday, any tomorrow—which we now realised simultaneously with the so-called present. It happened to be—so I felt—a particular tomorrow we realised, and it was something in the three of us (due, I mean, to the combination of our three personalities) that determined which particular tomorrow it was. The prisoner in space, his chains filed off, moves instinctively to the window of escape; and they, prisoners in time, moved now similarly to a window—of escape. . . . .

A flash of this escape from ordinary categories, of this "different" experience, had come to me as we left the railway carriage. It now grew brighter, more steady, more continuous. I seemed travelling in time, as one travels ordinarily in space. To the wingless creature crawling over fields the hedge behind it is past, the hedge beyond it future. It cannot conceive both hedges existing simultaneously. Then some miracle gives it wings. Hanging in the air, it sees both past and future existing simultaneously. Losing its wings once more, it crawls across the fields again. That air-experience now seems absurd, impossible, contradicting all established law. The same signpost points now as it always pointed—in one direction.

This analogy, though imperfect, occurred to me, while we brought up, but not even breathlessly, halfway down the field as already mentioned, and all I have attempted to describe took place in that brief interval of running.

Before entering that field with its rivers of gold, we had been leaning on a stile; we were leaning on that stile still. Or, it may be put otherwise: we were leaning on that stile again.

Similarly, the whole business of running, of passing the signs mentioned by the porter, the conversations, the emotions, everything in fact, were just about to happen all over again. More truly expressed, they were all happening still. Like Barton, in Malahide's previous phrase, it was all *there*. The hedge behind, the hedge in front, were both beneath us, existing simultaneously. At a particular spot in the hedge—a particular "tomorrow"—we paused . . . .

7

. . . At my side, touching my shoulders, Malahide and Forden were quietly discussing the way to Barton-in-Fabis, and, as I listened, there came over me again that touch of nausea. For, while flatly contradicting one another, they were yet in complete agreement.

It was at this instant the shock fell upon me with its glory and its terror.

My companions stood back to back. I was a yard or so to one side. They both now turned suddenly— but how phrase the incredible thing?—they both came at me, while at the same time they went away from me. A hand, endowed with consciousness, a hand being turned inside out like a glove, might feel what I felt.

I saw their two faces. A little more, a little less, and there must have been a bristling horror in the experience. As it was, I felt only that a sheet of wonder caught us up all three. The odour of burning that came with it did not terrify; that drift of yellow smoke, now deepening, did not wound. I accepted, I understood, there was even something in me had rejoiced.

In the twinkling of an eye, both men were marvellously changed: they stood before me, splendid and divine. I was aware of the complete being in each, the full, whole Self, I mean, instead of the minute fraction I had known hitherto. All that lay in them, either of strength or weakness, was magnificently fused. . . . The word "glory" flashed, followed immediately by a better word, and one that Malahide had already used. Its inadequacy was painful. Its third meaning, however, in that instant blazed. "Angels" in spite of everything, remains.

And I, too, moved—moved with them both, but in a way, and in a direction, I had never known before. The glove, the hand, being turned inside out, is what my pen writes down, but accurate description is not possible. I moved, at any rate, on—*on* with my two companions towards Barton.

"It's all one to me," I said, perfectly aware that I suddenly used the third meaning of the phrase, and that Malahide and Forden understood.

"I've just said that myself," the latter mentioned— and this again was true. The smile, the happiness, on his face carried the very spirit of that radiant April morning, the essence of spring, with its birds, its flowers, its dew, its careless wisdom.

"Such things," cried Malahide, "are painless after all. It comes on me like sleep upon a child. Ha, ha!" he laughed, in his wild, vehement way. "It's all one to me now too. Escape, by God!"

The stab of fierce emotion his language caused me passed and vanished; the afflicting memory of the burning odour was forgotten too. Everything, indeed, *was* one. Both men, I realised, gazed at me, smiling, wonderful, superb, and in their eyes a light, whose reflection apparently lay also in my own; an immense and awful pity that our everyday, unhappy, partial selves should ever have dared to masquerade as though they were complete and real. . . .

"God's pity," sang Malahide like a trumpet. "We shall have deserved it!"

"And the Devil's admiration," followed Forden's sweeter tones, as of a *vox humana*, both distant, yet like a lark against my ears. He was laughing with sheer music. "There was no terror. I knew it must be so. . . . Oh, the delicious liberty . . . at last!"

Both uttered simultaneously. In the same breath, anguish and happiness working together, my own voice cried aloud:

"We are, for once, whole-hearted!"

8

At the moment of actual experience a new category would not seem foolish or impossible. These qualities would declare themselves only when it passed away. This was what happened—gradually— to me now, and, alas, to my companions too. A searing pain accompanied the transition, but no shock of violence.

At the pinnacle there was a state of consciousness too strange, too "different," to be set down. The content of life, its liberty, its splendour, its characteristics of grandeur, even of divinity, were more than ordinary memory could retain. My own cry: "We are whole-hearted" must betray how pitiful description is. Thus, the lovely moment, for instance, when I first saw rivers of gold, kept repeating itself—because it gave me happiness, because it moved me. That field of golden buttercups was always—there. I lingered with it, came back to it, enjoyed it over and over again, yet with no sense of repetition. It was new and fresh each time. Now, Malahide and Forden, selecting other moments, chose these instead, and these, again, were moments easy to be remembered.

Their finer instances baffle memory, although I knew and shared them at the time. Forden, for some peculiar choice to himself, was in the mountains which he loved; his honeymoon presumably. Malahide, on the other hand, preferred his stars, though details of this have left me beyond recovery. . . Yet, while we lingered, respectively, among rivers of gold and stars and snowy peaks, we were solidly side by side in the actual present, crossing the country fields towards Barton-in-Fabis on this April morning.

The gradual passing of this state remains fairly clear in me.

There came signs, I remember, of distress and effort in our relationships. This, at least, was the first touch of sorrow that I noticed. I

72

was coming back to the surface, as it were. The change was more in myself than in the others. There was argument about footpath, sign-posts, and the way to Barton generally.

"The fellow has planted his last post," I heard Malahide complaining. "Now he'll begin pulling them all up again. He both wants us to get to Barton, yet doesn't want it." He paused. His usual laugh did not follow. "You know," he went on, his whisper choking a little oddly in his throat, "he rather—puts the wind up me." A spasm ran over his big body. Then suddenly, he added, half to himself, with an effort painfully like a gasp, "I can't get my breath—quite."

Forden spoke very quickly in his delicate way, resignation rather sweetly mingled in it: "Well, at any rate, we're all right so far, for I see the porter's farm and gate at last." He started and pointed. "Over there, you see." Only, instead of pointing across the fields, he—to my sharp dismay—looked and pointed straight into the sky above him.

It was the fear in Malahide that chiefly afflicted me. And the pain of this, I remember, caused me to make an effort—which was an unwise thing to do. I drew attention to the ordinary things about us:

"Look, there's a hill," I cried.

"God!" exclaimed Forden, with quiet admiration, "what amazing things you say!" While Malahide began to sing again with happiness.

His reaction to my sentence forced me to realise the increasing change in myself. As I uttered the words I knew their third meaning; in the plain sentences was something that equalled in value: "See! the Heavens are open. There is God!" My companions still heard this third meaning, for I saw the look of majesty in Malahide's great eyes, the love and beauty upon Forden's shining face. But, for myself, having spoken, there remained—suddenly—nothing more than a common-place low hill upon the near horizon. The gate and farm I saw as well. A feeling of tears rose in me, for the straining effort for recovery was without result, anguished and bitter beyond words.

I stole a glance at my companions. And that strange word Malahide had used came back to me, but with a deep, an awful sense of intoler-able regret, as though its third meaning were gone beyond recall, and only two rather empty and foolish syllables remained. . . .

It was passing, yes, for all three of us now; the gates of ivory were closing; there was confusion, and a rather crude foolishness. Oddly enough, it was Forden—seeing that he was altogether a slighter fellow than Malahide—it was Forden who rose most slowly to the surface. Very gradually indeed he left the deeps we had all known together. To

73

all that he now said and did Malahide responded with an aggravating giggle. He said such foolish things, confused, uncomfortable to listen to. His nerves showed signs of being frayed.

He became a trifle sullen, a little frightened as well, and in his gait and gesture lay a disconcerting hurry and uncertainty, as though, hesitating to make a decision of some vital sort, he was flurried, almost in a frenzy sometimes, trying vainly to escape. This stupid confusion in him afflicted me, but the effort to escape seemed to paralyse something in my mind. It was petrifying. And thus the sequence of what followed, proved extraordinarily difficult to remember afterwards. An atmosphere of sadness, of foreboding, of premonition came over me; there was desolation in my heart; there were stabs of horrible presentiment. All these, moreover, were ever vaguely related to one thing—that inexplicable faint odour of burning . . . .

What memory recalls can be told very briefly. It lies in my mind thus, condensed and swift:

The storm was natural enough, but, here again, the smell of burning alarmed and wrung me. It was faint, it was fugitive. Our mistake about the river had no importance, for the depression in the landscape might easily after all have held flowing water. The roofs, too, were not the roofs of Barton, but of a hamlet nestling among orchards, Clifden by name, and it was here, Forden informed us, he had first met his wife and had proposed to her; this also of no importance, except that he went on talking about it, and that it surprised him. He suddenly recognised the place, I mean. It increased his bewilderment, and is mentioned for that reason.

The storm, then, came abruptly. We had not seen it coming. Following a low line of hills, it overtook us from behind, bringing its own wind with it. The rustling of the leaves was the first thing I noticed. The trees about us began to shake and bend. The sparkling brilliance, I saw, had left the day; the sun shone dully; the fields were no longer radiant; the flowers, too, were gone, for we were crossing a ploughed field at the moment.

The discussion between us may be omitted; its confusion is really beyond me to describe. The storm, however, is easily described, for everyone has seen that curious thickening of the air on a day in high summer, when the clouds are not really clouds, but come as a shapeless, murky gloom, threatening a portentous downpour, while yet no single raindrop falls. In childhood we called it "blight," believing it to be composed of myriads of tiny insects. Lurid effects of lighting accompanied it, trees and roofs, against its dark background, looking as if stage flares illumined them. The whole picture, indeed, was theatrical in the extreme, artificial almost; but the aspect that I, personally, found so unwelcome, was that it laid over the sky an appearance of volumes of dense, heavy smoke. The idea of burning may, or may not, have been in my own mind only, for my companions made no comment on it. I cannot say. That it made my heart sink I remember clearly.

It was a sham storm, it had no meaning, nothing happened. Having accomplished its spectacular effect, it passed along the hills and dissipated, and the sun shone out with all its former brilliance. Yet, before it passed, certain things occurred; they came and went, it seemed to me afterwards, with the simultaneity of dream happenings. Forden, noticing the wall of gloom advancing, catching the noise of the trees as well, stopped dead in his tracks, and stared. He sniffed the air, but made no comment. An expression of utter bewilderment draped his face. He seemed once more bewitched. It was here the smell of burning came to me most strongly.

"Look out!" he cried, and started to run. He ran in front of us, we did not attempt to follow. But he ran in a circle, like a terrified animal. His figure went shifting quickly, silhouetted, like the trees and roofs, against the murky background of the low-hanging storm. A moment later he was beside us again, his face white, his eyes shining, his breath half-gone.

"Come on, old Fordy," said Malahide affectionately, taking him by the arm. He, for some reason, was not affected. "It's not going to rain, you know, and anyhow there's no good running. Let's sit down and eat our lunch." And he led the way across a few furrows to the hedge.

We ate our sandwiches and cake and apples. The sun shone hotly again. None of us smoked, I remember. For myself, the smell of burning had left something so miserable in me that I dared not smell even a lighted match. But no word was said by anybody in this, or in any other, sense. I kept my own counsel. . . . And it was while we lay resting idly, hardly speaking at all,. that a sound reached me from the other side of the hedge: a footstep in the flowered grass. My companions exchanged quick glances, I noticed, but I did not even turn my head. I did not dare.

"He's putting it in," whispered Malahide, a touch of the old vehemence in his eyes. "The last one!" Forden smiled, nodded his head, and was about to add some comment of his own, when the other interrupted brusquely:

"Is that the way to Barton?" he enquired suddenly in a louder voice, something challenging, almost truculent, in the tone. He jerked his head towards the gate we had recently come through. "Through that gate and past that farm, I mean?"

The answering voice startled me. It was the owner of the footsteps, of course, behind the hedge.

"No. That's a dead end," came in gruff but not unpleasant country tones.

There was no more than that. It was all natural enough. Yet a lump came up in my throat as I heard. I still dared not look round over my shoulder. I looked instead into Forden's face, so close beside me. "We're all right," he was saying, as he glanced up a little. "Don't struggle so. It's the way we've got to go . . ." and was about to say more, when a fit of coughing caught him, as though for a moment he were about to suffocate. I hid my eyes quickly; a feeling of horror and despair swept through me; for there was terror in the sound he made; but the next second, when I looked again, the coughing had passed, and I saw in his face an expression of radiant happiness; the eyes shone wonderfully, there was a delicate, almost unearthly, beauty on his features. I found myself trembling, utterly unnerved.

"We'd better be getting on," mentioned Malahide, in his abrupt, inconsequent fashion. "We mustn't miss that train back." And it was this unexpected change of key that enabled me at last to turn my head. I looked hurriedly behind the hedge. I was just in time to see a man, a farmer apparently, in the act of planting a post into the ground. He was pressing it down, at any rate, and much in the fashion of Malahide's former play about a "fellow who planted signposts." But he was planting—two. Side by side they already stood in the earth. One arm pointed right, the other left. They formed, thus, a cross.

The very same second, with a quiver in the air, as when two cinema pictures flash on each other's heels with extreme rapidity, I experienced an optical delusion. I must call it such, at any rate. The focus of my sight changed instantaneously. The man was already in the distance, diminished in outline, moving away across the bright fields of golden buttercups. I saw him as I had seen him once or twice before, earlier in the day, a moving figure in the grass; and when my eyes shifted back to examine the posts, there was but a single post—a signpost whose one arm bore in faded lettering the words: "*From* Barton." It pointed in the direction whence we had come. . . .

I followed my companions in a dream that is better left untouched by words. Led by Malahide, we passed through Clifden; we came to the Trent and were ferried across; and a little later we reached, as the porter had described, a Midland station called Attenborough. A train soon took us back to the town where we were playing. Malahide, without a word, vanished from our side the moment we left the carriage. I did not see him again until, dressed in his lordly costume, he stood in the wings that night, waiting impatiently for his entrance. I had walked home with Forden, flung myself on the bed, and dropped off into a deep two-hours' sleep.

9

A performance behind the scenes that night was more dramatic—to me, at least—than anything the enthusiastic audience witnessed from the front. The three of us met in the wings for the first time since Malahide had given us the slip at the station. High tea at six I had alone, Forden for some reason going to a shop for his meal. Malahide, for another reason, ate nothing. We met, anyhow, at our respective posts in the wings. Neither Forden nor I were on till late in the second act, and as we came down the rickety stairs from separate dressing-rooms, at the same moment it so chanced, I realised at once that he was as little inclined to talk as I was. My own mind was still too packed with the whirling wonder of the whole affair for utterance. We nodded, then dropped back towards the door through which he would presently make his entrance.

It was just then, while someone was whispering "He's giving a marvellous performance tonight," that Malahide swept by me from his exit and ran to his dressing-room for a hurried change.

"Hullo, Hubert!" he cried in his tempestuous way. "I say . . ." as though it surprised him to see me there. "By the by," he rattled on, stopping dead for a breathless second in the rush to his room, "there's a place called Barton I want to see—Barton-in-Fabis. Let's go tomorrow. There's a train at 10.15. Forden can come too!" And he was gone. Gone too, I realised with a dreadful sinking of the heart, a trembling of the nerves as well-utterly gone as though it had never happened, was all memory of the day's adventure. The mind in Malahide was blank as a clean-washed slate.

And Forden—standing close behind him within easy earshot—my eye fell upon Forden, who had heard every single word. I saw him stare and bite his lips. He passed a hand aimlessly across his forehead. His eyelids flickered. There was a quiver of the lips. In his old man's wig and make-up, he looked neither himself nor the part he was just about to play. Waiting there for his cue, now imminent, he stared fixedly at Malahide's vanishing figure, then at me, then blankly into space. He was like a man about to fall. He looked bewitched again.

A moment's intense strain shot across the delicate features. He made in that instant, I am convinced, a tremendous, a violent, effort to recapture something that evaded him, an effort that failed completely. The next second, too swift to be measurable, that amazing expression, the angel's, shone out amazingly. It flashed and vanished.

. . . His cue sounded. He, too, was gone.

How I made my own entrance, I hardly know. Five minutes later we met on the stage. He was normal. He was acting beautifully. His mind, like Malahide's, was a clean-washed slate.

<h2 style="text-align:center">10</h2>

My one object was to avoid speech with either Malahide or Forden. The former was on the stage until the end of the play, but the latter made no appearance in the last act. I slipped out the moment I was free to go. Malahide's door was ajar, but he did not see me. Foregoing supper, I was safely in bed when I heard Forden come upstairs soon after midnight. I fell into an uneasy sleep that must have been deeper, however, than it seemed, for I did not hear Malahide come in, but I was wide awake on the instant, dread clutching me with gripping force, when I heard Forden's voice outside my door.

"It's half-past nine!" he warned me. "We mustn't miss the train, remember!"

After gulping down some coffee, I went with him to the station, and he was normal and collected as you please. We chatted in our usual fashion. Clearly, his mind held no new, strange thing of any sort. Malahide was there before us . . . .

The day, for me, was a nightmare of appalling order. A kind of mystical horror held me in a vice.

Half-memories of bewildering and incredible things haunted me. The odour of burning, faint but unmistakable, was never absent . . . .

We took single tickets to Stanton, Malahide reading a pile of papers and commenting volubly on the criticisms of the play. A porter at the station gave us confused directions. We followed faulty signposts, ancient and illegible, losing ourselves rather stupidly . . . and I noticed a man—a farmer with a spud—wandering about the fields and making thrusts from time to time at thistles. A sham storm followed a low line of hills, but no rain fell, and the brilliance of the April day was otherwise unspoilt. Barton itself we never reached, but we crossed the Trent on our way to a station called Attenborough, first passing a hamlet, Clifden, where, Forden informed us, he had met the girl he later made his wife.

It was a dull and uninspired expedition, Malahide voluble without being articulate, Forden rather silent on the whole. . . and at the home station Malahide gave us the slip without a word . . . but during the entire outing neither one nor other betrayed the slightest hint of familiarity with anything they had known before. In myself the memory lay mercilessly sharp and clear. I noted each startling contrast between the one and other. At the end I was worn out, bone-tired, every nerve seemed naked . . . and, again, I left the theatre alone, ran home, and went supperless to bed.

My determination was to keep awake at all costs, but sleep caught me too easily, as I believed it was meant to catch me. No such little thing as a warning was allowed to override what had to be, what had already been.   In the early hours of the morning, about two o'clock, to be exact, I woke from a nightmare of overwhelming vividness. Wide awake I was, the instant I opened my eyes. The nightmare was one of suffocation. I was being suffocated, and I carried over into waking consciousness the smell of burning and the atmosphere of smoke. The room, I saw at once, *was* full of smoke, the burning was not a dream. I *was* being suffocated. But in my case the suffocation was not complete, whereas Malahide and Forden died, according to the doctors, in their sleep. They did not even wake. They knew no pain. . . .

Sand

As Felix Henriot came through the streets that January night the fog was stifling, but when he reached his little flat upon the top floor there came a sound of wind. Wind was stirring about the world. It blew against his windows, but at first so faintly that he hardly noticed it. Then, with an abrupt rise and fall like a wailing voice that sought to claim attention, it called him. He peered through the window into the blurred darkness, listening.

There is no cry in the world like that of the homeless wind. A vague excitement, scarcely to be analysed, ran through his blood. The curtain of fog waved momentarily aside. Henriot fancied a star peeped down at him.

"It will change things a bit—at last," he sighed, settling back into his chair. "It will bring movement!"

Already something in himself had changed. A restlessness, as of that wandering wind, woke in his heart—the desire to be off and away. Other things could rouse this wildness too: falling water, the singing of a bird, an odour of wood-fire, a glimpse of winding road. But the cry of wind, always searching, questioning, travelling the world's great routes, remained ever the master-touch. High longing took his mood in hand. Mid seven millions he felt suddenly—lonely.

I will arise and go now, for always night and day
I hear lake water lapping with low sounds by the shore;
While I stand on the roadway, or on the pavements grey,
I hear it in the deep heart's core.

He murmured the words over softly to himself. The emotion that produced Innisfree passed strongly through him. He too would be over the hills and far away. He craved movement, change, adventure— somewhere far from shops and crowds and motor-'busses. For a week the fog had stifled London. This wind brought life.

Where should he go? Desire was long; his purse was short.

He glanced at his books, letters, newspapers. They had no interest now. Instead, he listened. The panorama of other journeys rolled in colour through the little room, flying on one another's heels. Henriot enjoyed this remembered essence of his travels more than the travels themselves. The crying wind brought so many voices, all of them seductive:

There was a soft crashing of waves upon the Black Sea shores, where the huge Caucasus beckoned in the sky beyond; a rustling in the umbrella pines and cactus at Marseilles, whence magic steamers start about the world like flying dreams. He heard the plash of fountains upon Mount Ida's slopes, and the whisper of the tamarisk on Marathon. It was dawn once more upon the Ionian Sea, and he smelt the perfume of the Cyclades. Blue-veiled islands melted in the sunshine, and across the dewy lawns of Tempe, moistened by the spray of many waterfalls, he saw—Great Heavens above!—the dancing of white forms . . . or was it only mist the sunshine painted against Pelion?. . . "Methought, among the lawns together, we wandered underneath the young grey dawn. And multitudes of dense white fleecy clouds shepherded by the slow, unwilling wind. . . ."

And then, into his stuffy room, slipped the singing perfume of a wall-flower on a ruined tower, and with it the sweetness of hot ivy. He heard the "yellow bees in the ivy bloom." Wind whipped over the open hills—this very wind that laboured drearily through the London fog.

And—he was caught. The darkness melted from the city. The fog whisked off into an azure sky. The roar of traffic turned into booming of the sea. There was a whistling among cordage, and the floor swayed to and fro. He saw a sailor touch his cap and pocket the two-*franc* piece. The syren hooted—ominous sound that had started him on many a journey of adventure—and the roar of London became mere insignificant clatter of a child's toy carriages.

He loved that syren's call; there was something deep and pitiless in it. It drew the wanderers forth from cities everywhere: "Leave your known world behind you, and come with me for better or for worse! The anchor is up; it is too late to change. Only—beware! You shall know curious things—and alone!"

Henriot stirred uneasily in his chair. He turned with sudden energy to the shelf of guide-books, maps and timetables—possessions he

82

most valued in the whole room. He was a happy-go-lucky, adventure-loving soul, careless of common standards, athirst ever for the new and strange.

"That's the best of having a cheap flat," he laughed, "and no ties in the world. I can turn the key and disappear. No one cares or knows—no one but the thieving caretaker. And he's long ago found out that there's nothing here worth taking!"

There followed then no lengthy indecision. Preparation was even shorter still. He was always ready for a move, and his sojourn in cities was but breathing-space while he gathered pennies for further wanderings. An enormous kit-bag—sack-shaped, very worn and dirty—emerged speedily from the bottom of a cupboard in the wall. It was of limitless capacity. The key and padlock rattled in its depths. Cigarette ashes covered everything while he stuffed it full of ancient, indescribable garments. And his voice, singing of those "yellow bees in the ivy bloom," mingled with the crying of the rising wind about his windows. His restlessness had disappeared by magic.

This time, however, there could be no haunted Pelion, nor shady groves of Tempe, for he lived in sophisticated times when money markets regulated movement sternly. Travelling was only for the rich; mere wanderers must pig it. He remembered instead an opportune invitation to the Desert. "Objective" invitation, his genial hosts had called it, knowing his hatred of convention. And Helouan danced into letters of brilliance upon the inner map of his mind. For Egypt had ever held his spirit in thrall, though as yet he had tried in vain to touch the great buried soul of her. The excavators, the Egyptologists, the archaeologists most of all, plastered her grey ancient face with labels like hotel advertisements on travellers' portmanteaux. They told where she had come from last, but nothing of what she dreamed and thought and loved.

The heart of Egypt lay beneath the sand, and the trifling robbery of little details that poked forth from tombs and temples brought no true revelation of her stupendous spiritual splendour. Henriot, in his youth, had searched and dived among what material he could find, believing once—or half believing—that the ceremonial of that ancient system veiled a weight of symbol that was reflected from genuine supersensual knowledge. The rituals, now taken literally, and so pityingly explained away, had once been genuine pathways of approach. But never yet, and least of all in his previous visits to Egypt itself, had he discovered one single person, worthy of speech, who caught at his idea. "Curious," they said, then turned away—to go on digging in the sand. Sand smothered her world today. Excavators discovered skeletons. Museums everywhere stored them—grinning, literal relics that told nothing.

But now, while he packed and sang, these hopes of enthusiastic younger days stirred again—because the emotion that gave them birth was real and true in him. Through the morning mists upon the Nile an old pyramid bowed hugely at him across London roofs: "Come," he heard its awful whisper beneath the ceiling, "I have things to show you, and to tell." He saw the flock of them sailing the Desert like weird grey solemn ships that make no earthly port. And he imagined them as one: multiple expressions of some single unearthly portent they adumbrated in mighty form—dead symbols of some spiritual conception long vanished from the world.

"I mustn't dream like this," he laughed, "or I shall get absent-minded and pack fire-tongs instead of boots. It looks like a jumble sale already!" And he stood on a heap of things to wedge them down still tighter.

But the pictures would not cease. He saw the kites circling high in the blue air. A couple of white vultures flapped lazily away over shining miles. *Felucca* sails, like giant wings emerging from the ground, curved towards him from the Nile. The palm-trees dropped long shadows over Memphis. He felt the delicious, drenching heat, and the *Khamasin*, that over-wind from Nubia, brushed his very cheeks. In the little gardens the mish-mish was in bloom. . . . He smelt the Desert. . . . grey sepulchre of cancelled cycles. . . . The stillness of her interminable reaches dropped down upon old London. . . .

The magic of the sand stole round him in its silent-footed tempest. And while he struggled with that strange, capacious sack, the piles of clothing ran into shapes of gleaming Bedouin faces; London garments settled down with the mournful sound of camels' feet, half dropping wind, half water flowing underground—sound that old Time has brought over into modern life and left a moment for our wonder and perhaps our tears.

He rose at length with the excitement of some deep enchantment in his eyes. The thought of Egypt plunged ever so deeply into him, carrying him into depths where he found it difficult to breathe, so strangely far away it seemed, yet indefinably familiar. He lost his way. A touch of fear came with it.

"A sack like that is the wonder of the world," he laughed again, kicking the unwieldy, sausage-shaped monster into a corner of the room, and sitting down to write the thrilling labels: "Felix Henriot, Alexandria *via* Marseilles." But his pen blotted the letters; there was sand in it. He rewrote the words. Then he remembered a dozen things he had left out. Impatiently, yet with confusion somewhere, he stuffed them in. They ran away into shifting heaps; they disappeared; they emerged suddenly again. It was like packing hot, dry, flowing sand. From the pockets of a coat—he had worn it last summer down Dorset way—out trickled sand. There was sand in his mind and thoughts.

And his dreams that night were full of winds, the old sad winds of Egypt, and of moving, sifting sand. Arabs and Afreets danced amazingly together across dunes he could never reach. For he could not follow fast enough. Something infinitely older than these ever caught his feet and held him back. A million tiny fingers stung and pricked him. Something flung a veil before his eyes. Once it touched him—his face and hands and neck. "Stay here with us," he heard a host of muffled voices crying, but their sound was smothered, buried, rising through the ground. A myriad throats were choked. Till, at last, with a violent effort he turned and seized it. And then the thing he grasped at slipped between his fingers and ran easily away. It had a grey and yellow face, and it moved through all its parts. It flowed as water flows, and yet was solid. It was centuries old.

He cried out to it. "Who are you? What is your name? I surely know you. . . . but I have forgotten. . . .?"

And it stopped, turning from far away its great uncovered countenance of nameless colouring. He caught a voice. It rolled and boomed and whispered like the wind. And then he woke, with a curious shaking in his heart, and a little touch of chilly perspiration on the skin.

But the voice seemed in the room still—close beside him:

"I am the Sand," he heard, before it died away.

★★★★★★★★★★★★★★★★★

And next he realised that the glitter of Paris lay behind him, and a steamer was taking him with much unnecessary motion across a sparkling sea towards Alexandria. Gladly he saw the Riviera fade below the horizon, with its hard bright sunshine, treacherous winds, and its smear of rich, conventional English. All restlessness now had left him. True vagabond still at forty, he only felt the unrest and discomfort of life when caught in the network of routine and rigid streets, no chance of breaking loose. He was off again at last, money scarce enough indeed, but the joy of wandering expressing itself in happy emotions of release. Every warning of calculation was stifled. He thought of the American woman who walked out of her Long Island house one summer's day to look at a passing sail—and was gone eight years before she walked in again. Eight years of roving travel! He had always felt respect and admiration for that woman.

For Felix Henriot, with his admixture of foreign blood, was philosopher as well as vagabond, a strong poetic and religious strain sometimes breaking out through fissures in his complex nature. He had seen much life; had read many books. The passionate desire of youth to solve the world's big riddles had given place to a resignation filled to the brim with wonder. Anything *might* be true. Nothing surprised him. The most outlandish beliefs, for all he knew, might fringe truth somewhere. He had escaped that cheap cynicism with which disappointed men soothe their vanity when they realise that an intelligible explanation of the universe lies beyond their powers. He no longer expected final answers.

For him, even the smallest journeys held the spice of some adventure; all minutes were loaded with enticing potentialities. And they shaped for themselves somehow a dramatic form. "It's like a story," his friends said when he told his travels. It always was a story.

But the adventure that lay waiting for him where the silent streets of little Helouan kiss the great Desert's lips, was of a different kind to any Henriot had yet encountered. Looking back, he has often asked himself, "How in the world can I accept it?"

And, perhaps, he never yet has accepted it. It was sand that brought it. For the Desert, the stupendous thing that mothers little Helouan, produced it.

2

He slipped through Cairo with the same relief that he left the Riviera, resenting its social vulgarity so close to the imperial aristocracy of the Desert; he settled down into the peace of soft and silent little Helouan. The hotel in which he had a room on the top floor had been formerly a Khedivial Palace. It had the air of a palace still. He felt himself in a country-house, with lofty ceilings, cool and airy corridors, spacious halls. Soft-footed Arabs attended to his wants; white walls let in light and air without a sign of heat; there was a feeling of a large, spread tent pitched on the very sand; and the wind that stirred the oleanders in the shady gardens also crept in to rustle the palm leaves of his favourite corner seat. Through the large windows where once the *Khedive* held high court, the sunshine blazed upon *vistaed* leagues of Desert.

And from his bedroom windows he watched the sun dip into gold and crimson behind the swelling Libyan sands. This side of the pyramids he saw the Nile meander among palm groves and tilled fields. Across his balcony railings the Egyptian stars trooped down beside his very bed, shaping old constellations for his dreams; while, to the south, he looked out upon the vast untameable body of the sands that carpeted the world for thousands of miles towards Upper Egypt, Nubia, and the dread Sahara itself. He wondered again why people thought it necessary to go so far afield to know the Desert. Here, within half an hour of Cairo, it lay breathing solemnly at his very doors.

For little Helouan, caught thus between the shoulders of the Libyan and Arabian Deserts, is utterly sand-haunted. The Desert lies all round it like a sea. Henriot felt he never could escape from it, as he moved about the island whose coasts are washed with sand. Down each broad and shining street the two end houses framed a vista of its dim immensity—glimpses of shimmering blue, or flame-touched purple. There were stretches of deep sea-green as well, far off upon its bosom. The streets were open channels of approach, and the eye ran down them as along the tube of a telescope laid to catch incredible distance out of space.

Through them the Desert reached in with long, thin feelers towards the village. Its Being flooded into Helouan, and over it. Past walls and houses, churches and hotels, the sea of Desert pressed in silently with its myriad soft feet of sand. It poured in everywhere, through crack and slit and cranny. These were reminders of possession and ownership. And every passing wind that lifted eddies of dust at the street corners were messages from the quiet, powerful Thing that permitted Helouan to lie and dream so peacefully in the sunshine. Mere artificial oasis, its existence was temporary, held on lease, just for ninety-nine centuries or so.

This sea idea became insistent. For, in certain lights, and especially in the brief, bewildering dusk, the Desert rose—swaying towards the small white houses. The waves of it ran for fifty miles without a break. It was too deep for foam or surface agitation, yet it knew the swell of tides. And underneath flowed resolute currents, linking distance to the centre. These many Deserts were really one.

A storm, just retreated, had tossed Helouan upon the shore and left it there to dry; but any morning he would wake to find it had been carried off again into the depths. Some fragment, at least, would disappear. The grim Mokattam Hills were rollers that ever threatened to topple down and submerge the sandy bar that men called Helouan.

Being soundless, and devoid of perfume, the Desert's message reached him through two senses only—sight and touch; chiefly, of course, the former. Its invasion was concentrated through the eyes. And vision, thus uncorrected, went what pace it pleased. The Desert played with him. Sand stole into his being—through the eyes.

And so obsessing was this majesty of its close presence, that Henriot sometimes wondered how people dared their little social activities within its very sight and hearing; how they played golf and tennis upon reclaimed edges of its face, picnicked so blithely hard upon its frontiers, and danced at night while this stern, unfathomable Thing lay breathing just beyond the trumpery walls that kept it out. The challenge of their shallow admiration seemed presumptuous, almost provocative. Their pursuit of pleasure suggested insolent indifference. They ran fool-hardy hazards, he felt; for there was no worship in their vulgar hearts. With a mental shudder, sometimes he watched the cheap tourist horde go laughing, chattering past within view of its ancient, half-closed eyes. It was like defying deity.

For, to his stirred imagination the sublimity of the Desert dwarfed humanity. These people had been wiser to choose another place for the flaunting of their tawdry insignificance. Any minute this Wilderness, "huddled in grey annihilation," might awake and notice them . . . .!

In his own hotel were several "smart," so-called "Society" people who emphasised the protest in him to the point of definite contempt. Overdressed, the latest worldly novel under their arms, they strutted the narrow pavements of their tiny world, immensely pleased with themselves. Their vacuous minds expressed themselves in the slang of their exclusive circle—value being the element excluded. The pettiness of their outlook hardly distressed him—he was too familiar with it at home—but their essential vulgarity, their innate ugliness, seemed more than usually offensive in the grandeur of its present setting. Into the mighty sands they took the latest London scandal, gabbling it over even among the Tombs and Temples. And "it was to laugh," the pains they spent wondering whom they might condescend to know, never dreaming that they themselves were not worth knowing. Against the background of the noble Desert their titles seemed the cap and bells of clowns.

And Henriot, knowing some of them personally, could not always escape their insipid company. Yet he was the gainer. They little guessed how their commonness heightened contrast, set mercilessly thus beside the strange, eternal beauty of the sand.

Occasionally the protest in his soul betrayed itself in words, which of course they did not understand. "He is so clever, isn't he?" And then, having relieved his feelings, he would comfort himself characteristically:

"The Desert has not noticed them. The Sand is not aware of their existence. How should the sea take note of rubbish that lies above its tide-line?"

For Henriot drew near to its great shifting altars in an attitude of worship. The wilderness made him kneel in heart. Its shining reaches led to the oldest Temple in the world, and every journey that he made was like a sacrament. For him the Desert was a consecrated place. It was sacred.

And his tactful hosts, knowing his peculiarities, left their house open to him when he cared to come—they lived upon the northern edge of the oasis—and he was as free as though he were absolutely alone. He blessed them; he rejoiced that he had come. Little Helouan accepted him. The Desert knew that he was there.

★★★★★★★★★★★★★★★★

From his corner of the big dining-room he could see the other guests, but his roving eye always returned to the figure of a solitary man who sat at an adjoining table, and whose personality stirred his interest. While affecting to look elsewhere, he studied him as closely as might be. There was something about the stranger that touched his curiosity—a certain air of expectation that he wore. But it was more than that: it was anticipation, apprehension in it somewhere. The man was nervous, uneasy. His restless way of suddenly looking about him proved it. Henriot tried every one else in the room as well; but though his thought settled on others too, he always came back to the figure of this solitary being opposite, who ate his dinner as if afraid of being seen, and glanced up sometimes as if fearful of being watched. Henriot's curiosity, before he knew it, became suspicion. There was mystery here. The table, he noticed, was laid for two.

"Is he an actor, a priest of some strange religion, an enquiry agent, or just—a crank?" was the thought that first occurred to him. And the question suggested itself without amusement. The impression of subterfuge and caution he conveyed left his observer unsatisfied.

The face was clean shaven, dark, and strong; thick hair, straight

89

yet bushy, was slightly unkempt; it was streaked with grey; and an unexpected mobility when he smiled ran over the features that he seemed to hold rigid by deliberate effort. The man was cut to no quite common measure. Henriot jumped to an intuitive conclusion: "He's not here for pleasure or merely sight-seeing. Something serious has brought him out to Egypt."

For the face combined too ill-assorted qualities: an obstinate tenacity that might even mean brutality, and was certainly repulsive, yet, with it, an undecipherable dreaminess betrayed by lines of the mouth, but above all in the very light blue eyes, so rarely raised. Those eyes, he felt, had looked upon unusual things; "dreaminess" was not an adequate description; "searching" conveyed it better. The true source of the queer impression remained elusive. And hence, perhaps, the incongruous marriage in the face—mobility laid upon a matter-of-fact foundation underneath. The face showed conflict.

And Henriot, watching him, felt decidedly intrigued. "I'd like to know that man, and all about him." His name, he learned later, was Richard Vance; from Birmingham; a business man. But it was not the Birmingham he wished to know; it was the—other: cause of the elusive, dreamy searching. Though facing one another at so short a distance, their eyes, however, did not meet. And this, Henriot well knew, was a sure sign that he himself was also under observation. Richard Vance, from Birmingham, was equally taking careful note of Felix Henriot, from London.

Thus, he could wait his time. They would come together later. An opportunity would certainly present itself. The first links in a curious chain had already caught; soon the chain would tighten, pull as though by chance, and bring their lives into one and the same circle. Wondering in particular for what kind of a companion the second cover was laid, Henriot felt certain that their eventual coming together was inevitable. He possessed this kind of divination from first impressions, and not uncommonly it proved correct.

Following instinct, therefore, he took no steps towards acquaintance, and for several days, owing to the fact that he dined frequently with his hosts, he saw nothing more of Richard Vance, the business man from Birmingham. Then, one night, coming home late from his friend's house, he had passed along the great corridor, and was actually a step or so into his bedroom, when a drawling voice sounded close behind him. It was an unpleasant sound. It was very near him too—

"I beg your pardon, but have you, by any chance, such a thing as a compass you could lend me?"

The voice was so close that he started. Vance stood within touching distance of his body. He had stolen up like a ghostly Arab, must have followed him, too, some little distance, for further down the passage the light of an open door—he had passed it on his way—showed where he came from.

"Eh? I beg your pardon? A—compass, did you say?" He felt disconcerted for a moment. How short the man was, now that he saw him standing. Broad and powerful too. Henriot looked down upon his thick head of hair. The personality and voice repelled him. Possibly his face, caught unawares, betrayed this.

"Forgive my startling you," said the other apologetically, while the softer expression danced in for a moment and disorganised the rigid set of the face. "The soft carpet, you know. I'm afraid you didn't hear my tread. I wondered"—he smiled again slightly at the nature of the request—"if—by any chance—you had a pocket compass you could lend me?"

"Ah, a compass, yes! Please don't apologise. I believe I have one—if you'll wait a moment. Come in, won't you? I'll have a look."

The other thanked him but waited in the passage. Henriot, it so happened, had a compass, and produced it after a moment's search.

"I am greatly indebted to you—if I may return it in the morning. You will forgive my disturbing you at such an hour. My own is broken, and I wanted—er—to find the true north."

Henriot stammered some reply, and the man was gone. It was all over in a minute. He locked his door and sat down in his chair to think. The little incident had upset him, though for the life of him he could not imagine why. It ought by rights to have been almost ludicrous, yet instead it was the exact reverse—half threatening. Why should not a man want a compass? But, again, why should he? And at midnight? The voice, the eyes, the near presence—what did they bring that set his nerves thus asking unusual questions? This strange impression that something grave was happening, something unearthly—how was it born exactly? The man's proximity came like a shock. It had made him start. He brought—thus the idea came unbidden to his mind—something with him that galvanised him quite absurdly, as fear does, or delight, or great wonder. There was a music in his voice too—a certain—well, he could only call it lilt, that reminded him of plainsong, intoning, chanting. Drawling was *not* the word at all.

He tried to dismiss it as imagination, but it would not be dismissed.

The disturbance in himself was caused by something not imaginary, but real. And then, for the first time, he discovered that the man had brought a faint, elusive suggestion of perfume with him, an aromatic odour, that made him think of priests and churches. The ghost of it still lingered in the air. Ah, here then was the origin of the notion that his voice had chanted: it was surely the suggestion of incense. But incense, intoning, a compass to find the true north—at midnight in a Desert hotel!

A touch of uneasiness ran through the curiosity and excitement that he felt.

And he undressed for bed. "Confound my old imagination," he thought, "what tricks it plays me! It'll keep me awake!"

But the questions, once started in his mind, continued. He must find explanation of one kind or another before he could lie down and sleep, and he found it at length in—the stars. The man was an astronomer of sorts; possibly an astrologer into the bargain! Why not? The stars were wonderful above Helouan. Was there not an observatory on the Mokattam Hills, too, where tourists could use the telescopes on privileged days? He had it at last. He even stole out on to his balcony to see if the stranger perhaps was looking through some wonderful apparatus at the heavens.

Their rooms were on the same side. But the shuttered windows revealed no stooping figure with eyes glued to a telescope. The stars blinked in their many thousands down upon the silent Desert. The night held neither sound nor movement. There was a cool breeze blowing across the Nile from the Lybian Sands. It nipped; and he stepped back quickly into the room again. Drawing the mosquito curtains carefully about the bed, he put the light out and turned over to sleep.

And sleep came quickly, contrary to his expectations, though it was a light and surface sleep. That last glimpse of the darkened Desert lying beneath the Egyptian stars had touched him with some hand of awful power that ousted the first, lesser excitement. It calmed and soothed him in one sense, yet in another, a sense he could not understand, it caught him in a net of deep, deep feelings whose mesh, while infinitely delicate, was utterly stupendous. His nerves this deeper emotion left alone: it reached instead to something infinite in him that mere nerves could neither deal with nor interpret. The soul awoke and whispered in him while his body slept.

And the little, foolish dreams that ran to and fro across this veil of surface sleep brought oddly tangled pictures of things quite tiny and at the same time of others that were mighty beyond words. With these two counters Nightmare played. They interwove. There was the figure of this dark-faced man with the compass, measuring the sky to find the true north, and there were hints of giant Presences that hovered just outside some curious outline that he traced upon the ground, copied in some nightmare fashion from the heavens. The excitement caused by his visitor's singular request mingled with the profounder sensations his final look at the stars and Desert stirred. The two were somehow inter-related.

Some hours later, before this surface sleep passed into genuine slumber, Henriot woke—with an appalling feeling that the Desert had come creeping into his room and now stared down upon him where he lay in bed. The wind was crying audibly about the walls outside. A faint, sharp tapping came against the window panes.

He sprang instantly out of bed, not yet awake enough to feel actual alarm, yet with the nightmare touch still close enough to cause a sort of feverish, loose bewilderment. He switched the lights on. A moment later he knew the meaning of that curious tapping, for the rising wind was flinging tiny specks of sand against the glass. The idea that they had summoned him belonged, of course, to dream.

He opened the window, and stepped out on to the balcony. The stone was very cold under his bare feet. There was a wash of wind all over him. He saw the sheet of glimmering, pale Desert near and far; and something stung his skin below the eyes.

"The sand," he whispered, "again the sand; always the sand. Waking or sleeping, the sand is everywhere—nothing but sand, sand, Sand. . . ."

He rubbed his eyes. It was like talking in his sleep, talking to Someone who had questioned him just before he woke. But was he really properly awake? It seemed next day that he had dreamed it. Something enormous, with rustling skirts of sand, had just retreated far into the Desert. Sand went with it—flowing, trailing, smothering the world. The wind died down.

And Henriot went back to sleep, caught instantly away into unconsciousness; covered, blinded, swept over by this spreading thing of reddish brown with the great, grey face, whose Being was colossal yet quite tiny, and whose fingers, wings and eyes were countless as the stars.

But all night long it watched and waited, rising to peer above the little balcony, and sometimes entering the room and piling up beside his very pillow. He dreamed of Sand.

3

For some days Henriot saw little of the man who came from Birmingham and pushed curiosity to a climax by asking for a compass in the middle of the night. For one thing, he was a good deal with his friends upon the other side of Helouan, and for another, he slept several nights in the Desert.

He loved the gigantic peace the Desert gave him. The world was forgotten there; and not the world merely, but all memory of it. Everything faded out. The soul turned inwards upon itself.

An Arab boy and donkey took out sleeping-bag, food and water to the Wadi Hof, a desolate gorge about an hour eastwards. It winds between cliffs whose summits rise some thousand feet above the sea. It opens suddenly, cut deep into the swaying world of level plateaux and undulating hills. It moves about too; he never found it in the same place twice—like an arm of the Desert that shifted with the changing lights. Here he watched dawns and sunsets, slept through the mid-day heat, and enjoyed the unearthly colouring that swept day and night across the huge horizons. In solitude the Desert soaked down into him.

At night the jackals cried in the darkness round his cautiously-fed camp fire—small, because wood had to be carried—and in the day-time kites circled overhead to inspect him, and an occasional white vulture flapped across the blue. The weird desolation of this rocky valley, he thought, was like the scenery of the moon. He took no watch with him, and the arrival of the donkey boy an hour after sunrise came almost from another planet, bringing things of time and common life out of some distant gulf where they had lain forgotten among lost ages.

The short hour of twilight brought, too, a bewitchment into the silence that was a little less than comfortable. Full light or darkness he could manage, but this time of half things made him want to shut his eyes and hide. Its effect stepped over imagination. The mind got lost. He could not understand it. For the cliffs and boulders of discoloured limestone shone then with an inward glow that signalled to the Desert with veiled lanterns. The misshapen hills, carved by wind and rain into ominous outlines, stirred and nodded.

In the morning light they retired into themselves, asleep. But at dusk the tide retreated. They rose from the sea, emerging naked, threatening. They ran together and joined shoulders, the entire army of them. And the glow of their sandy bodies, self-luminous, continued even beneath the stars. Only the moonlight drowned it. For the moonrise over the Mokattam Hills brought a white, grand loveliness that drenched the entire Desert. It drew a marvellous sweetness from the sand. It shone across a world as yet unfinished, whereon no life might show itself for ages yet to come. He was alone then upon an empty star, before the creation of things that breathed and moved.

What impressed him, however, more than everything else was the enormous vitality that rose out of all this apparent death. There was no hint of the melancholy that belongs commonly to flatness; the sadness of wide, monotonous landscape was not here. The endless repetition of sweeping vale and plateau brought infinity within measurable comprehension. He grasped a definite meaning in the phrase "world without end": the Desert had no end and no beginning.

It gave him a sense of eternal peace, the silent peace that star-fields know. Instead of subduing the soul with bewilderment, it inspired with courage, confidence, hope. Through this sand which was the wreck of countless geological ages, rushed life that was terrific and uplifting, too huge to include melancholy, too deep to betray itself in movement. Here was the stillness of eternity. Behind the spread grey masque of apparent death lay stores of accumulated life, ready to break forth at any point. In the Desert he felt himself absolutely royal.

And this contrast of Life, veiling itself in Death, was a contradiction that somehow intoxicated. The Desert exhilaration never left him. He was never alone. A companionship of millions went with him, and he *felt* the Desert close, as stars are close to one another, or grains of sand.

It was the *Khamasin*, the hot wind bringing sand, that drove him in—with the feeling that these few days and nights had been immeasurable, and that he had been away a thousand years. He came back with the magic of the Desert in his blood, hotel-life tasteless and insipid by comparison. To human impressions thus he was fresh and vividly sensitive. His being, cleaned and sensitised by pure grandeur, "felt" people—for a time at any rate—with an uncommon sharpness of receptive judgment. He returned to a life somehow mean and meagre, resuming insignificance with his dinner jacket. Out with the sand he had been regal; now, like a slave, he strutted self-conscious and reduced.

But this imperial standard of the Desert stayed a little time beside him, its purity focussing judgment like a lens. The specks of smaller emotions left it clear at first, and as his eye wandered vaguely over the people assembled in the dining-room, it was arrested with a vivid shock upon two figures at the little table facing him.

He had forgotten Vance, the Birmingham man who sought the North at midnight with a pocket compass. He now saw him again, with an intuitive discernment entirely fresh. Before memory brought up her clouding associations, some brilliance flashed a light upon him.

"That man," Henriot thought, "might have come with me. He would have understood and loved it!" But the thought was really this—a moment's reflection spread it, rather: "He belongs somewhere to the Desert; the Desert brought him out here." And, again, hidden swiftly behind it like a movement running below water—"What does he want with it? What is the deeper motive he conceals? For there is a deeper motive; and it *is* concealed."

But it was the woman seated next him who absorbed his attention really, even while this thought flashed and went its way. The empty chair was occupied at last. Unlike his first encounter with the man, she looked straight at him. Their eyes met fully. For several seconds there was steady mutual inspection, while her penetrating stare, intent without being rude, passed searchingly all over his face. It was disconcerting. Crumbling his bread, he looked equally hard at her, unable to turn away, determined not to be the first to shift his gaze.

And when at length she lowered her eyes he felt that many things had happened, as in a long period of intimate conversation. Her mind had judged him through and through. Questions and answer flashed. They were no longer strangers. For the rest of dinner, though he was careful to avoid direct inspection, he was aware that she felt his presence and was secretly speaking with him. She asked questions beneath her breath. The answers rose with the quickened pulses in his blood. Moreover, she explained Richard Vance. It was this woman's power that shone reflected in the man. She was the one who knew the big, unusual things. Vance merely echoed the rush of her vital personality.

This was the first impression that he got—from the most striking, curious face he had ever seen in a woman. It remained very near him all through the meal: she had moved to his table, it seemed she sat beside him. Their minds certainly knew contact from that moment.

It is never difficult to credit strangers with the qualities and knowledge that oneself craves for, and no doubt Henriot's active fancy went busily to work. But, none the less, this thing remained and grew: that this woman was aware of the hidden things of Egypt he had always longed to know. There was knowledge and guidance she could impart. Her soul was searching among ancient things. Her face brought the Desert back into his thoughts. And with it came—the sand.

Here was the flash. The sight of her restored the peace and splendour he had left behind him in his Desert camps. The rest, of course, was what his imagination constructed upon this slender basis. Only— not all of it was imagination.

Now, Henriot knew little enough of women, and had no pose of "understanding" them. His experience was of the slightest; the love and veneration felt for his own mother had set the entire sex upon the heights. His affairs with women, if so, they may be called, had been transient—all but those of early youth, which having never known the devastating test of fulfilment, still remained ideal and superb. There was unconscious humour in his attitude—from a distance; for he regarded women with wonder and respect, as puzzles that sweetened but complicated life, might even endanger it. He certainly was not a marrying man! But now, as he felt the presence of this woman so deliberately possess him, there came over him two clear, strong messages, each vivid with certainty.

One was that banal suggestion of familiarity claimed by lovers and the like—he had often heard of it—"I have known that woman before; I have met her ages ago somewhere; she is strangely familiar to me"; and the other, growing out of it almost: "Have nothing to do with her; she will bring you trouble and confusion; avoid her, and be warned";—in fact, a distinct presentiment.

Yet, although Henriot dismissed both impressions as having no shred of evidence to justify them, the original clear judgment, as he studied her extraordinary countenance, persisted through all denials. The familiarity, and the presentiment, remained. There also remained this other—an enormous imaginative leap!—that she could teach him "Egypt."

He watched her carefully, in a sense fascinated. He could only describe the face as black, so dark it was with the darkness of great age. Elderly was the obvious, natural word; but elderly described the features only. The expression of the face wore centuries. Nor was it merely the coal-black eyes that betrayed an ancient, age-travelled soul behind them. The entire presentment mysteriously conveyed it.

This woman's heart knew long-forgotten things—the thought kept beating up against him. There were cheek-bones, oddly high, that made him think involuntarily of the well-advertised Pharaoh,

Ramases; a square, deep jaw; and an aquiline nose that gave the final touch of power. For the power undeniably was there, and while the general effect had grimness in it, there was neither harshness nor any forbidding touch about it. There was an implacable sternness in the set of lips and jaw, and, most curious of all, the eyelids over the steady eyes of black were level as a ruler. This level framing made the woman's stare remarkable beyond description. Henriot thought of an idol carved in stone, stone hard and black, with eyes that stared across the sand into a world of things non-human, very far away, forgotten of men. The face was finely ugly. This strange dark beauty flashed flame about it.

And, as the way ever was with him, Henriot next fell to constructing the possible lives of herself and her companion, though without much success. Imagination soon stopped dead. She was not old enough to be Vance's mother, and assuredly she was not his wife. His interest was more than merely piqued—it was puzzled uncommonly. What was the contrast that made the man seem beside her—vile? Whence came, too, the impression that she exercised some strong authority, though never directly exercised, that held him at her mercy?

How did he guess that the man resented it, yet did not dare oppose, and that, apparently acquiescing good-humouredly, his will was deliberately held in abeyance, and that he waited sulkily, biding his time? There was furtiveness in every gesture and expression. A hidden motive lurked in him; unworthiness somewhere; he was determined yet ashamed. He watched her ceaselessly and with such uncanny closeness.

Henriot imagined he divined all this. He leaped to the guess that his expenses were being paid. A good deal more was being paid besides. She was a rich relation, from whom he had expectations; he was serving his seven years, ashamed of his servitude, ever calculating escape—but, perhaps, no ordinary escape. A faint shudder ran over him. He drew in the reins of imagination.

Of course, the probabilities were that he was hopelessly astray—one usually is on such occasions—but this time, it so happened, he was singularly right. Before one thing only his ready invention stopped every time. This vileness, this notion of unworthiness in Vance, could not be negative merely. A man with that face was no inactive weakling. The motive he was at such pains to conceal, betraying its existence by that very fact, moved, surely, towards aggressive action. Disguised, it never slept. Vance was sharply on the alert. He had a plan deep out of sight. And Henriot remembered how the man's soft approach along the carpeted corridor had made him start. He recalled the quasi shock it gave him. He thought again of the feeling of discomfort he had experienced.

Next, his eager fancy sought to plumb the business these two had together in Egypt—in the Desert. For the Desert, he felt convinced, had brought them out. But here, though he constructed numerous explanations, another barrier stopped him. Because he *knew*. This woman was in touch with that aspect of ancient Egypt he himself had ever sought in vain; and not merely with stones the sand had buried so deep, but with the meanings they once represented, buried so utterly by the sands of later thought.

And here, being ignorant, he found no clue that could lead to any satisfactory result, for he possessed no knowledge that might guide him. He floundered—until Fate helped him. And the instant Fate helped him, the warning and presentiment he had dismissed as fanciful, became real again. He hesitated. Caution acted. He would think twice before taking steps to form acquaintance. "Better not," thought whispered. "Better leave them alone, this queer couple. They're after things that won't do you any good." This idea of mischief, almost of danger, in their purposes was oddly insistent; for what could possibly convey it? But, while he hesitated, Fate, who sent the warning, pushed him at the same time into the circle of their lives: at first tentatively— he might still have escaped; but soon urgently—curiosity led him inexorably towards the end.

4

It was so simple a manoeuvre by which Fate began the innocent game. The woman left a couple of books behind her on the table one night, and Henriot, after a moment's hesitation, took them out after her. He knew the titles—*The House of the Master*, and *The House of the Hidden Places*, both singular interpretations of the Pyramids that once had held his own mind spellbound. Their ideas had been since disproved, if he remembered rightly, yet the titles were a clue—a clue to that imaginative part of his mind that was so busy constructing theories and had found its stride. Loose sheets of paper, covered with notes in a minute handwriting, lay between the pages; but these, of course, he did not read, noticing only that they were written round designs of various kinds—intricate designs.

He discovered Vance in a corner of the smoking-lounge. The

woman had disappeared.

Vance thanked him politely. "My aunt is so forgetful sometimes," he said, and took them with a covert eagerness that did not escape the other's observation. He folded up the sheets and put them carefully in his pocket. On one there was an ink-sketched map, crammed with detail, that might well have referred to some portion of the Desert. The points of the compass stood out boldly at the bottom. There were involved geometrical designs again. Henriot saw them. They exchanged, then, the commonplaces of conversation, but these led to nothing further. Vance was nervous and betrayed impatience.

He presently excused himself and left the lounge. Ten minutes later he passed through the outer hall, the woman beside him, and the pair of them, wrapped up in cloak and ulster, went out into the night. At the door, Vance turned and threw a quick, investigating glance in his direction. There seemed a hint of questioning in that glance; it might almost have been a tentative invitation. But, also, he wanted to see if their exit had been particularly noticed—and by whom.

This, briefly told, was the first manoeuvre by which Fate introduced them. There was nothing in it. The details were so insignificant, so slight the conversation, so meagre the pieces thus added to Henriot's imaginative structure. Yet they somehow built it up and made it solid; the outline in his mind began to stand foursquare. That writing, those designs, the manner of the man, their going out together, the final curious look—each and all betrayed points of a hidden thing. Subconsciously he was excavating their buried purposes.

The sand was shifting. The concentration of his mind incessantly upon them removed it grain by grain and speck by speck. Tips of the smothered thing emerged. Presently a subsidence would follow with a rush and light would blaze upon its skeleton. He felt it stirring underneath his feet—this flowing movement of light, dry, heaped-up sand. It was always—sand.

Then other incidents of a similar kind came about, clearing the way to a natural acquaintanceship. Henriot watched the process with amusement, yet with another feeling too that was only a little less than anxiety. A keen observer, no detail escaped him; he saw the forces of their lives draw closer. It made him think of the devices of young people who desire to know one another, yet cannot get a proper introduction. Fate condescended to such little tricks. They wanted a third person, he began to feel. A third was necessary to some plan they had on hand, and—they waited to see if he could fill the place. This woman, with whom he had yet exchanged no single word, seemed so familiar to him, well known for years. They weighed and watched him, wondering if he would do.

None of the devices were too obviously used, but at length Henriot picked up so many forgotten articles, and heard so many significant phrases, casually let fall, that he began to feel like the villain in a machine-made play, where the hero for ever drops clues his enemy is intended to discover.

Introduction followed inevitably. "My aunt can tell you; she knows Arabic perfectly." He had been discussing the meaning of some local name or other with a neighbour after dinner, and Vance had joined them. The neighbour moved away; these two were left standing alone, and he accepted a cigarette from the other's case. There was a rustle of skirts behind them. "Here she comes," said Vance; "you will let me introduce you." He did not ask for Henriot's name; he had already taken the trouble to find it out—another little betrayal, and another clue.

It was in a secluded corner of the great hall, and Henriot turned to see the woman's stately figure coming towards them across the thick carpet that deadened her footsteps. She came sailing up, her black eyes fixed upon his face. Very erect, head upright, shoulders almost squared, she moved wonderfully well; there was dignity and power in her walk. She was dressed in black, and her face was like the night. He found it impossible to say what lent her this air of impressiveness and solemnity that was almost majestic. But there *was* this touch of darkness and of power in the way she came that made him think of some sphinx-like figure of stone, some idol motionless in all its parts but moving as a whole, and gliding across—sand. Beneath those level lids her eyes stared hard at him. And a faint sensation of distress stirred in him deep, deep down. Where had he seen those eyes before?

He bowed, as she joined them, and Vance led the way to the armchairs in a corner of the lounge. The meeting, as the talk that followed, he felt, were all part of a preconceived plan. It had happened before. The woman, that is, was familiar to him—to some part of his being that had dropped stitches of old, old memory.

Lady Statham! At first the name had disappointed him. So many folk wear titles, as syllables in certain tongues wear accents—without them being mute, unnoticed, unpronounced. Nonentities, born to names, so often claim attention for their insignificance in this way. But this woman, had she been Jemima Jones, would have made the name distinguished and select. She was a big and sombre personality. Why was it, he wondered afterwards, that for a moment something in him shrank, and that his mind, metaphorically speaking, flung up an arm in self-protection? The instinct flashed and passed. But it seemed to him born of an automatic feeling that he must protect—not himself, but the woman from the man. There was confusion in it all; links were missing.

He studied her intently. She was a woman who had none of the external feminine signals in either dress or manner, no graces, no little womanly hesitations and alarms, no daintiness, yet neither anything distinctly masculine. Her charm was strong, possessing; only he kept forgetting that he was talking to a—woman; and the thing she inspired in him included, with respect and wonder, somewhere also this curious hint of dread. This instinct to protect her fled as soon as it was born, for the interest of the conversation in which she so quickly plunged him obliterated all minor emotions whatsoever. Here, for the first time, he drew close to Egypt, the Egypt he had sought so long. It was not to be explained. He *felt* it.

Beginning with commonplaces, such as "You like Egypt? You find here what you expected?" she led him into better regions with "One finds here what one brings." He knew the delightful experience of talking fluently on subjects he was at home in, and to someone who understood. The feeling at first that to this woman he could not say mere anythings, slipped into its opposite—that he could say everything. Strangers ten minutes ago, they were at once in deep and intimate talk together. He found his ideas readily followed, agreed with up to a point—the point which permits discussion to start from a basis of general accord towards speculation.

In the excitement of ideas, he neglected the uncomfortable note that had stirred his caution, forgot the warning too. Her mind, moreover, seemed known to him; he was often aware of what she was going to say before he actually heard it; the current of her thoughts struck a familiar gait, and more than once he experienced vividly again the odd sensation that it all had happened before. The very sentences and phrases with which she pointed the turns of her unusual ideas were never wholly unexpected.

For her ideas were decidedly unusual, in the sense that she accepted without question speculations not commonly deemed worth consideration at all, indeed not ordinarily even known. Henriot knew them, because he had read in many fields. It was the strength of her belief that fascinated him. She offered no apologies. She knew. And while he talked, she listening with folded arms and her black eyes fixed upon his own, Richard Vance watched with vigilant eyes and listened too, ceaselessly alert. Vance joined in little enough, however, gave no opinions, his attitude one of general acquiescence.

Twice, when pauses of slackening interest made it possible, Henriot fancied he surprised another quality in this negative attitude. Interpreting it each time differently, he yet dismissed both interpretations with a smile. His imagination leaped so absurdly to violent conclusions. They were not tenable: Vance was neither her keeper, nor was he in some fashion a detective. Yet in his manner was sometimes this suggestion of the detective order. He watched with such deep attention, and he concealed it so clumsily with an affectation of careless indifference.

There is nothing more dangerous than that impulsive intimacy strangers sometimes adopt when an atmosphere of mutual sympathy takes them by surprise, for it is akin to the false frankness friends affect when telling "candidly" one another's faults. The mood is invariably regretted later. Henriot, however, yielded to it now with something like abandon. The pleasure of talking with this woman was so unexpected, and so keen.

For Lady Statham believed apparently in some Egypt of her dreams. Her interest was neither historical, archaeological, nor political. It was religious—yet hardly of this earth at all. The conversation turned upon the knowledge of the ancient Egyptians from an unearthly point of view, and even while he talked, he was vaguely aware that it was *her* mind talking through his own. She drew out his ideas and made him say them. But this he was properly aware of only afterwards—that she had cleverly, mercilessly pumped him of all he had ever known or read upon the subject. Moreover, what Vance watched so intently was himself, and the reactions in himself this remarkable woman produced. That also he realised later.

His first impression that these two belonged to what may be called the "crank" order was justified by the conversation. But, at least, it was interesting crankiness, and the belief behind it made it even fascinating. Long before the end he surprised in her a more vital form of his own attitude that anything *may* be true, since knowledge has never yet found final answers to any of the biggest questions.

He understood, from sentences dropped early in the talk, that she was among those few "superstitious" folk who think that the old Egyptians came closer to reading the eternal riddles of the world than any others, and that their knowledge was a remnant of that ancient Wisdom Religion which existed in the superb, dark civilization of the sunken Atlantis, lost continent that once joined Africa to Mexico. Eighty thousand years ago the dim sands of Poseidonis, great island adjoining the main continent which itself had vanished a vast period before, sank down beneath the waves, and the entire known world today was descended from its survivors.

Hence the significant fact that all religions and "mythological" systems begin with a story of a flood—some cataclysmic upheaval that destroyed the world. Egypt itself was colonised by a group of Atlantean priests who brought their curious, deep knowledge with them. They had foreseen the cataclysm.

Lady Statham talked well, bringing into her great dream this strong, insistent quality of belief and fact. She knew, from Plato to Donelly, all that the minds of men have ever speculated upon the gorgeous legend. The evidence for such a sunken continent—Henriot had skimmed it too in years gone by—she made bewilderingly complete. He had heard Baconians demolish Shakespeare with an array of evidence equally overwhelming. It catches the imagination though not the mind. Yet out of her facts, as she presented them, grew a strange likelihood. The force of this woman's personality, and her calm and quiet way of believing all she talked about, took her listener to some extent—further than ever before, certainly—into the great dream after her.

And the dream, to say the least, was a picturesque one, laden with wonderful possibilities. For as she talked the spirit of old Egypt moved up, staring down upon him out of eyes lidded so curiously level. Hitherto all had prated to him of the Arabs, their ancient faith and customs, and the splendour of the Bedouins, those Princes of the Desert. But what he sought, barely confessed in words even to himself, was something older far than this. And this strange, dark woman brought it close. Deeps in his soul, long slumbering, awoke. He heard forgotten questions.

Only in this brief way could he attempt to sum up the storm she roused in him.

She carried him far beyond mere outline, however, though afterwards he recalled the details with difficulty. So much more was suggested than actually expressed. She contrived to make the general modern scepticism an evidence of cheap mentality. It was so easy; the depth it affects to conceal, mere emptiness. "We have tried all things, and found all wanting"—the mind, as measuring instrument, merely confessed inadequate. Various shrewd judgments of this kind increased his respect, although her acceptance went so far beyond his own. And, while the label of credulity refused to stick to her, her sense of imaginative wonder enabled her to escape that dreadful compromise, a man's mind in a woman's temperament. She fascinated him.

The spiritual worship of the ancient Egyptians, she held, was a symbolical explanation of things generally alluded to as the secrets of life and death; their knowledge was a remnant of the wisdom of Atlantis. Material relics, equally misunderstood, still stood today at Karnac, Stonehenge, and in the mysterious writings on buried Mexican temples and cities, so significantly akin to the hieroglyphics upon the Egyptian tombs.

"The one misinterpreted as literally as the other," she suggested, "yet both fragments of an advanced knowledge that found its grave in the sea. The Wisdom of that old spiritual system has vanished from the world, only a degraded literalism left of its undecipherable language. The jewel has been lost, and the casket is filled with sand, sand, sand."

How keenly her black eyes searched his own as she said it, and how oddly she made the little word resound. The syllable drew out almost into chanting. Echoes answered from the depths within him, carrying it on and on across some Desert of forgotten belief. Veils of sand flew everywhere about his mind. Curtains lifted. Whole hills of sand went shifting into level surfaces whence gardens of dim outline emerged to meet the sunlight.

"But the sand may be removed." It was her nephew, speaking almost for the first time, and the interruption had an odd effect, introducing a sharply practical element. For the tone expressed, so far as he dared express it, disapproval. It was a baited observation, an invitation to opinion.

"We are not sand-diggers, Mr. Henriot," put in Lady Statham, before he decided to respond. "Our object is quite another one; and I believe—I have a feeling," she added almost questioningly, "that you might be interested enough to help us perhaps."

He only wondered the direct attack had not come sooner. Its bluntness hardly surprised him. He felt himself leap forward to accept it. A sudden subsidence had freed his feet.

Then the warning operated suddenly—for an instant. Henriot *was* interested; more, he was half seduced; but, as yet, he did not mean to be included in their purposes, whatever these might be. That shrinking dread came back a moment, and was gone again before he could question it. His eyes looked full at Lady Statham. "What is it that you know?" they asked her. "Tell me the things we once knew together, you and I. These words are merely trifling. And why does another man now stand in my place? For the sands heaped upon my memory are shifting, and it is *you* who are moving them away."

His soul whispered it; his voice said quite another thing, although the words he used seemed oddly chosen:

"There is much in the ideas of ancient Egypt that has attracted me ever since I can remember, though I have never caught up with anything definite enough to follow. There was majesty somewhere in their conceptions—a large, calm majesty of spiritual dominion, one might call it perhaps. I *am* interested."

Her face remained expressionless as she listened, but there was grave conviction in the eyes that held him like a spell. He saw through them into dim, faint pictures whose background was always sand. He forgot that he was speaking with a woman, a woman who half an hour ago had been a stranger to him. He followed these faded mental pictures, though he never caught them up. . . . It was like his dream in London.

Lady Statham was talking—he had not noticed the means by which she effected the abrupt transition—of familiar beliefs of old Egypt; of the Ka, or Double, by whose existence the survival of the soul was possible, even its return into manifested, physical life; of the astrology, or influence of the heavenly bodies upon all sublunar activities; of terrific forms of other life, known to the ancient worship of Atlantis, great Potencies that might be invoked by ritual and ceremonial, and of their lesser influence as recognised in certain lower forms, hence treated with veneration as the "Sacred Animal" branch of this dim religion. And she spoke lightly of the modern learning which so glibly imagined it was the animals themselves that were looked upon as "gods"—the bull, the bird, the crocodile, the cat.

"It's there they all go so absurdly wrong," she said, "taking the symbol for the power symbolised. Yet natural enough. The mind today wears blinkers, studies only the details seen directly before it. Had none of us experienced love, we should think the first lover mad. Few today know the Powers *they* knew, hence deny them. If the world were deaf it would stand with mockery before a hearing group swayed by an orchestra, pitying both listeners and performers. It would deem our admiration of a great swinging bell mere foolish worship of form

and movement. Similarly, with high Powers that once expressed themselves in common forms—where best they could—being themselves
bodiless. The learned men classify the forms with painstaking detail.
But deity has gone out of life. The Powers symbolised are no longer
experienced."

"These Powers, you suggest, then—their *Kas*, as it were—may
still—"

But she waved aside the interruption. "They are satisfied, as the
common people were, with a degraded literalism," she went on. "Nut
was the Heavens, who spread herself across the earth in the form of a
woman; Shu, the vastness of space; the ibis typified Thoth, and Hathor
was the Patron of the Western Hills; Khonsu, the moon, was personi-
fied, as was the deity of the Nile. But the high priest of Ra, the sun,
you notice, remained ever the Great One of Visions."

The High Priest, the Great One of Visions!—How wonderfully
again she made the sentence sing. She put splendour into it. The pictures shifted suddenly closer in his mind. He saw the grandeur of
Memphis and Heliopolis rise against the stars and shake the sand of
ages from their stern old temples.

"You think it possible, then, to get into touch with these High
Powers you speak of, Powers once manifested in common forms?"

Henriot asked the question with a degree of conviction and solemnity that surprised himself. The scenery changed about him as he
listened. The spacious halls of this former *khedivial* Palace melted into
Desert spaces. He smelt the open wilderness, the sand that haunted Helouan. The soft-footed Arab servants moved across the hall in
their white sheets like eddies of dust the wind stirred from the Libyan
dunes. And over these two strangers close beside him stole a queer,
indefinite alteration. Moods and emotions, nameless as unknown stars,
rose through his soul, trailing dark mists of memory from unfathomable distances.

Lady Statham answered him indirectly. He found himself wishing
that those steady eyes would sometimes close.

"Love is known only by feeling it," she said, her voice deepening
a little. "Behind the form you feel the person loved. The process is an
evocation, pure and simple. An arduous ceremonial, involving worship
and devotional preparation, is the means. It is a difficult ritual—the
only one acknowledged by the world as still effectual. Ritual is the
passage way of the soul into the Infinite."

He might have said the words himself. The thought lay in him

while she uttered it. Evocation everywhere in life was as true as assim-
ilation. Nevertheless, he stared his companion full in the eyes with a
touch of almost rude amazement. But no further questions prompted
themselves; or, rather, he declined to ask them. He recalled, somehow
uneasily, that in ceremonial the points of the compass have significance, standing for forces and activities that sleep there until invoked,
and a passing light fell upon that curious midnight request in the
corridor upstairs. These two were on the track of undesirable experiments, he thought. . . . They wished to include him too.

"You go at night sometimes into the Desert?" he heard himself
saying. It was impulsive and miscalculated. His feeling that it would
be wise to change the conversation resulted in giving it fresh impetus
instead.

"We saw you there—in the Wadi Hof," put in Vance, suddenly
breaking his long silence; "you too sleep out, then? It means, you
know, the Valley of Fear."

"We wondered—" It was Lady Statham's voice, and she leaned forward eagerly as she said it, then abruptly left the sentence incomplete.
Henriot started; a sense of momentary acute discomfort again ran over
him. The same second she continued, though obviously changing the
phrase—"we wondered how you spent your day there, during the
heat. But you paint, don't you? You draw, I mean?"

The commonplace question, he realised in every fibre of his being, meant something *they* deemed significant. Was it his talent for
drawing that they sought to use him for? Even as he answered with
a simple affirmative, he had a flash of intuition that might be fanciful,
yet that might be true: that this extraordinary pair were intent upon
some ceremony of evocation that should summon into actual physical
expression some Power—some type of life—known long ago to
ancient worship, and that they even sought to fix its bodily outline
with the pencil—his pencil.

A gateway of incredible adventure opened at his feet. He balanced
on the edge of knowing unutterable things. Here was a clue that
might lead him towards the hidden Egypt he had ever craved to know.
An awful hand was beckoning. The sands were shifting. He saw the
million eyes of the Desert watching him from beneath the level lids of
centuries. Speck by speck, and grain by grain, the sand that smothered
memory lifted the countless wrappings that embalmed it.

And he was willing, yet afraid. Why in the world did he hesitate
and shrink? Why was it that the presence of this silent, watching per-

sonality in the chair beside him kept caution still alive, with warning close behind? The pictures in his mind were gorgeously coloured. It was Richard Vance who somehow streaked them through with black. A thing of darkness, born of this man's unassertive presence, flitted ever across the scenery, marring its grandeur with something evil, petty, dreadful. He held a horrible thought alive. His mind was thinking venal purposes.

In Henriot himself imagination had grown curiously heated, fed by what had been suggested rather than actually said. Ideas of immensity crowded his brain, yet never assumed definite shape. They were familiar, even as this strange woman was familiar. Once, long ago, he had known them well; had even practised them beneath these bright Egyptian stars. Whence came this prodigious glad excitement in his heart, this sense of mighty Powers coaxed down to influence the very details of daily life? Behind them, for all their vagueness, lay an archetypal splendour, fraught with forgotten meanings. He had always been aware of it in this mysterious land, but it had ever hitherto eluded him.

It hovered everywhere. He had felt it brooding behind the towering Colossi at Thebes, in the skeletons of wasted temples, in the uncouth comeliness of the Sphinx, and in the crude terror of the Pyramids even. Over the whole of Egypt hung its invisible wings. These were but isolated fragments of the Body that might express it. And the Desert remained its cleanest, truest symbol. Sand knew it closest. Sand might even give it bodily form and outline.

But, while it escaped description in his mind, as equally it eluded visualisation in his soul, he felt that it combined with its vastness something infinitely small as well. Of such wee particles is the giant Desert born. . . .

Henriot started nervously in his chair, convicted once more of unconscionable staring; and at the same moment a group of hotel people, returning from a dance, passed through the hall and nodded him goodnight. The scent of the women reached him; and with it the sound of their voices discussing personalities just left behind. A London atmosphere came with them. He caught trivial phrases, uttered in a drawling tone, and followed by the shrill laughter of a girl. They passed upstairs, discussing their little things, like marionettes upon a tiny stage.

But their passage brought him back to things of modern life, and to some standard of familiar measurement. The pictures that his soul had gazed at so deep within, he realised, were a pictorial transfer caught incompletely from this woman's vivid mind. He had seen the Desert as the grey, enormous Tomb where hovered still the *Ka* of ancient Egypt. Sand screened her visage with the veil of centuries. But She was there, and She was living. Egypt herself had pitched a temporary camp in him, and then moved on.

There was a momentary break, a sense of abruptness and dislocation. And then he became aware that Lady Statham had been speaking for some time before he caught her actual words, and that a certain change had come into her voice as also into her manner.

5

She was leaning closer to him, her face suddenly glowing and alive. Through the stone figure coursed the fires of a passion that deepened the coal-black eyes and communicated a hint of light—of exaltation—to her whole person. It was incredibly moving. To this deep passion was due the power he had felt. It was her entire life; she lived for it, she would die for it. Her calmness of manner enhanced its effect. Hence the strength of those first impressions that had stormed him. The woman had belief; however wild and strange, it was sacred to her. The secret of her influence was—conviction.

His attitude shifted several points then. The wonder in him passed over into awe. The things she knew were real. They were not merely imaginative speculations.

"I knew I was not wrong in thinking you in sympathy with this line of thought," she was saying in lower voice, steady with earnestness, and as though she had read his mind. "You, too, know, though perhaps you hardly realise that you know. It lies so deep in you that you only get vague feelings of it—intimations of memory. Isn't that the case?"

Henriot gave assent with his eyes; it was the truth.

"What we know instinctively," she continued, "is simply what we are trying to remember. Knowledge is memory." She paused a moment watching his face closely. "At least, you are free from that cheap scepticism which labels these old beliefs as superstition." It was not even a question.

"I—worship real belief—of any kind," he stammered, for her words and the close proximity of her atmosphere caused a strange upheaval in his heart that he could not account for. He faltered in his speech. "It is the most vital quality in life—rarer than deity." He was using her own phrases even. "It is creative. It constructs the world anew—"

"And may reconstruct the old."

She said it, lifting her face above him a little, so that her eyes looked down into his own. It grew big and somehow masculine. It was the face of a priest, spiritual power in it. Where, oh where in the echoing Past had he known this woman's soul? He saw her in another setting, a forest of columns dim about her, towering above giant aisles. Again, he felt the Desert had come close. Into this tent-like hall of the hotel came the sifting of tiny sand. It heaped softly about the very furniture against his feet, blocking the exits of door and window. It shrouded the little present. The wind that brought it stirred a veil that had hung for ages motionless. . . .

She had been saying many things that he had missed while his mind went searching. "There were types of life the Atlantean system knew it might revive—life unmanifested today in any bodily form," was the sentence he caught with his return to the actual present.

"A type of life?" he whispered, looking about him, as though to see who it was had joined them; "you mean a—soul? Some kind of soul, alien to humanity, or to—to any forms of living thing in the world today?" What she had been saying reached him somehow, it seemed, though he had not heard the words themselves. Still hesitating, he was yet so eager to hear. Already he felt she meant to include him in her purposes, and that in the end he must go willingly. So strong was her persuasion on his mind.

And he felt as if he knew vaguely what was coming. Before she answered his curious question—prompting it indeed—rose in his mind that strange idea of the Group-Soul: the theory that big souls cannot express themselves in a single individual, but need an entire group for their full manifestation.

He listened intently. The reflection that this sudden intimacy was unnatural, he rejected, for many conversations were really gathered into one. Long watching and preparation on both sides had cleared the way for the ripening of acquaintance into confidence—how long he dimly wondered? But if this conception of the Group-Soul was not new, the suggestion Lady Statham developed out of it was both new and startling—and yet always so curiously familiar. Its value for him lay, not in far-fetched evidence that supported it, but in the deep belief which made it a vital asset in an honest inner life.

"An individual," she said quietly, "one soul expressed completely in a single person, I mean, is exceedingly rare. Not often is a physical instrument found perfect enough to provide it with adequate expression. In the lower ranges of humanity—certainly in animal and insect life—one soul is shared by many. Behind a tribe of savages stands one Savage. A flock of birds is a single Bird, scattered through the consciousness of all. They wheel in mid-air, they migrate, they obey the deep intelligence called instinct—all as one. The life of any one lion is the life of all—the lion group-soul that manifests itself in the entire *genus*. An ant-heap is a single Ant; through the bees spreads the consciousness of a single Bee."

Henriot knew what she was working up to. In his eagerness to hasten disclosure he interrupted—

"And there may be types of life that have no corresponding bodily expression at all, then?" he asked as though the question were forced out of him. "They exist as Powers—unmanifested on the earth today?"

"Powers," she answered, watching him closely with unswerving stare, "that need a group to provide their body—their physical expression—if they came back."

"Came back!" he repeated below his breath.

But she heard him. "They once had expression. Egypt, Atlantis knew them—spiritual Powers that never visit the world today."

"Bodies," he whispered softly, "actual bodies?"

"Their sphere of action, you see, would be their body. And it might be physical outline. So potent a descent of spiritual life would select materials for its body where it could find them. Our conventional notion of a body—what is it? A single outline moving altogether in one direction. For little human souls, or fragments, this is sufficient. But for vaster types of soul an entire host would be required."

"A church?" he ventured. "Some Body of belief, you surely mean?"

She bowed her head a moment in assent. She was determined he should seize her meaning fully.

"A wave of spiritual awakening—a descent of spiritual life upon a nation," she answered slowly, "forms itself a church, and the body of true believers are its sphere of action. They are literally its bodily expression. Each individual believer is a corpuscle in that Body. The Power has provided itself with a vehicle of manifestation. Otherwise, we could not know it. And the more real the belief of each individual, the more perfect the expression of the spiritual life behind them all. A Group-soul walks the earth. Moreover, a nation naturally devout could attract a type of Soul unknown to a nation that denies all faith. Faith brings back the gods. . . . But today belief is dead, and Deity has left the world."

She talked on and on, developing this main idea that in days of older faiths there were deific types of life upon the earth, evoked by worship and beneficial to humanity. They had long ago withdrawn because the worship which brought them down had died the death. The world had grown pettier. These vast centres of Spiritual Power found no "Body" in which they now could express themselves or manifest. . . . Her thoughts and phrases poured over him like sand. It was always sand he felt—burying the Present and uncovering the Past. . . .

He tried to steady his mind upon familiar objects, but wherever he looked Sand stared him in the face. Outside these trivial walls the Desert lay listening. It lay waiting too. Vance himself had dropped out of recognition. He belonged to the world of things today. But this woman and himself stood thousands of years away, beneath the columns of a Temple in the sands. And the sands were moving. His feet went shifting with them. . . .running down *vistas* of ageless memory that woke terror by their sheer immensity of distance. . . .

Like a muffled voice that called to him through many veils and wrappings, he heard her describe the stupendous Powers that evocation might coax down again among the world of men.

"To what useful end?" he asked at length, amazed at his own temerity, and because he knew instinctively the answer in advance. It rose through these layers of coiling memory in his soul.

"The extension of spiritual knowledge and the widening of life," she answered. "The link with the 'unearthly kingdom' wherein this ancient system went forever searching, would be re-established. Complete rehabilitation might follow. Portions—little portions of these Powers—expressed themselves naturally once in certain animal types, instinctive life that did not deny or reject them. The worship of sacred animals was the relic of a once gigantic system of evocation—not of monsters," and she smiled sadly, "but of Powers that were willing and ready to descend when worship summoned them."

Again, beneath his breath, Henriot heard himself murmur—his own voice startled him as he whispered it: "Actual bodily shape and outline?"

"Material for bodies is everywhere," she answered, equally low; "dust to which we all return; sand, if you prefer it, fine, fine sand. Life moulds it easily enough, when that life is potent."

A certain confusion spread slowly through his mind as he heard her. He lit a cigarette and smoked some minutes in silence. Lady Statham and her nephew waited for him to speak. At length, after some inner battling and hesitation, he put the question that he knew they waited for. It was impossible to resist any longer.

"It would be interesting to know the method," he said, "and to revive, perhaps, by experiment—"

Before he could complete his thought, she took him up:

"There are some who claim to know it," she said gravely—her eyes a moment masterful. "A clue, thus followed, might lead to the entire reconstruction I spoke of."

"And the method?" he repeated faintly.

"Evoke the Power by ceremonial evocation—the ritual is obtainable—and note the form it assumes. Then establish it. This shape or outline once secured, could then be made permanent—a mould for its return at will—its natural physical expression here on earth."

"Idol!" he exclaimed.

"Image," she replied at once. "Life, before we can know it, must have a body. Our souls, in order to manifest here, need a material vehicle."

"And—to obtain this form or outline?" he began; "to fix it, rather?"

"Would be required the clever pencil of a fearless looker-on—someone not engaged in the actual evocation. This form, accurately made permanent in solid matter, say in stone, would provide a channel always open. Experiment, properly speaking, might then begin. The cisterns of Power behind would be accessible."

"An amazing proposition!" Henriot exclaimed. What surprised him was that he felt no desire to laugh, and little even to doubt.

"Yet known to every religion that ever deserved the name," put in Vance like a voice from a distance. Blackness came somehow with his interruption—a touch of darkness. He spoke eagerly.

To all the talk that followed, and there was much of it, Henriot listened with but half an ear. This one idea stormed through him with an uproar that killed attention. Judgment was held utterly in abeyance. He carried away from it some vague suggestion that this woman had hinted at previous lives she half remembered, and that every year she came to Egypt, haunting the sands and temples in the effort to recover lost clues. And he recalled afterwards that she said, "This all came to me as a child, just as though it was something half remembered." There was the further suggestion that he himself was not unknown to her; that they, too, had met before.

But this, compared to the grave certainty of the rest, was merest fantasy that did not hold his attention. He answered, hardly knowing what he said. His preoccupation with other thoughts deep down was so intense, that he was probably barely polite, uttering empty phrases, with his mind elsewhere. His one desire was to escape and be alone, and it was with genuine relief that he presently excused himself and went upstairs to bed. The halls, he noticed, were empty; an Arab servant waited to put the lights out. He walked up, for the lift had long ceased running.

And the magic of old Egypt stalked beside him. The studies that had fascinated his mind in earlier youth returned with the power that had subdued his mind in boyhood. The cult of Osiris woke in his blood again; Horus and Nephthys stirred in their long-forgotten centres. There revived in him, too long buried, the awful glamour of those liturgal rites and vast body of observances, those spells and formulae of incantation of the oldest known recension that years ago had captured his imagination and belief—the Book of the Dead. Trumpet voices called to his heart again across the Desert of some dim past. There were forms of life—impulses from the Creative Power which is the Universe—other than the soul of man. They could be known. A spiritual exaltation, roused by the words and presence of this singular woman, shouted to him as he went.

Then, as he closed his bedroom door, carefully locking it, there stood beside him—Vance. The forgotten figure of Vance came up close—the watching eyes, the simulated interest, the feigned belief, the detective mental attitude, these broke through the grandiose panorama, bringing darkness. Vance, strong personality that hid behind assumed nonentity for some purpose of his own, intruded with sudden violence, demanding an explanation of his presence.

And, with an equal suddenness, explanation offered itself then and there. It came unsought, its horror of certainty utterly unjustified; and it came in this unexpected fashion:

Behind the interest and acquiescence of the man ran—fear: but behind the vivid fear ran another thing that Henriot now perceived was vile. For the first time in his life, Henriot knew it at close quarters, actual, ready to operate. Though familiar enough in daily life to be of common occurrence, Henriot had never realised it as he did now, so close and terrible. In the same way he had never *realised* that he would die—vanish from the busy world of men and women, forgotten as though he had never existed, an eddy of wind-blown dust. And in the man named Richard Vance this thing was close upon blossom. Henriot could not name it to himself. Even in thought it appalled him.

115

He undressed hurriedly, almost with the child's idea of finding safety between the sheets. His mind undressed itself as well. The business of the day laid itself automatically aside; the will sank down; desire grew inactive. Henriot was exhausted. But, in that stage towards slumber when thinking stops, and only fugitive pictures pass across the mind in shadowy dance, his brain ceased shouting its mechanical explanations, and his soul unveiled a peering eye. Great limbs of memory, smothered by the activities of the Present, stirred their stiffened lengths through the sands of long ago—sands this woman had begun to excavate from some far-off pre-existence they had surely known together. Vagueness and certainty ran hand in hand. Details were unrecoverable, but the emotions in which they were embedded moved.

He turned restlessly in his bed, striving to seize the amazing clues and follow them. But deliberate effort hid them instantly again; they retired instantly into the subconsciousness. With the brain of this body, he now occupied, they had nothing to do. The brain stored memories of each life only. This ancient script was graven in his soul. Subconsciousness alone could interpret and reveal. And it was his subconscious memory that Lady Statham had been so busily excavating.

Dimly it stirred and moved about the depths within him, never clearly seen, indefinite, felt as a yearning after unrecoverable knowledge. Against the darker background of Vance's fear and sinister purpose—both of this present life, and recent—he saw the grandeur of this woman's impossible dream, and *knew*, beyond argument or reason, that it was true. Judgment and will asleep, he left the impossibility aside, and took the grandeur. The Belief of Lady Statham was not credulity and superstition; it was Memory. Still to this day, over the sands of Egypt, hovered immense spiritual potencies, so vast that they could only know physical expression in a group—in many. Their sphere of bodily manifestation must be a host, each individual unit in that host a corpuscle in the whole.

The wind, rising from the Lybian wastes across the Nile, swept up against the exposed side of the hotel, and made his windows rattle—the old, sad winds of Egypt. Henriot got out of bed to fasten the outside shutters. He stood a moment and watched the moon floating down behind the Sakkara Pyramids. The Pleiades and Orion's Belt hung brilliantly; the Great Bear was close to the horizon. In the sky above the Desert swung ten thousand stars. No sounds rose from the streets of Helouan. The tide of sand was coming slowly in.

And a flock of enormous thoughts swooped past him from fields of this unbelievable, lost memory. The Desert, pale in the moon, was co-extensive with the night, too huge for comfort or understanding, yet charged to the brim with infinite peace. Behind its majesty of silence lay whispers of a vanished language that once could call with power upon mighty spiritual Agencies. Its skirts were folded now, but, slowly across the leagues of sand, they began to stir and rearrange themselves. He grew suddenly aware of this enveloping shroud of sand—as the raw material of bodily expression: Form.

The sand was in his imagination and his mind. Shaking loosely the folds of its gigantic skirts, it rose; it moved a little towards him. He saw the eternal countenance of the Desert watching him—immobile and unchanging behind these shifting veils the winds laid so carefully over it. Egypt, the ancient Egypt, turned in her vast sarcophagus of Desert, wakening from her sleep of ages at the Belief of approaching worshippers.

Only in this insignificant manner could he express a letter of the terrific language that crowded to seek expression through his soul.... He closed the shutters and carefully fastened them. He turned to go back to bed, curiously trembling. Then, as he did so, the whole singular delusion caught him with a shock that held him motionless. Up rose the stupendous apparition of the entire Desert and stood behind him on that balcony. Swift as thought, in silence, the Desert stood on end against his very face. It towered across the sky, hiding Orion and the moon; it dipped below the horizons. The whole grey sheet of it rose up before his eyes and stood. Through its unfolding skirts ran ten thousand eddies of swirling sand as the creases of its grave-clothes smoothed themselves out in moonlight. And a bleak, scarred countenance, huge as a planet, gazed down into his own....

Through his dreamless sleep that night two things lay active and awake....in the subconscious part that knows no slumber. They were incongruous. One was evil, small and human; the other unearthly and sublime. For the memory of the fear that haunted Vance, and the sinister cause of it, pricked at him all night long. But behind, beyond this common, intelligible emotion, lay the crowding wonder that caught his soul with glory:

The Sand was stirring, the Desert was awake. Ready to mate with them in material form, brooded close the *Ka* of that colossal Entity that once expressed itself through the myriad life of ancient Egypt.

6

Next day, and for several days following, Henriot kept out of the path of Lady Statham and her nephew. The acquaintanceship had grown too rapidly to be quite comfortable. It was easy to pretend that he took people at their face value, but it was a pose; one liked to know something of antecedents. It was otherwise difficult to "place" them. And Henriot, for the life of him, could not "place" these two. His Subconsciousness brought explanation when it came—but the Subconsciousness is only temporarily active. When it retired, he floundered without a rudder, in confusion.

With the flood of morning sunshine, the value of much she had said evaporated. Her presence alone had supplied the key to the cipher. But while the indigestible portions he rejected, there remained a good deal he had already assimilated. The discomfort remained; and with it the grave, unholy reality of it all. It was something more than theory. Results would follow—if he joined them. He would witness curious things.

The force with which it drew him brought hesitation. It operated in him like a shock that numbs at first by its abrupt arrival, and needs time to realise in the right proportions to the rest of life. These right proportions, however, did not come readily, and his emotions ranged between sceptical laughter and complete acceptance. The one detail he felt certain of was this dreadful thing he had divined in Vance. Trying hard to disbelieve it, he found he could not. It was true. Though without a shred of real evidence to support it, the horror of it remained. He knew it in his very bones.

And this, perhaps, was what drove him to seek the comforting companionship of folk he understood and felt at home with. He told his host and hostess about the strangers, though omitting the actual conversation because they would merely smile in blank miscomprehension. But the moment he described the strong black eyes beneath the level eyelids, his hostess turned with a start, her interest deeply roused: "Why, it's that awful Statham woman," she exclaimed, "that must be Lady Statham, and the man she calls her nephew."

"Sounds like it, certainly," her husband added. "Felix, you'd better clear out. They'll bewitch you too."

And Henriot bridled, yet wondering why he did so. He drew into his shell a little, giving the merest sketch of what had happened. But he listened closely while these two practical old friends supplied him with information in the gossiping way that human nature loves. No doubt there was much embroidery, and more perversion, exaggeration too, but the account evidently rested upon some basis of solid foundation for all that. Smoke and fire go together always.

"He *is* her nephew right enough," Mansfield corrected his wife, before proceeding to his own man's form of elaboration; "no question about that, I believe. He's her favourite nephew, and she's as rich as a pig. He follows her out here every year, waiting for her empty shoes. But they *are* an unsavoury couple. I've met 'em in various parts, all over Egypt, but they always come back to Helouan in the end. And the stories about them are simply legion. You remember—" he turned hesitatingly to his wife—"some people, I heard," he changed his sentence, "were made quite ill by her."

"I'm sure Felix ought to know, yes," his wife boldly took him up, "my niece, Fanny, had the most extraordinary experience." She turned to Henriot. "Her room was next to Lady Statham in some hotel or other at Assouan or Edfu, and one night she woke and heard a kind of mysterious chanting or intoning next her. Hotel doors are so dreadfully thin. There was a funny smell too, like incense of something sickly, and a man's voice kept chiming in. It went on for hours, while she lay terrified in bed—"

"Frightened, you say?" asked Henriot.

"Out of her skin, yes; she said it was so uncanny—made her feel icy. She wanted to ring the bell, but was afraid to leave her bed. The room was full of—of things, yet she could see nothing. She *felt* them, you see. And after a bit the sound of this sing-song voice so got on her nerves, it half dazed her—a kind of enchantment—she felt choked and suffocated. And then—" It was her turn to hesitate.

"Tell it all," her husband said, quite gravely too.

"Well—something came in. At least, she describes it oddly, rather; she said it made the door bulge inwards from the next room, but not the door alone; the walls bulged or swayed as if a huge thing pressed against them from the other side. And at the same moment her windows—she had two big balconies, and the venetian shutters were fastened—both her windows *darkened*—though it was two in the morning and pitch dark outside. She said it was all *one* thing— trying to get in; just as water, you see, would rush in through every hole and opening it could find, and all at once. And in spite of her terror—that's the odd part of it—she says she felt a kind of splendour in her—a sort of elation."

"She saw nothing?"

"She says she doesn't remember. Her senses left her, I believe—though she won't admit it."

"Fainted for a minute, probably," said Mansfield.

"So, there it is," his wife concluded, after a silence. "And that's true. It happened to my niece, didn't it, John?"

Stories and legendary accounts of strange things that the presence of these two brought poured out then. They were obviously somewhat mixed, one account borrowing picturesque details from another, and all in disproportion, as when people tell stories in a language they are little familiar with. But, listening with avidity, yet also with uneasiness, somehow, Henriot put two and two together. Truth stood behind them somewhere. These two held traffic with the powers that ancient Egypt knew.

"Tell Felix, dear, about the time you met the nephew—horrid creature—in the Valley of the Kings," he heard his wife say presently. And Mansfield told it plainly enough, evidently glad to get it done, though.

"It was some years ago now, and I didn't know who he was then, or anything about him. I don't know much more now—except that he's a dangerous sort of charlatan-devil, *I* think. But I came across him one night up there by Thebes in the Valley of the Kings—you know, where they buried all their Johnnies with so much magnificence and processions and masses, and all the rest. It's the most astounding, the most haunted place you ever saw, gloomy, silent, full of gorgeous lights and shadows that seem alive—terribly impressive; it makes you creep and shudder. You feel old Egypt watching you."

"Get on, dear," said his wife.

"Well, I was coming home late on a blasted lazy donkey, dog-tired into the bargain, when my donkey boy suddenly ran for his life and left me alone. It was after sunset. The sand was red and shining, and the big cliffs sort of fiery. And my donkey stuck its four feet in the ground and wouldn't budge. Then, about fifty yards away, I saw a fellow—European apparently—doing something—Heaven knows what, for I can't describe it—among the boulders that lie all over the ground there. Ceremony, I suppose you'd call it. I was so interested that at first, I watched. Then I saw he wasn't alone.

"There were a lot of moving things round him, towering big things, that came and went like shadows. That twilight is fearfully bewildering; perspective changes, and distance gets all confused. It's fearfully hard to see properly. I only remember that I got off my donkey and went up closer, and when I was within a dozen yards of him—well, it sounds such rot, you know, but I swear the things suddenly rushed off and left him there alone. They went with a roaring noise like wind; shadowy but tremendously big, they were, and they vanished up against the fiery precipices as though they slipped bang into the stone itself. The only thing I can think of to describe 'em is—well, those sand-storms the *Khamasin* raises—the hot winds, you know."

"They probably *were* sand," his wife suggested, burning to tell another story of her own.

"Possibly, only there wasn't a breath of wind, and it was hot as blazes—and—I had such extraordinary sensations—never felt anything like it before—wild and exhilarated—drunk, I tell you, drunk."

"You saw them?" asked Henriot. "You made out their shape at all, or outline?"

"Sphinx," he replied at once, "for all the world like sphinxes. You know the kind of face and head these limestone strata in the Desert take—great visages with square Egyptian head-dresses where the driven sand has eaten away the softer stuff beneath? You see it everywhere—enormous idols they seem, with faces and eyes and lips awfully like the sphinx—well, that's the nearest I can get to it." He puffed his pipe hard. But there was no sign of levity in him. He told the actual truth as far as in him lay, yet half ashamed of what he told. And a good deal he left out, too.

"She's got a face of the same sort, that Statham horror," his wife said with a shiver. "Reduce the size, and paint in awful black eyes, and you've got her exactly—a living idol." And all three laughed, yet a laughter without merriment in it.

"And you spoke to the man?"

"I did," the Englishman answered, "though I confess I'm a bit ashamed of the way I spoke. Fact is, I was excited, thunderingly excited, and felt a kind of anger. I wanted to kick the beggar for practising such bally rubbish, and in such a place too. Yet all the time—well, well, I believe it was sheer funk now," he laughed; "for I felt uncommonly queer out there in the dusk, alone with—with that kind of business; and I was angry with myself for feeling it. Anyhow, I went up—I'd lost my donkey boy as well, remember—and slated him like a dog. I can't remember what I said exactly—only that he stood and stared at me in silence.

"That made it worse—seemed twice as real then. The beggar said no single word the whole time. He signed to me with one hand to clear out. And then, suddenly out of nothing—she—that woman—appeared and stood beside him. I never saw her come. She must have been behind some boulder or other, for she simply rose out of the ground. She stood there and stared at me too—bang in the face. She was turned towards the sunset—what was left of it in the west—and her black eyes shone like—ugh! I can't describe it—it was shocking."

"She spoke?"

"She said five words—and her voice—it'll make you laugh—it was metallic like a gong: 'You are in danger here.' That's all she said. I simply turned and cleared out as fast as ever I could. But I had to go on foot. My donkey had followed its boy long before. I tell you—smile as you may—my blood was all curdled for an hour afterwards."

Then he explained that he felt some kind of explanation or apology was due, since the couple lodged in his own hotel, and how he approached the man in the smoking-room after dinner. A conversation resulted—the man was quite intelligent after all—of which only one sentence had remained in his mind.

"Perhaps you can explain it, Felix. I wrote it down, as well as I could remember. The rest confused me beyond words or memory; though I must confess it did not seem—well, not utter rot exactly. It was about astrology and rituals and the worship of the old Egyptians, and I don't know what else besides. Only, he made it intelligible and almost sensible, if only I could have got the hang of the thing enough to remember it. You know," he added, as though believing in spite of himself, "there *is* a lot of that wonderful old Egyptian religious business still hanging about in the atmosphere of this place, say what you like."

"But this sentence?" Henriot asked. And the other went off to get a note-book where he had written it down.

"He was jawing, you see," he continued when he came back, Henriot and his wife having kept silence meanwhile, "about direction being of importance in religious ceremonies, West and North symbolising certain powers, or something of the kind, why people turn to the East and all that sort of thing, and speaking of the whole Universe as if it had living forces tucked away in it that expressed themselves somehow when roused up. That's how I remember it anyhow. And then he said this thing—in answer to some fool question probably that I put." And he read out of the note-book:

"'You were in danger because you came through the Gateway of the West, and the Powers from the Gateway of the East were at that moment rising, and therefore in direct opposition to you.'"

Then came the following, apparently a simile offered by way of explanation. Mansfield read it in a shamefaced tone, evidently prepared for laughter:

"'Whether I strike you on the back or in the face determines what kind of answering force I rouse in you. Direction is significant.' And he said it was the period called the Night of Power—time when the Desert encroaches and spirits are close."

And tossing the book aside, he lit his pipe again and waited a moment to hear what might be said. "Can you explain such gibberish?" he asked at length, as neither of his listeners spoke. But Henriot said he couldn't. And the wife then took up her own tale of stories that had grown about this singular couple.

These were less detailed, and therefore less impressive, but all contributed something towards the atmosphere of reality that framed the entire picture. They belonged to the type one hears at every dinner party in Egypt—stories of the vengeance mummies seem to take on those who robbed them, desecrating their peace of centuries; of a woman wearing a necklace of scarabs taken from a princess's tomb, who felt hands about her throat to strangle her; of little *Ka* figures, Pasht goddesses, amulets and the rest, that brought curious disaster to those who kept them. They are many and various, astonishingly circumstantial often, and vouched for by persons the reverse of credulous.

The modern superstition that haunts the Desert gullies with Afreets has nothing in common with them. They rest upon a basis of indubitable experience; and they remain—inexplicable. And about the personalities of Lady Statham and her nephew they crowded like flies attracted by a dish of fruit. The Arabs, too, were afraid of her. She had difficulty in getting guides and *dragomen*.

"My dear chap," concluded Mansfield, "take my advice and have nothing to do with 'em. There *is* a lot of queer business knocking about in this old country, and people like that know ways of reviving it somehow. It's upset you already; you looked scared, I thought, the moment you came in." They laughed, but the Englishman was in earnest. "I tell you what," he added, "we'll go off for a bit of shooting together. The fields along the Delta are packed with birds now: they're home early this year on their way to the North. What d'ye say, eh?"

But Henriot did not care about the quail shooting. He felt more inclined to be alone and think things out by himself. He had come to his friends for comfort, and instead they had made him uneasy and excited. His interest had suddenly doubled. Though half afraid, he longed to know what these two were up to—to follow the adventure to the bitter end. He disregarded the warning of his host as well as the premonition in his own heart. The sand had caught his feet.

There were moments when he laughed in utter disbelief, but these were optimistic moods that did not last. He always returned to the feeling that truth lurked somewhere in the whole strange business, and that if he joined forces with them, as they seemed to wish, he would witness—well, he hardly knew what—but it enticed him as danger does the reckless man, or death the suicide. The sand had caught his mind.

He decided to offer himself to all they wanted—his pencil too. He would see—a shiver ran through him at the thought—what they saw, and know some eddy of that vanished tide of power and splendour the ancient Egyptian priesthood knew, and that perhaps was even common experience in the far-off days of dim Atlantis. The sand had caught his imagination too. He was utterly sand-haunted.

7

And so, he took pains, though without making definite suggestion, to place himself in the way of this woman and her nephew—only to find that his hints were disregarded. They left him alone, if they did not actually avoid him. Moreover, he rarely came across them now. Only at night, or in the queer dusk hours, he caught glimpses of them moving hurriedly off from the hotel, and always Desertwards. And their disregard, well calculated, enflamed his desire to the point when he almost decided to propose himself. Quite suddenly, then, the idea flashed through him—how do they come, these odd revelations, when the mind lies receptive like a plate sensitised by anticipation?— that they were waiting for a certain date, and, with the notion, came Mansfield's remark about "the Night of Power," believed in by the old Egyptian Calendar as a time when the supersensuous world moves close against the minds of men with all its troop of possibilities.

And the thought, once lodged in its corner of imagination, grew strong. He looked it up. Ten days from now, he found, Leyel-el-Sud would be upon him, with a moon, too, at the full. And this strange hint of guidance he accepted. In his present mood, as he admitted, smiling to himself, he could accept anything. It was part of it, it belonged to the adventure. But even while he persuaded himself that it was play, the solemn reality, of what lay ahead increased amazingly, sketched darkly in his very soul.

These intervening days he spent as best he could—impatiently, a prey to quite opposite emotions. In the blazing sunshine he thought of it and laughed; but at night he lay often sleepless, calculating chances of escape. He never did escape, however. The Desert that watched little Helouan with great, unwinking eyes watched also every turn and twist he made. Like this oasis, he basked in the sun of older time, and dreamed beneath forgotten moons. The sand at last had crept into his inmost heart. It sifted over him.

Seeking a reaction from normal, everyday things, he made tourist trips; yet, while recognising the comedy in his attitude, he never could lose sight of the grandeur that banked it up so hauntingly. These two contrary emotions grafted themselves on all he did and saw. He crossed the Nile at Bedrashein, and went again to the Tomb-World of Sakkara; but through all the chatter of veiled and helmeted tourists, the *bandar-log* of our modern Jungle, ran this dark under-stream of awe their monkey methods could not turn aside. One world lay upon another, but this modern layer was a shallow crust that, like the phenomenon of the "Desert-film," a mere angle of falling light could instantly obliterate.

Beneath the sand, deep down, he passed along the Street of Tombs, as he had often passed before, moved then merely by historical curiosity and admiration, but now by emotions for which he found no name. He saw the enormous *sarcophagi* of granite in their gloomy chambers where the sacred bulls once lay, swathed and embalmed like human beings, and, in the flickering candle light, the mood of ancient rites surged round him, menacing his doubts and laughter.

The least human whisper in these subterraneans, dug out first four thousand years ago, revived ominous Powers that stalked beside him, forbidding and premonitive. He gazed at the spots where Mariette, unearthing them forty years ago, found fresh as of yesterday the marks of fingers and naked feet—of those who set the sixty-five ton slabs in position. And when he came up again into the sunshine, he met the eternal questions of the pyramids, overtopping all his mental horizons. Sand blocked all the avenues of younger emotion, leaving the channels of something in him incalculably older, open and clean swept.

He slipped homewards, uncomfortable and followed, glad to be with a crowd—because he was otherwise alone with more than he could dare to think about. Keeping just ahead of his companions, he crossed the Desert edge where the ghost of Memphis walks under rustling palm trees that screen no stone left upon another of all its mile-long populous splendours. For here was a vista his imagination could realise; here he could know the comfort of solid ground his feet could touch. Gigantic Ramases, lying on his back beneath their shade and staring at the sky, similarly helped to steady his swaying thoughts. Imagination could deal with these.

And daily thus he watched the busy world go to and fro to its scale of tips and bargaining, and gladly mingled with it, trying to laugh and study guidebooks, and listen to half-fledged explanations, but always seeing the comedy of his poor attempts. Not all those little donkeys, bells tinkling, beads shining, trotting beneath their comical burdens to the tune of shouting and belabouring, could stem this tide of deeper things the woman had let loose in the subconscious part of him. Everywhere he saw the mysterious camels go slouching through the sand, gurgling the water in their skinny, extended throats. Centuries passed between the enormous knee-stroke of their stride. And, every night, the sunsets restored the forbidding, graver mood, with their crimson, golden splendour, their strange green shafts of light, then—sudden twilight that brought the Past upon him with an awful leap.

Upon the stage then stepped the figures of this pair of human beings, chanting their ancient plainsong of incantation in the moonlit Desert, and working their rites of unholy evocation as the priests had worked them centuries before in the sands that now buried Sakkara fathoms deep.

Then one morning he woke with a question in his mind, as though it had been asked of him in sleep and he had waked just before the answer came. "Why do I spend my time sight-seeing, instead of going alone into the Desert as before? What has made me change?"

This latest mood now asked for explanation. And the answer, coming up automatically, startled him. It was so clear and sure—had been lying in the background all along. One word contained it:

Vance.

The sinister intentions of this man, forgotten in the rush of other emotions, asserted themselves again convincingly. The human horror, so easily comprehensible, had been smothered for the time by the hint of unearthly revelations. But it had operated all the time. Now it took the lead. He dreaded to be alone in the Desert with this dark picture in his mind of what Vance meant to bring there to completion. This abomination of a selfish human will returned to fix its terror in him.

To be alone in the Desert meant to be alone with the imaginative picture of what Vance—he knew it with such strange certainty—hoped to bring about there.

There was absolutely no evidence to justify the grim suspicion. It seemed indeed far-fetched enough, this connection between the sand and the purpose of an evil-minded, violent man. But Henriot saw it true. He could argue it away in a few minutes—easily. Yet the instant thought ceased, it returned, led up by intuition. It possessed him, filled his mind with horrible possibilities. He feared the Desert as he might have feared the scene of some atrocious crime. And, for the time, this dread of a merely human thing corrected the big seduction of the other—the suggested "supernatural."

Side by side with it, his desire to join himself to the purposes of the woman increased steadily. They kept out of his way apparently; the offer seemed withdrawn; he grew restless, unable to settle to anything for long, and once he asked the porter casually if they were leaving the hotel. Lady Statham had been invisible for days, and Vance was somehow never within speaking distance. He heard with relief that they had not gone—but with dread as well. Keen excitement worked in him underground. He slept badly. Like a schoolboy, he waited for the summons to an important examination that involved portentous issues, and contradictory emotions disturbed his peace of mind abominably.

8

But it was not until the end of the week, when Vance approached him with purpose in his eyes and manner, that Henriot knew his fears unfounded, and caught himself trembling with sudden anticipation—because the invitation, so desired yet so dreaded, was actually at hand. Firmly determined to keep caution uppermost, yet he went unresistingly to a secluded corner by the palms where they could talk in privacy. For prudence is of the mind, but desire is of the soul, and while his brain of today whispered wariness, voices in his heart of long ago shouted commands that he knew he must obey with joy.

It was evening and the stars were out. Helouan, with her fairy twinkling lights, lay silent against the Desert edge. The sand was at the flood. The period of the Encroaching of the Desert was at hand, and the deeps were all astir with movement. But in the windless air was a great peace. A calm of infinite stillness breathed everywhere. The flow of Time, before it rushed away backwards, stopped somewhere between the dust of stars and Desert. The mystery of sand touched every street with its unutterable softness.

And Vance began without the smallest circumlocution. His voice was low, in keeping with the scene, but the words dropped with a sharp distinctness into the other's heart like grains of sand that pricked the skin before they smothered him. Caution they smothered instantly; resistance too.

"I have a message for you from my aunt," he said, as though he brought an invitation to a picnic. Henriot sat in shadow, but his companion's face was in a patch of light that followed them from the windows of the central hall. There was a shining in the light blue eyes that betrayed the excitement his quiet manner concealed. "We are going—the day after tomorrow—to spend the night in the Desert; she wondered if, perhaps, you would care to join us?"

"For your experiment?" asked Henriot bluntly.

Vance smiled with his lips, holding his eyes steady, though unable to suppress the gleam that flashed in them and was gone so swiftly. There was a hint of shrugging his shoulders.

"It is the Night of Power—in the old Egyptian Calendar, you know," he answered with assumed lightness almost, "the final moment of Leyel-el-Sud, the period of Black Nights when the Desert was held to encroach with—with various possibilities of a supernatural order. She wishes to revive a certain practice of the old Egyptians. There *may* be curious results. At any rate, the occasion is a picturesque one—better than this cheap imitation of London life." And he indicated the lights, the signs of people in the hall dressed for gaieties and dances, the hotel orchestra that played after dinner.

Henriot at the moment answered nothing, so great was the rush of conflicting emotions that came he knew not whence. Vance went calmly on. He spoke with a simple frankness that was meant to be disarming. Henriot never took his eyes off him. The two men stared steadily at one another.

"She wants to know if you will come and help too—in a certain way only: not in the experiment itself precisely, but by watching merely and—" He hesitated an instant, half lowering his eyes.

"Drawing the picture," Henriot helped him deliberately.

"Drawing what you see, yes," Vance replied, the voice turned graver in spite of himself. "She wants—she hopes to catch the outlines of anything that happens—"

"Comes."

"Exactly. Determine the shape of anything that comes. You may

128

remember your conversation of the other night with her. She is very certain of success."

This was direct enough at any rate. It was as formal as an invitation to a dinner, and as guileless. The thing he thought he wanted lay within his reach. He had merely to say yes. He did say yes; but first he looked about him instinctively, as for guidance. He looked at the stars twinkling high above the distant Libyan Plateau; at the long arms of the Desert, gleaming weirdly white in the moonlight, and reaching towards him down every opening between the houses; at the heavy mass of the Mokattam Hills, guarding the Arabian Wilderness with strange, peaked barriers, their sand-carved ridges dark and still above the Wadi Hof.

These questionings attracted no response. The Desert watched him, but it did not answer. There was only the shrill whistling cry of the lizards, and the sing-song of a white-robed Arab gliding down the sandy street. And through these sounds he heard his own voice answer: "I will come—yes. But how can I help? Tell me what you propose—your plan?"

And the face of Vance, seen plainly in the electric glare, betrayed his satisfaction. The opposing things in the fellow's mind of darkness fought visibly in his eyes and skin. The sordid motive, planning a dreadful act, leaped to his face, and with it a flash of this other yearning that sought unearthly knowledge, perhaps believed it too. No wonder there was conflict written on his features.

Then all expression vanished again; he leaned forward, lowering his voice.

"You remember our conversation about there being types of life too vast to manifest in a single body, and my aunt's belief that these were known to certain of the older religious systems of the world?"

"Perfectly."

"Her experiment, then, is to bring one of these great Powers back—we possess the sympathetic ritual that can rouse some among them to activity—and win it down into the sphere of our minds, our minds heightened, you see, by ceremonial to that stage of clairvoyant vision which can perceive them."

"And then?" They might have been discussing the building of a house, so naturally followed answer upon question. But the whole body of meaning in the old Egyptian symbolism rushed over him with a force that shook his heart. Memory came so marvellously with it.

"If the Power floods down into our minds with sufficient strength for actual form, to note the outline of such form, and from your drawing model it later in permanent substance. Then we should have means of evoking it at will, for we should have its natural Body—the form it built itself, its signature, image, pattern. A starting-point, you see, for more—leading, she hopes, to a complete reconstruction."

"It might take actual shape—assume a bodily form visible to the eye?" repeated Henriot, amazed as before that doubt and laughter did not break through his mind.

"We are on the earth," was the reply, spoken unnecessarily low since no living thing was within earshot, "we are in physical conditions, are we not? Even a human soul we do not recognise unless we see it in a body—parents provide the outline, the signature, the sigil of the returning soul. This," and he tapped himself upon the breast, "is the physical signature of that type of life we call a soul. Unless there is life of a certain strength behind it, no body forms. And, without a body, we are helpless to control or manage it—deal with it in any way. We could not know it, though being possibly *aware* of it."

"To be aware, you mean, is not sufficient?" For he noticed the italics Vance made use of.

"Too vague, of no value for future use," was the reply. "But once obtain the form, and we have the natural symbol of that particular Power. And a symbol is more than image, it is a direct and concentrated expression of the life it typifies—possibly terrific."

"It may be a body, then, this symbol you speak of."

"Accurate vehicle of manifestation; but 'body' seems the simplest word."

Vance answered very slowly and deliberately, as though weighing how much he would tell. His language was admirably evasive. Few perhaps would have detected the profound significance the curious words he next used unquestionably concealed. Henriot's mind rejected them, but his heart accepted. For the ancient soul in him was listening and aware.

"Life, using matter to express itself in bodily shape, first traces a geometrical pattern. From the lowest form in crystals, upwards to more complicated patterns in the higher organisations—there is always first this geometrical pattern as skeleton. For geometry lies at the root of all possible phenomena; and is the mind's interpretation of a living movement towards shape that shall express it." He brought his eyes closer to the other, lowering his voice again. "Hence," he said softly, "the signs

130

in all the old magical systems—skeleton forms into which the Powers evoked descended; outlines those Powers automatically built up when using matter to express themselves. Such signs are material symbols of their bodiless existence. They attract the life they represent and interpret. Obtain the correct, true symbol, and the Power corresponding to it can approach—once roused and made aware. It has, you see, a ready-made mould into which it can come down."

"Once roused and made aware?" repeated Henriot questioningly, while this man went stammering the letters of a language that he himself had used too long ago to recapture fully.

"Because they have left the world. They sleep, unmanifested. Their forms are no longer known to men. No forms exist on earth today that could contain them. But they may be awakened," he added darkly. "They are bound to answer to the summons, if such summons be accurately made."

"Evocation?" whispered Henriot, more distressed than he cared to admit.

Vance nodded. Leaning still closer, to his companion's face, he thrust his lips forward, speaking eagerly, earnestly, yet somehow at the same time, horribly: "And we want—my aunt would ask—your draughtsman's skill, or at any rate your memory afterwards, to establish the outline of anything that comes."

He waited for the answer, still keeping his face uncomfortably close.

Henriot drew back a little. But his mind was fully made up now. He had known from the beginning that he would consent, for the desire in him was stronger than all the caution in the world. The Past inexorably drew him into the circle of these other lives, and the little human dread Vance woke in him seemed just then insignificant by comparison. It was merely of Today.

"You two," he said, trying to bring judgment into it, "engaged in evocation, will be in a state of clairvoyant vision. Granted. But shall I, as an outsider, observing with unexcited mind, see anything, know anything, be aware of anything at all, let alone the drawing of it?"

"Unless," the reply came instantly with decision, "the descent of Power is strong enough to take actual material shape, the experiment is a failure. Anybody can induce subjective vision. Such fantasies have no value though. They are born of an overwrought imagination." And then he added quickly, as though to clinch the matter before caution and hesitation could take effect: "You must watch from the heights above. We shall be in the valley—the Wadi Hof is the place. You must not be too close—"

"Why not too close?" asked Henriot, springing forward like a flash before he could prevent the sudden impulse.

With a quickness equal to his own, Vance answered. There was no faintest sign that he was surprised. His self-control was perfect. Only the glare passed darkly through his eyes and went back again into the sombre soul that bore it.

"For your own safety," he answered low. "The Power, the type of life, she would waken is stupendous. And if roused enough to be at-tracted by the patterned symbol into which she would decoy it down, it will take actual, physical expression. But how? Where is the Body of Worshippers through whom it can manifest? There is none. It will, therefore, press inanimate matter into the service. The terrific impulse to form itself a means of expression will force all loose matter at hand towards it—sand, stones, all it can compel to yield—everything must rush into the sphere of action in which it operates. Alone, we at the centre, and you, upon the outer fringe, will be safe. Only—you must not come too close."

But Henriot was no longer listening. His soul had turned to ice. For here, in this unguarded moment, the cloven hoof had plainly shown itself. In that suggestion of a particular kind of danger Vance had lifted a corner of the curtain behind which crouched his horrible intention. Vance desired a witness of the extraordinary experiment, but he desired this witness, not merely for the purpose of sketching possible shapes that might present themselves to excited vision. He desired a witness for another reason too. Why had Vance put that idea into his mind, this idea of so peculiar danger? It might well have lost him the very assistance he seemed so anxious to obtain.

Henriot could not fathom it quite. Only one thing was clear to him. He, Henriot, was not the only one in danger.

They talked for long after that—far into the night. The lights went out, and the armed patrol, pacing to and fro outside the iron railings that kept the Desert back, eyed them curiously. But the only other thing he gathered of importance was the ledge upon the cliff-top where he was to stand and watch; that he was expected to reach there before sunset and wait till the moon concealed all glimmer in the western sky, and—that the woman, who had been engaged for days in secret preparation of soul and body for the awful rite, would not be visible again until he saw her in the depths of the black valley far

132

below, busy with this man upon audacious, ancient purposes.

9

An hour before sunset Henriot put his rugs and food upon a donkey, and gave the boy directions where to meet him—a considerable distance from the appointed spot. He went himself on foot. He slipped in the heat along the sandy street, where strings of camels still go slouching, shuffling with their loads from the quarries that built the pyramids, and he felt that little friendly Helouan tried to keep him back. But desire now was far too strong for caution. The Desert tide was rising. It easily swept him down the long white street towards the enormous deeps beyond. He felt the pull of a thousand miles before him; and twice a thousand years drove at his back.

Everything still basked in the sunshine. He passed Al Hayat, the stately hotel that dominates the village like a palace built against the sky; and in its pillared colonnades and terraces he saw the throngs of people having late afternoon tea and listening to the music of a regimental band. Men in flannels were playing tennis, parties were climbing off donkeys after long excursions; there was laughter, talking, a babel of many voices. The gaiety called to him; the everyday spirit whispered to stay and join the crowd of lively human beings. Soon there would be merry dinner-parties, dancing, voices of pretty women, sweet white dresses, singing, and the rest. Soft eyes would question and turn dark. He picked out several girls he knew among the palms. But it was all many, oh so many leagues away; centuries lay between him and this modern world. An indescribable loneliness was in his heart. He went searching through the sands of forgotten ages, and wandering among the ruins of a vanished time. He hurried. Already the deeper water caught his breath.

He climbed the steep rise towards the plateau where the Observatory stands, and saw two of the officials whom he knew taking a siesta after their long day's work. He felt that his mind, too, had dived and searched among the heavenly bodies that live in silent, changeless peace remote from the world of men. They recognised him, these two whose eyes also knew tremendous distance close. They beckoned, waving the straws through which they sipped their drinks from tall glasses. Their voices floated down to him as from the star-fields. He saw the sun gleam upon the glasses, and heard the clink of the ice against the sides. The stillness was amazing. He waved an answer, and passed quickly on. He could not stop this sliding current of the years.

133

The tide moved faster, the draw of piled-up cycles urging it. He emerged upon the plateau, and met the cooler Desert air. His feet went crunching on the "Desert-film" that spread its curious dark shiny carpet as far as the eye could reach; it lay everywhere, unswept and smooth as when the feet of vanished civilizations trod its burning surface, then dipped behind the curtains Time pins against the stars. And here the body of the tide set all one way. There was a greater strength of current, draught and suction. He felt the powerful undertow. Deeper masses drew his feet sideways, and he felt the rushing of the central body of the sand. The sands were moving, from their foundation upwards. He went unresistingly with them.

Turning a moment, he looked back at shining little Helouan in the blaze of evening light. The voices reached him very faintly, merged now in a general murmur. Beyond lay the strip of Delta vivid green, the palms, the roofs of Bedrashein, the blue laughter of the Nile with its flocks of curved felucca sails. Further still, rising above the yellow Libyan horizon, gloomed the vast triangles of a dozen Pyramids, cutting their wedge-shaped clefts out of a sky fast crimsoning through a sea of gold. Seen thus, their dignity imposed upon the entire landscape. They towered darkly, symbolic signatures of the ancient Powers that now watched him taking these little steps across their damaged territory.

He gazed a minute, then went on. He saw the big pale face of the moon in the east. Above the ever-silent Thing these giant symbols once interpreted, she rose, grand, effortless, half-terrible as themselves. And, with her, she lifted up this tide of the Desert that drew his feet across the sand to Wadi Hof. A moment later he dipped below the ridge that buried Helouan and Nile and Pyramids from sight. He entered the ancient waters. Time then, in an instant, flowed back behind his footsteps, obliterating every trace. And with it his mind went too. He stepped across the gulf of centuries, moving into the Past. The Desert lay before him—an open tomb wherein his soul should read presently of things long vanished.

The strange half-lights of sunset began to play their witchery then upon the landscape. A purple glow came down upon the Mokattam Hills. Perspective danced its tricks of false, incredible deception. The soaring kites that were a mile away seemed suddenly close, passing in a moment from the size of gnats to birds with a fabulous stretch of wing. Ridges and cliffs rushed close without a hint of warning, and level places sank into declivities and basins that made him trip and stumble. That indescribable quality of the Desert, which makes timid souls avoid the hour of dusk, emerged; it spread everywhere, undisguised. And the bewilderment it brings is no vain, imagined thing, for it distorts vision utterly, and the effect upon the mind when familiar sight goes floundering is the simplest way in the world of dragging the anchor that grips reality. At the hour of sunset this bewilderment comes upon a man with a disconcerting swiftness. It rose now with all this weird rapidity. Henriot found himself enveloped at a moment's notice.

But, knowing well its effect, he tried to judge it and pass on. The other matters, the object of his journey chief of all, he refused to dwell upon with any imagination. Wisely, his mind, while never losing sight of it, declined to admit the exaggeration that over-elaborate thinking brings. "I'm going to witness an incredible experiment in which two enthusiastic religious dreamers believe firmly," he repeated to himself. "I have agreed to draw—anything I see. There may be truth in it, or they may be merely self-suggested vision due to an artificial exaltation of their minds. I'm interested—perhaps against my better judgment. Yet I'll see the adventure out—because I *must.*"

This was the attitude he told himself to take. Whether it was the real one, or merely adopted to warm a cooling courage, he could not tell. The emotions were so complex and warring. His mind, automatically, kept repeating this comforting formula. Deeper than that he could not see to judge. For a man who knew the full content of his thought at such a time would solve some of the oldest psychological problems in the world. Sand had already buried judgment, and with it all attempt to explain the adventure by the standards acceptable to his brain of today. He steered subconsciously through a world of dim, huge, half-remembered wonders.

The sun, with that abrupt Egyptian suddenness, was below the horizon now. The pyramid field had swallowed it. Ra, in his golden boat, sailed distant seas beyond the Libyan wilderness. Henriot walked on and on, aware of utter loneliness. He was walking fields of dream, too remote from modern life to recall companionship he once had surely known. How dim it was, how deep and distant, how lost in this sea of an incalculable Past! He walked into the places that are soundless. The soundlessness of ocean, miles below the surface, was about him. He was with One only—this unfathomable, silent thing where nothing breathes or stirs—nothing but sunshine, shadow and the wind-borne sand. Slowly, in front, the moon climbed up the eastern sky, hanging above the silence—silence that ran unbroken across the horizons to where Suez gleamed upon the waters of a sister sea in motion.

That moon was glinting now upon the Arabian Mountains by its desolate shores. Southwards stretched the wastes of Upper Egypt a thousand miles to meet the Nubian wilderness. But over all these separate Deserts stirred the soft whisper of the moving sand—deep murmuring message that Life was on the way to unwind Death. The Ka of Egypt, swathed in centuries of sand, hovered beneath the moon towards her ancient tenement.

For the transformation of the Desert now began in earnest. It grew apace. Before he had gone the first two miles of his hour's journey, the twilight caught the rocky hills and twisted them into those monstrous revelations of physiognomies they barely take the trouble to conceal even in the daytime. And, while he well understood the eroding agencies that have produced them, there yet rose in his mind a deeper interpretation lurking just behind their literal meanings. Here, through the motionless surfaces, that nameless thing the Desert ill conceals urged outwards into embryonic form and shape, akin, he almost felt, to those immense deific symbols of Other Life the Egyptians knew and worshipped. Hence, from the Desert, had first come, he felt, the unearthly life they typified in their monstrous figures of granite, evoked in their stately temples, and communed with in the ritual of their Mystery ceremonials.

This "watching" aspect of the Libyan Desert is really natural enough; but it is just the natural, Henriot knew, that brings the deepest revelations. The surface limestones, resisting the erosion, block themselves ominously against the sky, while the softer sand beneath sets them on altared pedestals that define their isolation splendidly. Blunt and unconquerable, these masses now watched him pass between them. The Desert surface formed them, gave them birth. They rose, they saw, they sank down again—waves upon a sea that carried forgotten life up from the depths below. Of forbidding, even menacing type, they somewhere mated with genuine grandeur.

Unformed, according to any standard of human or of animal faces, they achieved an air of giant physiognomy which made them terrible. The unwinking stare of eyes—lidless eyes that yet ever succeed in hiding—looked out under well-marked, level eyebrows, suggesting a vision that included the motives and purposes of his very heart. They looked up grandly, understood why he was there, and then—slowly withdrew their mysterious, penetrating gaze.

The strata built them so marvellously up; the heavy, threatening brows; thick lips, curved by the ages into a semblance of cold smiles; jowls drooping into sandy heaps that climbed against the cheeks; protruding jaws, and the suggestion of shoulders just about to lift the entire bodies out of the sandy beds—this host of countenances conveyed a solemnity of expression that seemed everlasting, implacable as Death. Of human signature they bore no trace, nor was comparison possible between their kind and any animal life. They peopled the Desert here. And their smiles, concealed yet just discernible, went broadening with the darkness into a Desert laughter. The silence bore it underground. But Henriot was aware of it. The troop of faces slipped into that single, enormous countenance which is the visage of the Sand. And he saw it everywhere, yet nowhere.

Thus, with the darkness grew his imaginative interpretation of the Desert. Yet there was construction in it, a construction, moreover, that was *not* entirely his own. Powers, he felt, were rising, stirring, wakening from sleep. Behind the natural faces that he saw, these other things peered gravely at him as he passed. They used, as it were, materials that lay ready to their hand. Imagination furnished these hints of outline, yet the Powers themselves were real. There *was* this amazing movement of the sand. By no other manner could his mind have conceived of such a thing, nor dreamed of this simple, yet dreadful method of approach.

Approach! that was the word that first stood out and startled him. There was approach; something was drawing nearer. The Desert rose and walked beside him. For not alone these ribs of gleaming limestone contributed towards the elemental visages, but the entire hills, of which they were an outcrop, ran to assist in the formation, and were a necessary part of them. He was watched and stared at from behind, in front, on either side, and even from below. The sand that swept him on, kept even pace with him. It turned luminous too, with a patchwork of glimmering effect that was indescribably weird; lanterns glowed within its substance, and by their light he stumbled on, glad of the Arab boy he would presently meet at the appointed place.

The last torch of the sunset had flickered out, melting into the wilderness, when, suddenly opening at his feet, gaped the deep, wide gully known as Wadi Hof. Its curve swept past him.

This first impression came upon him with a certain violence: that the desolate valley rushed. He saw but a section of its curve and sweep, but through its entire length of several miles the *wadi* fled away. The moon whitened it like snow, piling black shadows very close against the cliffs. In the flood of moonlight, it went rushing past. It was emptying itself.

For a moment the stream of movement seemed to pause and look up into his face, then instantly went on again upon its swift career. It was like the procession of a river to the sea. The valley emptied itself to make way for what was coming. The approach, moreover, had already begun.

Conscious that he was trembling, he stood and gazed into the depths, seeking to steady his mind by the repetition of the little formula he had used before. He said it half aloud. But, while he did so, his heart whispered quite other things. Thoughts the woman and the man had sown rose up in a flock and fell upon him like a storm of sand. Their impetus drove off all support of ordinary ideas. They shook him where he stood, staring down into this river of strange invisible movement that was hundreds of feet in depth and a quarter of a mile across.

He sought to realise himself as he actually was today—mere visitor to Helouan, tempted into this wild adventure with two strangers. But in vain. That seemed a dream, unreal, a transient detail picked out from the enormous Past that now engulfed him, heart and mind and soul. *This* was the reality.

The shapes and faces that the hills of sand built round him were the play of excited fancy only. By sheer force he pinned his thought against this fact: but further he could not get. There *were* Powers at work; they were being stirred, wakened somewhere into activity. Evocation had already begun. That sense of their approach as he had walked along from Helouan was not imaginary. A descent of some type of life, vanished from the world too long for recollection, was on the way—so vast that it would manifest itself in a group of forms, a troop, a host, an army. These two were near him somewhere at this very moment, already long at work, their minds driving beyond this little world. The valley was emptying itself—for the descent of life their ritual invited.

And the movement in the sand was likewise true. He recalled the sentences the woman had used. "My body," he reflected, "like the bodies life makes use of everywhere, is mere upright heap of earth and dust and—sand. Here in the Desert is the raw material, the greatest store of it in the world."

And on the heels of it came sharply that other thing: that this descending Life would press into its service all loose matter within its reach—to form that sphere of action which would be in a literal sense its Body.

In the first few seconds, as he stood there, he realised all this, and realised it with an overwhelming conviction it was futile to deny. The fast-emptying valley would later brim with an unaccustomed and terrific life. Yet Death hid there too—a little, ugly, insignificant death. With the name of Vance, it flashed upon his mind and vanished, too tiny to be thought about in this torrent of grander messages that shook the depths within his soul. He bowed his head a moment, hardly knowing what he did. He could have waited thus a thousand years it seemed. He was conscious of a wild desire to run away, to hide, to efface himself utterly, his terror, his curiosity, his little wonder, and not be seen of anything. But it was all vain and foolish. The Desert saw him. The Gigantic knew that he was there. No escape was possible any longer. Caught by the sand, he stood amid eternal things. The river of movement swept him too.

These hills, now motionless as statues, would presently glide forward into the cavalcade, sway like vessels, and go past with the procession. At present only the contents, not the frame, of the *wadi* moved. An immense soft brush of moonlight swept it empty for what was on the way.... But presently the entire Desert would stand up and also go.

Then, making a sideways movement, his feet kicked against something soft and yielding that lay heaped upon the Desert floor, and Henriot discovered the rugs the Arab boy had carefully set down before he made full speed for the friendly lights of Helouan. The sound of his departing footsteps had long since died away. He was alone.

The detail restored to him his consciousness of the immediate present, and, stooping, he gathered up the rugs and overcoat and began to make preparations for the night. But the appointed spot, whence he was to watch, lay upon the summit of the opposite cliffs. He must cross the *wadi* bed and climb. Slowly and with labour he made his way down a steep cleft into the depth of the Wadi Hof, sliding and stumbling often, till at length he stood upon the floor of shining moonlight. It was very smooth; windless utterly; still as space; each particle of sand lay in its ancient place asleep. The movement, it seemed, had ceased.

He clambered next up the eastern side, through pitch-black shadows, and within the hour reached the ledge upon the top whence he could see below him, like a silvered map, the sweep of the valley bed. The wind nipped keenly here again, coming over the leagues of cooling sand. Loose boulders of splintered rock, started by his climbing, crashed and boomed into the depths. He banked the rugs behind him, wrapped himself in his overcoat, and lay down to wait.

Behind him was a two-foot crumbling wall against which he leaned; in front a drop of several hundred feet through space. He lay upon a platform, therefore, invisible from the Desert at his back. Below, the curving *wadi* formed a natural amphitheatre in which each separate boulder fallen from the cliffs, and even the little *silla* shrubs the camels eat, were plainly visible. He noted all the bigger ones among them. He counted them over half aloud.

And the moving stream he had been unaware of when crossing the bed itself, now began again. The *wadi* went rushing past before the broom of moonlight. Again, the enormous and the tiny combined in one single strange impression. For, through this conception of great movement, stirred also a roving, delicate touch that his imagination felt as bird-like. Behind the solid mass of the Desert's immobility flashed something swift and light and airy. Bizarre pictures interpreted it to him, like rapid snap-shots of a huge flying panorama: he thought of darting dragon-flies seen at Helouan, of children's little dancing feet, of twinkling butterflies—of birds. Chiefly, yes, of a flock of birds in flight, whose separate units formed a single entity. The idea of the Group-Soul possessed his mind once more. But it came with a sense of more than curiosity or wonder. Veneration lay behind it, a veneration touched with awe. It rose in his deepest thought that here was the first hint of a symbolical representation. A symbol, sacred and inviolable, belonging to some ancient worship that he half remembered in his soul, stirred towards interpretation through all his being.

He lay there waiting, wondering vaguely where his two companions were, yet fear all vanished because he felt attuned to a scale of things too big to mate with definite dread. There was high anticipation in him, but not anxiety. Of himself, as Felix Henriot, indeed, he hardly seemed aware. He was someone else. Or, rather, he was himself at a stage he had known once far, far away in a remote pre-existence. He watched himself from dim summits of a Past, of which no further details were as yet recoverable.

Pencil and sketching-block lay ready to his hand. The moon rose higher, tucking the shadows ever more closely against the precipices. The silver passed into a sheet of snowy whiteness, that made every boulder clearly visible. Solemnity deepened everywhere into awe. The *wadi* fled silently down the stream of hours. It was almost empty now. And then, abruptly, he was aware of change. The motion altered somewhere. It moved more quietly; pace slackened; the end of the procession that evacuated the depth and length of it went trailing past and turned the distant bend.

"It's slowing up," he whispered, as sure of it as though he had watched a regiment of soldiers filing by. The wind took off his voice like a flying feather of sound.

And there *was* a change. It had begun. Night and the moon stood still to watch and listen. The wind dropped utterly away. The sand ceased its shifting movement. The Desert everywhere stopped still, and turned.

Some curtain, then, that for centuries had veiled the world, drew softly up, leaving a shaded vista down which the eyes of his soul peered towards long-forgotten pictures. Still buried by the sands too deep for full recovery, he yet perceived dim portions of them—things once honoured and loved passionately. For once they had surely been to him the whole of life, not merely a fragment for cheap wonder to inspect. And they were curiously familiar, even as the person of this woman who now evoked them was familiar. Henriot made no pretence to more definite remembrance; but the haunting certainty rushed over him, deeper than doubt or denial, and with such force that he felt no effort to destroy it.

Some lost sweetness of spiritual ambitions, lived for with this passionate devotion, and passionately worshipped as men today worship fame and money, revived in him with a tempest of high glory. Centres of memory stirred from an age-long sleep, so that he could have wept at their so complete obliteration hitherto. That such majesty had departed from the world as though it never had existed, was a thought for desolation and for tears. And though the little fragment he was about to witness might be crude in itself and incomplete, yet it was part of a vast system that once explored the richest realms of deity. The reverence in him contained a holiness of the night and of the stars; great, gentle awe lay in it too; for he stood, aflame with anticipation and humility, at the gateway of sacred things.

And this was the mood, no thrill of cheap excitement or alarm to weaken in, in which he first became aware that two spots of darkness he had taken all along for boulders on the snowy valley bed, were actually something very different. They were living figures. They moved. It was not the shadows slowly following the moonlight, but the stir of human beings who all these hours had been motionless as stone. He must have passed them unnoticed within a dozen yards when he crossed the *wadi* bed, and a hundred times from this very ledge his eyes

141

had surely rested on them without recognition. Their minds, he knew full well, had not been inactive as their bodies. The important part of the ancient ritual lay, he remembered, in the powers of the evoking mind.

Here, indeed, was no effective nor theatrical approach of the principal figures. It had nothing in common with the cheap external ceremonial of modern days. In forgotten powers of the soul its grandeur lay, potent, splendid, true. Long before he came, perhaps all through the day, these two had laboured with their arduous preparations. They were there, part of the Desert, when hours ago he had crossed the plateau in the twilight. To them—to this woman's potent working of old ceremonial—had been due that singular rush of imagination he had felt. He had interpreted the Desert as alive.

Here was the explanation. It *was* alive. Life was on the way. Long latent, her intense desire summoned it back to physical expression; and the effect upon him had steadily increased as he drew nearer to the centre where she would focus its revival and return. Those singular impressions of being watched and accompanied were explained. A priest of this old-world worship performed a genuine evocation; a Great One of Vision revived the cosmic Powers.

Henriot watched the small figures far below him with a sense of dramatic splendour that only this association of far-off Memory could account for. It was their rising now, and the lifting of their arms to form a slow revolving outline, that marked the abrupt cessation of the larger river of movement; for the sweeping of the *wadi* sank into sudden stillness, and these two, with motions not unlike some dance of deliberate solemnity, passed slowly through the moonlight to and fro. His attention fixed upon them both. All other movement ceased. They fastened the flow of Time against the Desert's body.

What happened then? How could his mind interpret an experience so long denied that the power of expression, as of comprehension, has ceased to exist? How translate this symbolical representation, small detail though it was, of a transcendent worship entombed for most so utterly beyond recovery? Its splendour could never lodge in minds that conceive Deity perched upon a cloud within telephoning distance of fashionable churches. How should he phrase it even to himself, whose memory drew up pictures from so dim a past that the language fit to frame them lay unreachable and lost?

Henriot did not know. Perhaps he never yet has known. Certainly, at the time, he did not even try to think. His sensations remain his own—untranslatable; and even that instinctive description the mind gropes for automatically, floundered, halted, and stopped dead. Yet there rose within him somewhere, from depths long drowned in slumber, a reviving power by which he saw, divined and recollected—remembered seemed too literal a word—these elements of a worship he once had personally known.

He, too, had worshipped thus. His soul had moved amid similar evocations in some aeonian past, whence now the sand was being cleared away. Symbols of stupendous meaning flashed and went their way across the lifting mists. He hardly caught their meaning, so long it was since, he had known them; yet they were familiar as the faces seen in dreams, and some hint of their spiritual significance left faint traces in his heart by means of which their grandeur reached towards interpretation. And all were symbols of a cosmic, deific nature; of Powers that only symbols can express—prayer-books and sacraments used in the Wisdom Religion of an older time, but today known only in the decrepit, literal shell which is their degradation.

Grandly the figures moved across the valley bed. The powers of the heavenly bodies once more joined them. They moved to the measure of a cosmic dance, whose rhythm was creative. The Universe partnered them.

There was this transfiguration of all common, external things. He realised that appearances were visible letters of a soundless language, a language he once had known. The powers of night and moon and Desert sand married with points in the fluid stream of his inmost spiritual being that knew and welcomed them. He understood.

Old Egypt herself stooped down from her uncovered throne. The stars sent messengers. There was commotion in the secret, sandy places of the Desert. For the Desert had grown Temple. Columns reared against the sky. There rose, from leagues away, the chanting of the sand.

The temples, where once this came to pass, were gone, their ruin questioned by alien hearts that knew not their spiritual meaning. But here the entire Desert swept in to form a shrine, and the Majesty that once was Egypt stepped grandly back across ages of denial and neglect. The sand was altar, and the stars were altar lights. The moon lit up the vast recesses of the ceiling, and the wind from a thousand miles brought in the perfume of her incense. For with that faith which shifts mountains from their sandy bed, two passionate, believing souls invoked the Ka of Egypt.

And the motions that they made, he saw, were definite harmonious patterns their dark figures traced upon the shining valley floor. Like the points of compasses, with stems invisible, and directed from the sky, their movements marked the outlines of great signatures of power—the sigils of the type of life they would evoke. It would come as a Procession. No individual outline could contain it. It needed for its visible expression—many. The descent of a group-soul, known to the worship of this mighty system, rose from its lair of centuries and moved hugely down upon them. The Ka, answering to the summons, would mate with sand. The Desert was its Body.

Yet it was not this that he had come to fix with block and pencil. Not yet was the moment when his skill might be of use. He waited, watched, and listened, while this river of half-remembered things went past him. The patterns grew beneath his eyes like music. Too intricate and prolonged to remember with accuracy later, he understood that they were forms of that root-geometry which lies behind all manifested life. The mould was being traced in outline. Life would presently inform it. And a singing rose from the maze of lines whose beauty was like the beauty of the constellations.

This sound was very faint at first, but grew steadily in volume. Although no echoes, properly speaking, were possible, these precipices caught stray notes that trooped in from the further sandy reaches. The figures certainly were chanting, but their chanting was not all he heard. Other sounds came to his ears from far away, running past him through the air from every side, and from incredible distances, all flocking down into the *wadi* bed to join the parent note that summoned them. The Desert was giving voice. And memory, lifting her hood yet higher, showed more of her grey, mysterious face that searched his soul with questions. Had he so soon forgotten that strange union of form and sound which once was known to the evocative rituals of olden days?

Henriot tried patiently to disentangle this Desert-music that their intoning voices woke, from the humming of the blood in his own veins. But he succeeded only in part. Sand was already in the air. There was reverberation, rhythm, measure; there was almost the breaking of the stream into great syllables. But was it due, this strange reverberation, to the countless particles of sand meeting in mid-air about him, or—to larger bodies, whose surfaces caught this friction of the sand and threw it back against his ears? The wind, now rising, brought particles that stung his face and hands, and filled his eyes with a minute fine dust that partially veiled the moonlight. But was not something

144

larger, vaster these particles composed now also on the way?

Movement and sound and flying sand thus merged themselves more and more in a single, whirling torrent. But Henriot sought no commonplace explanation of what he witnessed; and here was the proof that all happened in some vestibule of inner experience where the strain of question and answer had no business. One sitting beside him need not have seen anything at all. His host, for instance, from Helouan, need not have been aware. Night screened it; Helouan, as the whole of modern experience, stood in front of the screen. This thing took place behind it. He crouched motionless, watching in some reconstructed ante-chamber of the soul's pre-existence, while the torrent grew into a veritable tempest.

Yet Night remained unshaken; the veil of moonlight did not quiver; the stars dropped their slender golden pillars unobstructed. Calmness reigned everywhere as before. The stupendous representation passed on behind it all.

But the dignity of the little human movements that he watched had become now indescribable. The gestures of the arms and bodies invested themselves with consummate grandeur, as these two strode into the caverns behind manifested life and drew forth symbols that represented vanished Powers. The sound of their chanting voices broke in cadenced fragments against the shores of language. The words Henriot never actually caught, if words they were; yet he understood their purport—these Names of Power to which the type of returning life gave answer as they approached. He remembered fumbling for his drawing materials, with such violence, however, that the pencil snapped in two between his fingers as he touched it. For now, even here, upon the outer fringe of the ceremonial ground, there was a stir of forces that set the very muscles working in him before he had become aware of it. . . .

Then came the moment when his heart leaped against his ribs with a sudden violence that was almost pain, standing a second later still as death. The lines upon the valley floor ceased their maze-like dance. All movement stopped. Sound died away. In the midst of this profound and dreadful silence the sigils lay empty there below him. They waited to be in-formed. For the moment of entrance had come at last. Life was close.

And he understood why this return of life had all along suggested a Procession and could be no mere momentary flash of vision. From such appalling distance did it sweep down towards the present.

Upon this network, then, of splendid lines, at length held rigid, the entire Desert reared itself with walls of curtained sand, that dwarfed the cliffs, the shouldering hills, the very sky. The Desert stood on end. As once before he had dreamed it from his balcony windows, it rose upright, towering, and close against his face. It built sudden ramparts to the stars that chambered the thing he witnessed behind walls no centuries could ever bring down crumbling into dust.

He himself, in some curious fashion, lay just outside, viewing it apart. As from a pinnacle, he peered within—peered down with straining eyes into the vast picture-gallery Memory threw abruptly open. And the picture spaced its noble outline thus against the very stars. He gazed between columns, that supported the sky itself, like pillars of sand that swept across the field of vanished years. Sand poured and streamed aside, laying bare the Past.

For down the enormous vista into which he gazed, as into an avenue running a million miles towards a tiny point, he saw this moving Thing that came towards him, shaking loose the countless veils of sand the ages had swathed about it. The *Ka* of buried Egypt wakened out of sleep. She had heard the potent summons of her old, time-honoured ritual. She came. She stretched forth an arm towards the worshippers who evoked her. Out of the Desert, out of the leagues of sand, out of the immeasurable wilderness which was her mummied Form and Body, she rose and came. And this fragment of her he would actually see—this little portion that was obedient to the stammered and broken ceremonial. The partial revelation he would witness—yet so vast, even this little bit of it, that it came as a Procession and a host.

For a moment there was nothing. And then the voice of the woman rose in a resounding cry that filled the *wadi* to its furthest precipices, before it died away again to silence. That a human voice could produce such volume, accent, depth, seemed half incredible. The walls of towering sand swallowed it instantly. But the Procession of life, needing a group, a host, an army for its physical expression, reached at that moment the nearer end of the huge avenue. It touched the Present; it entered the world of men.

10

The entire range of Henriot's experience, read, imagined, dreamed, then fainted into unreality before the sheer wonder of what he saw. In the brief interval it takes to snap the fingers the climax was thus so hurriedly upon him. And, through it all, he was clearly aware of the pair of little human figures, man and woman, standing erect and commanding at the centre—knew, too, that she directed and controlled, while he in some secondary fashion supported her—and ever watched. But both were dim, dropped somewhere into a lesser scale. It was the knowledge of their presence, however, that alone enabled him to keep his powers in hand at all. But for these two *human* beings there within possible reach, he must have closed his eyes and swooned.

For a tempest that seemed to toss loose stars about the sky swept round about him, pouring up the pillared avenue in front of the procession. A blast of giant energy, of liberty, came through. Forwards and backwards, circling spirally about him like a whirlwind, came this revival of Life that sought to dip itself once more in matter and in form. It came to the accurate out-line of its form they had traced for it. He held his mind steady enough to realise that it was akin to what men call a "descent" of some "spiritual movement" that wakens a body of believers into faith—a race, an entire nation; only that he experienced it in this brief, concentrated form before it has scattered down into ten thousand hearts.

Here he knew its source and essence, behind the veil. Crudely, unmanageable as yet, he felt it, rushing loose behind appearances. There was this amazing impact of a twisting, swinging force that stormed down as though it would bend and coil the very ribs of the old stubborn hills. It sought to warm them with the stress of its own irresistible life-stream, to beat them into shape, and make pliable their obstinate resistance. Through all things the impulse poured and spread, like fire at white heat.

Yet nothing visible came as yet, no alteration in the actual landscape, no sign of change in things familiar to his eyes, while impetus thus fought against inertia. He perceived nothing formal. Calm and untouched himself, he lay outside the circle of evocation, watching, waiting, scarcely daring to breathe, yet well aware that any minute the scene would transfer itself from memory that was subjective to matter that was objective.

And then, in a flash, the bridge was built, and the transfer was accomplished. How or where he did not see, he could not tell. It was there before he knew it—there before his normal, earthly sight. He saw it, as he saw the hands, he was holding stupidly up to shield his face. For this terrific release of force long held back, long stored up, latent for centuries, came pouring down the empty *wadi* bed prepared for its reception. Through stones and sand and boulders it came in an impetuous hurricane of power. The liberation of its life appalled him. All that was free, untied, responded instantly like chaff; loose objects fled towards it; there was a yielding in the hills and precipices; and even in the mass of Desert which provided their foundation. The hinges of the Sand went creaking in the night. It shaped for itself a bodily outline.

Yet, most strangely, nothing definitely moved. How could he express the violent contradiction? For the immobility was apparent only—a sham, a counterfeit; while behind it the essential *being* of these things did rush and shift and alter. He saw the two things side by side: the outer immobility the senses commonly agree upon, *and* this amazing flying-out of their inner, invisible substance towards the vortex of attracting life that sucked them in. For stubborn matter turned docile before the stress of this returning life, taught somewhere to be plastic. It was being moulded into an approach to bodily outline. A mobile elasticity invaded rigid substance. The two officiating human beings, safe at the stationary centre, and himself, just outside the circle of operation, alone remained untouched and unaffected. But a few feet in any direction, for any one of them, meant—instantaneous death. They would be absorbed into the vortex, mere corpuscles pressed into the service of this sphere of action of a mighty Body. . . .

How these perceptions reached him with such conviction, Henriot could never say. He knew it, because he *felt* it. Something fell about him from the sky that already paled towards the dawn. The stars themselves, it seemed, contributed some part of the terrific, flowing impulse that conquered matter and shaped itself this physical expression.

Then, before he was able to fashion any preconceived idea of what visible form this potent life might assume, he was aware of further change. It came at the briefest possible interval after the beginning—this certainty that, to and fro about him, as yet however indeterminate, passed Magnitudes that were stupendous as the Desert. There was beauty in them too, though a terrible beauty hardly of this earth at all. A fragment of old Egypt had returned—a little portion of that vast Body of Belief that once was Egypt. Evoked by the worship of one human heart, passionately sincere, the Ka of Egypt stepped back to visit the material it once informed—the Sand.

Yet only a portion came. Henriot clearly realised that. It stretched forth an arm. Finding no mass of worshippers through whom it might express itself completely, it pressed inanimate matter thus into its service.

Here was the beginning the woman had spoken of—little opening clue. Entire reconstruction lay perhaps beyond.

And Henriot next realised that these Magnitudes in which this group-energy sought to clothe itself as visible form, were curiously familiar. It was not a new thing that he would see. Booming softly as they dropped downwards through the sky, with a motion the size of them rendered delusive, they trooped up the Avenue towards the central point that summoned them. He realised the giant flock of them—descent of fearful beauty—outlining a type of life denied to the world for ages, countless as this sand that blew against his skin. Careering over the waste of Desert moved the army of dark Splendours, that dwarfed any organic structure called a body, men have ever known. He recognised them, cold in him of death, though the outlines reared higher than the pyramids, and towered up to hide whole groups of stars. Yes, he recognised them in their partial revelation, though he never saw the monstrous host complete. But, one of them, he realised, posing its eternal riddle to the sands, had of old been glimpsed sufficiently to seize its form in stone—yet poorly seized, as a doll may stand for the dignity of a human being or a child's toy represent an engine that draws trains. . . .

And he knelt there on his narrow ledge, the world of men forgotten. The power that caught him was too great a thing for wonder or for fear; he even felt no awe. Sensation of any kind that can be named or realised left him utterly. He forgot himself. He merely watched. The glory numbed him. Block and pencil, as the reason of his presence there at all, no longer existed. . . .

Yet one small link remained that held him to some kind of consciousness of earthly things: he never lost sight of this—that, being just outside the circle of evocation, he was safe, and that the man and woman, being stationary in its untouched centre, were also safe. But—that a movement of six inches in any direction meant for any one of them instant death.

What was it, then, that suddenly strengthened this solitary link so that the chain tautened and he felt the pull of it? Henriot could not say. He came back with the rush of a descending drop to the realisation—dimly, vaguely, as from great distance—that he was with these two, now at this moment, in the Wadi Hof, and that the cold of dawn was in the air about him. The chill breath of the Desert made him shiver.

But at first, so deeply had his soul been dipped in this fragment of ancient worship, he could remember nothing more. Somewhere lay a little spot of streets and houses; its name escaped him. He had once been there; there were many people, but insignificant people. Who were they? And what had he to do with them? All recent memories had been drowned in the tide that flooded him from an immeasurable Past.

And who were they—these two beings, standing on the white floor of sand below him? For a long time, he could not recover their names. Yet he remembered them; and, thus robbed of association that names bring, he saw them for an instant naked, and knew that one of them was evil. One of them was vile. Blackness touched the picture there. The man, his name still out of reach, was sinister, impure and dark at the heart. And for this reason, the evocation had been partial only. The admixture of an evil motive was the flaw that marred complete success.

The names then flashed upon him—Lady Statham—Richard Vance.

Vance! With a horrid drop from splendour into something mean and sordid, Henriot felt the pain of it. The motive of the man was so insignificant, his purpose so atrocious. More and more, with the name, came back—his first repugnance, fear, suspicion. And human terror caught him. He shrieked. But, as in nightmare, no sound escaped his lips. He tried to move; a wild desire to interfere, to protect, to prevent, flung him forward—close to the dizzy edge of the gulf below. But his muscles refused obedience to the will. The paralysis of common fear rooted him to the rocks.

But the sudden change of focus instantly destroyed the picture; and so vehement was the fall from glory into meanness, that it dislocated the machinery of clairvoyant vision. The inner perception clouded and grew dark. Outer and inner mingled in violent, inextricable confusion. The wrench seemed almost physical. It happened all at once, retreat and continuation for a moment somehow combined. And, if he did not definitely see the awful thing, at least he was aware that it had come to pass. He knew it as positively as though his eye were glued against a magnifying lens in the stillness of some laboratory. He witnessed it.

The supreme moment of evocation was close. Life, through that awful sandy vortex, whirled and raged. Loose particles showered and pelted, caught by the draught of vehement life that moulded the substance of the Desert into imperial outline—when, suddenly, shot the little evil thing across that marred and blasted it.

Into the whirlpool flew forward a particle of material that was a human being. And the Group-Soul caught and used it.

The actual accomplishment Henriot did not claim to see. He was a witness, but a witness who could give no evidence. Whether the woman was pushed of set intention, or whether some detail of sound and pattern was falsely used to effect the terrible result, he was helpless to determine. He pretends no itemised account. She went. In one second, with appalling swiftness, she disappeared, swallowed out of space and time within that awful maw—one little corpuscle among a million through which the Life, now stalking the Desert wastes, moulded itself a troop-like Body. Sand took her.

There followed emptiness—a hush of unutterable silence, stillness, peace. Movement and sound instantly retired whence they came. The avenues of Memory closed; the Splendours all went down into their sandy tombs. . . .

★★★★★★★★★★★★★★★

The moon had sunk into the Libyan wilderness; the eastern sky was red. The dawn drew out that wondrous sweetness of the Desert, which is as sister to the sweetness that the moonlight brings. The Desert settled back to sleep, huge, unfathomable, charged to the brim with life that watches, waits, and yet conceals itself behind the ruins of apparent desolation. And the *wadi*, empty at his feet, filled slowly with the gentle little winds that bring the sunrise.

Then, across the pale glimmering of sand, Henriot saw a figure moving. It came quickly towards him, yet unsteadily, and with a hurry that was ugly. Vance was on the way to fetch him. And the horror of the man's approach struck him like a hammer in the face. He closed his eyes, sinking back to hide.

But, before he swooned, there reached him the clatter of the murderer's tread as he began to climb over the splintered rocks, and the faint echo of his voice, calling him by name—falsely and in pretence—for help.

The Man Who Lived Backwards

If it is true that most people have one secret they never share, it is also true that many have an experience they never tell, not so much from fear of ridicule or being disbelieved as from utter inability to describe it intelligibly. Language has grown gradually: it describes the experience of the race; anything beyond human experience exposes the poverty of language at once. No words exist.

Professor Zeitt had something of the sort, it seems. He was an ardent physicist, astrophysics his speciality; he knew all about waves, he was one of the few who really understood Relativity; he was a wireless expert, too. If Jeans, Whitehead and Eddington were in his pocket, the mystery of space-time was in his mind. He chatted as easily about other dimensions in time as most people do about shares and commodities. Conceptions of time beyond our one-dimensional kind were always in his thoughts.

He was also an experimenter; he made, it appears, audacious experiments, some of them psychological. That he ever suffered from overwork, from cerebral excitement of a rather dangerous sort, 1s open to question. To myself, who enjoyed the privilege, or suffered the affliction, of hearing his experience, there seemed no sign of delusion, hallucination, or mental disturbance. I remain convinced that he told me something that had actually happened—to an able, clear-headed, if unusual man

It happened to him on a winter's night as he sat alone in his flat—a Sunday evening, the servants out, and his wife away in Paris. His married life was unhappy, childless, ill-assorted. He had made a mistake. There was another girl he should have chosen. Now, at forty, he realised this, though without undue bitterness, for he blamed himself. Her money had made his career possible. This particular day had been passed in strenuous exercise. His body, he admits, was over-tired, perhaps, but his mind, at any rate, was resting delightfully—he was read-

153

ing a story of crime over the fire—delicious relaxation, he called it. The room was dim, only the reading-lamp turned on. Facing him in the wall was a long pier glass.

The book, *It Doesn't Pay*, was the life of a burglar told by himself— Black, if memory serves me, the author—and he was near the end. In his mind, as he read the last chapter, stretched a picture of the man's whole life, not actually realised, perhaps, but lying there in perspective. Like a map, it existed serially and all at once, though he now focused attention on its close. As a cinema screen, it could have turned back, of course, and repeated any particular section. The whole of the burglar's life lay between the book covers; it was present, any portion of it accessible by turning back the pages.

Its end was vivid at the moment merely because he, Zeitt, focused attention upon that part, that moment. And so, as was usual with him, he realised that his own life, similarly, existed serially, complete, the whole map there, while he was conscious of himself at the moment called forty, merely because he focused attention on that moment. Only, in his own case, time made turning back impossible. If time had another dimension, he could have turned back to earlier sections.

He admits his general awareness of this idea in the background of his mind. For it was habitual. Such ideas lay always in his thought. But at the moment, thought and interest were centred on Black's adventures, these other ideas not consciously to the fore—when in the semi-darkened room suddenly drew his attention. The room, he felt positive, altered; and this alteration was in his immediate surroundings. Very close to him this abrupt change had come about. And he looked up from his page, startled a little, "as though an unexpected sound had disturbed me," were his words, "something, anyhow, that *drew* my attention actively."

The winter's night was still, the Sunday traffic negligible, the flat empty, yet he was positive that someone stood in the room in close proximity to him. As he raised his eyes, he looked automatically at the reflection of himself in the pier glass opposite. He saw himself deep in the easy chair, the open book on his knee, the shaded lamp behind his head, and at the same instant saw also the reflection of a tall, straight figure that passed swiftly behind his chair from right to left. Simultaneously with this, and before thought had time to spread, he felt something that, he declares, he had never felt before, something entirely new. Accustomed mentally to contemplate ultimate zero and the colds of outer space, he was instantly conscious now that all about

154

him, in brain and nerves as well, was a sudden cold of another kind altogether, a kind hitherto unexperienced.

This cold brought horror with it. He felt as if hanging in interstellar space, adrift from all known moorings, on the brink of something that horrified because it was utterly unknown. By "unknown" he meant he had never experienced it himself. There was no "up" or "down," because there was nothing to which "up" or "down" could be referred; similarly, "backwards" or "forwards" held no meaning. Nor could he know whether he was in motion or stationary. He was merely "relative." With a tremendous effort, however, he managed to cling tenaciously with his ordinary mind to ordinary, familiar standards. In the first second all this came to him.

At the same time, he knew that the figure, now passing behind his chair, would appear in a fractional moment beside or in front of him, and even as he realised this, it happened. The figure moved beside him, then in front, then stopped and looked at him. Expecting his muscles somehow to be paralysed by the shock of unusual fear, and that he would be unable to move, he now found that this was not the case. As he saw the tall, straight figure come to a dead stop in front of him, not two feet away, he rose quickly to his feet and faced it. The book fell to the carpet with a thud. It was a young man he looked at straight in the eyes.

He was able, even at this moment, to note his sensations. The habit of years worked truly. The intense, strange, different cold, he thus asserts, persisted. It numbed something in him that must have otherwise reasoned, reflected, criticised. These faculties, at any rate, did not function. All that happened seemed not natural, supernatural. The sensation of unbelievable fear that had turned him dizzy was gone. Having terrorised him, it disappeared. His breath became oddly, immensely accelerated. An idea of death slipped his thought. But all these, passing, left an exhilaration beyond all words.

It was under this intensification of consciousness that he then at once began to speak. The figure spoke, too. They spoke together. He emphasised this simultaneous utterance, though the spoken words were not always quite identical:

"Of course, I know you. I know who you are," he said. "You are myself."

The figure, a young man in a light, summery suit, smiled eagerly.

"I was twenty-five then," said Zeitt. "I *am* twenty-five," said the other. And, as they uttered together, came all the emotions of troubled love, of doubt, of being drawn in two different directions by worldly considerations and by personal inclination, with all the fever of a young man's indecision.

"If only I could see ahead," Zeitt heard himself saying, while simultaneously sounded: "*If only I could go back.*"

They looked into each other's eyes while uttering the next words, identical words this time:

"I exist at that point where my attention is fixed at a given moment. But there's really no need to. I can choose my moment, alter my attention—forwards or backwards. Can't I?"

The young figure smiled, a curiously passionate expression in the eyes. In Zeitt rose the tumultuous passion for a girl, as against the affection and respect of another girl whose worldly possessions would enable him to follow his dream.

"I can go backwards or forwards," both spoke together, "by changing my type of consciousness. It's open. It's here, it's now, both accessible, as between the covers of a book—if only I escape from being fixed on a point so stupidly. If only I knew how."

"I *do*," grinned the other, while Zeitt laughed audibly, a laugh of audacious triumph, using the same words exactly. "I do."

"I can change my consciousness, make it different," cried Zeitt. "I see the way. My life is serial, all at once, whole. I am not fixed at any point. I am in time of two dimensions."

"I *always am*," said the other, bending his head down to read a letter, whose wet ink still glistened.

"I will destroy it. I won't send it," exclaimed Zeitt, despising himself for proposing to a girl he did not really love.

The young figure tore the letter he held into tiny pieces and turned to throw them into the fire. But there was no fire, only a gas stove burning, and the room was a shabby lodging-house room. Zeitt gazed about him. The picture of the girl he really loved possessed his mind. "I'll go to her—go back to her. I'll go tomorrow." His speech fumbled slightly.

"*I'll go to her now*," said the figure decisively, his young face alight, as he moved across the faded carpet to a waste-paper basket beside the draughty window.

"I'll change it—change the past," and Zeitt realised he was shouting now aloud, amazing joy and wonder in him, as he watched the shower of small, torn bits of paper flutter down.

The figure came suddenly very close, so close that there seemed hardly room to stand without touching, as though space could not possibly contain both of them on that one spot, then closer still, all over one another.

"*That would be too dislocating—for others—and until all can do it,*" sounded the voice very faintly. Professor Zeitt declares it sounded inside himself. "*I'll make the effort, anyhow. A result of sorts may come.*" The voice died out. The figure was no longer there.

Zeitt, the physicist, found himself alone. He stooped down and picked up the fallen book. The heat of the blazing coal fire scorched his face, but did not affect the curious internal cold that lay, like a touch from interstellar space, over his entire being. He turned on all the lights, and before sitting down to finish Black's book, he wrote down the dialogue and description as given above. It was bald, but as accurate as he could make it.

Long afterwards, as I listened to his account, watching his face, I saw a light in his eyes I have never seen before in any human eyes.

"The major part of the experience," he added, "the *important* part," he emphasised, "is beyond any power or words at my command."

The distinguished man, now famous and happily remarried, smiled as he said this. He shivered a little. "They'd say I dreamed it," he remarked, shrugging his shoulders. Yet within a few short weeks of the experience, his wife had run off with another man, and Professor Zeitt, finding the girl he loved a widow, had married her.

S. O. S.

It is a question how many witnesses shall be required to establish the veracity of an occurrence so singular, especially when one of such witnesses is a dog.

Three of us, two men and a girl, had skimmed the snow-covered Jura slopes on our skees since noon, arriving toward four o'clock at the deserted chalet where the fourth was to meet us. Upon the arrival of that fourth hung all the future happiness of the girl, and he was to come from a village far away on the other side. The Christmas rendezvous had been carefully arranged.

We had brought provisions for making a hot supper in the empty building, a lonely farmhouse used only in summer, and our plan was to skee back all together by moonlight.

"Put on your extra sweaters before you begin to cool," said the older man, coming round the corner with an armful of logs from the frozen woodpile. "I'll get the fire going. Here, Dot,"—turning to his niece—"stack your skees, and get the food out. He'll be hungry as a bear."

The three of us bustled about over the crisp snow, and the older man had a wood fire blazing upon the great open hearth in less than ten minutes. The interior of the big room lit up, shadows flew overhead among the rafters, and shafts of cheery yellow light flashed even into the recesses of the vaulted barn that opened out into the cowsheds in the rear. Outside, the dusk visibly deepened from one minute to the next.

The cold was bitter; but our heated bodies fairly steamed. The big St. Bernard ran, sniffing and prancing, after each of us in turn, and from time to time flew up the mounds of snow outside, where he stood, with head flung back and muzzle up, staring against the sunset. He knew perfectly well that someone else was expected and the direction from which he would come. The effect of the firelight streaming through door and cracks of muffled window into the last hour of daylight was peculiar; night and day met together on the threshold of the chalet, under the shadows of that enormous snow-laden roof.

For the sun was now below the rim of the Suchet ridges, flaming with a wonderful sheet of red and yellow light over the huge white plateau, and the isolated trees threw vague shadows that easily ran into a length of half a kilometre. Rapidly they spread, assuming monstrous shapes, half animal, half human; then, deceiving the sight, merged into the strange uniform glow that lies upon a snow-field in the twilight. The forest turned purple; the crests of the pines cut into the sky like things of steel and silver. Everything shone, crackled, sparkled; the cold increased.

"Dorothy, where are you going?" sounded the older man's voice from the door, for the girl was out on her skees again. Her slim young figure, topped by the pointed, white snow-cap, was sprite-like.

"Just a little way over the slopes—to meet him," came her reply. She seemed to float above the snow, not on it.

With decision he called her in, and it was the warning in his tone that perhaps made her obey.

"Better rest," he said briefly; "we've got a long run home in the moonlight." On her skees she came "sishing" back down the gleaming slope to his side, neat and graceful, her shadow shooting ahead like black lightning, enormously elongated. "The Creux du Van precipices, besides, lie over that way," he continued. "They begin without warning—a sheer drop, and nothing to show the edge."

"I know them," she said, pouting a little.

"He knows them, too," her uncle answered, putting a hand on her shoulder. "He'll take the higher slopes. He'll get around all right." He had noticed the look in her soft, brown eyes that betrayed—it was the merest passing lash—an eagerness lying too close upon the verge of anxiety. "Harry knows these ridges even better than I do."

He helped her stack the skees, then turned to whistle in the dog, which had stayed behind on the summit of the slope she had just left, and it was at this instant, I think, that I first suddenly became aware of an unusual significance lying behind the little scene. Such moments are beyond explanation or analysis; one can only report them. They pertain, some hold, to a kind of vision. I can merely affirm that the flash came to me in this wise: I saw the big dog, his outline sharply silhouetted against the skyline and his head turned westward, refusing for the first time that day to obey instantly a whistle that for him was a summons always to be obeyed.

His master, noticing nothing, had already gone inside; but the girl saw what I saw, caught a flash similar to my own, and recognised in the animal's insignificant disobedience a corroboration of something in herself that touched uneasiness. I cannot prove it—she has never spoken of it—only, as she stood there a moment, with the sunset in her face and her tumbled hair half over her eyes, I intercepted the swift glance that ran upward to the St. Bernard, travelled beyond him to the huge, distant snow-slopes, and then fell upon me.

It was love, perhaps, that carried and interpreted thus the instantaneous wireless message—the love that lay undelivered in my heart, as in her own, and, since she was foresworn already, lay unrecognised. In view of what followed, I cannot wholly say. My sight held clearer and steadier than her own, and it came to me that my strange perception, sharpened to bitter sweetness as if by sacrifice, approached possibly to some kind of inferior divination of the wounded soul. The next minute the great dog came bounding down, and we entered the chalet together, busying ourselves with fire, benches, table, and supper. The portable little kettle of aluminium already steamed upon the hearth.

With us—with myself, at any rate—came into the cosy fire-lit interior a sensation that was new. I felt the terror and desolation of these vast, snow-covered mountains, immense, trackless, silent, lying away from the world of men below the coming stars. Winter, like a winter of the polar regions, held them fast. In the brilliant sunshine of the day, they had been friendly, enticing, sympathetic.

Now, with the icy dusk creeping over their bare, white faces, the freezing wind sifting with long sighs through the forests below, and the silent Terror of the Frost stalking from cliff to ridge with his head among the stars, they turned terrible. With the coming of the night, they awoke to their true power. They showed their teeth. Our own insignificance became curiously emphasised. I thought of the Creux du Van precipices, sweeping crater-like with their semicircle of dark grandeur, a gulf of snow-drifts about their dreadful lips, six hundred feet of shadows yawning within, and shuddered.

"You're cold," said Dot, softly, pulling me to the fire, where she warmed her steaming boots. "I'm cold, too." We piled the wood on; the flames leaped and crackled; shadows flew among the rafters.

"Harry's due any minute," said her uncle. "We'll drop the eggs in as soon as we hear his whistle." He stooped down to pat the St. Bernard, which lay with head stretched on his fore paws before the fire, staring, listening. "You'll hear him first," he laughed cheerily, giving the beast a resounding pat. "Long before we do."

The dog growled low, making no other response to a caress that usually brought him leaping to his master's breast. We heard the wind keening round the wooden walls, rushing with a long faint whistle over the roof, and we drew closer to the fire. For a long time, no one spoke. The minutes passed and passed.

It was then, quite suddenly, that we heard a step in the snow; but not before the dog had heard it first and bounded to his feet with a growl that was more like a human roar than any animal sound I have ever heard. He fairly leaped toward the door, and the same second Dot and I were also upon our feet.

"What's the matter?" exclaimed her uncle, startled and surprised. "That's only wind, or snow falling from the roof."

Behind us the wooden walls gave out sharp, cracking reports as the heated air made them expand; but in my heart something turned into ice with a cold that lay beyond all cold of winter. The terror I at first experienced, however, was not for myself, but for this soft, brown-eyed little maid who shot so swiftly by me and opened the heavy door. I was ready there to catch her, ready to protect and shield, yet knowing by some strange authority within me that she stood already safe, held by a power that lay beyond all little efforts of my own.

For into that great, fire-lit interior stepped at once the figure of a peasant, large, uncouth, lumbering, his face curiously concealed either by the play of the shadows or by the fall of his hair and beard—to this day I know not which—filling the threshold with his bulk, the freezing wind rushing in past his great, sheathed legs, and an eddy of dry snow veiling him like a flying cloak beyond. He stood there a second with an atmosphere of power about him that seemed to dwarf everything, and of such commanding stature that into my mind, bewildered and confused a little with the sudden entrance, ran the thought of a bleak and towering peak of mountain.

It came to me that the chalet must crumble, the huge beams split, and fall upon our heads. There was a rush of freezing wind, a touch of ice, and at the same time I was aware of some strange, intolerable beauty, as of wild nature, that made me hide my eyes. It was only long afterward that I remembered there was no snow upon his feet, that his eyes remained hidden, and also that he spoke not a word.

"The door's blown open!" cried the uncle. "For God's sake—"

All this, moreover, in the tenth of the first second, for immediately

I saw that the St. Bernard was bounding round the figure with an unfeigned delight that knew no fear; and next, that he had stretched his arms out toward the girl with a gesture of tenderness and invitation possible only in this whole world to the arms of woman. Terrible, yet inconceivably winning, was that gesture, as of a child. And the same moment, to my amazement, she had leaped forward and was gone. With her, barking and leaping, went the St. Bernard dog.

"Dot, you silly child, where in the world are you going? Do shut the door! It's not Harry yet. It was a false alarm." It was the matter-of-fact tone of her uncle's voice that let me into the secret—that only she, I, and the dog had witnessed anything at all.

"I'll go with her and see her safe," I shouted back, and it was only then, as I turned toward the door again after saying it, that I understood there was no one standing there, and that her leap had been really a springing run toward the corner where her skees lay. Already, I saw, they were on her feet. She was away. I saw the dog bounding over the frozen slope beside her. He was a little in front. He held her skirt in his teeth, guidingly. In that pale wintry light of the rising moon, I saw their two outlines against the snow. They were alone.

"Bring brandy and a blanket!" I had the sense to call back into the room, and was after her in my turn. But the frozen fastenings of my skees had never seemed so obstinate. It was a whole minute before I was whizzing down the mile-long slope. The speed was tremendous, and the skees skidded on the crust. She left only faint indications of her trail. It was the barking of the dog that guided me best, and far away below me in the yellow moonlight the little speeding spot of black that showed me where she flew, heading straight for the Creux du Van.

At any other time, such a descent as we two then made would have been sheer lunacy, even in daylight. The tearing speed, the angle of the huge slope, the iciness of that gleaming crust, all were invitations to disaster; and with the gaping chasm of the Creux du Van lying waiting at the bottom, it was simply a splendid race into suicide. The water poured from my eyes, the frozen mounds whipped by like giant white waves, and no sooner was the black line of some isolated pine-tree sighted than it was past, like the telegraph-poles to an express-train. Only the yellow face of the big rising moon held steady.

She had soon outstripped the dog, and as I shot past him, wildly cantering, with his tongue out and steaming, open jaws, he caught vainly at my *puttees*. The next moment he was a hundred yards behind me. But Dot, guided by some power that the mountains put into her little feet, knew her direction well, and went as straight as a die to the edge of the awful gulf; then stopped dead, buried to her neck in a drift that climbed wave-like upon the very lips of the chasm. It stopped her, as ten minutes before it had also stopped another, coming down from the slopes that lay to the westward. I saw the hole of the valley gaping at our very feet as a successful "telemark" flung me backward beside her just in the nick of time.

"Quick!" I heard her cry. "He's still sliding!" It was then that I realised that the third body, lying there unconscious where the drift had likewise stopped it, was slowly moving with the weight of snow toward the edge. One skee already projected horribly over the actual brink. I heard a mass of snow detach itself and drop even as she said it.

It took less than a second to detach my belt and fasten it to his leg; but even then, I firmly believe the strain of our slow pulling must have landed us all three into the gulf below had not the arrival of the St. Bernard put a different complexion upon the scene. It was the grandest thing I have ever witnessed. A second, he stood there, the supreme instinct of his noble race judging the problem. He knew the softness of the drift that must engulf him if he advanced; he also saw it sliding. Very slowly, like a courageous human being, on all fours, calculating distance, angle, and tensions, as it were, by his superb animal divination, he crawled round to another side. He crept gingerly along the very edge. His teeth fastened upon the boot and skee-straps. We pulled together. God! I cannot understand to this day how it was that the four of us were not gone! He knew, that splendid dumb creature. We merely followed his magnificent lead.

A moment later we were safe on hard, solid snow. As we lay back exhausted, the snow immediately at our feet slid with a hiss, and disappeared into the valley hundreds of feet below. But the St. Bernard, still pulling carefully and gently by himself, was next busily licking the boy's white face and breathing his heat upon him, when help arrived with the brandy and the blankets. I believe it was the tireless and incessant attentions of that great dog that really saved the life, for he lay upon the form with his whole body, keeping him warm, and letting go only when he understood that the blankets and our arms, carrying him to the chalet, might replace own self-sacrificing love.

"I heard a voice crying outside the door in the wind," she told me afterward. "It was his voice, you see, and it called me by name. I don't know what guided me to the place, for I think I shut my eyes the whole way till I fell at his side."

The Man Who Was Milligan

Milligan looked round the dingy rooms with an appraising air, while the landlady stood behind him, wondering whether he would decide to take them. She stood with her arms crossed; her eye was observant. She, in her turn, was appraising Milligan, of course. He was a cleric in a tourist agency, and in his spare time he wrote stories for the cinema. What attracted him just now in the very ordinary lodgings was the big folding-doors. All he really needed was a bed-sitting-room, with breakfast, but he suddenly saw himself sitting in that front room writing his scenarios—successfully at last. It was rather tempting. He would be a literary man—with a study! "Your price seems a trifle high, Mrs.—er—?" he opened the bargain.

"Bostock, sir, Mrs. Bostock," she informed him, then recited her tale of woe about the high cost of living. It was unnecessary recitation, for Milligan was not listening, having already decided in his mind to take the rooms.

While Mrs. Bostock droned monotonously on, his eye fell casually upon a picture that hung above the plush mantelpiece—a Chinese scene showing a man in a boat upon a little lake. He glanced at it, no more than that. It was better than glancing at Mrs. Bostock. The landlady, however, instantly caught that glance and noticed its direction,

"Me 'usband"—she switched off her main theme—"brought it 'ome from China. From Hong-Kong, I *should* say." And the way she aspirated the "H" in Hong made Milligan smile. He perceived that she was proud of the picture evidently.

"It's wonderful," he said. "Probably it's worth something, too. These Chinese drawings—some of 'em—are very rare, I believe."

The little picture was worth perhaps two shillings, and he knew it; but he had found his way to Mrs. Bostock's heart, and, incidentally, had persuaded her to take a shilling off the rent. The picture, he felt sure, had been stolen by her late husband, a sea captain. To her it was a kind of nest-egg. If she ever found herself in difficulties, it would fetch money. Milligan, by chance, had stumbled upon what he called a good line."

Being an honest creature, he had no wish to use his knowledge, but every week thereafter, almost every day, indeed, some remark concerning the Chinese drawing passed between them: with the natural result that, while it bored him a good deal, he cultivated the theme, and in so doing gazed much and often at the Chinaman. That Celestial, sitting in the boat with his back to the room, rowing, rowing eternally across the placid lake without advancing, he came to know in every detail.

Every time Mrs. Bostock chatted with him, his eye wandered from her grimy visage to the drawing. He used it to end the chat with.

"I like your picture so much," he observed. "It's nice to live with." He put it straight, he flicked dust from the frame with his handkerchief. "It's so much better than these modern things. It's worth a bit—I dare say—"

It chanced, at the time, that Lafcadio Hearn, the writer about Japan, was in his mind. He had once arranged a successful trip to Japan for a client of his firm, and the client had made him a present of one of Hearn's strange and wonderful books. It was hardly in the line of Milligan's reading, for it had no "film value," and he had sold the book—a collection of Chinese stories—to a second-hand bookseller for a shilling. But he had glanced at it first, and a story in it had remained sharply in his mind: a story about a picture of a man in a boat. An observer, watching the picture, had seen the man move. The man actually began to row. Finally, the man rowed right out of the picture and into the place—a temple—where the observer stood.

Milligan thought it foolish, yet his memory retained the details vividly. They stuck in his head. The graphic description was realistic. Milligan caught himself thinking of it every time he met a Chinaman in the street, every time he sold a ticket to China or Japan. It rose, it flitted by, it vanished. The memory persisted. And the moment his eye first saw Mrs. Bostock's treasure over the plush mantelpiece, this vivid memory of Hearn's story had again risen, flitted by, and vanished. It betrayed its vitality, at any rate. Wonderful chap, that Hearn, thought Milligan.

All this was natural enough, without mystery, without a hint of anything queer or out of the ordinary. What was a little queer—it struck Milligan so, at any rate—was an idea that began to grow in him from the very first week of his tenancy.

"That *might* be the very drawing the fellow wrote about," occurred to him one night as he laboured at a lurid scenario which was to make his fortune. "Not impossible at all. It's an old picture probably. Exactly what Hearn described, too. I wonder! Why not?"

Why not, indeed? A fellow—especially a literary fellow—should use his imagination. Milligan used his. Sometimes he used it in prolonged labour till the early hours. The gas-light flickered across his pages, across that lake in China, across the boat, across the back and arms and pigtail of that diminutive Chinaman who rowed eternally over a placid Chinese lake without advancing an inch. The scenario of the moment brought in China, aptly enough. A glance at the picture, he found, was not unhelpful in the way of stimulating a flagging imagination.

Milligan glanced often. The gas-light was always flickering. Shadows were for ever shifting to and fro across Mrs, Bostock's worthless nest-egg. It was easy to imagine that the boat, the water, even the figure moved. Those dancing shadows! How they played about the arms, the back, the outline of the boat, the oars!

And when it was two in the morning, and the London streets lay hushed, and a great stillness blanketed the whole city, Milligan felt even a little thrilled. It was, he thought, "imaginative," to catch these slight, elusive movements in the drawing. He imagined the fellow rowing about, changing his position, landing. It helped his own mood, his incidents, his atmosphere.

"That man's alive!" he whispered to himself. "By Jove! He moves in the picture. His place changes. It's an inspiration. I must use it somehow!—"And imagination, eerily stimulated in the deep silence of the sleeping city, was at work again.

This was the beginning of the strange adventure which befell the literary Milligan, whose imagination worked in the stillness of the small hours, but whose scenarios were never used.

"For why write scenarios," he said to me, "when you can *live* them?"

In Peking, ten or twelve years later, he said this to me, and I am probably the only person to whom this scenario he "lived" was ever confided.

In Peking his name was not Milligan at all. He was not working in a tourist agency. He was a rich man, aged thirty-eight, a "figure" in the English community there, a man of influence and position. But all that does not matter. What matters is the story of how he came to be in China at all—and this he does not know. He does not know how he came to be in China at all. There is no recollection of the journey even. Nor can he state precisely how he began the speculations and enterprises that made him prosperous, beyond that he suddenly found himself concerned in big, fortunate undertakings in the Chinese city.

There is this deep gap in the years.

"Loss of memory, I suppose they call it," he mentioned, after our chance acquaintanceship had grown into a friendship that gave me his confidence. What he *could* tell he told me frankly and without reserve, glad to talk of it, I think, to someone who did not mock, and making no condition of secrecy, moreover.

There was some link, apparently, between myself and the man who had been Milligan. Chance, that some call destiny, revealed it. And, as I listened to his amazing tale, I swore that on my return to London I would visit Mrs. Bostock and buy the picture. I wanted that Chinese drawing badly. I wanted to examine it myself. Her nest-egg at last should be worth something, as Milligan, ten years before, had told her.

What happened was, apparently, as follows: Milligan, first of all, discovered in himself, somewhat suddenly it seemed, a new interest in China and things Chinese. If the birth of this interest was abrupt, its growth was extremely rapid. China fairly leapt at him. He read books, talked with travellers, studied the map, the history, the civilisation of China. The psychology of the Celestial race absorbed him. The subject obsessed him. He longed to go to China. It became a yearning that left him no peace day or night. In practical terms of time, money and opportunity, the journey was, of course, impossible. He lived on in London, but actually he lived already in China, for where a man's thought is there shall his consciousness be also.

All this I could readily understand, for others, similarly, have felt the call and spell of countries like Egypt, Africa, the desert. There was nothing incomprehensible nor peculiar in the fascination China exercised upon the imaginative Milligan. It was his business, moreover, to sell exciting tickets to travellers, and China happened to have fired his particular temperament. Natural enough!

Natural enough, too, that, through this, the picture in his lodgings should have acquired more meaning for him, and that he should have studied it more closely and more frequently. It was the only Chinese object he had within constant reach, and he told me at wearisome length how he knew every tiniest detail of the drawing, and how it became for him a kind of symbol, almost a kind of sacred symbol, upon which he focussed his intense desires—frustrated desires. Wearisome, yes, until he reached a point in his story that suddenly galvanised my interest, so that I began to listen with uncommon, if a rather creepy, curiosity.

The picture, he informed me, altered. There was movement among its details that he already knew by heart.

"*Movement!*" he half-whispered to me, his eyes shining, a faint shudder running through his big body.

The sincerity of deep conviction with which he described what happened left a lasting impression on my mind. His words, his manner, conveyed the truth of a genuine experience. Hitherto only the back of the man's head had been visible. Then, one night, Milligan saw his profile. The face was turned. It now looked a little over the shoulder, and towards the room.

From this moment, though he never detected actual movement when it occurred, the alteration in the drawing was marked and rapid. The face retained its new position; the angle of the profile did not widen, but the position of oars and boat, the attitude of arms and back, their size as well, these now changed from day to day.

There was a dreadful rapidity about these changes. The figure of the Chinaman grew bigger; the boat grew bigger too. They were coming nearer. "I had the awful conviction," whispered the man who had been Milligan, "that they were coming—to fetch me. I used to get all of a sweat each time I saw the size and nearness grow. It was appalling, but also it was delightful somehow—"

I permitted myself a question: "Did your landlady notice it too?" I enquired, concealing my scepticism.

"Mrs. Bostock was ill in bed the whole time. She never came into the room once."

"The servant?" I persisted. "Or any of your friends?"

He hesitated. "The girl who did the room," he said honestly, "observed nothing. She gave notice suddenly without a reason. So did the next girl. I never asked them anything. As for my friends"—he smiled faintly—"I was too scared—to bring them in."

"You were afraid they might *not* see what you saw?"

He shrugged his shoulders. "It scared me," he repeated, looking past me towards the shuttered windows of his study where we sat.

The account he gave of it all made my flesh creep even in that bright Peking sunshine. He certainly described what he saw, or believed he saw, as, day after day, night after night, that man rowed his boat slowly, slowly, surely, surely, very gradually, but with remorseless purpose, nearer, nearer—and nearer. The lodger watched. He also waited.

"The man," he whispered, "was rowing into the room. It was his purpose to row into the room. He was coming to fetch me" And he mopped his forehead at the thought of what had happened ten years ago.

Suddenly he leant forward.

"In the end," his thin voice rattled almost against my face, "he—did fetch me. I'm in that picture with him now. I'm not in China, as *you* think I am. This"—he tapped his chest, the chest of a successful business man—"is not me. I'm not Milligan. Milligan is in that picture with the Chinaman. He's in that boat, sitting beside him, motionless. Being stared at by a succession of lodgers. Sitting in that stiff little boat. Very tiny. Not dead, but captive. Sitting without breath. Without feeling. Painted, yet alive. Caught on the surface of that placid Chinese lake until time or death dissolve the drawing—"

I thought he was going to faint, but, oddly enough, I did *not* think him merely mad. His mood, his crawling horror, his intense sincerity took me bodily into his own deep nightmare. He recovered quickly. He was a man who had himself always well in hand. He told me the end at once.

He had been to a dance and he came home tired, sober, having well enjoyed himself, it seems, about four in the morning. The time was early spring, and dawn was just giving faint signs of breaking, but the hall and passage of the house were still dark.

He entered his room and lit the gas, going at once to the mirror to have a look at himself. This was the first thing he did, he assured me, and in the mirror, he saw, behind himself, the boat and the Chinaman, both of them—gigantic.

Gigantic was the word he used, though he used it, of course, relatively. The Chinaman was standing in the room. He was in the lake in front of the plush mantelpiece. The wall was gone—there was a sort of hazy space. Close at the Chinaman's heels lay the boat, both oars resting sideways on the water, their heads still in the rowlocks. Water was up to his feet, to Milligan's feet, for he not only felt his shoes soaked through, but he also heard the lapping sound of diminutive wavelets on the "shore."

He gave a great sigh. No cry, either of terror or surprise, he said, escaped him. His only sound was this great sigh—of acceptance, of resignation, of a mind benumbed and yet secretly delighted. The big Chinaman beckoned, smiled, nodded his yellow face, retreating very slowly as he did so. And Milligan obeyed. He followed. He stepped into the boat. The Chinaman took up the oars, and rowed him slowly, very slowly, across the placid lake, into the picture and out of his familiar, known surroundings, rowed him slowly, very slowly, into the land of his heart's deep desire.

★★★★★★★★★★★★★★★★★

All the way home to England in the steamer this strangest of strange narratives haunted me. I still saw the man who was Milligan sitting in the study of his big, expensive house as he told it to me. His shrewd business brain had built that house; the fortune he had made provided the good lunch and cigars we had enjoyed together. From the moment of entering the boat his memory had remained a blank. Continuity of personality though still, it seemed to me, rather uncertain somewhere, had revived only when he was already a rich man who had spent years in China. This big gap in the years remains.

In my mind lay every detail of the story; in my pocket-book lay the address of Mrs. Bostock's rooms. I prayed heaven she might still be living, even if aged and crumpled by ten more English winters.

I had arranged to cable "Milligan" at once; we had selected the very words I was to use: "Two figures in boat," or "One figure in boat." He asked for the message in these words. Fortune favoured me; I found the rooms; Mrs. Bostock was alive; the rooms were unoccupied; I looked over them; I saw—the picture.

Before visiting Mrs. Bostock's however. I had visited the newspaper files in the British Museum, and the "Disappearance of James Milligan" was there for all to read. Millions had evidently read it. It had been *the* news of the day. Columns of space were devoted to it; dozens of false clues were started; crime was suggested, of course. His disappearance was complete. Milligan was a case of "sunk without trace," with a vengeance.

It was in the dingy front room that I experienced what was perhaps the most vivid thrill of wonder life has ever given me. I stood, appraising the room as a would-be lodger. Behind me, her arms crossed, appraising me in turn just as she had appraised her former lodger of ten years ago, stood Mrs. Bostock. Probably I looked more prosperous than he had looked; her attitude, at any rate, was attentive to a fault. Why I should have trembled a little is hard to say, but self-control was certainly not as full as it might have been, for my voice shook a trifle as, at length, I drew her attention with calculated purpose to the picture above the plush mantelpiece. I praised it.

"Me 'usband brought it back from Hong-Kong," I heard her say.

My breath caught a little, so that there was a slight pause before I said the next thing. My voice went slightly husky.

"I have a collection of Chinese drawings," I mentioned. "If you cared to sell, perhaps—"

"Oh, many 'as wanted to buy it," she lied easily, hoping to increase its value.

I mentioned five pounds. I mentioned another figure too—the figure in the boat.

"That single figure," I explained in as calm a tone as I could muster, "is so good, you see. The Chinese artists never overcrowded their paintings. Now, if—instead of that single figure—there were two"—I moved closer to the picture, hoping she would follow—"the value," I went on, "would, of course, be less."

Mrs. Bostock had followed me. I had tempted her greed; I had tested her truth as well. We stood side by side immediately beneath the drawing. We examined it together.

At the mention of five pounds the woman had given a little gasp, jerking her body at the same time. Now, at such close quarters with the thing she hoped to sell me, her voice was dumb at first. At first. For a moment later a strange sound escaped her lips, a sound that was meant to be a cry, but only succeeded in being a wheezy struggle to get her breath. Her mouth opened wide, her eyes popped almost from her face. She staggered, recovered her balance by putting a hand on my arm for support, then stepped still nearer to the mantelpiece and thrust her head and shoulders close against the drawing. Her blind eyes peered. Her skin was already white.

"Two of 'em!" she exclaimed in a terrified whisper. "Two of 'em, so 'elp me, Gawd! And the other's *him!*"

I was ready to support. I had expected her to collapse perhaps. I felt rather like collapsing myself. She swayed, turning her horror-stricken countenance to mine.

"Mr. Milligan!" she screamed aloud, then, her voice returning in full volume: "It's Mr. Milligan. All this time that's where 'e's been. And I never noticed it till now!"

She swooned away.

The second figure faced the room, for the boat was in the position of being pushed by the oars, not rowed. The features were unmistakable... Half an hour later I sent a cable to Peking; "*Two figures in boat.*"

The real climax, I think, came three days later, when, with the picture safely in my rooms, I had arranged for "specialists" to call and examine it. A chemist, an experienced dealer, and a sort of expert psychic investigator were already upstairs when I reached my flat.

The picture was in my bedroom. I had examined it myself—examined Milligan's face and figure—hour after hour, my flesh crawling, my hair almost rising, as I did so. My guests were in the sitting-room, the servant informed me, handing me a telegram as I hurried up in the lift. My three friends were already known to each other, and, after apologising for the delay, I brought in the drawing and laid it before them on the small table. I intended to tell them the story after their examination; the psychic investigator I meant to keep when the other two had left. Setting the drawing in front of them, I looked over their shoulders at it.

There was only one figure—the Chinaman. He sat alone in the little boat. He was rowing, not pushing; his back was to the room.

The dealer said the drawing was worth a shilling; the chemist said nothing; I, too, said nothing; but the psychic investigator turned sharply and complained that I was hurting him. My hand, it seems, had clutched the shoulder nearest to me, and it happened to be his. I allowed him to leave when the other two left...

I was alone. I remembered the telegram. More to steady my mind than for any interest I felt in it, my fingers tore it open. It was a cablegram from—Peking, signed by a friend of Milligan and myself:

"Milligan died heart failure yesterday."

The Lane That Ran East and West

1

The curving strip of lane, fading into invisibility east and west, had always symbolized life to her. In some minds, life pictures itself a straight line, uphill, downhill, flat, as the case may be; in hers it had been, since childhood, this sweep of country lane that ran past her cottage door. In thick white summer dust, she invariably visualized it, blue and yellow flowers along its untidy banks of green. It flowed, it glided, sometimes it rushed. Without a sound it ran along past the nut trees and the branches where honeysuckle and wild roses shone. With every year now its silent speed increased.

From either end she imagined, as a child, that she looked over into outer space—from the eastern end into the infinity before birth, from the western into the infinity that follows death. It was to her of real importance.

From the veranda the entire stretch was visible, not more than five hundred yards at most; from the platform in her mind, whence she viewed existence, she saw her own life, similarly, as a white curve of flowering lane, arising she knew not whence, gliding whither she could not tell. At eighteen she had paraphrased the quatrain with a smile upon her red lips, her chin tilted, her strong grey eyes rather wistful with yearning—

Into this little lane, and why not knowing,
Nor whence, like water willy-nilly flowing,
And out again—like dust along the waste,
I know not whither, willy-nilly blowing.

At thirty she now repeated it, the smile still there, but the lips not quite so red, the chin a trifle firmer, the grey eyes stronger, clearer, but charged with a more wistful and a deeper yearning.

It was her turn of mind, imaginative, introspective, querulous per-

175

haps, that made the bit of running lane significant. Food with the butcher's and baker's carts came to her from its eastern, its arriving end, as she called it; news with the postman, adventure with rare callers. Youth, hope, excitement, all these came from the sunrise. Thence came likewise spring and summer, flowers, butterflies, the swallows. The fairies, in her childhood, had come that way too, their silver feet and gossamer wings brightening the summer dawns; and it was but a year ago that Dick Messenger, his car stirring a cloud of thick white dust, had also come into her life from the space beyond the sunrise.

She sat thinking about him now—how he had suddenly appeared out of nothing that warm June morning, asked her permission about some engineering business on the neighbouring big estate over the hill, given her a dog-rose and a bit of fern-leaf, and eventually gone away with her promise when he left. Out of the eastern end he appeared; into the western end he vanished.

For there was this departing end as well, where the lane curved out of sight into the space behind the yellow sunset. In this direction went all that left her life. Her parents, each in turn, had taken that way to the churchyard. Spring, summer, the fading butterflies, the restless swallows, all left her round that western curve. Later the fairies followed them, her dreams one by one, the vanishing years as well—and now her youth, swifter, ever swifter, into the region where the sun dipped nightly among pale rising stars, leaving her brief strip of life colder, more and more unlit.

Just beyond this end she imagined shadows.

She saw Dick's car whirling towards her, whirling away again, making for distant Mexico, where his treasure lay. In the interval he had found that treasure and realised it. He was now coming back again. He had landed in England yesterday.

Seated in her deckchair on the veranda, she watched the sun sink to the level of the hazel trees. The last swallows already flashed their dark wings against the fading gold. Over that western end tomorrow or the next day, amid a cloud of whirling white dust, would emerge, again out of nothingness, the noisy car that brought Dick Messenger back to her, back from the Mexican expedition that ensured his great new riches, back into her heart and life. In the other direction she would depart a week or so later, her life in his keeping, and his in hers. . . . . and the feet of their children, in due course, would run up and down the mysterious lane in search of flowers, butterflies, excitement, in search of life.

She wondered . . . and as the light faded her wondering grew deeper. Questions that had lain dormant for twelve months became audible suddenly. Would Dick be satisfied with this humble cottage which meant so much to her that she felt she could never, never leave it? Would not his money, his new position, demand palaces elsewhere? He was ambitious. Could his ambitions set an altar of sacrifice to his love? And she—could she, on the other hand, walk happy and satisfied along the western curve, leaving her lane finally behind her, lost, untravelled, forgotten? Could she face this sacrifice for him? Was he, in a word, *the* man whose appearance out of the sunrise she had been watching and waiting for all these hurrying, swift years?

She wondered. Now that the decisive moment was so near, unhappy doubts assailed her. Her wondering grew deeper, spread, enveloped, penetrated her being like a gathering darkness. And the sun sank lower, dusk crept along the hedgerows, the flowers closed their little burning eyes. Shadows passed hand in hand along the familiar bend that was so short, so soon travelled over and left behind that a mistake must ruin all its sweetest joy. To wander down it with a companion to whom its flowers, its butterflies, its shadows brought no full message, must turn it chill, dark, lonely, colourless. . . . Her thoughts slipped on thus into a soft inner reverie born of that scented twilight hour of honeysuckle and wild roses, born too of her deep self-questioning, of wonder, of yearning unsatisfied.

The lane, meanwhile, produced its customary few figures, moving homewards through the dusk. She knew them well, these familiar figures of the countryside, had known them from childhood onwards—labourers, hedgers, ditchers and the like, with whom now, even in her reverie, she exchanged the usual friendly greetings across the wicket-gate. This time, however, she gave but her mind to them, her heart absorbed with its own personal and immediate problem.

Melancey had come and gone; old Averill, carrying his hedger's sickle-knife, had followed; and she was vaguely looking for Hezekiah Purdy, bent with years and rheumatism, his tea-pail always rattling, his shuffling feet making a sorry dust, when the figure she did not quite recognize came into view, emerging unexpectedly from the sunrise end. Was it Purdy? Yes—no—yet, if not, who was it? Of course, it must be Purdy. Yet while the others, being homeward bound, came naturally from west to east, with this new figure it was otherwise, so that he was half-way down the curve before she fully realised him. Out of the eastern end the man drew nearer, a stranger therefore; out of the unknown regions where the sun rose, and where no shadows were, he moved towards her down the deserted lane, perhaps a trespasser, an intruder possibly, but certainly an unfamiliar figure.

Without particular attention or interest, she watched him drift nearer down her little semi-private lane of dream, passing leisurely from east to west, the mere fact that he was there establishing an intimacy that remained at first unsuspected. It was her eye that watched him, not her mind. What was he doing here, where going, whither come, she wondered vaguely, the lane both his background and his starting-point? A little by-way, after all, this haunted lane. The real world, she knew, swept down the big high-road beyond, unconscious of the humble folk its unimportant tributary served. Suddenly the burden of the years assailed her. Had she, then, missed life by living here?

Then, with a little shock, her heart contracted as she became aware of two eyes fixed upon her in the dusk. The stranger had already reached the wicket-gate and now stood leaning against it, staring at her over its spiked wooden top. It was certainly not old Purdy. The blood rushed back into her heart again as she returned the gaze. He was watching her with a curious intentness, with an odd sense of authority almost, with something that persuaded her instantly of a definite purpose in his being there. He was waiting for her—expecting her to come down and speak with him, as she had spoken with the others. Of this, her little habit, he made use, she felt. Shyly, half-nervously, she left her deck-chair and went slowly down the short gravel path between the flowers, noticing meanwhile that his clothes were ragged, his hair unkempt, his face worn and ravaged as by want and suffering, yet that his eyes were curiously young. His eyes, indeed, were full brown smiling eyes, and it was the surprise of his youth that impressed her chiefly. That he could be tramp or trespasser left her. She felt no fear.

She wished him "Good evening" in her calm, quiet voice, adding with sympathy, "And who are you, I wonder? You want to ask me something?" It flashed across her that his shabby clothing was somehow a disguise. Over his shoulder hung a faded sack. "I can do something for you?" she pursued inquiringly, as was her kindly custom. "If you are hungry, thirsty, or——"

It was the expression of vigour leaping into the deep eyes that stopped her. "If you need clothes," she had been going to add. She was not frightened, but suddenly she paused, gripped by a wonder she could not understand.

And his first words justified her wonder. "*I* have something for you," he said, his voice faint, a kind of stillness in it as though it came through distance. Also, though this she did not notice, it was an educated voice, and it was the absence of surprise that made this detail too natural to claim attention. She had expected it. "Something to give you. I have brought it for you," the man concluded.

"Yes," she replied, aware, again without comprehension, that her courage and her patience were both summoned to support her. "Yes," she repeated more faintly, as though this was all natural, inevitable, expected. She saw that the sack was now lifted from his shoulder and that his hand plunged into it, as it hung apparently loose and empty against the gate. His eyes, however, never for one instant left her own. Alarm, she was able to remind herself, she did not feel. She only recognized that this ragged figure laid something upon her spirit she could not fathom, yet was compelled to face.

His next words startled her. She drew, if unconsciously, upon her courage:

"A dream."

The voice was deep, yet still with the faintness as of distance in it. His hand, she saw, was moving slowly from the empty sack. A strange attraction, mingled with pity, with yearning too, stirred deeply in her. The face, it seemed, turned soft, the eyes glowed with some inner fire of feeling. Her heart now beat unevenly.

"Something—to—sell to me," she faltered, aware that his glowing eyes upon her made her tremble. The same instant she was ashamed of the words, knowing they were uttered by a portion of her that resisted, and this was not the language he deserved.

He smiled, and she knew her resistance a vain make-believe he pierced too easily, though he let it pass in silence.

"There is, I mean, a price—for every dream," she tried to save herself, conscious delightfully that her heart was smiling in return.

The dusk enveloped them, the corncrakes were calling from the fields, the scent of honeysuckle and wild roses lay round her in a warm wave of air, yet at the same time she felt as if her naked soul stood side by side with this figure in the infinitude of space beyond the sunrise end. The golden stars hung calm and motionless above them.

"That price"—his answer fell like a summons she had actually expected—"you pay to another, not to me." The voice grew fainter, farther away, dropping through empty space behind her. "All dreams are but a single dream. You pay that price to——"

179

Her interruption slipped spontaneously from her lips, its inevitable truth a prophecy:

"To myself!"

He smiled again, but this time he did not answer. His hand, instead, now moved across the gate towards her.

And before she quite realised what had happened, she was holding a little object he had passed across to her. She had taken it, obeying, it seemed, an inner compulsion and authority which were inevitable, fore-ordained. Lowering her face, she examined it in the dusk—a small green leaf of fern—fingered it with tender caution as it lay in her palm, gazed for some seconds closely at the tiny thing. . . . When she looked up again the stranger, the seller of dreams, as she now imagined him, had moved some yards away from the gate, and was moving still, a leisurely quiet tread that stirred no dust, a shadowy outline soft with dusk and starlight, moving towards the sunrise end, whence he had first appeared.

Her heart gave a sudden leap, as once again the burden of the years assailed her. Her words seemed driven out:

"Who are you? Before you go—your name! What is your name?"

His voice, now faint with distance as he melted from sight against the dark fringe of hazel trees, reached her but indistinctly, though its meaning was somehow clear:

"The dream," she heard like a breath of wind against her ear, "shall bring its own name with it. I wait. . . ." Both sound and figure trailed off into the unknown space beyond the eastern end, and, leaning against the wicket-gate as usual, the white dust settling about his heavy boots, the tea-pail but just ceased from rattling, was—old Purdy.

Unless the mind can fix the reality of an event in the actual instant of its happening, judgment soon dwindles into a confusion between memory and argument. Five minutes later, when old Purdy had gone his way again, she found herself already wondering, reflecting, questioning. Yearning had perhaps conjured with emotion to fashion both voice and figure out of imagination, out of this perfumed dusk, out of the troubled heart's desire. Confusion in time had further helped to metamorphose old Purdy into some legendary shape that had stolen upon her mood of reverie from the shadows of her beloved lane. . . . Yet the dream she had accepted from a stranger hand, a little fern leaf, remained at any rate to shape a delightful certainty her brain might criticize while her heart believed.

The fern leaf assuredly was real. A fairy gift! Those who eat of this fern-seed, she remembered as she sank into sleep that night, shall see the fairies! And, indeed, a few hours later she walked in dream along the familiar curve between the hedges, her own childhood taking her by the hand as she played with the flowers, the butterflies, the glad swallows beckoning while they flashed. Without the smallest sense of surprise or unexpectedness, too, she met at the eastern end—two figures. They stood, as she with her childhood stood, hand in hand, the seller of dreams and her lover, waiting since time began, she realised, waiting with some great unuttered question on their lips. Neither addressed her, neither spoke a word. Dick looked at her, ambition, hard and restless, shining in his eyes; in the eyes of the other—dark, gentle, piercing, but extraordinarily young for all the ragged hair about the face the shabby clothes, the ravaged and unkempt appearance—a brightness as of the coming dawn.

A choice, she understood, was offered to her; there was a decision she must make. She realised, as though some great wind blew it into her from outer space, another, a new standard to which her judgment must inevitably conform, or admit the purpose of her life evaded finally. The same moment she knew what her decision was. No hesitation touched her. Calm, yet trembling, her courage and her patience faced the decision and accepted it. The hands then instantly fell apart, unclasped. One figure turned and vanished down the lane towards the departing end, but with the other, now hand in hand, she rose floating, gliding without effort, a strange bliss in her heart, to meet the sunrise.

"He has awakened . . . so he cannot stay," she heard, like a breath of wind that whispered into her ear. "I, who bring you this dream—I wait."

She did not wake at once when the dream was ended, but slept on long beyond her accustomed hour, missing thereby Melancey, Averill, old Purdy as they passed the wicket-gate in the early hours. She woke, however, with a new clear knowledge of herself, of her mind and heart, to all of which in simple truth to her own soul she must conform. The fern-seed she placed in a locket attached to a fine gold chain about her neck. During the long, lonely, expectant yet unsatisfied years that followed she wore it day and night.

2

She had the curious feeling that she remained young. Others grew older, but not she. She watched her contemporaries slowly give the signs, while she herself held stationary. Even those younger than herself went past her, growing older in the ordinary way, whereas her heart, her mind, even her appearance, she felt certain, hardly aged at all. In a room full of people, she felt pity often as she read the signs in their faces knowing her own unchanged. Their eyes were burning out, but hers burned on. It was neither vanity nor delusion, but an inner conviction she could not alter.

The age she held to was the year she had received the fern-seed from old Purdy, or rather, from an imaginary figure her reverie had set momentarily in old Purdy's place. That figure of her reverie, the dream that followed, the subsequent confession to Dick Messenger, meeting his own half-way—these marked the year when she stopped growing older. To that year she seemed chained, gazing into the sunrise end—waiting, ever waiting.

Whether in her absent-minded reverie she had actually plucked the bit of fern herself, or whether, after all, old Purdy had handed it to her, was not a point that troubled her. It was in her locket about her neck still, day and night. The seller of dreams was an established imaginative reality in her life. Her heart assured her she would meet him again one day. She waited. It was very curious, it was rather pathetic. Men came and went, she saw her chances pass; her answer was invariably "No."

The break came suddenly, and with devastating effect. As she was dressing carefully for the party, full of excited anticipation like some young girl still, she saw looking out upon her from the long mirror a face of plain middle-age. A blackness rose about her. It seemed the mirror shattered. The long, long dream, at any rate, fell in a thousand broken pieces at her feet. It was perhaps the ball dress, perhaps the flowers in her hair; it may have been the low-cut gown that betrayed the neck and throat, or the one brilliant jewel that proved her eyes now dimmed beside it—but most probably it was the tell-tale hands, whose ageing no artifice ever can conceal. The middle-aged woman, at any rate, rushed from the glass and claimed her.

It was a long time, too, before the signs of tears had been carefully obliterated again, and the battle with herself—to go or not to go—was decided by clear courage. She would not send a hurried excuse of illness, but would take the place where she now belonged. She saw herself, a fading figure, more than half-way now towards the sunset end, within sight even of the shadowed emptiness that lay beyond the sun's dipping edge. She had lingered over-long, expecting a dream to confirm a dream; she had been oblivious of the truth that the lane went rushing just the same. It was now too late. The speed increased. She had waited, waited for nothing. The seller of dreams was a myth. No man could need her as she now was.

Yet the chief ingredient in her decision was, oddly enough, itself a sign of youth. A party, a ball, is ever an adventure. Fate, with her destined eyes aglow, may be bidden too, waiting among the throng, waiting for that very one who hesitates whether to go or not to go. Who knows what the evening may bring forth? It was this anticipation, faintly beckoning, its voice the merest echo of her shadowy youth, that tipped the scales between an evening of sleepless regrets at home and hours of neglected loneliness, watching the young fulfil the happy night. This and her courage weighed the balance down against the afflicting weariness of her sudden disillusion.

Therefore, she went, her aunt, in whose house she was a visitor, accompanying her. They arrived late, walking under the awning alone into the great mansion. Music, flowers, lovely dresses, and bright happy faces filled the air about them. The dancing feet, the flashing eyes, the swing of the music, the throng of graceful figures expressed one word—pleasure. Pleasure, of course, meant youth. Beneath the calm summer stars youth realised itself prodigally, reckless of years to follow. Under the same calm stars, some fifty miles away in Kent, her stretch of deserted lane flowed peacefully, never pausing, passing relentlessly out into unknown space beyond the edge of the world. A girl and a middle-aged woman bravely watched both scenes.

"Dreadfully overcrowded," remarked her prosaic aunt. "When I was a young thing there was more taste—always room to dance, at any rate."

"It is a rabble rather," replied the middle-aged woman, while the girl added, "but I enjoy it." She had enjoyed one duty-dance with an elderly man to whom her aunt had introduced her. She now sat watching the rabble whirl and laugh. Her friend, behind unabashed lorgnettes, made occasional comments.

"There's Mabel. Look at her frock, will you—the naked back. The way he holds her, too!"

She looked at Mabel Messenger, exactly her own age, wife of the successful engineer, yet bearing herself almost like a girl.

"*He's* away in Mexico, as usual," went on her aunt, "with somebody else, also as usual."

"I don't envy her," mentioned the middle-aged woman, while the girl added, "but she did well for herself, anyhow."

"It's a mistake to wait *too* long," was a suggestion she did not comment on.

The host's brother came up and carried off her aunt. She was left alone. An old gentleman dropped into the vacated chair. Only in the centre of the brilliantly lit room was there dancing now; people stood and talked in animated throngs, every seat along the walls, every chair and sofa in alcove corners occupied. The landing outside the great flung doors was packed; some, going on elsewhere, were already leaving, but others arriving late still poured up the staircase. Her loneliness remained unnoticed; with many other women, similarly stationed behind the whirling, moving dancers, she sat looking on, an artificial smile of enjoyment upon her face, but the eyes empty and unlit.

Two pictures she watched simultaneously—the gay ballroom and the lane that ran east and west.

Midnight was past and supper over, though she had not noticed it. Her aunt had disappeared finally, it seemed. The two pictures filled her mind, absorbed her. What she was feeling was not clear, for there was confusion in her between the two scenes somewhere—as though the brilliant ballroom lay set against the dark background of the lane beneath the quiet stars. The contrast struck her. How calm and lovely the night lane seemed against this feverish gaiety, this heat, this artificial perfume, these exaggerated clothes. Like a small, rapid cinema-picture the dazzling ballroom passed along the dark throat of the deserted lane. A patch of light, alive with whirling *animalculæ*, it shone a moment against the velvet background of the midnight country-side. It grew smaller and smaller. It vanished over the edge of the departing end. It was gone.

Night and the stars enveloped her, and her eyes became accustomed to the change, so that she saw the sandy strip of lane, the hazel bushes, the dim outline of the cottage. Her naked soul, it seemed again, stood facing an infinitude. Yet the scent of roses, of dew-soaked grass came to her. A blackbird was whistling in the hedge. The eastern end showed itself now more plainly. The tops of the trees defined themselves. There came a glimmer in the sky, an early swallow flashed past against a streak of pale sweet gold. Old Purdy, his tea-pail faintly rattling, a stir of thick white dust about his feet, came slowly round the curve. It was the sunrise.

A deep, passionate thrill ran through her body from head to feet. There was a clap beside her—in the air it seemed—as though the wings of the early swallow had flashed past her very ear, or the approaching sunrise called aloud. She turned her head—along the brightening lane, but also across the gay ballroom. Old Purdy, straightening up his bent shoulders, was gazing over the wicket-gate into her eyes.

Something quivered. A shimmer ran fluttering before her sight. She trembled. Over the crowd of intervening heads, as over the spiked top of the little gate, a man was gazing at her.

Old Purdy, however, did not fade, nor did his outline wholly pass. There was this confusion between two pictures. Yet this man who gazed at her was in the London ballroom. He was so tall and straight. The same moment her aunt's face appeared below his shoulder, only just visible, and he turned his head, but did not turn his eyes, to listen to her. Both looked her way; they moved, threading their way towards her. It meant an introduction coming. He had asked for it.

She did not catch his name, so quickly, yet so easily and naturally the little formalities were managed, and she was dancing. The same sweet, dim confusion was about her. His touch, his voice, his eyes combined extraordinarily in a sense of complete possession to which she yielded utterly. The two pictures, moreover, still held their place. Behind the glaring lights ran the pale sweet gold of a country dawn; woven like a silver thread among the strings she heard the blackbirds whistling; in the stale, heated air lay the subtle freshness of a summer sunrise. Their dancing feet bore them along in a flowing motion that curved from east to west.

They danced without speaking; one rhythm took them; like a single person they glided over the smooth, perfect floor, and, more and more to her, it was as if the floor flowed with them, bearing them along. Such dancing she had never known. The strange sweetness of the confusion that half-entranced her increased—almost as though she lay upon her partner's arms and that he bore her through the air. Both the sense of weight and the touch of her feet on solid ground were gone delightfully. The London room grew hazy, too; the other figures faded; the ceiling, half transparent, let through a filtering glimmer of the dawn. Her thoughts—surely, he shared them with her—went out floating beneath this brightening sky. There was a sound of wakening birds, a smell of flowers.

They had danced perhaps five minutes when both stopped abruptly as with one accord.

"Shall we sit it out—if you've no objection?" he suggested in the very instant that the same thought occurred to her. "The conservatory, among the flowers," he added, leading her to the corner among

185

scented blooms and plants, exactly as she herself desired. There were leaves and ferns about them in the warm air. The light was dim. A streak of gold in the sky showed through the glass. But for one other couple they were alone.

"I have something to say to you," he began. "You must have thought it curious—I've been staring at you so. The whole evening I've been watching you."

"I—hadn't noticed," she said truthfully, her voice, as it were, not quite her own. "I've not been dancing—only once, that is."

But her heart was dancing as she said it. For the first time she became aware of her partner more distinctly—of his deep, resonant voice, his soldierly tall figure, his deferential, almost protective manner. She turned suddenly and looked into his face. The clear, rather penetrating eyes reminded her of someone she had known.

At the same instant he used her thought, turning it in his own direction. "I can't remember, for the life of me," he said quietly, "where I have seen you before. Your face is familiar to me, oddly familiar—years ago—in my first youth somewhere."

It was as though he broke something to her gently—something he was sure of and knew positively, that yet might shock and startle her.

The blood rushed from her heart as she quickly turned her gaze away. The wave of deep feeling that rose with a sensation of glowing warmth troubled her voice. "I find in you, too, a faint resemblance to—someone I have met," she murmured. Without meaning it she let slip the added words, "when I was a girl."

She felt him start, but he saved the situation, making it ordinary again by obtaining her permission to smoke, then slowly lighting his cigarette before he spoke.

"You must forgive me," he put in with a smile, "but your name, when you were kind enough to let me be introduced, escaped me. I did not catch it."

She told him her surname, but he asked in his persuasive yet somehow masterful way for the Christian name as well. He turned round instantly as she gave it, staring hard at her with meaning, with an examining intentness, with open curiosity. There was a question on his lips, but she interrupted, delaying it by a question of her own. Without looking at him she knew and feared his question. Her voice just concealed a trembling that was in her throat.

"My aunt," she agreed lightly, "is incorrigible. Do you know I didn't catch yours either? Oh—I meant your surname," she added, confusion gaining upon her when he mentioned his first name only.

He became suddenly more earnest, his voice deepened, his whole manner took on the guise of deliberate intention backed by some profound emotion that he could no longer hide. The music, which had momentarily ceased, began again, and a couple, who had been sitting out diagonally across from them, rose and went out. They were now quite alone. The sky was brighter.

"I must tell you," he went on in a way that compelled her to look up and meet his intent gaze. "You really must allow me. I feel sure somehow, you'll understand. At any rate," he added like a boy, "you won't laugh."

She believes she gave the permission and assurance. Memory fails her a little here, for as she returned his gaze, it seemed a curious change came stealing over him, yet at first so imperceptibly, so vaguely, that she could not say when it began, nor how it happened.

"Yes," she murmured, "please——" The change defined itself. She stopped dead.

"I know now where I've seen you before. I remember." His voice vibrated like a wind in big trees. It enveloped her.

"Yes," she repeated in a whisper, for the hammering of her heart made both a louder tone or further words impossible. She knew not what he was going to say, yet at the same time she knew with accuracy. Her eyes gazed helplessly into his. The change absorbed her. Within his outline she watched another outline grow. Behind the immaculate evening clothes, a ragged, unkempt figure rose. A worn, ravaged face with young burning eyes peered through his own. "Please, please," she whispered again very faintly. He took her hand in his.

His voice came from very far away, yet drawing nearer, and the scene about them faded, vanished. The lane that curved east and west now stretched behind him, and she sat gazing towards the sunrise end, as years ago when the girl passed into the woman first.

"I knew—a friend of yours—Dick Messenger," he was saying in this distant voice that yet was close beside her, "knew him at school, at Cambridge, and later in Mexico. We worked in the same mines together, only he was contractor and I was—in difficulties. That made no difference. He—he told me about a girl—of his love and admiration, an admiration that remained, but a love that had already faded."

She saw only the ragged outline within the well-groomed figure of the man who spoke. The young eyes that gazed so piercingly into hers belonged to him, the seller of her dream of years before. It was to this ragged stranger in her lane she made her answer:

"I, too, now remember," she said softly. "Please go on."

"He gave me his confidence, asking me where his duty lay, and I told him that the real love comes once only; it knows no doubt, no fading. I told him this——"

"We both discovered it in time," she said to herself, so low it was scarcely audible, yet not resisting as he laid his other hand upon the one, he already held.

"I also told him there was only one true dream," the voice continued, the inner face drawing nearer to the outer that contained it. "I asked him, and he told me—everything. I knew all about this girl. Her picture, too, he showed me."

The voice broke off. The flood of love and pity, of sympathy and understanding that rose in her like a power long suppressed, threatened tears, yet happy, yearning tears like those of a girl, which only the quick, strong pressure of his hands prevented.

"The—little painting—yes, I know it," she faltered.

"It saved me," he said simply. "It changed my life. From that moment I began—living decently again—living for an ideal." Without knowing that she did so, the pressure of her hand upon his own came instantly. "He—he gave it to me," the voice went on, "to keep. He said he could neither keep it himself nor destroy it. It was the day before he sailed. I remember it as yesterday. I said I must give him something in return, or it would cut friendship. But I had nothing in the world to give.

"We were in the hills. I picked a leaf of fern instead. 'Fern-seed,' I told him, 'it will make you see the fairies and find your true dream.' I remember his laugh to this day—a sad, uneasy laugh. 'I shall give it to her,' he told me, 'when I give her my difficult explanation.' But I said, 'Give it with my love, and tell her that I wait.' He looked at me with surprise, incredulous. Then he said slowly, 'Why not? If—if only you hadn't let yourself go to pieces like this!'"

An immensity of clear emotion she could not understand passed over her in a wave. Involuntarily she moved closer against him. With her eyes unflinchingly upon his own, she whispered: "You were hungry, thirsty, you had no clothes. . . . You waited!"

"You're reading my thoughts, as I knew one day you would." It seemed as if their minds, their bodies too, were one, as he said the words. "You, too—you waited." His voice was low.

There came a glow between them as of hidden fire; their faces shone; there was a brightening as of dawn upon their skins, within their eyes, lighting their very hair. Out of this happy sky his voice floated to her with the blackbird's song:

"And that night I dreamed of you. I dreamed I met you in an English country lane."

"We did," she murmured, as though it were quite natural.

"I dreamed I gave you the fern leaf—across a wicket-gate—and in front of a little house that was our home. In my dream—I handed to you—a dream——"

"You did." And as she whispered it the two figures merged into one before her very eyes. "See," she added softly, "I have it still. It is in my locket at this moment, for I have worn it day and night through all these years of waiting." She began fumbling at her chain.

He smiled. "Such things," he said gently, "are beyond me rather. I have found you. That's all that matters. That"—he smiled again—"is real at any rate."

"A vision," she murmured, half to herself and half to him, "I can understand. A dream, though wonderful, is a dream. But the little fern you gave me," drawing the fine gold chain from her bosom, "the actual leaf I have worn all these years in my locket!"

He smiled as she held the locket out to him, her fingers feeling for the little spring. He shook his head, but so slightly she did not notice it.

"I will prove it to you," she said. "I must. Look!" she cried, as with trembling hand she pressed the hidden catch. "There! There!"

With heads close together they bent over. The tiny lid flew open. And as he took her for one quick instant in his arms the sun flashed his first golden shaft upon them, covering them with light. But her exclamation of incredulous surprise he smothered with a kiss. For inside the little locket there lay—nothing. It was quite empty.

Elsewhere and Otherwise

1

Among the genuinely strange stories of the world the strangest are those concerned with total disappearance. Apart from murders and destruction, where bodies are variously done away with, these "total disappearances" stand by themselves. Hi presto! and the fellow is gone, leaving not a wrack behind. The class, naturally, is small. Sydney Mantravers certainly belonged to it.

His case is interesting because, after a total disappearance of four years or so, he re-appeared. Not only did he re-appear, but he tried hard to tell me where he had been and what he had been doing during his long absence. He failed. Such experiences apparently seem uncommunicable in any language at the disposal of humanity, since they transcend anything humanity has undergone. The necessary words have not yet been coined. Before he could satisfy the thousand questions, I burned to ask him, questions, too, he might in time have partly answered, he was gone again, this time, as we say, for good.

I saw him go, I also saw him return: that is, I saw him disappear and re-appear. This was my unsought, unwelcome privilege. I was with him when he went, I was there when he came back. That final going in death robbed him, I firmly believe, of a burden of intense and marvellous confession, while it robbed me, but in particular robbed Dr. Vronski, his fellow student, of a rich harvest that was almost within my grasp—a revelation possibly that might have extended the present knowledge of the race.

Sydney Mantravers remains for me an extraordinary, even terrible problem. The mere mention of his name brings back the haunting radiance of his skin and eyes, the breath of some unearthly atmosphere which stimulates, while yet it cools, the blood. Eyes, skin and those thousand unanswered questions will haunt me till I, too, enter that silent darkness which makes reappearance apparently impossible.

His story is not really complicated. It is only that the sequence of its details covers a considerable time, a somewhat extensive field as well. It is best to tell it precisely as it happened. It began, then, in a London club, of which we were both members, and the occasion was August 4th, the night of the Ultimatum. War had been declared. England was at war with Germany. It was a night, as all remember, of intense excitement, of strange exaltation. Emotion was deep and real. It was not personal emotion. All of us, old and young, thought first of the country.

Mantravers, a distant cousin, was over sixty; I was a young officer of twenty-five. He had always been kind to me, I knew him fairly well, he had given me good tips in days gone by, we were friends of a kind, and his knowledge of life, as a rich, travelled, experienced bachelor, had often stood me in good stead. I respected, if rather dreaded, him, dreaded, that is, his strange highbrow theories, his attainments in higher physics, his amazing ideas about space and time and what not. Occasionally, he would pour something of all this into me, leaving me breathless, uneasy, perhaps a little scared.

My main interests being horses, women, money and personal advancement, the dread of his intellectual attainments was understandable, but he declared he liked to talk to me because, if ignorant, I was what he called "open-minded and intelligent," while I think he twigged some secret curiosity in me at the same time. I used to think of those occasional talks as "trying it on the dog," but when once I mentioned this, he shook his head. "No, no," he said, "it's not that. You happen to have an unusual mind, an original make-up. If you were trained a bit, I could tell you more. You could do things. Your ignorance is to the good, for you would have nothing to un-learn."

His greatest friend was a certain Dr. Vronski, whom I knew slightly too, another "advanced intellectual" whose experiments with glands, hypnotism, yoga, and other adventures into difficult fields brought him more than once into conflict with the Law. Vronski, I saw rarely, he never favoured me with special talks, but he treated me with a certain courtesy, almost a touch of deference in his manner somewhere, as though I interested him as a specimen, or as someone with possibilities that must be watched, at any rate, not damaged, this attitude due, I felt sure, to things my cousin had said about me. I was, naturally, in the confidence of neither. I mention this strange Dr. Vronski because of the role he inevitably played.

Another odd thing I must mention too at this point—the astonishing fact that Mantravers, already over sixty, looked even younger than Vronski, who was forty perhaps. My cousin's youthful air, indeed, was a standing joke almost. Not looked merely—he was young. He had not aged for years; for a quarter of a century, the story ran, he had not changed. Yet, when I caught up with the tale and its undeniable evidence, I had the convinced intuition that this amazing preservation had its mysterious roots, not in any experiment with glands, but in some secret adventure or discovery that had been undertaken by this amazing pair, had failed in Vronski's case, yet succeeded with my cousin. Sydney Mantravers, to put it ridiculously, had arrested decay, that gradual decay which we call growing older, for something like a score of years.

This was uppermost in my mind, even a rather dreadful barrier between us, each time we met and talked. Owing to my age much of the evidence, of course, was hearsay. Yet his curious youthfulness at sixty never failed to rise in my mind, often to strike me in the face with its uncanniness. He had somehow escaped a good twenty-five years of life. It was present in my mind when the Ultimatum came.

In the club, then, that night of strain and tension, I chanced to be sitting with him when the news we had all been waiting for came in—that war had been declared. We were all "worked up" and above ourselves. Mantravers, too, was all worked up—but, as I suddenly discovered with a shock, not about the declaration of war. He was stirred and excited about quite another matter, a wholly personal matter.

It was this difference of key that isolated him oddly from what all were feeling at the moment. While my mind was occupied entirely with questions about England, the Empire, our army and navy, with my own immediate prospects as a soldier as well, he kept asking me questions about some trivial personal matter. It got on my nerves a bit. Too excited to be puzzled, I felt first exasperated, then angry. He kept asking me if I remembered someone called Defrayne. But the name conveyed nothing to me. I had never heard it, and in any case what could it matter at such a time—unless, perhaps, this Defrayne had something to do with the war.

"He was in the 9th, you know," said Mantravers, as though Defrayne did, after all, have something to say to the war. I hardly listened, I was barely polite, my interest was so entirely elsewhere. The only point I noticed as curious, and had been aware of, indeed, even before— though the excitement had prevented my paying special attention to it—was the colour of my cousin's face. His skin was dead

193

white of rather a ghastly kind. "Try and remember," he urged. "Look back a bit. He was in your regiment. You must have heard of him." But I listened through a chorus of other voices, for we were all talking at once. . .

It was well after midnight, "God Save the King" already sung, when, to my surprise, Mantravers begged me to walk home with him, since it was on my own way, and when we reached his door asked, even insisted, that I should come in. He wished to tell me something. Once in his room, a drink before us, I remember that a sensation of discomfort, almost of alarm, came over me, and that I began to watch him more closely. My own preoccupation was still entirely with the war, of course.

Literally, I could think of nothing else. Yet his first question, since I had naturally expected something about Germany at least, returned to his own personal affair: "You tell me," he began in a low and rather tense voice, "that you don't recall Defrayne?" I did not, and I told him so again bluntly enough, exasperation and impatience showing plainly. I had hoped for something very different.

"Then—if you don't mind—I'll tell you something," he said, and there was a nervous hesitation, almost a demand for sympathy, in his manner that made me wonder. The pallor in his face again struck me sharply. "I must tell someone," he went on, "and you're the sort of listener I want. You're ignorant and simple, but you're open-minded." He paused for a second or two. "It's about Defrayne and myself," he added, almost in a whisper, and for some reason I felt a sudden shiver run down my back. It was due, this shiver, I verily believe, to an abrupt realisation that he looked twenty-five years younger than he was. I knew this in a general way, had wondered at it often enough. I now realised it. I felt at any rate this passing shiver.

2

Let me say at once that this announcement both bored and half in-furiated me, so that at first I listened perfunctorily—for what possible interest could Defrayne, whoever he was, have now?—but that later, if considerably later, my interest was so deeply caught that the war, with all it meant, slipped into the background. Strange, how many different things the mind can think of at the same time, how many different, even opposing, emotions it can hold simultaneously: the nearest ap-proach to four-dimensional time and space we know, perhaps. The thing he had to tell was so literally beyond belief that had he told it a week, even twenty-four hours before, it must have seemed wholly beyond belief, and I should have thought him mad.

Yet now, as I stared and listened, one ear cocked for the street where shouting, tumult and the National Anthem were still audible, I discovered that I did not entirely disbelieve. Nor did I, as must have been the case even the night before, regard my cousin as the victim of an elaborate hallucination, his mind deranged. On the contrary, I found myself listening to something that I felt was not necessarily impossible. And the idea dawned upon me, then, that this shock of the war, which in my case was profound and real, had worked in me some swift curious change. I felt in some way older, more developed. The shock had matured me abruptly, as it were with a jump. A new understanding of Mantravers was born in me. I understood, for instance, his reputation for giving "easy advice," for saying what the other fellow wanted to hear, rather than what he thought himself.

His immense knowledge of life had always brought people in trouble to him, young people especially. "Go and ask Mantravers, he'll tell you what to do," was a commonplace, though it would have been more correct to say "he'll tell you what you want to hear." I now realised suddenly that this was no false friendliness in him, nor lack of principle exactly, but was due rather to his deep understanding sympathy. He put himself so completely in the other fellow's shoes that he thought the other fellow's thoughts instead of his own. It was his own power of imaginative sympathy that sent him wrong. As my preoccupation with the war now slipped further and further into the background it flashed upon me, too, that after all I did perhaps remember having heard of Defrayne.

I did not know even how the name was spelt, when suddenly there leaped into my mind the word "de Frasne," and I dimly recalled that a young officer in my regiment, of that name pronounced Defrayne, had committed suicide a good many years ago. It was well before my time, but I had heard the case spoken of. In trouble about money, a woman, questions of personal honour involved, the young subaltern had put a bullet through his temple. But he had gone to see Mantravers first. As I listened to the tense, low-pitched voice in the chair opposite to mine, details filled in the story by degrees.

A good many years before, it appeared, young de Frasne had come to ask his advice. The young fellow had involved himself in a terrible mess, yet without having done anything wrong actually. Appearances were hopelessly against him. In a tragic mood, the youngster expected, wanted, tragic advice, and Mantravers took up his case with his usual intense sympathy. He felt, that is, exactly what young de Frasne felt. "Some chaps," he had suggested, "placed as you are, might, of course, rank honour higher than life. . ."

Young de Frasne went white. "You mean . . .?" he asked grimly. "There's always the emergency exit, isn't there?"

Mantravers mentioned, lending himself fully to the other's theatrical state of mind. It never occurred to him, he swore, that the stricken youngster would take his advice seriously. "I really thought," he now told me in his flat, "that he'd go home feeling himself a stage hero—then think out another way. He would come back in the morning. But he did not come back next morning, nor any other morning."

Mantravers, forgetting all about the interview to which he had not attached much importance, went to India that same week. He never heard till he came back to England a year later, and then he only heard it casually, that the young fellow had put a bullet in his brain. The lad had passed from his memory. He forgot even what he looked like. It gave him a horrid turn, he assured me, when he learned the truth, "for in a way, you see," he explained, "I felt responsible."

"That was some years ago," he was saying, my attention not yet wholly caught, "twenty or possibly twenty-five, and, as I've told you, I'd forgotten even what he looked like. My memory for faces is shocking. Last year in Dinard I talked and smoked, gambled too, with a delightful fellow whose face I remembered, but whose name, and where we had met, escaped me utterly, a fellow who knew me well too. He turned out to be the Italian barber in Regent Street who cuts my hair. . ."

"Yes, yes," I put in, making a show of interest, "but I'm rather like that, too."

He stared at me a moment. "Maybe," he countered briefly. "But a week ago," he went on, his face paler but his eyes oddly bright, "the same sort of thing happened to me again—at a party—and it turned out to be the last person in the world I expected."

I had not been listening properly, my thoughts still running on the war and what was coming, but the way he said this gave me a jolt for some reason. I felt a crawling again at the roots of my hair. I asked what he meant exactly.

"I went," he said in a lowered voice, "to an evening party an At Home of sorts, and as usual I ran into all kinds of people who knew me, but whose names—and where I had met them—I could not for the life of me remember. Among them was a young chap whose face I certainly knew, knew it as well as I know yours. But his name, or where we had met before, escaped me utterly. He seemed uncommonly pleased to run across me. It was quite awkward. He didn't say much, but what he did say was to the point. 'You've forgotten me,' he said, 'but I've been waiting for this chance. I've got a debt I want to repay.'

Having forgotten who he was, yet ashamed to let him see it, I murmured something vague about dining together some night. To my great embarrassment, he jumped at it. I was in a fix, you see. He was so determined, so intense. No memory of any debt occurred to me. I gave him my restaurant address, an Italian place near Leicester Square, and when he asked for a date, I rashly said that I was there most nights and that he would be very welcome. . . and then, as I was edging off, hoping to escape him, I found instead that he had somehow escaped me. He just melted away. The crowd was pretty thick, a regular crush, and how he managed it so quickly and cleverly puzzled me. One minute he was at my side, touching actually, the next—he wasn't——"

"He didn't say any more, you mean? Not even goodbye?" My interest was caught and held increasingly now.

Mantravers shook his head. "Just that he'd be there—and he was gone," came the reply. "And would you believe it," he went on, his eyes fixed hard on mine, "the very next night in my Italian restaurant, who should walk in but this very fellow. He came straight to my table too—and there I was, not knowing his name, or where we had met before, or what I could say to him, or what he wanted. It was a hell of a fix, eh? I felt an acute discomfort. This talk of a debt he had to settle was part of it, for I had a horrid feeling that I *ought* to remember something."

I watched my cousin more and more closely as my interest deepened, and the legend about his having somehow beaten time by twenty-five years came back to me Sharply. Very forcibly, unpleasantly too, it struck me, not that he could have passed for forty instead of sixty, but that he literally *was* forty instead of sixty—as though decay had been arrested. I cannot say why this conviction came over me so overwhelmingly just at this particular moment, nor can I explain why the roots of my hair began to crawl again. I only knew that I was vividly aware of it, and that a faint, unpleasant touch of chill came with it.

"You know," he went on, "how one is sometimes aware of things, little, trivial things, I mean, without actually noticing them? Well," he explained, "I noticed in this way one or two odd little details. Not important things, mind you. The important thing was to remember his name, where we had met, under what circumstances, but instead of that I noticed his old-fashioned dinner-jacket, the crease down the *side* of his trousers, his pumps—all of them details of dress no longer used. They had passed away—before your time, of course—but——"

"He dined with you? You dined together, I mean?" I brought him back. I was impatient. The cold I felt increased.

Mantravers shrugged his shoulders: his face seemed to grow paler still.

"He sat at my table," he replied, "for I couldn't help myself." His voice went lower than ever, and he looked over his shoulder. "I told the waiter to lay another place, and while that was being done, we talked. He talked, rather."

"Of course, you remembered then gradually? The talk brought him back?"

Again, he shook his head. "That's the odd part of it. The feeling of familiarity, of knowing him quite well, grew stronger and stronger, yet never fulfilled itself. It got no further. Something in my mind deliberately concealed him from me. Kept him hidden. You have guessed, of course, already. But I didn't—till the end." A perceptible shiver ran through his body. "All I knew was that while he talked, I was longing and longing to get rid of him, hoping he would go, wondering what I could do to bring this about, but listening all the time to what he said—as though I couldn't help myself and bad to listen."

He stopped and took a gulp of his whisky. asked what kind of things the unwelcome, half-recognised guest talked about. What did he say? It was plain that my cousin wanted to keep this back, while eager at the same time to tell it. He betrayed a touch of embarrassment, of awkwardness, almost of shyness.

"Well, sort of personal things," he brought it out at length hesitatingly, "said no one gave better advice than I did, it was a privilege to talk to me, that I had helped him once, and that now he could do the same for me—and owed it to me. That was what I disliked so— owed it to me—because—because our troubles were similar. *That*, he repeated more than once, was why he was able to come at all."

He raised his glass again, but did not drink.

"It was then," he whispered almost, "that was the first time, I mean, I began to feel jumpy."

"Jumpy!" To tell the truth I felt jumpy myself as I listened.

The strange maturity, the sudden growth in myself already referred to, began to work in me, bringing a sharper, deeper insight with it, so that I knew, as with a flash of clairvoyance, that Mantravers himself was in some kind of personal trouble. Abruptly, this revelation came, a sense of discomfort with it, for I understood that he was both anxious to tell it and not to tell it. I waited. In the end, of course, he told it, and it involved a woman, money, honour, and all in a distinctly unpleasant way that heaped appearances—though he had done no dishonourable act—against him. Only the bare outline was given to me, the outline of a very nasty fix.

"To my utter astonishment," Mantravers went on, "the fellow referred to this, as though he knew all about it. He did know all about it. It amazed me; I was flabbergasted. I felt as if hypnotised, for he had a dreadfully insistent way with him, so that I *had* to listen. And my eyes kept wandering to a dull red mark he had in his right temple. I had not noticed it before. It seemed to glow. It fascinated me, that mark, and from time to time the fellow's hand, as he passed it across his forehead, let his fingers trail and linger over it, deliberately, I could have sworn. He saw my eye on it. 'I've been waiting a long time for this,' he said. 'It was difficult to arrange, but now you're in much the same boat I was in once; now I can give you advice so that you'll understand.'

"A sort of icy smile ran over his face. 'You see,' he added, 'by rights I ought to have stayed here another twenty-five years. My life would have run to fifty-one.' And with that he abruptly stood up to go. The red mark on his temple glowed and spread a little. I got up too. 'Meet me in my house tomorrow,' he said, 'meet me at six o'clock,' a strange compelling power in his voice and fixed staring eyes. 'I shall be there waiting for you.' With that he turned, I saw the red mark flame out and die away, I saw him walk across the floor between the tables and go out of the restaurant."

It was only at this final moment, my cousin assured me, his voice a whisper now, that he recognised de Frasne, as though the shutter that all this time had deliberately hidden him from memory, was lifted, also deliberately. Yet no shock accompanied the revelation. His attention, rather, was drawn to quite normal things about him—the waiter, though he had laid a second cover, as bidden, was hovering near, saying something, asking, indeed, whether he should bring the soup since perhaps the expected gentleman was not coming after all, and a moment later serving the single plate and clearing away the second unwanted cover.

I sat silent for some minutes, finding nothing to say, wishing only that my cousin would remove his fixed stare from my face, and relieved when at last he did so and raised his glass and drank. Yet a lot of things crowded jostling in my mind during that brief silence. While resisting with all my might the shivers down my spine, my main thought, the one that obsessed me chiefly, was, oddly enough, not the wild, forbidding story itself, but that other, almost equally sinister legend about my cousin's personal appearance.

His story bewildered me beyond anything I could understand, of course, but it was this point of his physical preservation that for some reason kept intruding dominatingly, forcing its way see other thoughts and feelings. That he actually looked, and was, a whole generation younger than he had the right to be, that he had evaded, as it were, the march and decay of something like twenty-five years, that those missing years lay in wait for him, ready to pounce, and that this period was just about what de Frasne would have lived had he not killed himself—it was impossible and outrageous ideas of this kind that whirled through my mind in such a torrent that I felt as though I were going mad. I made a violent effort to get myself in hand.

Mantravers' eyes were off me for a moment while he raised his glass, but as he drank, his stare fixed me again over the tumbler's rim. I remember shaking myself free, shaking myself, as it were, mentally and physically, opening my mouth to speak.

Mantravers was before me, however. "I'm going to the house," he said quietly, his voice no longer whispering. "I shall keep the appointment. I must, you see."

It gave me a shock to hear him, but his next words brought back another thing I dreaded more—the long cold shuddering down my spine.

"I want you to come with me—in case I go."

It was the last word that made the shudder repeat itself, and so uncontrollably that my hand was trembling as I lifted my own glass. That "go" was for some reason awful, so that I dared not question even....

Mantravers had my promise before I left his flat, though it took him the best part of an hour to obtain it.

The turmoil in my young mind is understandable without detailed description. England was at war with Germany, I was in the army, my regiment absorbed my thoughts ... For a couple of hours Mantravers had torn my interest away to his own amazing story, but the moment I left him the war and its immediate personal claims returned. I cursed myself for having given that promise. At the same time, I was gripped by the unusual tale. I had a deep respect for my cousin. If his reputation, with its semi-legendary atmosphere of suggesting the impossible and supernatural, made me uneasy in his presence, his personality impressed me to a point that made me feel he was not quite as other men are.

He was un-ordinary in some peculiar way, extremely gifted, of course, as well; I knew his courage; I looked up to him. His invitation probably flattered me into the bargain. . . I was a little scared, to tell the truth, rather as a schoolboy might be scared, and the idea occurred to me to get in touch with Dr. Vronski, his friend and companion in adventure. I felt the need of advice. Time, however, made this out of the question. I expected to get my army orders any moment.

In the end I kept my promise, kept the appointment punctually.

And, once again, the first thing that impressed me when we met in the club was his uncommon, even uncanny, youthfulness. I swear he might have been my captain. I mention this particularly because of what came later, if a good deal later, and that it should have struck me so vividly, that at first it ousted my thoughts and fears of the adventure to follow, is worth emphasis. Coming straight from a feverish, excited day full of thoughts about kit, orders, fighting, France, even about being killed, I found myself registering first this conviction, this positive certainty, that he had somehow managed to evade a long toll of years.

His air and attitude, his very atmosphere, conveyed this ridiculous assurance in a way I cannot describe, though the unwelcome shiver it caused in my spine is easily told. A moment later, then, I found myself, instantly and unaccountably, swept up into his mood, into his stream of thought and feeling, so that this world's affairs, even a war with Germany, seemed somehow of less account than what he had afoot. His face, curiously unlined and young, was also distinctly pale, there was a shrinking in his manner. Had I not known his courage, I should perhaps have credited him with what we youngsters called "cold feet."

"I'm obliged to you," he remarked quietly, "for being so punctual. But I knew you would not fail me. It's rather out of your categories, you see," he added after a slight hesitation, "this proposed visit of mine." What he meant precisely, God only knows: I only know myself that I was aware of a queer pang as of something that both attracted and repelled me with a certain violence—by which I mean, perhaps, that I both understood yet did not understand. It was the part of me that understood that attracted me.

201

We set out on foot at once for a walk of a mile or two to de Frasne's house in Bayswater. All these years it had remained empty, apparently neither sold nor rented. The region, prosaic and respectable, reassured me, for how could anything "unearthly" happen in Bayswater? He had the key, he mentioned. And the only other remark he made during that walk of ours over half an hour was a curious one, uttered with breaks and at intervals moreover, for I said nothing: "If what I think is true," came in that low voice that again rather gave me the creeps, "young de Frasne . . . since his death . . . has been in other time and space . . . When he said that he had been waiting for me . . . it was really I who . . . had been waiting for him . . ."

And then suddenly, as I made no comment, he raised his voice almost to a shout that made me start. "You follow me?" he cried. I managed a reply of sorts. I was following, of course. "I didn't mean literally," he explained, lowering his voice; "I meant—do you understand?" My face, doubtless, gave my answer clearly enough. "No, no, how could you?" he went on, half to himself. "You've never transcended human experience, so you couldn't. Naturally, you couldn't. You only know time in a line, as past, present, future. Vronski and I have known it . . . otherwise . . . in two dimensions, two at least . . . A changed consciousness—that's the trick, you see—can function in different time . . . . elsewhere and otherwise——"

A sudden flash came to me, so that I stopped him on the pavement.

"Living backwards *or* forwards, you mean?" I cried.

He stared at me with a kind of exultation. I remember the pallor of his skin, the brightness in his eyes. "I imagine parallel is the right, the better word," he said, with a kind of odd breathlessness, and then he added quickly, "I felt sure—I always knew—you had it in you—somewhere. Death of unexpected kind, selfinflicted, before the natural moment, I mean. . . and I showed him the way . . . would make this possible probably . . ."

His voice died away into undistinguishable phrases mumbled below his breath. We hurried on. I grunted, stared, and mopped my face. There was only one horror in me—that he would explain more clearly what was in him. I went ahead of him, going faster and faster.

We reached the street, he found the number, we stopped outside an empty house that showed distinct evidence of long neglect, smothered in boards and signs of house-agents. Mantravers went up the eight steps, I following him. He put the key in the door, opened it, then handed me the key.

He gave me a searching look, a sort of frozen smile on his lips, his pallor very marked. "You needn't come in with me," he whispered, "and you needn't lock the door. Keep the key. I'm going in alone. I *think* I know what I'm in for," he added, "but remember, if I'm right in my conjecture, no one need look for me. I shall, at any rate, be *here*."

He looked me straight in the eyes, and his skin was white as linen. He was not frightened. He struck me as a man in a dream, but an awful, icy dream that shattered ordinary experience. The door banged behind him. I stuck my ear close and listened intently. I heard his footsteps clearly as they went across the carpetless hall, then up the wooden stairs, then along a landing, fainter and fainter, after which came silence. I found myself in a shudder, standing on the outer steps, trembling all over, excited beyond words, my heart positively thumping, my forehead wet with perspiration. I waited some fifteen minutes. There was not a sound from inside the house. The traffic went past noisily. It was already after sunset, the dusk falling. I decided to go in. I put in the key, pushed the door open and walked cautiously inside. I closed the door behind me.

Daylight still hung about in palish patches, but there were shadows too. The hall gaped as though about to utter, but no sound came. Peering into two large empty unfurnished rooms, I went slowly upstairs, the stairs he had trodden just before me, along the deserted landing, passing from failing light across little gulfs of shadow. Everything gaped, gaped with emptiness, dust lay all over, decay, neglect, cobwebs, silence, vacancy, motionless air and musty odours—otherwise nothing. All windows everywhere were closed and fastened. I felt my skin crawl with goose-flesh, and the hair moved on my scalp.

I persisted. I searched every single room, even the attics and the kitchen and scullery below. I called aloud. I waited, listening. I stared and watched. Taking quick steps, I then paused, every sense alert, intent. I called again, but no answer came. No hint of a human presence was discoverable. I searched, as the saying is, from roof to cellar. That I found the courage to do so seems to me now the proof of my intensely alive curiosity, even of something in me that believed, and hoped, and perhaps expected—to find a clue . . .

Half an hour later I stood on the outer steps again in the evening air, the street now draped with dusk turning towards night. I decided I must find Dr. Vronski. I must see him at once, without delay. He, rather than the police, was the one to be informed. But at my rooms I found peremptory orders that admitted of no delay or compromise.

I left England a few hours later, the key still in my pocket, the door it belonged to unlocked. There had just been time for me to send a hasty letter to Dr. Vronski giving the facts as I knew them, and for a word of reply to reach me:

"No cause for anxiety. I've heard from S. M. Do your job—but don't forget him."

With this measure of relief—for I should otherwise have thought that Mantravers had shot himself or leaped from a window to his death—I crossed the Channel, an insignificant unit in that heroic B.E.F. Since Vronski had "heard from him," he was still alive—somewhere.

What happened to men's minds during those four years lies, of course, beyond easy understanding—by those who never experienced the strains and stresses they were subject to. Any man capable of going over the 'edge, went over it. For myself, I cannot say. After a year's anguish, tension, suffering that I swear lie beyond human expression in words, I was taken prisoner, and for the next three years I languished in a German prison camp. Nothing can extenuate or excuse the inhuman horror of a bad German prison camp. My own was of the worst. Any prisoner who survived the process that stunned, stupefied, brutalised his soul, had in him something unusual. The life taught him to search the very marrow of his soul's bones to find relief from daily and nightly torture of excruciating kind.

My point here is that, while I could not honestly find myself unusual in any way, I did find relief; and I found a good deal of this relief in speculating about escape—but I mean escape in space and time. Any real relief inside that barbed wire had to be of mental or spiritual kind, imaginative if you will. The point is that I found it to some extent in speculating about the wild ideas of Vronski and Mantravers. My mind, quite possibly, went a bit over the edge, as I called it above, though I cannot judge of that.

My speculations, such as they were, began after a letter I received from Dr. Vronski, it ran briefly, also disconnectedly, since the censor's attentions had maimed it badly:

You will like to know about your cousin. The police gave up the search long ago. The Courts have given leave now to assume him dead. But I know he is. . . not dead. . . conceivably within reach even. He is not unhappy, nor is he happy, for he is different. I am not in communication with him, but I know . . .

alive and well ... will come back when you come back ... you, so to speak, the point in our space and time ... point he left at . . . Shown the way by de Frasne into other conditions. He is, for the moment, elsewhere and otherwise ... for him literally for a moment only. If this reaches you, do not worry ... think about it only ... no help from you needed, but sympathetic thought of most concentrated kind can keep open. . . .

And the letter closed thus abruptly as though the censor rather late in the day imagined a code.

I had years of "sympathetic thought," stimulated by fierce mental and physical anguish of distinctly "concentrated" kind.

Let us leave it at that. . . .

Mantravers had disappeared, leaving not a wrack behind. Hi presto! and the fellow was gone. He vanished—into an empty and unfurnished house. He was just over sixty when he went, and he was just over sixty when he returned. I was present when he returned and I can testify. I knew him before and after. The clothes he went in were the clothes he came back in— an everyday tweed suit with a blue bow tie. He had been away for over four years. He came into view again, reemerged into our ordinary three-dimensional categories, into our ordinary life and world that is, precisely and exactly as he left it—almost. Changes of a kind there were, but to describe them here would be to anticipate unduly. They shall be told in their proper place and sequence. . .

Other letters from Vronski reached me in my prison camp, though most of them, since they dealt with "escape," were too censored to be intelligible. A book or two came as well, articles and pamphlets, undoubtedly sent by him. My mind, whether "over the edge" or not, being neither mathematical nor metaphysical, made little headway with them, though I read—waded through them rather—with undeniable interest and excitement. Other cases of "total disappearance" were discussed and analysed, and such cases, apparently, were not so rare as I had imagined.

There were certain places, certain spots of loneliness on the world's surface, regions of wild and hostile desolation, regions avoided rather by commonplace humanity, where such queer "vanishings" had occurred too frequently to be normally explained, and my mind, "ignorant but open," simple certainly, struggled with these strange and semi-marvellous accounts, accounts, moreover, painfully documented with names and dates and other evidence we usually accept as honest.

Such disappearances, however, hardly applied, I felt, to a Bayswater street and a dwelling-house plastered with agents' boards. It was the deeper, more philosophical articles that held my interest chiefly, the writers who suggested that "escape" from the limited life we know was possible, desirable as well. Life, declared one writer, was nothing but a prison-house, a cage, and we were wise to admit frankly that it was horrible. We were prisoners in it, slaves, caught helplessly by the bars of space and time which were our ghastly limitations.

Yet a way of escape, "though few there be that find it," offered, the ABC of this way being to "go against nature," since nature kept us stupefied within our bars. The great majority, of course, dominated by the herd instinct, obeyed the shibboleths of the herd. These never could, because they never wanted to, escape. Only the few who re-sisted the stunning, deadening influence of the herd, of nature, need ever dare to make the attempt . . .

A strange new world of possibilities opened before me. I did not close my mind against them, but merely wondered, dreamed, and speculated. Did I actually make tactical attempts, following the guard-ed hints and clues, attempts to practise in my own being the amazing rules laid down? I had these awful, bitter hours to fill as best I could. Physical efforts were not' available, I must fill my life mentally, imagi-natively, or else, as we described it among ourselves, and as I saw hap-pening daily, hourly, among my fellow-prisoners, "go potty." My long sleepless nights, my days of endless anguish, sought what alleviation they could find. . .

Another dimension in space was easier to conceive, I found, than another dimension in time. Moreover, among my fellow-prisoners, was a professor of sorts, a Russian, to whom I talked a good deal, and he tried to explain the space business to me with at least a glimmer-ing of success. He showed me how a fellow could be in two places at once, in London, say, and Calcutta. Taking a sheet of paper from some old letter, he marked Calcutta at one end and London at the other. He told me to imagine people living on the surface of this sheet, people who knew only length and breadth—a world of two dimensions. "Of height, remember," he warned me in his broken English, "they know nothing. They have no perception of height—cannot even think of it. They are two-dimensional beings in a two-dimensional world."

Well, I understood that all right.

"A fellow in their world," he explained, "can be in London or in

Calcutta, but he cannot be in both." It was obvious enough.

Then he bent the sheet of paper. He doubled it together, so that the spot of London and the spot of Calcutta lay cheek by jowl. They coincided.

"In bending the sheet," he added, "I have made it pass through height, of course."

I agreed.

"Yet, in the result, Calcutta and London lie together. The man in Calcutta is in London too. He is in two places at once."

We glared at one another. "It is only an analogy, of course," he reminded me, "and it has the fallacy that all analogies must hold."

I got an inkling of what he meant, but when he talked in similar fashion about time, I could not follow him. It gave me a sick headache merely.

From the books I read and the thoughts I thought, I gathered anyhow that brains, tongues and pens have speculated freely enough as about these very rare "total disappearances." I gathered likewise that such speculations were somewhat negligible, and that only a mere handful who had made practical experiments—among them undoubtedly Vronski and my cousin—could offer anything of tangible value. Among the sparse elect, none the less, I caught strange whispers. A notion grew in the deepest part of me that another dimension in space could explain this wiping out of a physical body, and that such a one, dropping away into a direction at right angles to the three we know so well, drops obviously and naturally clean out of sight. He passes into a region no sense of ours can ever plumb. Out of our known, familiar space he has dropped elsewhere—and otherwise as well, since a new direction in space involves necessarily a new dimension in time.

Time, as we know it, runs forward only in a line; but in two dimensions it would run backwards, or parallel as well. Not only could he be in two places at once, but he could be also in two times at once. He could do two things—two things otherwise mutually self-exclusive—at once.

"At any given moment," said my fellow-prisoner, "you have a choice of doing several things. Of these you choose one. Actually, you might choose any of the others. You select one, however, and do it. That one thing actualises."

I nodded, as much as my approaching headache allowed.

"Now, listen: In time of more than one dimension you could

choose more than one thing. You could do several things at once—and they all would actualise. . . ."

At which point my sick headache usually developed suddenly, so that my friend continued to talk without my understanding.

I acquired, at any rate, a sort of smattering of comprehension.

"Anyone escaping into other time and space," he finished later, "would come back, you see, at the point he left, even if years of *our* time had passed meanwhile—years or a few minutes only. . . ."

Such explanations, I found, supported themselves, loosely enough, with the jargon of Relativity. Einstein, the magician thinker, was called in to help. To me it remained a "line of speculation," than which the sober mind would say no more.

Mantravers, at any rate, disappeared . . . and since he vanished when war was declared, and reappeared shortly after the Armistice, there were those who sneered that he had been in hiding. This was untrue, absurd as well. No more patriotic Englishman ever lived. Nor was his courage questionable. The date of his going and returning had nothing to do with the War. The Great War, indeed, was almost a trivial item in his strange experience, and his disappearance I incline to think, was enforced, and singularly enforced.

★★★★★★★★★★★★★★★★★

It was January 1919, when I found myself in London again. My intention, backed by a deep instinct, was to go back to the house where Sydney Mantravers had left me standing on the steps: to enter the building, if still unoccupied; to walk through all its rooms and passages again. I wished to do this alone, and to do it before I had spoken with Dr. Vronski, or even seen him. Vronski's talk and information could come later. I kept my return secret from him.

If I never quite explained or justified this deep instinct even to myself, I recognised that no mere morbid curiosity lay in it anywhere. Clearest in my mind was the desire to make this visit and inspection before I became immersed again in the world of ordinary everyday affairs, that is, before some inner mood or attitude acquired in my years of solitude had dissipated. During those prison years of introspection, thought, speculation, even of experiment as well, something had come to life in me that contact with the bustling outer world, I knew, must smash to pieces.

It was as though I had dreamed of another order of existence, had even fringed the perception of entirely new categories. Two sets of values at any rate, appeared in some depth of my being that was only accessible to me with the greatest difficulty and effort. I was aware of them, no more than that; the slightest mistake, of clumsiness or stupidity, on my part would send them plunging for ever beyond my reach. This extremely delicate balance I perceived. The disappearance of Mantravers was concerned with the set of values I had dreamed of, possibly just begun to understand, to acquire even, in my bitter years of prison life. My instinct was to visit the house while this still remained and before its fading, already in progress, resulted in complete forgetfulness.

Did I expect to see him too, actually to see some figure or outline of the man who had disappeared over four years ago and was now legally dead? I cannot truthfully say, although I believe some uncanny, rather awful hope lurked deep down in me. . . .I reached London at noon, my return to England, my presence in town, a well-kept secret; not wasting a minute I was walking up the Bayswater side-street by the afternoon, the January daylight already fading, and it must have been close on four o'clock when the house came into view, plastered, I noticed, still with agents' boards, and therefore unlet, unoccupied. The stained and dirty window-panes had no blinds, the patchy walls showed no signs of recent paint, the air of neglect and disuse were the same as before, only more marked.

The key, in case of need, the very key my cousin had handed to me himself, was in my pocket, kept carefully all these years. In the pocket of my mackintosh my fingers gripped it tightly, even a trifle feverishly, as though it might somehow melt away and defeat my purpose. I kept feeling it over, indeed, as a man might finger banknotes to make quite sure he still had them safely. A definite realisation, moreover, came to me as I walked up the steps—that I was both exhilarated and frightened, and that while the exhilaration contained an immense, a biting curiosity, the fear was partly due to a sudden wave of depression that had come upon me.

Was this depression, this lowering of vitality, I remember asking myself, similar to what the two ladies experienced just as they passed the threshold into their unique other worldly Adventure in Versailles? The vivid detail rose up from my reading in my prison camp. It was certainly not a physical fear, it was perhaps a mental, a spiritual hint of terror, as best I could diagnose it, for the idea appeared that my ordinary equipment of mind and body contained no weapon to help me in what *might* be coming. Yet a touch of horror I had known before "going over the top" seemed in it too. My hand, at any rate, was trembling as I took the big key and began to fit it into the lock of the front door—at which very moment a noise of tapping on glass somewhere above me made me pause.

It sounded like fingers drumming or tapping faintly on a window-pane. Startled, I looked up quickly, and there, at a window on the second floor, two storeys above, I saw a face peering down at me through the dusty pane, a face I recognised, the face of my cousin, Sydney Mantravers. Looking over his shoulder, and also staring down at me, was the outline of a second face, but a face that was wholly strange to me. I had just time to note that it wore a small moustache, when both the faces withdrew sharply backwards from the window so that they were no longer visible, and it was in this same instant that my fingers, fumbling with the key automatically, discovered that that door was not locked at all but was indeed already open into the hall.

It is astonishing what thoughts, and how trivial ones at that, start up in the mind as it meets an unusual shock or crisis, for at this moment when an unearthly acceptance and a vehement incredulity clashed together, the one definite impression I could recognise was—that youthful appearance. This flashed over me even as the faces of both withdrew, and it was not the visage of a possible de Frasne, dead these thirty years and more, that made my flesh creep, but the unquestionable assurance that Mantravers, whom I knew to be over sixty, looked hardly forty. The amazing fact that he had "disappeared" for an interval of four years seemed left out of account at this instant; it was the uncanny air of having missed decay for a generation that leaped back into my mind with horror.

Then, before I knew what my shaking legs were doing, they had taken me automatically into the hall, and the front door closed behind me with a bang. Standing there in the semi-darkness, it was all I could do to hold myself together, and I mean my "self" precisely, for at first everything I was accustomed to hold on to in a time of stress seemed wavering like a jelly that must any instant dissolve. To hold myself steady, to keep control, was what occupied my mind in that first moment of entering the hall; there was no room in me for anything but this tremendous effort; and in making it, a cold perspiration burst out all over my skin. I only recall that the exhilaration had left me entirely, while the depression had greatly intensified. The curiosity, if of rather an icy kind, remained, but it was fed by a lowering vitality.

The house, as I went in, was very still, no sound audible. It was also dark, all outlines heavily draped, no edges visible. I stood stock still, shivering and afraid, even unable, to move. I could not stir a foot. There was a queer sense that everything had stopped moving the instant I came in, that a crowd had rushed into hiding, that my arrival was anticipated by a fraction of a second; but this, I knew, was due to imagination only. Actually, nothing but emptiness and vacancy surrounded me. The gloom concealed no living thing.

An unoccupied, unfurnished house at the best of times is a ghostly, even a hostile place, but this particular one wrapped in the wintry dusk, turned the perspiration cold against my skin. The conviction that upstairs, perhaps even now watching me, was a man who had been "dead" four years, a companion with him who had left the world by suicide long before him, that this awful pair hidden among the untenanted rooms above, stood waiting to look me in the eyes, perchance to touch me, ask me questions, reveal their knowledge and their presence—this all gave me a sensation of dread and horror that paralysed my muscles. I stood there as though turned into stone, while the echoes from the banging door rolled on through the series of unoccupied halls and chambers, then died away into a silence that was even worse.

Had I seen Mantravers at that moment, heard his descending step, or caught the sound of his voice calling me by name, I believe my heart must have stopped dead. Already it was beating like a troubled engine, my breathing difficult as well. Afraid to go forward, afraid to turn back and go out, my shaking body leaning for support against the wall, stood where it was, my powers of self-control gone all to pieces.

What on earth was I to do next? The answer came unexpectedly. A light flashed suddenly across the ceiling, darting its bright beam swiftly from point to point, and with it came the sound of footsteps. Someone was moving cautiously along the landing above, and the flash came obviously from a shifting electric torch. I slipped back into the corner, every nerve taut with horrified anticipation.

"Who's there?" called a man's voice loudly. "Who is it?"

I made an attempt to answer, but no sound left my throat. The same second the steps quickened, left the upper landing, and began to come down the carpetless stairs. I saw the dark outline of a man shading his eyes with one hand from the glare of a torch he shifted to and fro in front of him. He came down slowly, cautiously, treading each board with care. A dozen steps from the bottom he stopped and turned the full light of the brilliant torch upon me where I crouched in the angle against the wall. I stood helpless in this dazzling blaze, the stream showing me up mercilessly from head to foot, the man who held it of course invisible.

"Oh, it's you!" came a voice of startled surprise. "So, you're back in England! That explains it. . ." as the speaker turned the light upon himself, so that I recognised, with a surprise equal to his own, but with a relief he could hardly have guessed, the face and figure of Dr. Vronski.

I could think of nothing to say or do except what I *did* say and do:

I pointed overhead. "Hush! Hush!" I cried in a stifled whisper. "He's up there. I've just seen him. He tapped on the window—beckoned. He's come back, by God————"

"Who?" he asked, his voice, it seemed to me, strangely calm, his manner quiet and matter of fact, the odd composure of the man adding to my horror.

"Mantravers," I whispered. "I saw him at the window. He tapped. Somebody was with him. Up there on the next floor close behind you."

He did not even turn. He had reached my side by now. His face was close to mine, so that I saw the fierce light shining in his eyes, but there was no excitement in him. Cold and collected as a fish he seemed.

"He is expecting you," he said, as quietly as you please. "The other will not stay————stay *here*, I mean. He has led him to the point where *you* are needed. The point you left him at four years ago." His eyes ran over me like a moving flame. "To him—remember if you can—it's not even a minute."

I felt my body slipping down against the wall as though my legs were gone. The whole house, it seemed, was listening to our whispered words. I heard the staircase creak. The rumble of street traffic was audible outside. I caught myself thinking that I would have given my very soul to see an omnibus, a good, everyday red omnibus, a taxi cab, a policeman. What was to come next, I dared not even think about. Vronski stood close beside me, our shoulders touching. His unescapable eyes ran over me in liquid fire. What would he say next? What would he ask of me?

And then a crackling voice rang out upstairs, a voice I knew and recognised. Though a curious distance was in it, yet a distance that could not muffle, it was sharp and distinct. It called my name.

"Come," said Vronski calmly. "You must come up and help him. He is expecting you."

212

It came over me suddenly that the entire experience was a dream. Things in a dream happened just like this. The sense of surprise, the power of criticism, are absent. Mantravers, Vronski, myself were all figures in a dream. The whole business belonged to a dream. I, the dreamer, should presently wake up. Yet while this thought flashed, its opposite, appearing concurrently, flashed with it: that my consciousness, namely, had changed, and that I was beyond the emotions that pertain to normal consciousness. As consciousness changes, grows, the universe it perceives grows and changes with it. . . .

"In a sense that's exactly true," I heard Vronski murmur as we crossed the silent hall, and it did not occur to me as in the least odd that he should know what I was thinking. "We *are* in a dream-world here and now, a dream condition, a dream civilisation. We are, that is, so little conscious that what we think real is actually hardly more than a dream-state . . ." and his voice died away among the shadows.

I heard this without an atom of surprise, without a tremor of disbelief. Philosophical talk at such a moment! And yet somehow occasioning no astonishment! Obviously, the experience was all a dream.

"He woke up," the voice ran on as we reached the staircase, "and consequently he disappeared. That is, he left our dream-conditions."

I could not quite follow that. I was suddenly stiff with terror too, thinking of the man waiting for us up that dark flight of stairs. It seemed absurd and horrible, comic and tragic, that we should be exchanging philosophical comments at such a moment.

"He became aware of other conditions, though these are about us always, and only a change in our perceptive apparatus is needed————"

I gave a little sharp cry unwittingly, as though the terror had crawled into my throat, and his voice fell away while he took my arm firmly, for I had stumbled over the first step as we began to mount the staircase. "Don't be frightened, don't feel fear, or anything negative," he concluded, his arm preventing me falling. "Feel sympathy, curiosity, interest, even scepticism if you like. But don't feel fear," he repeated. "I have come to this house four times a week ever since he left us. I have sat here waiting, hoping for hours on end, without result, though once—once only—I saw de Frasne—rushing— rushing with the speed of light and through every room and passage simultaneously—rushing, I tell you, with etheric speed, etheric omnipresence—but of him, no sign, and I knew at last that only you could get him back, because you were with him when he went. You are a signpost, if you like, the point of departure and so the point of return—of simultaneous return. Above all, therefore, feel no fear, for fear repels and blocks————"

A cry interrupted this amazing flow. It sounded overhead again, in the dark space of the landing. It called my name, but it was fainter than before and held a curious touch of fading distance. We were halfway up the stairs. I stopped dead.

"Answer him, answer," urged Vronski quickly, almost passionately. "Say you're here." And making a great effort, I obeyed.

"I'm here, Sydney, I'm coming to you," my voice rose out of some kind of automatism. "Hold on!" And Vronski, hastening his step, dragged me with him.

"Remember," he whispered in my ear, "remember all he says, for he can tell marvellous things, though probably to you only."

We reached the landing, and Vronski flashed his torch along the corridor, flooding it with light, illuminating several doors, a whole series of doors belonging, apparently, to bedrooms, and one of these doors stood open. It was standing ajar. These details showed up with vivid clearness instantly, but it was something else I saw simultaneously that my attention fastened on with immediate horror, although horror is not the accurate word, since the amazement in me—I can only call it an explosion of amazement—was of too vast, too strange a kind to include a negative emotion such as horror. For I saw several figures, a series of them, all moving with great rapidity, moving in the three directions known to us, up, down, across, yet all moving in some incredible manner simultaneously—a figure I recognised, the figure of de Frasne.

It is of course impossible to describe, it lies entirely beyond words, beyond our three-dimensional experience, which is all we have. For, in addition to this multiplication of one figure into numerous duplicates, it, or they, were moving in other places than this stretch of illuminated corridor. They moved along other passages, through other rooms on floors upstairs and downstairs, moved up and down between floors and ceilings elsewhere in the house. They were, in fact, all over the building, and in the same instant, while yet the whole series of figures, as I have said, was always one and the same, the figure of de Frasne.

Pages of description cannot make any clearer this instant flash that overwhelmed me with complete conviction. I know what I witnessed, and I know that this certainty of positive knowledge lay in me. No surprise accompanied it, no touch of criticism, as in a dream I accepted it merely as true and possible. There was in me, perhaps, a momentary extension of consciousness, a change of consciousness, that involved some sudden awareness of a changed, extended universe. It went as quickly as it came. I had, in any case, no instant for reflection.

The figures vanished. Round the door that was standing ajar, peering at us, fingers gripping the edge, I saw the face of Sydney Mantravers. Vronski saw it too, though whether he had seen de Frasne or not I did not know, and, feeling me shrink back involuntarily, he pulled me sharply, even violently forward, so that together we took half a dozen rapid steps in the direction of the face. I saw the hand that gripped the edge of the door advance; it pushed out; an arm came next; the face, with shoulders behind it followed; the entire figure pushed into full view. There was a blaze.

"Hold out your hand," Vronski whispered. "Say something. A welcome."

As in a nightmare, I made the effort. My own hand moved out. My voice spoke, made a sound at any rate, a hoarse whisper, half choked with terror: "Here I am, Sydney. Come on—come back to me—back to us."

It seemed to me my mind and senses were registering only certain things of limited kind, and that a whole world of other occurrences going on at the same time about me now passed entirely unrecognised. While aware of their existence, I could not perceive them.

The full-length figure then drove forward at what seemed terrific speed through the now wide-open door. There was a rush, a roar too, I believe, as though a comet swept through space, and I felt my hand grasped in a clutch of ice, while a tremendous blow seemed to strike me, not in the face and chest alone and not outward only, but over my whole body, and somehow inside as well, knocking me backwards as with some gigantic energy behind it. I reeled at the shock.

I lost my balance. As I fell against the wall at my back, I saw the face and figure of Mantravers come rushing at me with the speed and power as of some awful projectile. I cannot over-emphasise this impression of appalling speed and power. In the flash of a second it happened. Memory and consciousness then collapsed together simultaneously, but before the darkness swept over me, I caught the laughter of both men on the tail of broken sentences.

". . . . too much for him, but I'm here again. . . he's got me out . . . damned idiot to come. . . just going back into sleep once more . . . de

215

Frasne refused . . . enjoying his boyhood too much. . . ."

The words roared past me like a clap of thunder, but the heavy thump I heard was evidently my own body as it reached the floor.

"Hold on for God's sake don't forget grip your memory hold on to *that*——tell us all you can——" I just caught in Vronski's voice as I sank into oblivion.

★★★★★★★★★★★★★★★★

Memory, apparently, is but a clumsy, ineffective process. No man can recall accurately the details of the accident that knocked him out. People who claim to remember past lives usually have blank minds about what happened a month ago. At any rate, to remember in a calm moment what occurred in a time of violent stress seems quite impossible. The chief detail I recalled clearly of this amazing scene was that Mantravers looked exactly the same as when I had last seen him four years before, but that his face had a brilliant whiteness and that he was thin to emaciation. Against the surrounding darkness of the landing, he looked radiant, he shone, he rushed at me like a stream of lightning. And hence, of course, the blaze already mentioned.

His words, the words of Vronski too, held equally clear and definite, audible memories being perhaps more vividly impressed than visual ones. His return to our three-dimensional conditions he regarded thus as a limitation of life and an idiotic one, for it was "falling into sleep again." The glimpse accorded me, moreover, of the conditions he had left, conditions possible to an extended consciousness, were "too much" for me, while de Frasne, being in different time, could choose his period at will, and preferred his "boyhood" years to anything to be found in our world. Yet of those few pregnant words I caught, it was the word "here" that impressed me most. My cousin said "here" as though he had never left or gone away.

It was later that I was able to note and label other changes. . . .

If his clothing betrayed no passage of the years, there were alterations in his appearance that impressed me profoundly. These testified to something, though what this something was I leave to others cleverer than myself. He looked no older, I can swear to that. He still wore, indeed, that air of mighty resistance to the years already mentioned before he vanished, that extraordinary retention of youth, as though the usual decay had hardly touched him for a generation, as though this natural process had been arrested in his physical being. And this resistance to time, even with these four years added, was what struck me as his radiant face rushed at me in that empty house. I have thought later, if a good deal later, that in earlier experiments with Vronski, he had so outdistanced his companion, left him so far behind, that intelligible communication between the two had blocked. Myself, ignorant, untrained, sympathetic and openminded, he could make contact with, while Vronski, stopped at a certain point, lay out of his reach. . . .

Yet, if he looked no older, he certainly did look different. Different is the word, though to analyse this difference precisely puzzles me completely. Things had passed over him, he had enjoyed, suffered, worn, while it was not, I swear, the physical envelope that had worn, and his body at 64 looked 40 still. There lay the imprint of signatures on his soul perhaps, of vigils due to an intensity of experience ordinary humans cannot know. I say "perhaps," for it is imagination that interprets such strange markings, and I cannot expect the report of my imagination to pass as evidence.

Were I forced to find strictly truthful terms, I should say that Mantravers during this four years' interlude which left him physically untouched, had inwardly endured things we may hardly guess at, much less define, things possible only to an altered consciousness in altered conditions of space and time, and whether in the body or out of the body, to borrow from an expert, we need not dare to fathom, since they are not knowable to our three-dimensional faculties. Personally, I phrased it thus—that he had been out of the cage we know as life and living. He had escaped.

The fact remains that, of outward physical signs, his face and skin alone at first betrayed him—their incalculable, sweet, fiery radiance. It was this effect of light that had struck me so vividly, even with a burst of horror, before, an instant later, I lost consciousness.

This momentary weakness in myself I have always bitterly regretted, for it robbed me of witnessing any coherent interchange of words and action between Vronski and himself. Its duration was brief, yet long enough for several minutes to have passed, during which we all three reached the hall below. Vronski was chafing my hands. I opened my eyes. "I'm going to find a taxi," he said clearly, as soon as he saw I was all right. "Wait here with your cousin." He placed the hand of Mantravers in my own, and the front door closed behind him with a bang, leaving us together, sitting side by side on two wooden chairs.

Some wholesome magic lay perhaps in that word "taxi," for a measure of control came back to me, though of those next minutes I remember only one thing clearly: that while I searched feverishly, frantically even, for something to say, or rather to ask, a thousand questions boiling in me, Mantravers spoke himself. In the gloom of that dreary hall, lit only by a gleam through the narrow windows from the street, he turned his radiant face towards me. The blaze had dimmed, but it still shone as with an interior lamp.

"I have been awake," he said quietly, sadly, " but I am now falling back into sleep again. I have been elsewhere and otherwise, but time now separates things idiotically here. I've been out of the cage. . . .'"

He said much more, his words, each like a great eagle on the wing, rushing past me, into some region where I could not follow. For understanding left me, even while something just beyond reason beckoned dangerously. With those shining eyes fixed on my own, I felt myself caught up, rapt away, ravished into something beyond experience. Only the feeblest flash of his meaning came—namely, that our earthly consciousness, even at its best and highest, is so limited that it is little better than a state of dream, and that his return to it was like falling into sleep. But before I could frame a single question, much less utter an intelligible comment, the front door had opened again, and I heard Vronski's rather harsh voice calling: "The taxi's here. Come on!"

★★★★★★★★★★★★★★★★★

Mantravers was legally dead; in the eyes of authority, he had no existence; he could neither be taxed, fined, nor arrested and imprisoned. He lived—went to bed, rather, and stayed there—in Dr. Vronski's house in Westminster, and to me, ignorant, stupid, scared, but "open-minded," was allotted by Vronski the task of watching over him. "He'll talk to *you*, at least he *may*," said Vronski, emphasising "you" and "may," "if he talks at all. Not," he added bluntly, resentfully a trifle too, "because you know anything, or will even understand what he says, but because you're a link of sorts, a link with his dream-existence *here*, you see, before he left."

I was too uneasy to feel flattered, as I listened, but it did occur to me to ask why he, Vronski, couldn't be that link himself. His reply only set my mind going in whirls and whorls. He couldn't, he explained, because he, Vronski, was still in the state of sleep—what most people called life, whereas Mantravers had been "awake for a long time, for twenty-five years or more. I woke up for moments, but I never could hold it. I dropped back again into—into *this*," and he waved his arms over London, as it were. "He left me more than a quarter of a century ago, a whole generation. But *you*," he looked hard at me with a bitter envy in both voice and eyes, "though you don't know it"—he hesitated a moment—"are more awake than I—for longer periods anyhow." He turned away with a half angry shrug. "Anyhow, he may talk to you, and if he does, treasure his words like gold. I can't get a syllable out of him."

He gazed at me with that horrible envy in his eyes. It made me shiver to hear him, and though I longed to ask him about those twenty-five years, missing years as it were, I could not bring myself to do so.

"You have," he went on more quietly, "an amazing privilege—a chance in a thousand million. Think of it—a man, a human, who has tasted other time and space. You may hear something about existence outside our categories altogether. Make a note of—of everything, especially of what you don't understand. The more it contradicts our logic and experience, the more valuable it may be. Nonsense, sheer nonsense, here will be right, remember. . . ."

Much more in similar vein he impressed upon me, as he installed me in the dressing-room leading out of the "sick man's" chamber in his luxurious house, the very house, I knew, where he and my cousin had carried on their audacious experiments of years ago. I listened, listened closely, saying hardly anything myself, while in my mind, or in some part of me that somehow remained aloof, unfrightened, the calmest of calm spectators, I was perfectly aware that Vronski and I were talking in a dream, and that our three-dimensional consciousness was little better than a dream state.

The journey in the taxi, to go back a bit, left few clear impressions in me; I was too scared, too utterly nonplussed at the moment to focus attention or reflection. Mantravers, emaciated, limp and so strangely shining, lay back in his corner beside his former friend. He rarely spoke a word. I watched him as I might have watched a nightmare figure. This dream-texture wove itself through the whole journey.

The taxi, I remember, drove dangerously fast, so that, as in the cinema stunt-pictures, crashes which seemed unavoidable were just avoided by a hair's breadth and the stream of vehicles rushed past us in a dreadful sequence. I was clutching for safety at everything within reach, when my cousin spoke. "Why doesn't the man start?" he asked impatiently. "He's got three directions to choose from, hasn't he, and the house can't come to us—down here, at any rate, it can't. I'm there already anyhow, if he only knew it." He gave a queer little gulp of laughter, turning to me with a look that set my shivers going again. "I knew it, knew it perfectly, you see, before I came back into this, but I'm losing it now, it's going again." His piercing, fiery eyes were full upon me; he drew a profound sigh of weariness, of disgust, of pity.

"The cage is about me, the stupid, futile cage. It's time that does it, it's your childish linear time, time in a single line. In such a limited state it's not even being awake, just trivial dreaming, almost death and the voice died off into a whisper. He closed his eyes, leaning back into his corner.

I saw Vronski clutch him. "Remember," Vronski shouted, "try to remember! You're back in three-dimensional space and one-dimensional time now—and with me. I'm Vronski—Nicholas Vronski—your old friend. You remember our talks, our speculations, our experiments!"

There was no response, not even a turn of the head. But one of those flashes I had actually no right to, came to me, and I understood that Mantravers, back now in conditions he had long escaped, found himself so caged and limited that he felt helpless. After the intensity, the difference, the power and liberty he had known, the experiences of our existence were as the unreal phantasmagoria of a dream. "It's all leaving me," he murmured once. "I'm forgetting, forgetting. It's awful, awful. It was always difficult to hold it. I can't hold it now. Yet I had a flash, a minute—four years, as you think it here."

The taxi, escaping a hundred deaths, stopped suddenly, and then Vronski, grabbing my arm painfully hard as we got out, whispered something about "get all he says, make notes, remember every word, hold on to him," and somehow, we were, all three, inside the house.

Such is my brief recollection, half hazy, half vivid, of that frightful journey. So perturbed and upset I was that I only vaguely recall that Vronski provided a meal of sorts, put Mantravers to bed, and fixed me up in the dressing-room with only a door between. It all happened with the rapidity of that stunt cinema-picture almost; these little details of preparation, eating a meal, providing me with pyjamas, paper and pencil, and a dozen other necessary matters, all went past with extraordinary swiftness, as though, perhaps, I hardly noticed them attentively enough to take them in.

It seemed but a few minutes, when he stood at the door, giving me final injunctions before he left me alone for the night. "I'm best out of sight, in the background anyhow," he whispered. "Ring for all you want. My manservant is used to anything at any hour. I must go now. I must notify the authorities, of course, for one thing. Keep your door ajar, and watch and listen. Be ready. Your position, your privilege, your duty. . . ." The words poured out feverishly jumbled, there was so much he wanted to say. He shrugged his shoulders, and adding that he would look in again at midnight, he was gone.

He did come back at midnight, a couple of hours later, and entering my room on tiptoe, seemed relieved to hear that there had been no waking yet, hardly a movement of the sleeping body even. "He may sleep for hours," he told me, "for days, even for weeks, like others before him. But I doubt it. His case is not of that sort. He'll wake up right enough before too long, and you must be the first person he sees."

My shudder was noticeable evidently. He eyed me keenly, alive to my exhaustion. "You—you will stick it, won't you?" he asked, almost piteously.

I looked into those beseeching eyes. The pallid face, wasted with intense desire, distraught, scarred by experiments of nameless kind, the face of a man who had not spared himself in the search for what he deemed knowledge, made an almost violent appeal. The pain, too, was there, the sense of loss, the anguish due to being robbed of refreshment poignantly expected, earned—robbed by another whom, moreover, he considered, at the least, unworthy.

I asked a few questions. He answered them. It all still seemed to me a dream of marvellous, even supernatural sort, a dream I could only partially recover. It seems so today, indeed, more than ever.

"I'm scared," I whispered.

"You well may be," he whispered back.

I gave my promise, if fearfully, yet at the same time eagerly as well.

"Scared," that little trivial word, was the one that hung echoing in the air during the hours of my long vigil. I dreaded the awakening, yet longed for it. My mind was a turmoil. Contradictions raged in me. Mantravers, they said, had of course been in hiding all these years—yet his very clothes hanging over the chair, denied it. It was all a tricky hallucination of my own mind—my recent war experiences denied that still more decisively. The alternative was staggering, more than my faculties could hold or deal with—that my cousin, sleeping calmly in that bed, had left our space and time for a period of four years, and that before this complete disappearance, as a preliminary to it, by way of training possibly, he had escaped our time, while still occupying our space, for a far longer period, for some twenty-five years, an entire generation.

When he woke up in that bed across the floor, woke out of this interval of readjustment which was an earthly sleep, he might tell me something, things of unexampled, fearful interest—*me*, because though ignorant I was open-minded, not knowing enough even to have prejudices. . . .

With books I could not read, with pencil and writing-pad in hand, I sat peering through the half-open door. I could easily see the emaciated, shining face, the collar of blue pyjamas round the neck, the nose buried in the pillow, the counterpane rising and falling with the steady breathing. No other movement came, no sound, no gentle snoring even; he might pass his life away, it seemed to me, dying in his sleep. He looked as if he could never wake, as if he did not mean to, certainly did not want to, wake. What dying might mean to him, I dared not think. Once I crept in on tiptoe, and looked closer, standing within two feet of the bed. God—that strange radiance! Even the transparent eyelids glowed, as though the eyeballs underneath looked through at me. I felt "seen through," my very soul examined. I returned again and again, stealthily, as though irresistibly attracted, fascinated. I hoped he would never wake, I hoped he would, I sat with nerves on edge, with senses painfully alert, too frightened to feel fear.

The hours passed slowly. No sound penetrated from the London streets. It seemed the silence deepened to something beyond silence. Beneath the surface the turmoil in my mind ran helter-skelter among a thousand thoughts and pictures, playing pitch-and-toss with my years in the prison camp, with my reading, with my own strange experiments in escape. . . . I wondered, wondered, for wonder seemed the single attitude that held calm and steady in me.

For the hundredth time I went over my brief talk with Vronski just before he left, the few wild questions I had put, the startling replies. Incoherent and almost childish that exchange seemed now. Was there anything in particular I should look for, I had asked, apart from noting what my cousin might say?

And Vronski, eyeing me hungrily, had hesitated a moment, as though reflecting deeply. "A change," he had said at length, "an alteration—of unexpected kind—a sudden—possibly a very shocking one." Into my mind leaped the idea of mania. "No, not that," came the reply, reading my thoughts again. "I mean that its suddenness, its rapidity—you might find shocking." It was nothing mental, I realised.

"Oh, physical then?" I asked with a little gasp impossible to repress, and he had nodded, the expression on his face dreadful almost, because a queer superior smile lay mingled in it. "He might appear suddenly—rather—different," his words came slowly. I guessed faintly at what his allusion meant perhaps. I recalled, all in a flash, the stories, my own casual observations in the past, the fact that for a generation Mantravers had not grown older, and the unnatural horror of it came back to me like ice. And Vronski's slow words were still dropping from his lips in whispers. "The stresses and energies where he has been, lie beyond anything we can know or imagine. Their removal *here* may result in abrupt collapse of even dreadful kind. The price must be paid—paid back!—in our *time*, of course." His voice became almost inaudible. "It may be sudden," I just caught, "what we call sudden."

The talk ran in a ceaseless circle through my mind, round and round, till any meaning it might have held was lost, as I sat there watching the sleeper's bed. My armchair was against the open door. The silence deepened, the cold increased, the city traffic lay dead, no birds awake, no wind astir. No hint of sleep came near me. If he wakened—should I dare to ask the thousand questions raging in my mind, dare to frame a single one of them? He did not stir an inch, he did not turn over, trunk and head and limbs lay motionless, and I doubt if my eyes ever left his face for more than a few seconds at a time.

So long this silence and immobility continued that, beginning to feel nothing would ever happen again, I glanced at my wrist-watch, noting that it was close upon four in the morning, the hour when human vitality sinks to its lowest ebb, and thinking that daylight must presently come filtering through the blinds. I can swear that my eyes did not leave his face for longer than ten seconds at most, but it was in this very brief interval I became aware of a sudden movement in the still room. I started, gave a jerk as though a bullet had passed through me, while my questions fled like a flock of terrified sheep. The movement was of the slightest, but it was real—the opening of his eyelids. Mantravers was staring at me across the floor. And accompanying this movement was a low sound that came at me like a bell—his voice.

Caution, circumspection, sensible action, all forsook me in that instant, and fear went with them: memory of detailed instruction vanished utterly; caught in a wave of passionate and overwhelming curiosity, I sprang to my feet, obeying instinctively my dominating impulse. I was across the strip of intervening carpet in a second, I rushed up to the bed; with barely a foot between our two faces, I plumped out my first question, regardless of all else. It was what, above all, I wanted to know, apparently, for it burst out like an automatic explosion.

'How did you do it, Sydney—keep young—arrest age and decay, I mean, for twenty-five years on end?"

The question had spurted spontaneously out of my "subconscious," of course, where it had lain so long, perplexingly unanswered; for I had no thought of asking it till then, and there were others I *had* meant to put.

Those strange electric eyes gazed into mine. He spoke, and his voice again was like a bell: "A man in his own place," he answered with a curious gentleness, "is the ruler of his fate. And I found mine."

"How—how did you get there?" came from my lips, stupidly enough.

"By leaving—this—this imagery." He made a slight, even a tiny, gesture with his arm, yet it was as though he swept away the house, London, England itself and all it stood for in ordinary experience. Imagery! I almost felt myself swept with it into something beyond all trivial, confined and relative conditions I had hitherto mistaken for reality and life. Though my mind and emotions were a boiling cauldron, little clear and steady in them, another question rising to the surface shot out of its own accord.

"Our knowledge, then—science————"

An extraordinarily sweet expression stole upon his face. He gently shook his head. "Unreal," rang the voice, though fainter than before, "and part of the dream we ourselves create. The How is nothing— mere effects. Here we can dream effects only. Knowledge and reality can be known only in the Why—the world of causes. . . ."

On the last three words the bell-like quality grew fainter, fading from his voice, the eyelids dropped slowly over the terrific eyes. I searched for one more question among the hundreds I longed to ask, but found no single word. He lay quite still again, apart from the gentle rise and fall of the body that breathed equably in what men call physical sleep. The queer notion came to me that he had not really wakened at all, that Mantravers in his totality had certainly not been there, nor gazed at me, nor spoken, but that only a fraction of his being, using the familiar terms of limited human intelligence, had brushed my mind in passing.

True enough, of course, the fragment that was spoken, for even I grasped that, and classifying effects can bring no knowledge of reality. Science, which explains how a thing happens, can tell nothing as to why it happens, nor has normal human consciousness any faculty for apprehending this region of causes. Had he, then, experienced that, dwelt in that, known reality face to face?

I remember withdrawing softly, as a giddy man withdraws cautiously from the edge of a precipice that makes him tremble. Quickly,

I jotted down the brief exchange in a hand that shook a little. I sank back into my deep armchair with the strange assurance that it would be long before he really woke. I fell asleep. It was, this time, Vronski's sharp, practical voice that startled me.

"Humph! So, you *had* to sleep, of course," he exclaimed in a whispered voice between a snap and a growl, yet somehow not unkindly. "It's six o'clock, you know. You've lost something, probably." He had already examined the sleeper, I knew, for he came to me out of the bedroom. His fearful eagerness was pathetic.

I shook my head, wide awake on the instant, all my faculties about me. I pushed my notes towards him.

"What?" he whispered. "He's waked then—and spoken? You heard it? You put questions—good ones? You understood—something?" He seized the notes as a famished man might snatch at food, his hand shaking, while he eyed my face and the paper alternately like a hungry wolf. I told him briefly what had occurred, as he read the sentences over and over again, first very rapidly to take in their general sense, then very slowly, reflectively, laboriously even. They were laconic enough, but I filled in the blanks in a whisper. His hunger, his envy, his greed to know, again touched my pity. I felt ashamed of being so unworthy a go-between.

"Yes, yes, of course," he was mumbling, as though speaking to himself rather than to me, "but we both knew that. We've been there before together already. The *why* of things, rather than the futile *how* that science gabbles. That's the first result of a changed, a different consciousness. But he's been beyond that—far, far beyond it. That's what I want to know—what the new faculties that come with a changed consciousness reveal —beyond the region of causes even. . . ."

His speech grew so rapid, so involved, I could not follow it. On his face the ravaged look intensified. He kept one eye, none the less, both ears as well, I knew, upon the inner room, and then suddenly glanced sharply back at me, as though my presence had just occurred to him. "There was more, much more, he wanted—tried—to say, wasn't there?" he shot at me. A quick smile of apology, of courtesy, accompanied it.

"That's the impression made upon me," I agreed. "He knew things impossible—utterly impossible—to communicate in ordinary words."

Vronski fell silent, thoughtful, for a moment, then went on again, as though talking to himself rather than to me:

"He *was* awake, of course, awake here in our sense," he muttered.

"Just for those moments he was awake here—but to him that would be falling asleep again. He was talking in his sleep. He had already waked up out of all this long ago—waked up a second time. To come back to conditions here would be falling asleep again." His meaning was quite clear to me. Ordinary waking every morning is merely the gain of increased and clearer consciousness; to wake up then a second time involves a yet greater gain. "If he had talked nonsense, instead of sense," Vronski was whispering to himself, "he could have told more. Yes, yes, as you felt, he was just talking in his sleep," again picking an earlier thought out of my own mind. "A man in his own place," he repeated, "is ruler of his fate."

I stared stupidly, perhaps, yet not as stupidly as I doubtless looked. I realised, at least, that from the point of view of a *different* consciousness having new faculties, our own best scientific dicta must be childishly inadequate and false, But I found no useful word to say. Fatigue, too, began to stupefy me. "It was a good question all the same," he went on, "the one you put. Our three-dimensional consciousness has no faculty that can know anything of a universe that is certainly many-dimensional. Our best knowledge is a dream, born of dream-minds in a dream-civilisation. To tell us *how* water runs downhill is to tell us nothing—*why* it runs downhill is godlike." He looked me over as man might regard a stupid employee who had done his best, and then suddenly something I found awful crept into the face.

"I doubt, I doubt now our getting anything," he whispered lower than before, and the voice made me think of ice. "He'll wake of course, right enough, but—but he'll leave us before he can—speak. Leave finally I mean," his voice breaking queerly. "Just pay his debt and go before we can get a word. The debt——twenty-five years—twenty-five stolen years. Taken from here, they can only be repaid here. In our time, I mean—for where he has been they are not even a moment——"

He stopped, he stood stock-still. He looked me over again, but with an intensity and thoroughness that made me avoid an inspection I found too much. I trembled a little in spite of myself.

"Something I could understand?" I stammered. "You mean—I should witness it?"

The expression that frightened me was gone: he was still grave, extremely perplexed, but his look became human, sympathetic, gentle towards me, as he nodded his head in answer. "Yes," he murmured, "witness it, and with your own eyes." I left it there, asking no further question because I dared not, and he went on quickly: "If he wakes, have questions ready. Avoid his eyes, I advise. Hang on firmly, tightly, to your own personality. Grip yourself like iron. Ask him"—he reflected a moment—"ask if he knows death—if he can speak of the War—if love, *Love*, mind you—exists with value—if—if——"

He shrugged his great shoulders; the tired eyes that had not closed all night gave me a warmer look. "Oh, ask your own questions," he added almost hopelessly. "Just ask what occurs to you. And if anything— happens, call me up instantly. The telephone is at your hand. I shall be near—in this building." He read the shock in my face, of course. "Can you stand it?" he asked suddenly, moving away towards the door, my heart sinking as I noticed it.

I nodded stiffly. "Sudden, swift repayment, you mean?" I stammered. His head bowed as he turned the handle.

"Departure—final departure?" I heard my own horrified whisper. "All those years—in just a moment?" For I caught his meaning, such was the intensity of his mind. With a shock I caught it. Decay and age involve considerable time, as I understood time, for normal life lays such process so gradually, slowly, softly on us all. Years compressed into a moment could only be appalling.

Vronski, now half out of the room, his face a mask of white, answered below his breath, a mere whisper that was dreadful with a kind of spiritual pain:

"If at all—it must be very rapid, may seem almost instantaneous," came the syllables across the quiet air. "Sweet, too, if terrible. The questions first, remember—if you can." And the door closed noiselessly behind him.

Alone again, after taking the coffee he had left me in a thermos, I tried to think out the questions I would ask. Something, perhaps subconscious guidance, assured me my cousin would not wake for hours. Were our deeper selves in telepathic communication possibly? I cannot say, I did not even try to think. At the time I was sure of nothing except that it was safe for me to take my rest and sleep, and this I therefore did, opening my eyes again after what must have been many hours, for it was well on into the short winter afternoon and dusk had come. My mind felt clear, it felt also calm, and this calmness I noticed with something of surprise.

It has always seemed to me remarkable, indeed, that my nerves and faculties supported the entire experience as they did, and that I did not, almost literally, lose my senses. The riot of tearing emotions

I certainly had known, bewilderment, excitement, a raging curiosity and fear beyond easy description, but deep within me all the time was some centre that held steady enough, some part of me that observed and judged, burned with a clear light, and even, for intolerable flashes, understood.

When I woke, at any rate, there was no violence of feeling in me, the tumult had died down, and only two words seemed to ring on hauntingly in my mind, with some touch of the turmoil that had first accompanied them. The combination, "sweet and terrible," was unusual still, but the horror with which I had first heard them did not now appear. And, after a cautious inspection of the sleeper and the bed in the next room to assure myself that there was no sign of change as yet, I bent my mind to the framing of the questions as best I might.

Yet behind each attempt, and despite my strongest effort to deny it, rose always the ghost of an expectant dread—the dread that before there was time to ask a single one, perhaps, something would happen to prevent, something to render replies impossible, something rapid, sweet and terrible. And this ghost of twenty-five years to be repaid I could not lay, it waved a shroud, as it were, above each word my pencil traced.

Within its limitations, none the less, my mind worked reasonably well, though the difficulty of choosing words and subject were too much for me. The subject was so vast, the field it might cover so inexhaustible. All the great adventuring Discovers, from Buddha to Christ, I remembered, used childish local parables to convey something they themselves knew that yet lay beyond language, beyond any faculties their listeners possessed. How might I, thus, explain to a dog, watching me turn mere pages, that I am deeply immersed in the soul-fortunes of a dozen living characters? And how similarly, could I, the dog this time, ask intelligently about a superhuman experience? I fell back, at last, upon questions of a very simple kind.

I would ask for information on what I called "man-in-the-street" matters, questions about what a commonplace mind like my own would like to know. If Mantravers had actually changed his type of consciousness so that his new faculties made him free of time in more than our one dimension, and in space of more than three, what could he report intelligibly about his experiences? Was he conscious, for instance, of being away from ordinary London life, or was he living both lives simultaneously, one life parallel to the other ? Was there continuity of memory and personality, was the duration long or short and what did he *do*, feel, suffer and enjoy?

I longed to know whether his experiences and reactions in this state of "elsewhere and otherwise" were commensurable with our three-dimensional existence, and while I knew it could not possibly be so I had this burning curiosity to hear what he might say. Did he look forward into a future and back into a past, or were these both simultaneously accessible in the sense that a biography, from child-hood to old age, lie between the covers of a book, for the reader to choose any period he will? If, too, the future was accessible to him *now*, as we say, could he thence influence, even alter, the past? Above all, I longed to know about what, on earth, is called happiness. Having risen above the world of effects which is human knowledge, into the world of causes, which is reality, did he gain satisfaction, rest for the spirit, peace?

I laid my pencil down, having covered sheet upon sheet with ques-tions I knew to be futile—because I should never ask them. They were worthless, in any case, because unanswerable. I challenged myself, as I challenge anybody, to think of better ones. He had no terms, I had no terms, in which comprehensible answers could be given and under-stood. The Great War? Pain? Sleep? Love?—I drew my pencil through at least a hundred such, and leaned back in my chair to await events. . . .

Dusk was falling, the room darkening, shadows gathering, and my eyes, ever on the mysterious sleeper, saw details of wall and furniture less clearly now. Outlines of bed and chairs and windows faded, the silhouette of the sheets above the sleeper became filmed, there was a blur over the entire room, yet I had the queer feeling that this was less due to the waning light than to a lack of reality in the objects themselves. Each picture lost vividness because it was but a transient appearance of something more real that lay behind, something the senses never knew because no sense could apprehend directly. The idea came, then vanished again.

At the same time, I became aware of an invading stupor stealing over me, a stupor I fought against with all my power— not sleep or exhaustion of physical kind, but a dulling of my surface consciousness, as though some brighter faculty beyond it were trying to assert itself.

That I resisted was, I came to believe long afterwards, a mistake; I here missed an opportunity, offered directly or indirectly by Mantra-vers. I can only guess at this. It was fear that prevented. Remembering Vronski's vehement warning, I held on to myself as tightly as I could, afraid of losing grip upon my personality. I was afraid, too, of being caught unawares, of being taken by surprise, suddenly horrified at the sight of the sleeper rising from his bed, coming across the room, standing beside me, looking down into my face. . . . And, it seemed, a long period passed, whose duration quite escaped my measurement, for though I can swear I did not sleep I recall that my eyes now opened with a sudden start, and my ears similarly became sharply alert. Had twelve hours passed or twenty-four, or a few minutes only? It was the first definite thought that came to me—was it evening still, or early morning? The same thin layer as of dusk or twilight lay upon the room, but objects were more plainly visible than before. There was a light somewhere, it seemed.

The questions rose, but there was no time to satisfy them, for the nerves of sight and hearing were too insistent for me to think of anything else. There had, once again, been sound and movement. I looked, I listened, with all my power. The sleeping man was sitting up in his bed, that bell-like resonance vibrated in the air, the syllables of my name still echoed, I saw the figure, half upright, like some awful deity upon its throne, and the same second, the first instant of paralysis having passed, I had sprung to my feet. And it was at this moment, as I dashed across the carpet, that I heard a cock crow in the distance, and knew that it was early morning.

"Come to me, come quickly," rang the bell-like voice, "before I leave. Let the useless questions go. Just come to me."

I was already beside the bed. He was sitting up, leaning back upon his hands. I had the extraordinary impression he was going to rise and take the air. The radiance in his eyes and face and skin were marvellous. I saw a dark blue stain glow out upon his right temple, then fade away. It was like a bullet wound. All memory of my questions had wholly vanished. "Dying—you mean?" came automatically from my lips. "Is it—death?"

And then he laughed. His eyes ran over my face, the eyes I had been told to avoid.

" My second death. There are so many. This is the life I owed de Frasne. All the lives are simultaneous——"

A flow of words that rushed on I cannot remember, even if I registered them. They held no meaning for me—in the instant of utterance, that is, they held a meaning I understood, as in a timeless flash, but meaning and understanding were gone again as soon as born. Only the shattering effect remained, as of something better left untold, unknown. The laughter, too, unnerved me, that sweet, careless, unearthly laughter that seemed to break up and destroy whatever was left of coherence in me.

"Tell us," I believe I cried, "tell me—before you go." I know that something of the sort burst from me. I can still hear my hoarse, breathless cry saying this. I was shaking with terror at the same time lest he touch me, for his hand came groping towards me where I stood against the bed. It seemed to me that if he touched me, my being somehow must dissolve. It seemed my very self was threatened, while yet that threatened self, trembling in the balance, understood why "life must be lost to find it," and that my courage failed. The awful yearning and the awful dread were there. It was the bell-like voice, with its sound of death or freedom, that caught me back into my pitiful restricted cage again, though not before I had realised something of the loneliness, the deific beauty and glory in that loss of self without which no heaven is attainable.

"Stop thinking," was what I caught of his answer. "Behind thought lies the entrance. Reason and thinking hold us in the life of least importance. Go behind both to find the beginning—behind the mind—into a different way. You will find several lives together and at once—and more than one kind of death. . . ."

His meaning, at the moment, flashed like lightning across my understanding, but his eyes were now holding mine, and I could not speak. Did his conditions flow over into me? Did I borrow some faint reflection of what he knew, of where he was, of a difference he tried to convey? I cannot say. Words left my mind, for they were useless, vain, meaningless. No words existed anywhere—the few he used are reported as feebly, inaccurately, as those I fought to choose for myself. The mind, as an instrument, lay helpless, withered. His eyes held mine. I looked, that is, straight into his own. And I understood—oh, so easily and clearly and simply then——that my full earth-life was but a fraction, a trivial rivulet, that ran parallel with numerous other streams that were deeper, mightier, more important. It was a question of focusing upon this little rivulet, or spreading attention and consciousness over them all, yet simultaneously.

In his eyes I read this fantastic but literal certainty. I became aware of stresses of a kind never before experienced. No mental or emotional tension life had brought me hitherto, either by way of love, hate, passion, yearning, fear, was akin to it. I was stretched and altered, altered above all, in my deepest essential being, and yet such alteration was easy, natural, right, while entirely new, and different to anything I could, imaginatively or intellectually, have even supposed possible. For above all I noticed this—that it was unlike anything my mind could have even imagined.

I watched him, and as I watched the light, I had already noticed in the room increased a little, as though it came closer. Its origin I had not guessed, though I certainly had not fancied it, and it was, I knew, external to himself. Both bed and occupant became a shade clearer. I stared with intense and feverish attention. I could have sworn there was a change, the flutter of a change. That was the word—it fluttered, then was gone. But it returned, this faint, fluttering difference. I noticed it a second time. It was lost again. Something touched the face, there was a change upon the features. It vanished. With it came over me a rushing instinct that I must be quick, I must act instantly, or the opportunity would be lost for ever.

This certainty swept me like an icy wind, and the ghostly dread I could not lay moved down the air. What Vronski feared might happen was on the way, closer, nearer, even imminent. I must plunge in as best I could, and I made the effort, as the hundred questions flew past me in their glittering series. I picked one out, then another, and another, but could not speak them, could not utter even a sound, for all were useless, meaningless, and the awful flutter, meanwhile, had reappeared, this time lingering. Thought froze in me. I closed my eyes a second.

It was his quiet laughter that made me open them again the next moment. The light had come closer than before, and the ghastly signature upon his face, I saw, had deepened. I actually saw it spring back, this fluttering alteration, to settle like a great bright insect on the face. He was speaking, but the bell-like note had left the voice, and then the lips stopped moving, the eyes lost their terrible radiance, the whole skin paled, the arms supporting the body sagged.

"Christ!" I heard my voice with a stifled shriek, his curious light laughter still audible across it: It was that same happy, careless laughter, no pain, not even anxiety, possible with such a sound, a laughter of relief rather. And the voice came with it as a bell ringing across great distances: "Ah, *that* above all else, the way of light," reached my ears faintly, brokenly, a profound wavering sigh accompanying it. "I will tell you, tell all I can—show you the escaping way—the *why*——" the syllables dying into incoherence then, so that I bent over to catch the scarcely audible whisper that almost stopped my heart. Though confused, words running into each other, their meaning penetrated: "a moment—a moment only—I must first pay back the stolen years—

now and here. After that I will tell——"

The whisper died out because the lips through which it came were gone already. I remember an odd sound behind me, an increase of light as well, but it was impossible to turn my head. The horror of what Vronski's cryptic words had suggested was nothing to the horror of what I saw. I stared. The whole dreadful sight came, it seemed, in a single second.

Twenty-five years rushed on him in a single moment. He did not stare back because the eyes, following the lips, were no longer there to stare with. The features all ran away together. In the space of a few seconds, fifteen perhaps at most, Sydney Mantravers aged twenty-five years, became a quarter of a century older.

The accumulation of this period's decay was upon him, all over him, with an abrupt, appalling rush. The skin grew loose and wrinkled, changing, even hiding the eyes so that it seemed they disappeared; the muscles slackened, sprayed, sagged away, chin and neck showing it most clearly. There was a ghastly crumpling together of the entire physical frame. The shrivelling seemed intensified by its swiftness. I remember that no comprehensible feeling was in me, horror having passed into something else, and similarly, no thought took the brain.

The "bends" rose as a picture, because probably my mind contained it as the only comparable human experience, the hideous "bends" that divers know on rising too rapidly from deep waters before the decompression can be applied, or, when caught unawares in too great depths, the frame is jellied, the entire body crammed up into the helmet. There rose another picture too—of a mummy exposed suddenly to air and damp becoming a little heap of dust soon after. These awful pictures rose, then vanished, as though the mind automatically searched for a parallel.

Though it was not quite so, the body none the less collapsed in a dreadful, stupid heap before my eyes, the last detail to suffer change being the small red bruise that glowed in the right temple before it too was gone. One feeble breath rose from the huddled shape upon the sheets, one last fluttering breath escaped the dried and shrunken flesh that had been lips, bearing with extreme faintness a ghost of happy laughter, and just reaching my ears as I bent closer above the dissolving face: "a moment . . . only a moment... and I will tell you . . . escaping way . . . elsewhere and otherwise . . ."

Loud and quite clear behind my back, as the light came closer suddenly, was the piteous, convulsive sound of Vronski's sobbing, beyond which again, the faint clear note as of a ringing bell that died away into the silence.

Chemical

It is odd how trivial a thing can cause a first, instinctive dislike: the way a man wears his hat, the smirk with which a woman uses her mirror and lipstick in a public place—and aversion is suddenly aroused. Later knowledge may justify this first dislike, but the actual start has been the merest triviality.

Some think, however, this cause has not been so trivial as it appears; that gesture, being an unconscious expression of the entire personality, may betray far more than speech, which is calculated. Moleson, thinking over the brusqueness of the stranger on the doorstep, the unnecessary way he pushed ahead of him and up the stairs, his whole air, indeed, of general resentment and disapproval, found himself recalling a rather significant answer that a very wise old man had once given in his hearing to a commonplace question. The question was not his own: he was listening to two friends discussing a third.

"Everything indicates," said the first, carelessly enough, "that I ought to like X. I have nothing against him. Quite the reverse, in fact. Yet I do not like him. I simply cannot like him, try as I will. Now—why don't I?"

"Your dislike," was the reply, "is probably chemical. Merely chemical."

This came back to Moleson's mind now, as he unpacked his things and arranged himself in the top-floor bed-sitting-room he had engaged that afternoon. It was in Bloomsbury, close to the British Museum. The November twilight was setting in; the gas, electric light stopping at the second floor, was poor; his reading lamp was not yet unpacked. "Chemical! . . ." he thought. "I wonder!. . . ." as he looked out a moment into the rather dismal street, where the museum buildings blocked the sky with their sombre and formidable mass. He had, of course, the layman's vague knowledge of the loves and hates of atoms, their intense attraction and repulsion for each other, the dizzy rapidity with which they rushed towards, or away from, those they respectively liked or disliked. Had all the atoms of which he was composed, then, turned their backs instinctively upon those which made up the stranger's body, racing away at a headlong speed that caused him this acute and positive discomfort? Was his instantaneous loathing "merely chemical"? . . .

As he bustled about arranging his things, his dislike of the fellow remained vivid and persistent. The recent scene again passed through his mind in detail.

He had called in the morning and interviewed Mrs. Smith, with the result: "Not at the moment, sir, I 'aven't got a room free"; then, after a rather curious hesitation, "But later a little, maybe"; then more hesitation; "This afternoon, per'aps—I—I might be able to manage it—if you could make it convenient—to call in again . . ."; whereupon, seeing that the house was so admirably close to the Reading Room where his daily work would be, Moleson offered to pay in advance, but was then quick enough to see that it was not the question of money alone that troubled the woman. Her hesitation, he perceived, was not mere independence, nor was it due to his unprosperous appearance. She wanted a lodger, clearly enough—if she could "manage it," whatever that might mean—and it was not himself that she objected to. It was, he felt sure, a calculation of sorts she was trying to make in her own mind. He wisely decided to give her time to make it.

"I'll look in again," he said, "about three o'clock, say," and he added, with his pleasant smile, that most of his time would be spent working in the Museum opposite.

It was on his return in the afternoon that the scene occurred.

He had rung the bell, and was waiting just inside the narrow hall while the maid hurried downstairs to fetch Mrs. Smith, the street door still ajar behind him, when somebody, another lodger evidently, pushed past brusquely, offensively, almost resentfully, half shoving him, yet without actual contact, from where he stood at the foot of the stairs—slightly in the way, perhaps—and without so much as by your leave. There might, of course, have been a grunt of apology, for Moleson was a little deaf, but the man's attitude made it unlikely, and the pose of the head and shoulders, the face being turned away and not visible, was far more of resentful disapproval than of apology.

Moleson, on the instant, loathed him, not because of the rudeness, but because of some presentment his appearance offered that stirred an intense, instinctive dislike amounting to positive repulsion. A moment later, when Mrs. Smith arrived, panting and labouring, the man was up the stairs and out of sight, but at first the impression left was so vivid that Moleson would not have been altogether displeased if he had heard that no room was, after all, available. The contrary, however, took place. A bargain was struck, money passed hands, and the room was his.

The majority of young men in these circumstances would probably have given their attention to the land lady, to whom money must be paid, and on whose good will they must depend for their comfort and the like. Moleson, instead, found himself thinking only of this rude fellow lodger. Over his dinner in a neighbouring restaurant, he reflected that his sudden dislike was odd; he had never set eyes upon the fellow before, and so far, had not even seen the face nor heard the voice, yet this loathing had leaped into being. Revulsion, he called it. Its oddness, of course, lay in this want of proportion.

He gave a passing thought, too, to his landlady, yet chiefly using her as a means of comparison with the other. Her rather sombre visage, an over whelming melancholy in it, though certainly not attractive, woke nothing stronger in him than a vague, tolerant sympathy. He felt no dislike, at any rate; she merely didn't matter; a worthy soul, he decided, worn into sadness by life. Whereas the other human being gave him this instinctive, deep revulsion. Chemical? He wondered. For why, if chemical, should one unpleasing soul wake pity, and another, equally unpleasing, stir violent antipathy? . . .

Over his coffee, he dismissed the little puzzle. His room was admirably close to the museum; Bloomsbury liked him; and it was the number in the street—No. 11—his Manchester friend and employer had mentioned. The price, too, suited him, for money was scarce, otherwise he would not be "devilling" for another man—looking up certain seventeenth-century facts for a writer who would probably clear £1,000 over his silly book, yet "must be sure of my dates and facts, you know. Your expenses and £5 a week, if you'll do it for me. . ." The street and number, close to the Museum, were added. Young Moleson, ignorant of London, jumped at it.

It was some years before our Great Date this happened. Jim Moleson, engaged to a sweet girl, and now married to her, told me the details recently. The war intervened, of course. He had learnt something. At that time, I should have described him as highly strung, sensitive at any rate, imaginative certainly, poetic probably. I, his senior by a quarter of a century, rather believed he wrote "Celtic" poetry in his bedroom. The war undeceived us about that type, revealed them rather: their amazing courage, the splendour of their "imagination," translated into reckless, inspired action.

Jim, anyhow, was always headstrong, fierce-tempered, "nasty" once his feelings were stirred, only these feelings were usually for others— for a lame dog, an injured cat, a bird in a cage, an overworked horse. Slights, even insults to himself he could stand, to the point of cowardice, some thought; but this was wrong; he was easy-going to that point; beyond it he saw red and—killed. This savage temper, rarely roused, and then with a curious suddenness, was an item I overlooked. But it was a human, not merely an animal, temper.

His work at the museum, apparently, absorbed him; no more painstaking and accurate "devil" ever devilled; and he got back to his room, tired mentally and physically. A nice-looking, upstanding lad with his mop of dark hair and blue eyes, he soon made a friend of Mrs. Smith—over his letters first: "Lef' at No. 7," she informed him, the printed name of his employer's Institute on the envelope catching her trained, if mournful, eye perhaps. "The postman arst me, and I thought they was for you," she explained.

So, his slight deafness had again betrayed him, and his employer had said "No. 7," instead of "No. 11." They talked on a bit. He had the feeling *she* wanted to talk a bit, but wanted to talk about something in particular, and to him. He explained about the letters and his troublesome deafness in one ear; he heard her say "your glass of porter" when she actually said, "hot bathwater," and then, after a nice little chat about the weather, prices, and "'ow times was changing," he noticed that she suddenly stuck.

This was after a week in the house, he told me. The appalling melancholy of her face came over him, but rather in a new way; he realised it in some personal sense, I think, as they stood awkwardly staring at one another, each waiting for the other to speak, so that through his sensitive, imaginative mind ran the thought: "That's no ordinary sadness, I'll be bound! . . ."—and then *he* stuck.

The impulse to say something kind rose in him, only he could think of nothing to say, nothing suitable. It was here he got his first clear, instinctive impression about this commonplace woman: that she was interested, namely, to ask some definite question of him, that, liking and trusting him, and, further, having watched carefully and waited anxiously the whole week, she now longed to put this definite query to him, yet was afraid. The same hesitation he had seen first on the doorstep showed itself in her face and sorrowful eyes.

He had been vaguely aware of this for some time evidently, but had not recognised it. It was not, he felt sure, any question about his comfort, for he was old enough to know that landladies rarely took that risk. Something, none the less, she wanted to know, something personal to himself. The suffering in her face made him wonder. A queer sympathy moved through him. He recalled the stationer round the corner in Bury Street, when he bought his paper and materials: "Oh yes, I know, sir; that's Mrs. Warley's," saying he would send the parcel round, and, being corrected: "No, Mrs. Smith's," he looked blank a moment, troubled a little, but in a kindly sense, before he agreed: "Oh yes, to be sure, sir—Mrs. Smith's—now. So, it is. . . . That "now" was suggestive. She had changed her name, married again, no doubt, yet there had been trouble of some sort, Moleson gathered. And, though he had not pursued the matter at the time, this little memory came back now, as he stood chatting with her, trying to think of something pleasant he might say. He wondered. . . . .

"I'm very comfortable," he said on impulse, presently, "The room's just what I wanted" and he was about to add some kind and soothing word when she interrupted in an eager way that startled him:

"Oh, then everything *is* all right, sir? There's nothing, I mean, interfering with your quiet? If anything annoys"—she changed the verb, before it was completed, to "disturbs," then stopped dead.

It was not the words—commonplace enough: it was her face that startled him. It had been on the tip of her tongue, he felt, so say "anyone" instead of "anything."

He knew it in his bones. Also, she could have cut off that tongue for having let it say what it had said. That, too, he perceived. This question she longed yet feared to ask had nearly slipped out in spite of herself. Her face, anyhow, betrayed an emotion that for an instant obliterated its usual sadness. It was the emotion of terror.

Moleson, as he caught it, felt shocked. The sharp instinct came suddenly to him that it was wiser not to ask. He cut the talk short, as nicely as he could. "Nothing, nothing," he replied, gave her his pleasant smile, and went up quickly to his room.

Her question was an approach to the real one she wanted so much to ask. That, of course, he realised. Terror lay in it; it was wrapped round with terror as in a cocoon. Once the cocoon burst, was broken, out would come all the hideous wriggling things that lay concealed inside. This was the feeling Moleson carried upstairs with him. It was as though he had just caught a glimpse, behind her suddenly pale skin, of the hideous wriggling things that caused her sadness and her terror. But another certainty lay in him too at this moment: the question she had asked, this preliminary question that was an approach to another, referred—he felt positive of it—to someone he particularly sought to keep out of his thoughts as much as ever he could. She referred, indirectly thus, to the other lodger.

It was his habit at night, after his dinner round the corner, to sort out the notes of his day's work before an early bed. Tonight, however, this talk stayed by him and prevented. He sat thinking about it. . . and eventually, it seems, thought circling and circling but coming to no satisfactory conclusion, of course, he dropped asleep, to wake very suddenly much later in a state of uncommon distress—"acute distress," he called it, "funk."

This, I think, is one of the most curious and betraying things about the whole business: that, even when he told it all to me later, he kept off that unpleasant lodger, as he called him—kept him so long in the background. He had begun by emphasising his unusual repulsion towards the fellow, dwelling upon it, stressing it, just as I have done in this written account. But then, when I was expecting the lodger to appear in some dreadful and dramatic guise—a sneakthief, a forger with coining apparatus, a blackmailer in league with Mrs. Warley-Smith (as I styled her), even a murderer hiding from the police with the woman's help—Moleson merely left him out.

He ignored him, made no mention of him. He talked about his work, about Mrs. Smith, his liking the house, yet disliking the room— feeling *it* disliked him and wanted him out—about anything except the sinister lodger. Having first firmly fixed him in my mind as an ominous character, he just left him there. Thus, when I tried to bring him to the point— this suggestive point of the sinister lodger, and a point he had himself established in opening his tale—he stopped abruptly, and stared into my face, his features working, his eyes gone positively googly. Some fear, I saw, still operated in him, unreleased. His face gave me a touch of gooseflesh. There was an ingredient of salutary "confession" in his delayed account, I began to gather. He lowered his voice. "I knew you'd ask that before long," he said. "You see—I shirked him myself,"

"Refused to acknowledge him, you mean?" I queried vaguely. "Tried to pretend he wasn't in the house?"

He nodded, looking down at his boots.

"You disliked him," I insisted, "to *that* point?" The expression in his eyes, as he glanced up quickly, answered me better than his words.

"It's unbelievable," he whispered, "how that fellow obsessed me. Obsessed is the term."

I asked if he saw him often.

"After that first encounter on the front-door steps— only twice, all told."

The intensity, a sort of inner secrecy in him still, made me hesitate, but as he said nothing, I presently asked boldly:

"But—in the end—you found out who he was, what he was doing there? In a word—why you loathed him so?" I got no straight answer, but I got the full story, told in his own evasive, curious way.

"I mentioned how I dropped asleep in my chair, and woke up suddenly feeling frightened," he went on. "Well—that's the point, you see."

"What is?" I asked, justifiably dense.

He cast his eyes down as though he were ashamed of it. "I'd been frightened all along," he muttered. "Damned frightened. Ever since I'd been in that awful house, I'd been frightened."

"Of—him?"

He nodded.

He believed he had discovered why the fellow resented his being there: it was because Moleson occupied his room. Mrs. Smith had hesitated that first morning whether she could turn him out or not— his rent probably overdue, and what not—but eventually had spoken to him—and Moleson, as described, cash in hand, had moved in. It was a sufficiently obvious explanation.

"But that didn't explain my own abhorrence—did it?"

Obviously not.

"He may have felt resentful, furious, because I'd got his room, but that couldn't have made me feel the physical repulsion, to the point of nausea, which I did feel. And dread too. I only saw him twice after that first meeting, but though I saw him so rarely, I knew he was in the house with me. I never forgot it. He was all over the house expresses it better. I was always expecting to meet him, to run across him on the stairs, to find him in the hall. When I came down the street, I imagined him standing on the doorstep, fumbling with his latchkey. When I went to my bath halfway down the stairs, I thought we should pass. At night, if I went out to post a letter; in the morning when I opened my door to take my hot water in. But, no; he made no sign, I did not meet him. What he did all day I have no notion: he never went out, so far as I saw or knew. But then I myself was out from nine to five, then again for my dinner between eight and nine, you see."

At a great rate he rattled this off. He gave me a good deal in a very few words.

A definite question halted his rambling account, though it was my object, otherwise, to hear the tale just as he cared to tell it.

"Describe him?" He repeated my words. "As I first saw him—— Oh yes. Though I didn't see the features, remember, that time." Then he startled me by raising his voice most unexpectedly in his excitement: "Misshapen!" he shouted in my face, so that I jumped. "Well, you asked me; and that's what I felt about him. But mentally, morally, rather than physically. That's the impression he made on me."

And then he barked out another word: "A monster!" A little shudder ran over him. "I didn't see the face," he went on, "because he didn't mean me to see it. He moved sideways, the shoulder next to me humped up a trifle so as to hide it. A bit of a beard I saw, or whiskers, straggly hair, anyhow, that left in my mind some faint notion of pretence, of a wig perhaps. But my mind at the moment was on my business with Mrs. Smith, and I wasn't trying to see what a stranger pushing rudely past me was like. I had no particular interest in him then. Clothes? . . . Oh, that I couldn't say with accuracy either, but a dark suit, and a bowler hat on his head. *Dark*," he emphasised, "the whole look and feel of the man was dark."

I was still anxiously waiting for that account of his waking up frightened in his chair, for my interest was now deeply held. But I was patient; I had to be. He went on to tell me how he was for ever expecting to see the man again, yet did not see him. This repetition, in the tale as he told it, was not redundant, though, when written, it may seem so. It led up with a bang, as it were, to the meeting—the sight, rather—when it came. Every morning on going out to his work he was positive he must pass the fellow on the darkish stairs, but the stairs were empty; on the landing when he opened his door, on the front-door steps when he returned in the evening, but landing and steps were unoccupied. He would have a good look at the door first from a little way up the street, before coming to it, for the dread of meeting was established, horribly established, in his being—"expectant dread," he called it. Then, suddenly, he did see him. This was the second time.

"I was hardly settled at my desk in the Reading Room," he described the incident, "when I found I'd left my employer's letter on the mantelpiece. It had questions for me to verify, you see. I hurried back for it. It only took five minutes—that's why the house suited me so—but I had a good squint first from a distance to see if the doorstep was free. No one was visible. I ran up. Just as I slipped my latchkey in, I glanced up—something made me—and there he was, staring down at me from the window—*my* window."

"In your room!"

"I saw the face for the first time, but only for a second, just long enough for our eyes to meet. He withdrew it instantly—awfully quick, I mean. It was dark, unshaven, the beard not a real intended beard. I saw hanging lips. No, it was not what you'd call an evil face, not in that sense, but it was dreadful in the sense of being out of relation with any world I knew. Horrible, appalling, in that way. It was a mad face. Behind its darkness there was white—the white of terror. The face was all I really saw, with just a bit of the neck that had a thin red scarf about it. . . . The key dropped out of my fingers with a clatter on the steps.

"I was shaking all over. "Ferreting about in *my* room! . . . was my first thought—the room that used to be his! . . . But a second thought came with it simultaneously, and it was this second thought that unsettled me most, I believe. I realised in a flash that the fellow had been actually watching me ever since my arrival, keeping out of my way on purpose, waiting an opportunity, waiting for me to go out—oh, I can't describe it exactly—but he knew my every movement, I mean."

"You rushed up——?" I interrupted. It was a stupid question, but the dread of this mysterious lodger in my mind excited me.

Moleson hesitated. "I've got a vile temper, you know," he said, shyly rather, as though I was not supposed to be aware of this; "*vile*," he repeated with emphasis and a touch of shame, "curiously sudden too——"

"That brute in your own room," I helped him. For a moment I feared I was to hear of a violent assault.

"I was up those stairs in a second or two," he went on, "and the first thing I noticed on getting to the top was that my door was moving. There was no one on the landing. The room itself was empty." He paused, looking at me significantly. "The fellow," he then added, "'had got out—just in time." Again, he paused for a moment. "I shouldn't have waited to ask any questions, you know."

I knew he meant it, but I was glad to have been spared details of an ugly assault. This savage temper in Moleson always alarmed me rather. I verily believe he would have done the fellow in. His face, as

243

he told it, betrayed him. By this time, moreover, I already had a shrewd suspicion of what was to prove the explanation of this unpleasant and mysterious lodger: a mad mind certainly, a maniac probably (I had glimpses of a homicidal maniac), he would turn out to be the son of Mrs. Smith. That I was partly right, yet at the same time curiously wrong, is a tribute perhaps to the unconscious skill with which Moleson told his story, concealing its climax admirably, yet disdaining to mislead me by using false clues.

The crime of murder, at any rate, was meanwhile spared him. The room was empty, nothing had apparently been touched, and the corridor was empty too. His suggestion of having been "watched" I disregarded. Later, however, I inclined to accept it.

"Across my landing," Moleson continued, "was one door only—the door of what I felt convinced was his room. It was closed. My first instinct was to bang at it and ask him what the devil . . . Well"—he laughed a little—"I didn't do it, that's all. My anger had cooled down somehow. I just snatched up the letter I'd come to fetch and went back to the Museum Reading Room."

I looked at him, impressed by his admirable brevity, thinking of the M.C. gained in Flanders, of that runaway he once stopped, of the two hefty ruffians he fought, half killing one of them, in a Surrey lane when they objected to his interfering on behalf of their overloaded horses. He had various things to his credit of this sort, and he was delicate, of slight build, no muscles or brawn at all. Moleson, with his fierce, perhaps great, spirit, was not negligible. Any story he told, I mean, had value. . . . . ."Now," I thought to myself, "at last we'll get to this business about waking up frightened!" Not a bit of it. He must tell me something about Mrs. Smith first. And though it delayed the thing I wanted to hear, it was worth listening to.

Poor lodging-houses have secrets, secret lodgers, as well, no doubt. His room was cheap, too cheap. But it was not his business, after all. "Better leave it at that!" he decided. Only one thing troubled me about Mrs. Smith—her interest, namely, in ascertaining if he was "not interfered with"—as though she had rather expected that he *would* be disturbed. Her phrase had anchored itself in his mind; he was always recalling it; he couldn't forget it apparently. Why should he be interfered with"? What—who—should interfere with him? Who, indeed, he reflected, but this man? This man who had been turned out for him? This man whose room he now undoubtedly occupied?

And so it was that, since Mrs. Smith came to no closer terms with the real question she longed to ask, he now, for his part, decided to come to closer terms with the question *he* wanted to ask: "Who is your other lodger?" For the floor below being empty, he knew there was none but himself and this other lodger in the house.

After various hints, suggestions and the rest, chances he provided but she did not take, the expression in her face invariably making him pause—after numerous futile leads, he came abruptly one day to the direct question. Tired of fencing, a touch of his queer anger stirred in him. He made up his mind to know whether her feelings were upset or not. He put the direct question, though he did it delicately enough:

"By the by," he said, as they were in the narrow hall, money having just passed, "I meant to ask you sooner, Mrs. Smith—my typewriter at night—does it disturb anyone? The gentleman opposite, I mean?"

If he was prepared for evasion of some kind, he was certainly not prepared for the answer he received.

"She denied there being any gentleman opposite at all?" I asked, as Moleson hesitated, wondering, I fancied, how best to make her answer sound credible to a Philistine like myself.

"She *didn't* answer," he said briefly. "Her face turned white as a sheet. She fell back against the hat rack. She screamed. It was a curious scream, rather low, not noisy a bit. And it was pain, not fear. She was hurt, terribly hurt. She began to cry...."

Further explanation of the amazing collapse, beyond that her "'eart caught me sudden—it's always been weak"—there was none. It was in this brief fashion that Moleson related the incident, then left it there without another word—as I, too, must therefore leave it.

★★★★★★★★★★★★★★★

For some days after that nothing happened. He did not see the lodger. He avoided the landlady. He began to look forward to the end of his stay, hurrying his work at the Museum purposely. But his mind was for ever going back, he says, to that odd question about being "interfered with," and one night in particular, as he sat over his notes after dinner, memory carried him away rather forcibly, rather persistently, to that phrase which had started his original uneasiness. He sat in his chair, lolling back, and thinking about it, wondering afresh about this mysterious lodger, about what he did, why he hid so carefully, why he watched him. The old notions slipped through his mind, for no new ones occurred to him: was he a coiner of counterfeit money, a blackmailer, a lunatic, a man wanted by the police, a man who ought by rights to be shut up, a suicidal maniac ... and so, eventually, he dropped asleep in his chair. . . to wake up suddenly "frightened, and in acute distress."

So, at last, we had got to it.

It was late. The night was very still, all noises in the street had stopped. No footsteps even were audible on the pavement through the open window. "I woke up cold," he said, "cold to the bone. The room, in spite of the warm summer air, was icy. I was shivering."

And at first, rather bewildered after his sleep, he sat there listening, waiting, wondering why he felt cold, wondering for some minutes what the matter was. That something was the matter, he felt sure. Something had been happening, had just happened, while he was asleep. But what? He collected his senses, remembering exactly where he was. Details, of course, came back quickly then. He says the first thing he noticed was that a change had come over the room. The room was somehow different. It had curiously altered. When he dropped off to sleep it had been one thing, now it was another. He glanced about him, searching uncomfortably for evidence of this change, but finding no single detail altered, nothing out of place, the furniture exactly as it always was—until his eye rested on the door. The door, he phrased it, "drew" his attention, although a closed door—and it was closed now—must always, it seemed to me, look much the same.

"Well," he said, "it didn't." He used the tone of challenge, anticipating disbelief. "That door," he declared, "had been opened and shut while I was asleep." He waited a moment. "It had only just been shut—that very second."

The imaginative statement struck me as singularly dramatic. Proof, of course, was not possible, yet a door, I reflected, is easily the most significant feature of a house, opened, closed, tapped on, locked; it is a frontier, a threshold, and when passed, either in exit or entrance, leads necessarily to other conditions of living, to other states of mind, since it leads to other people and other atmosphere. I could understand in a fashion that Moleson used those words. He rather convinced me, I mean, that he was possibly right.

"That's what made you wake," I offered, filling the pause he left.

"Yes," he returned flatly. "While I slept, that door had been opened, someone had looked in, come in, moved about the room, done something, then gone out again—gone out just that instant."

Aware of this change in the room, or in the atmosphere about him, he sat for some time staring at that door. He listened intently. A glance at his wristwatch showed that it was two in the morning, so that he had slept several hours. The deep silence of the house came over him unpleasantly, and his distress, instead of passing, increased. He found himself still shivering. But a moment later his cold skin turned hot and broke out in a profuse perspiration—at a sound. It was a sound he recognised, having heard it before: the dragging of furniture or luggage across the landing, of heavy and awkward articles, difficult to move. He had heard it already several times, late at night, early in the morning, through his dreams as well, and he had always ascribed it to the lodger, busy arranging things in his room opposite, and using the landing sometimes in so doing.

He had paid no particular attention to it, beyond a passing annoyance at the choice of hours, and the sounds had usually ceased after a few minutes at the most. Now, however, he was conscious of a difference, for in the first place it was two in the morning, when ordinary people were asleep; secondly, he realised distinctly, it was not furniture or luggage being moved—it was a piece of luggage, a heavy piece, for the sound was unmistakable. He thought of a trunk or portmanteau. Moreover—it was going on immediately outside his own door.

"The fellow was dragging this luggage of his across the landing just beyond my door," Moleson underlined the fact. "At two o'clock in the morning, if you please!"

The first effect upon him was one of a queer paralysis, mental and physical. He could neither think nor move.

"I just sat listening to the fellow dragging his great bag, or whatever it was, across the landing—dragging it, I supposed, towards his own room opposite. Then, very gradually, my mental numbness lifted, and I found myself wondering *why*. At two in the morning! Dragging luggage about! What was he doing with luggage on the landing of a Bloomsbury lodging-house at that unearthly hour? So close to my own door too? The bumping and scraping were audible enough; there was no pretence of doing it quietly. Where was he taking his luggage from? Where to? My mind worked quickly, once it started. A score of questions rushed over me. What could it be, this bag, this portmanteau, this heavy bundle so difficult to move? What could it contain? What had he put inside it? Taken?"

"Taken? . . ." I repeated, not quite following him.

"Some of the questions racing through my mind," he explained, "brought a kind of answer with them. That's the only way I can put it," he added apologetically, a sop to me, the sceptical recipient of his confession.

"*What* had he taken?" he repeated, looking at me rather hard.

I had no notion.

"But I had," said Moleson with decision, interpreting my blank expression.

"I guessed at once—half guessed, at least."

He had me at a loss there, I admit; but I made no comment, merely nodding my head affirmatively. His next words took me completely by surprise:

"His great bag or bundle, whatever it was," whispered Moleson, "contained something he had just taken out of my room. While I slept, the fellow had sneaked in, crept about, found what he wanted, taken it, and sneaked out again with it—in his bag."

Again, I made no comment, the explanation being too preposterous to argue about. Moleson, besides, was now too earnest and convinced—he knew, remember, the climax, whereas I was still in ignorance—too eager to make his full confession for me to interfere and cavil with commonplace criticism. It might have stopped him, for one thing. . . .

"You missed anything?" I asked, no actual disbelief in my face or voice. I had to repeat it before he replied, and his reply, when it came, again took me by surprise. Also, it sent a shiver through me, as though the hair were moving on my scalp.

"What he had taken," he told me in a lowered voice, and speaking very slowly, "was not in my room at that time—when I fell asleep, I mean. But it had been there —some time before."

The statement, naturally, left me without a rejoinder. I lit a cigarette and waited in silence.

"At that moment," he went on impressively, still in his whisper, and loathing coming into his face with a leap, as it were, "I knew—he was a—horror. Oh, in every meaning of the word. And a queer, sudden revulsion rushed over me—the intense desire to see him close, to look at him face to face, to speak to him—I never once heard his voice, you know—to—yes, even to touch the brute; and in so doing—somehow—God knows how—to get rid of him. So far, he had avoided me deliberately. All this time he had evaded, escaped me. He *meant* to avoid and escape me, but now at last I had him close—a few feet away—busy, occupied, within reach, unable to get away—if I just opened that door. I need only open that door, and I should see him— catch him in the act."

Longing to ask 'In what act?' I ventured instead "You felt angry all of a sudden?" and hit the mark better than I knew.

He admitted it, ashamed a little, with a nod. "I felt cold all over, mind you," he went on, always in that low voice, "scared as well, really scared, but at the same time, as you say, I felt"—he chose a queer word—"vicious. Exasperated, too, a bit. I wanted to be done with it. I wanted to get at the fellow. Why the devil should he make this infernal row at two in the morning? How dared he? How dared he come into another man's room, even if it had once been his own? Why should he watch me, bother me, haunt me, get into my mind—and all the rest of it? Yes"—with a touch of fierceness—"you're right—I did feel angry all of a sudden. I decided abruptly I'd go out———"

"Open that door?"—I simply couldn't keep it back. Personally, I should *not* have opened that door at two in the morning under the circumstances.

"Yes, open the door, go out, and tell the brute to go to hell. I decided to do that—and more———"

I knew what that "more" meant.

"———but when I tried to get up from my chair, I found I couldn't move. I just sat there, furiously angry, struggling—like a mechanical doll whose machinery had run down. I was dying to get at the fellow. I was perspiring all over. I felt that if he answered back, showed any insolence, I'd—strangle him—just go for him and be done with it. Throttle the devil! I felt my fingers at his throat, the prickle of his filthy beard, saw his hanging lips drop wider as he fought for breath, his beastly eyes bulge out, his face turn black—oh, I was in this odd, sudden fury, I admit—and yet—I couldn't move an inch.

"Perhaps—probably—I made a noise of some kind— cursed aloud most likely, but anyhow the sound of the dragging luggage suddenly stopped. A deep, rather an extraordinary silence followed. I could hear the blood beating in my head. I sat fixed in my chair like a dummy, staring at the door. Only that door separated us. He existed there—breathing, vivid, intense—a few feet from where I sat rigid in my chair, unable to get at him, unable to move a muscle. He seemed to exert some tremendous pressure on me, paralysing my will, holding me helpless where I was."

Moleson mopped his forehead a moment.

"I was so angry," he went on, rather breathless now in his excitement, as though he lived over again his fury and exasperation, "that I felt murder in me. Positively, I felt myself a murderer."

Curiously, he stopped dead suddenly. A look of shyness came over him. He stared at me, I stared back at him. Such language, of course, in anybody else, would have been merely extravagant, hysterical. In his case it was real. I knew his sudden, ungovernable temper; I knew, too, he was ashamed of it. In a less civilised country he must always have been in trouble with his gun. He was the type that saw red and killed. And a quick flash of understanding somehow came into me, so that I guessed in that instant the explanation both of his abrupt pause and of his queer shyness. Having this dangerous thing in himself, he recognised it in others too. That sympathy existed.

"Yes—that's how I knew," he muttered, looking down, having guessed my thought. "Chemical," he went on below his breath. "It's opposites that attract, but likes that repel."

"What was *he*?" I asked, fumbling with my cigarette.

"A murderer," he said, quietly. "I felt the same."

★★★★★★★★★★★★★★★

I waited in silence, wondering what he was going to tell me. His face was rather white, his excitement only kept under by his doubt of being believed. It was best now, I felt, to ask no questions. In his own way he would presently go on. But curiosity, I confess, devoured me. Did he open that door? Did he see the other fellow, speak to him, touch him, perhaps go for him?

His own mind, however, was an odd psychological revelation—of himself.

"And the instant I realised *that*," he went on, "the power to move came back to me. My muscles acted. The pressure the fellow exerted was lifted, because we understood one another. There was that ghastly sympathy between us. I got out of my chair and crossed the floor. I reached the door. Then I stopped a moment and listened. He, too, I knew, was listening a few inches away from my face, nothing but half an inch of thin boards between us, listening to my movements, bending to the keyhole probably, crouching, his luggage neglected for a moment while he waited to see what I was going to do. A second later I caught the handle, turned it, and flung the door wide open with a rush.

"There he was before me. Quite close. He was bending down, exactly as I had imagined, crouching, his head lowered; and at his feet, less than a yard beyond me, I saw on the floor the dark blotch that was his luggage.

"What happened then happened so quickly that it seemed less than a second. From the stooping position he did not rise, nor make any attempt to rise. One hand, still stretched out upon the bag, began to work. He pulled at it. He had been pulling at it when I opened the door, and he went on pulling at it—dragging it, dragging it away from me, away from the door, and across the landing floor. I, for my part, had one hand raised to strike, to clutch, to kill, if necessary, but my hand did not fall. I did nothing violent, because I made in that very instant a horrible discovery. I suddenly realised that he did not see me. He had not noticed me. He was not aware of my being there close beside him. He did not react to my presence in any way because he was simply not conscious of it. He continued doing what he had been doing just before—dragging his luggage across the landing floor. I saw the dark mass of it go hitching along in jerks as he pulled. It was very heavy.

"And this—this not being aware of me, I mean—came as a tremendous shock. The surprise of it, perhaps. It was the last thing in the world I'd expected. I had rather looked for something sudden, violent. I was prepared for it. This way he just ignored me turned me cold. It struck me as unnatural. I stood and stared, for I didn't know what else to do, and my body was trembling, and I felt queerly uncertain of my legs. I watched him go on dragging at that heavy thing, which I now saw was not luggage after all, not ordinary luggage, at least. It was neither bag nor portmanteau, nor anything like that. It was a sack of awkward shape and out line.

"It was unpleasant, I thought, the way it bulged. But more than that, more than unusual, it gave me a turn—I felt it somewhere awful. And realising this, I made an unconscious movement evidently, for I felt my breath catch, and I must have staggered a little. I caught at the edge of the door to steady myself, and the door, naturally, yielded with my weight; I lurched with it, sideways at first, then a little outwards as the door came with me, and then—forwards. Before I could recover balance, I was against him. I was right into him.

"But I didn't fall. I didn't, thank God, collide with the monstrous creature and his awful sack, but I was so close against him that the shock of finding nothing solid—there was no substance there at all— stopped my heart for a second. It seemed to rush up into my throat. Then my breath came back, and I let out a yell into the night that must have been heard in the street. At which moment, still dragging at his bundle, he made a sudden, rather violent, movement. He turned in a new way. I saw his face clearly.

"By 'clearly' I mean close—dreadfully close. It was turned up, but

I saw it obliquely rather, a kind of sideways glimpse, and even then he wasn't looking *at* me. The light from the open door behind fell on it, and I saw the eyes, blazing eyes, the hanging lips, the white skin smudged with unshaven hair of the growing black beard, and—to my utter amazement—tears upon the cheeks. It was a maniac's face, if ever I saw one. The other thing that I saw clearly was that the thin red scarf about the neck was not a scarf at all. It was a thin red line of contused blood in the flesh of the neck itself, a line that only a rope, drawn very tightly, could have made."

Moleson stopped then and sank back in his chair, looking away from me, and glad, I think, that he had got so far without interruption. His words and manner, his facial expression above all, conveyed his horror far better than his jerked-out sentences. I smoked a moment in silence, handing him a cigarette too, which he refused. But he said nothing for some little time, while I also kept back a dozen questions that rushed up in me.

"What happened then?" I ventured at length. "What did you do?"

"Nothing," he replied briefly, looking up at me again, his manner now quiet and collected. "I did nothing. It seemed, somehow, there was nothing I wanted to do. A feeling I must shout, strike out, do something violent passed. What was done next, *he* did. I merely looked on and watched. There was no emotion in me of any sort. I was just numb. My whole consciousness, I think, was in my eyes. I stared. . . as he went on dragging that heavy mass across the landing, always a little farther from me, hitching and shoving it along with great effort —towards the door of his room. Then he opened the door, but the light from my room did not reach to it, and as it was not lit inside, I saw nothing but a black space.

"I watched. I saw everything he did, every movement he made. He stepped to one side, across the bundle, so that he was then pushing instead of dragging. His whole body was bent double with the effort to get the thing through the door and inside the room. Apparently, it was difficult to do. He accomplished it after several minutes. The sack, it seemed, made one or two little movements of its own—jerks. He closed the door, putting his weight against it heavily from outside, and then—after that—well—he wasn't there anymore."

"He'd gone into the room?"

Moleson shrugged his shoulders. "Can't say," he answered rather curtly. "I tell you he simply wasn't there. I couldn't see him anymore. I'd lost sight of him." He added sheepishly: "Something happened to my eyes, I suppose. I didn't see him go—but he *was* gone."

Fully five minutes passed, Moleson then told me slowly, before he could think, much less move. He was struck dumb with terror and amazement. He felt stupid, empty of life, unable to act at all.

"It may have been five minutes," he said, "but it may just as well have been twenty—for all I know. The only thing I remember clearly is that my awful yell—that wild shriek I let out into the night some time before—still seemed to me echoing through the house and down the stairs. I had a feeling it must have been heard in the street and the police would be in. But nothing happened. The fellow's disappearance bewildered me to a point I can't describe properly. I *knew* I hadn't been dreaming, but I knew damned little else, it seems to me.

"I moved at last, after a bit. I moved backwards. I threw my own door as wide as it would go, so as to get all the light there was, and the light streamed across the landing and fell on the door—his door. I knew I was going to open that door. I had to."

His pluck hardly surprised me, for I already knew it. I admired it. Nothing in this world or the next could have induced me to go near that door, much less open it. Moleson, however, did more: he went over and knocked loudly against its boards.

"The sound echoed," he told me, "but not inside. It echoed down the stairs, I mean. The boards sounded dull. That dullness explained itself," he added, with a quick glance up at me as though, of course, I understood what he meant. But I did not understand, and my eye brows went up in query and response. "It wasn't an ordinary door," he said.

"You—opened it?" I had no inkling what he meant.

"I guessed it wasn't a proper door," he replied, changing his adjective, but leaving me more ignorant than before. "I felt that some time before."

"Sham? . . ."

"Not an ordinary door into an ordinary room," he replied, with a hint of impatience at my stupidity. "When I knocked," he went on, "and got no answer, I knew I was right. The dead sound proved it."

"Oh! . . ."

"Yes," he went on quietly, "the dead muffled sound it made. I waited a moment. Then I opened it. It was the door of a cupboard—a rather shallow cupboard." He paused, then said something that made my blood curdle: "That's why the creature had to shove it in so hard—*stuff* it in—to make it stay——"

"Upright? . . ." I gasped, catching the ghastly meaning at last.

"Upright," was all he replied.

★★★★★★★★★★★★★★★★

The dusk was now fallen into our room between us, and I saw the glow of my cigarette-end in the mirror, behind his chair. It had been a dreadful story. I longed for light and a glass of whisky. Moleson had so convinced me of the truth, the reality, of his confession, yet I got the feeling that he hoped I would tear it to pieces and demolish it utterly, proving to his satisfaction how absurd it all was, and using nice words like hallucination, overwrought nerves and the like.

Instead, I remained rather quiet and noncommittal, and certainly dumb; I could not honestly comfort him in the way he wished.

"I told you," he resumed, his voice much lower now, "that I imagined that shriek of mine still echoing in the house and down the stairs? Well, a few moments later, while I still stood glaring at that ghastly cupboard, all black and empty . . . I heard a sound on the stairs. It was below me, coming nearer. I couldn't move— not an inch, one way or the other. I was just stuck to the floor. But I felt sure of one thing—it wasn't"—but he couldn't say the word he meant, the word in his mind—"it wasn't——" He stuck again.

"*Who* was it?" I asked quickly, eager to help him, but to help myself at the same time.

"First I saw the light," he said, "the light of a candle, evidently, flickering on the wall, then on the ceiling. Next came the shadow, enormously magnified and grotesque. Then came a large white face of melancholy and terror mixed, looming at me over the banisters. There was a thin voice:

"'. . . . interfered with. . .' I heard from what seemed an immense distance. . . . 'He showed hisself, then, did he? . . . May God forgive me. . .' and something about a 'broken promise' and a 'room I didn't oughter 'ave let to anyone. . . .' And then, as, to my shame, I felt myself being helped up from the floor—for I had no idea I had let my legs give way like that—something—oh, horrible and dreadful—about '. . . they 'anged him for it; oh, they 'anged him at the Scrubs . . . it was 'is own father, you see. . . . and now over twenty years ago. . .'"

There were gulping sounds, he remembers, and these odd, broken words.

Moleson, curiously enough, had never gone to the trouble to verify anything, and it was my vile curiosity that had to find its own satisfaction. The British Museum where he had worked so hard, gave me certain facts in the newspapers of long before the war. The "Warley Parricide," I discovered, and the unpleasant details about how the body was found stuffed upright into a cupboard, and how the public signed a petition and the lawyers urged homicidal mania, but without the intended result.

LEONAUR

ALSO FROM LEONAUR
AVAILABLE IN SOFTCOVER OR HARDCOVER WITH DUST JACKET

MR MUKERJI'S GHOSTS *by S. Mukerji*—Supernatural tales from the British Raj period by India's Ghost story collector.

KIPLINGS GHOSTS *by Rudyard Kipling*—Twelve stories of Ghosts, Hauntings, Curses, Werewolves & Magic.

THE COLLECTED SUPERNATURAL AND WEIRD FICTION OF WASHINGTON IRVING: VOLUME 1 *by Washington Irving*—Including one novel 'A History of New York', and nine short stories of the Strange and Unusual.

THE COLLECTED SUPERNATURAL AND WEIRD FICTION OF WASHINGTON IRVING: VOLUME 2 *by Washington Irving*—Including three novelettes 'The Legend of the Sleepy Hollow', 'Dolph Heyliger', 'The Adventure of the Black Fisherman' and thirty-two short stories of the Strange and Unusual.

THE COLLECTED SUPERNATURAL AND WEIRD FICTION OF JOHN KENDRICK BANGS: VOLUME 1 *by John Kendrick Bangs*—Including one novel 'Toppleton's Client or A Spirit in Exile', and ten short stories of the Strange and Unusual.

THE COLLECTED SUPERNATURAL AND WEIRD FICTION OF JOHN KENDRICK BANGS: VOLUME 2 *by John Kendrick Bangs*—Including four novellas 'A House-Boat on the Styx', 'The Pursuit of the House-Boat', 'The Enchanted Typewriter' and 'Mr. Munchausen' of the Strange and Unusual.

THE COLLECTED SUPERNATURAL AND WEIRD FICTION OF JOHN KENDRICK BANGS: VOLUME 3 *by John Kendrick Bangs*—Including twor novellas 'Olympian Nights', 'Roger Camerden: A Strange Story', and ten short stories of the Strange and Unusual.

THE COLLECTED SUPERNATURAL AND WEIRD FICTION OF MARY SHELLEY: VOLUME 1 *by Mary Shelley*—Including one novel 'Frankenstein or the Modern Prometheus', and fourteen short stories of the Strange and Unusual.

THE COLLECTED SUPERNATURAL AND WEIRD FICTION OF MARY SHELLEY: VOLUME 2 *by Mary Shelley*—Including one novel 'The Last Man', and three short stories of the Strange and Unusual.

THE COLLECTED SUPERNATURAL AND WEIRD FICTION OF AMELIA B. EDWARDS *by Amelia B. Edwards*—Contains two novelettes 'Monsieur Maurice', and 'The Discovery of the Treasure Isles', one ballad 'A Legend of Boisguilbert' and seventeen short stories to cill the blood.

LEONAUR

ALSO FROM LEONAUR
AVAILABLE IN SOFTCOVER OR HARDCOVER WITH DUST JACKET

THE COMPLETE FOUR JUST MEN: VOLUME 2 *by Edgar Wallace*—*The Law of the Four Just Men & The Three Just Men*—disillusioned with a world where the wicked and the abusers of power perpetually go unpunished, the Just Men set about to rectify matters according to their own standards, and retribution is dispensed on swift and deadly wings.

THE COMPLETE RAFFLES: 1 *by E. W. Hornung*—*The Amateur Cracksman & The Black Mask*—By turns urbane gentleman about town and accomplished cricketer, life is just too ordinary for Raffles and that sets him on a series of adventures that have long been treasured as a real antidote to the 'white knights' who are the usual heroes of the crime fiction of this period.

THE COMPLETE RAFFLES: 2 *by E. W. Hornung*—*A Thief in the Night & Mr Justice Raffles*—By turns urbane gentleman about town and accomplished cricketer, life is just too ordinary for Raffles and that sets him on a series of adventures that have long been treasured as a real antidote to the 'white knights' who are the usual heroes of the crime fiction of this period.

THE COLLECTED SUPERNATURAL AND WEIRD FICTION OF WILKIE COLLINS: VOLUME 1 *by Wilkie Collins*—Contains one novel 'The Haunted Hotel', one novella 'Mad Monkton', three novelettes 'Mr Percy and the Prophet', 'The Biter Bit' and 'The Dead Alive' and eight short stories to chill the blood.

THE COLLECTED SUPERNATURAL AND WEIRD FICTION OF WILKIE COLLINS: VOLUME 2 *by Wilkie Collins*—Contains one novel 'The Two Destinies', three novellas 'The Frozen deep', 'Sister Rose' and 'The Yellow Mask' and two short stories to chill the blood.

THE COLLECTED SUPERNATURAL AND WEIRD FICTION OF WILKIE COLLINS: VOLUME 3 *by Wilkie Collins*—Contains one novel 'Dead Secret,' two novelettes 'Mrs Zant and the Ghost' and 'The Nun's Story of Gabriel's Marriage' and five short stories to chill the blood.

FUNNY BONES *selected by Dorothy Scarborough*—An Anthology of Humorous Ghost Stories.

MONTEZUMA'S CASTLE AND OTHER WEIRD TALES *by Charles B. Cory*—Cory has written a superb collection of eighteen ghostly and weird stories to chill and thrill the avid enthusiast of supernatural fiction.

SUPERNATURAL BUCHAN *by John Buchan*—Stories of Ancient Spirits, Uncanny Places & Strange Creatures.

www.ingramcontent.com/pod-product-compliance
Lightning Source LLC
Chambersburg PA
CBHW050500260626
47157CB00004B/1127